THE FIRES OF FREEDOM

THE FIRES OF FREEDOM

FREEDOM FLEET BOOK II

DANIEL ARENSON

PROLOGUE
The Ghost in the Machine

The Nazis prowled the shadowy hallways of the space station, hunting a ghost.

This whole place is full of ghosts, Wolfgang thought. He was a big, powerful warrior clad in battle armor, and a helmet like a steel skull covered his head. In his youth, he had broken the skulls of boys and beasts with his bare hands. As a young trooper, he had faced hordes of screaming barbarians and scuttling alien spiders. As Grand Admiral of the Weltraumwaffe, he had hurled armadas against enemy fleets. Dammit, he was the son of the führer of the Fatherworld. Yet here in this dusky corridor, trapped in a space station light-years from home, Wolfgang König shivered.

This place was wrong. A place that should not be. A shadow universe beyond space and time and understanding. They had passed through the looking glass and were navigating the clockwork innards of a strange machine. A space station? No. This was a labyrinth. A mechanical maze. A prison born of the twisted mind of Lucifer himself.

And *he* was out there. In this station. Lurking in the shadows. Waiting.

The ghost.

"We should never have come back," Wolfgang muttered. "We should have left him here to haunt his tomb."

The memories rose like spirits in the darkness. A month ago, Wolfgang had invaded this space station. He had slain every soldier and spacer in his path. Finally only the station commander had remained alive. And his family. Well, the family not for very long. How that woman and her children had screamed! How the torture had deformed them!

"Kill me," Commander Ishmael Jordan had begged. "Let me die with them."

Wolfgang had only scoffed, leaving the wretched subhuman behind. Leaving him to rot in a space station that would become his tomb. Triumphant, Wolfgang had flown onward to Earth, determined to crush the blue planet.

Well, Earth still stood. The subhumans still resisted. And now Wolfgang was back in this wretched, floating hellhole at Alpha Centauri. The orders had come from dear Onkel Dieter himself, High Commander of the Wehrmacht. Wolfgang's uncle. And superior officer.

"You abandoned a working space station?" Dieter had cried. "Near our only portal into the impure universe? Return at once to retake the prize you so carelessly abandoned."

The old fool! Dieter was seventy years old, gangling and gray, a living corpse. The old goat was commander of the armed forces, a lofty position, but Dieter craved more. How the old man lusted for his brother's throne! How bitter he was that Helmut, not Dieter, commanded the Fatherworld! And so Dieter took out all that venom on his nephew.

He doesn't care about Toliman Station, Wolfgang thought. *He just wants to humiliate me. He sits safe in the Fatherworld while I'm here in Unreineland, and—*

A howl sounded in the depths.

Wolfgang froze. He stood paralyzed in the dark tunnel of the station. His fellow Aryans froze behind him. Eight others had joined him on this ghost hunt. Six were big, hulking men, elite warriors of the Waffen-SS. One was a monk in dark robes. And one was a little girl.

The howl went on and on. A howl of pain, it seemed. Or

perhaps of rage. The longer it continued and the more Wolfgang listened, the less human the howl seemed. It sounded like the raw cry of an animal. Or perhaps the undead.

Finally the sound died. The echoes faded like wisps of fog. For a moment the silence lingered, a deathly stillness like a tomb after the widow had gone hoarse from weeping and returned home to grieve in shadow, leaving only death in the graveyard, only a white somber nothingness under the moonlight and mist.

And it was the little girl in their group, a pale child with black pigtails and a dark dress, who broke the silence.

"It's him," little Greta said in a singsong voice. *"Der schwarzer geist."*

Wolfgang could not help but shudder. He hoped his armor hid the tremble that ran along his limbs.

"The Black Ghost isn't real, little one," he said to the child. "Just a myth. There are no such things as ghosts."

The Burned One stared from the shadows of his hood. He was always staring, that one. That hood was like a cave, and the creature inside like a dark wolf awaiting prey. Only his eyes were visible in the blackness, glittering like blue marbles. His hand reached out, hidden within a custom glove with only three fingers. He wrapped that strange talon around his daughter's shoulder, perhaps seeking to soothe the girl. And from that hood like a predator's den, those flaming orbs stared at Wolfgang.

"Oh, there are ghosts in the shadows, dear cousin," the Burned One hissed. "And there are things worse than ghosts."

His voice was soft, raspy, slurred. The fire had taken his lips. Along with most of his face, several fingers and toes, and much of his skin. Wolfgang was thankful for the shadows. He didn't like looking at the Burned Ones. Even a Burned One who shared his last name. Yes, this creature before him was a König. A shame upon the dynasty, if you asked Wolfgang. How could a dynasty that prided itself on Aryan purity, that exterminated cripples, allow such a hideous monstrosity to bear its name? And yet the cult of Aschenfeuer lived by a different standard.

They were fanatics. It was a disgrace that his own cousin, his own blood, had joined the Aschenfeuer order. The Burned Ones believed that Hitler himself lived in all fire. The Eternal Führer's body was embalmed and entombed in Berlin, forever preserved and displayed. But that was only a shell, the Burned Ones claimed. Hitler's soul lived in flame.

According to these sly, scarred monks, the fire revealed all. The fire peeled back all pretension and preening. To serve, one must step willingly into the flame. In the conflagration they were judged. The fire chose some acolytes to death, allowing them to join Hitler's soul in the ever-raging holocaust. Others emerged from the inferno, scarred and purified, and donned the black robes. It was a strange life, one Wolfgang did not understand. He was a soldier, a man of the sword.

But a sword cannot cut a ghost, he thought. And so he had brought Scarfather Ludwig König, a servant of the Imperishable Flame.

"You mean demons," Wolfgang said to the Burned One.

Ludwig's eyes glittered. Wolfgang glimpsed the hint of a thin, lipless smile, a smile that was all gums and crooked teeth.

"There are beasts between the universes that have no name, Cousin. And no words in any human tongue can describe their horror. But fear not. We do not deal with such a being here."

Wolfgang's muscles relaxed. "So the killer in the shadows—he's mortal? Even after all the bodies we found, even after all the troopers he killed—he's just a man?"

The Burned One shook his hooded head. "No longer. He was once a man, perhaps. But some things break men. Some things shatter and reshape them into something new. You mutilated and tortured this man's family to death, yes?"

"It was my daughter, Eva, who did the dirty work. But yes,

I ordered it done." Wolfgang raised his chin. "It's no more than he deserved. You are right. He is no man but a subhuman. More an animal than a man. You should have seen his skin, Ludwig. As black as your robes."

The Burned One licked the scarred fringes of his lipless mouth. "Ah, so sweet little Eva got to play. I've seen your daughter's work. She's not merely a torturer. She's an artist. And great art can break down men. As you broke this man, this Ishmael. As surely as the fire broke me. As surely as the fire shall someday break my daughter." He stroked the girl's hair. "I arose from the ashes purified, a being of firelight to cast back the darkness. And this creature we hunt—he retreated into the shadows after breaking, and in the dark pits of his grief, he became a beast."

Wolfgang listened again to the station's ambiance. He heard the distant hum of machinery. The rattle of air through the vents. All the normal sounds of a space station. But no more howls. No more ghosts in the night. Wolfgang frowned and tilted his head. Was that breathing in the depths? Or just the machinery? Dammit, it was too dark. Why couldn't the engineers get the lights back on? And why was it so damn cold?

"Well, at least he's not a demon," Wolfgang muttered. "Come on. Let's keep going. He's down here somewhere. You all heard him howling."

He kept walking, heading deeper into the shadowy station. The others followed close behind. What a motley crew they made! One admiral who had faced armadas yet feared ghosts in the shadows. Six hulking brutes trained to torture and kill, Sig runes crackling upon their breastplates. A Burned One, his humanity seared away. And a little girl, doomed to the fire. Onward through Toliman they went, moving ever deeper into the bowels of this space station, plunging into the darkest pits of the machine. A tale from his childhood returned to Wolfgang. A tale from ancient

Greece. Daedalus had been tasked with running a string through
the coiling innards of a seashell. The craftsman tied a thread to an
ant, and enticed by the promise of honey, the insect crawled
through the pearly labyrinth, pulling the string all the way through.
That was how Wolfgang imagined himself and his crew. As ants.
Just little ants moving through a seashell. But this shell did not
gleam like mother-of-pearl. It was a mechanical shell, a place of
darkness and decay.

None of this is right, Wolfgang thought, struck with vertigo.
Instead of walking down a horizontal tunnel, he suddenly felt as if
the tunnel were vertical, a shaft, and he was hanging above the pit
like a man dangling above a well. No, none of this was right. They
shouldn't even be here.

He didn't mean aboard Toliman. Wolfgang existed to
board enemy ships and stations and seize them for the
Fatherworld. He thrived behind enemy lines. It wasn't the station
that sent shivers down his spine, dark and coiling as Toliman
might be. It was this universe. This parallel dimension. Everything
here felt wrong, as if Wolfgang had stepped through a reflection
within a reflection, a looking glass within a looking glass.
Somehow he just didn't fit.

And there is another me out there, he thought. *My doppelgänger.
My reflection. Myself—my own enemy. A leader named Bastian King.
Someday I must face my shadow . . . and kill him.*

* * * * *

"Are you all right, sir?"

The soft, girlish voice pierced the haze of Wolfgang's
thoughts. He looked down to see his cousin's kid. Fräulein Greta's
large, lavender eyes shone from the shadows. Her face was like
ivory, still hinting at the strength of the beast it had thrust from,
but now smoothed and carved into the face of a doll. That was

the dichotomy of Fräulein Greta, a creature both girlish and monstrous, a child of innocence doomed to someday burn.

Wolfgang tried to muss her hair. But pulled tight into its pigtails, that hair felt like stretched copper wires. "Of course I'm all right."

"I saw you tremble," the child said. Her eyes wouldn't break contact. Wouldn't even blink. They were like lanterns, like purple planets in the depths.

A few glances passed among the troops. The SS always thought themselves superior to the Wehrmacht. Wolfgang could imagine the goons smirking behind their skull visors. Ha! An admiral of the Wehrmacht, trembling?

Wolfgang could have remained in Ops, safe within the control center of the station. He could have let the SS goons go alone to explore the shadowy bowels of Toliman. But he had insisted on joining the hunt. The last time Wolfgang had sent men into the tunnels, they never returned. Later he found only mangled corpses, barely recognizable as men. Something in the shadows had torn them apart. So much for the Waffen-SS being superior fighters. If you wanted to do a job right, you must do it yourself.

"Perhaps I did tremble," Wolfgang said to the odd child. "I admit, I was worried about the SS troopers with us. They tend not to fare well in these tight spots." He glanced toward the troopers and winked.

They snorted, but they relaxed, and the tension eased in the tunnel. The Wehrmacht and Waffen-SS often bantered this way, bragging about which force was stronger (of course it was the Wehrmacht). Sometimes the feuds got heated, leading to duels and even deaths, but usually they were good-natured. This was familiar. This was safe. This—

A howl.

A howl pierced the shadows, louder than before, closer. It

11

weaved all around them, spinning, coming from above one moment, below the other, then morphing into deep laughter. That laughter was like thunder rolling over a midnight sea at storm, a dark ocean with coiling, scaly reptiles churning in its depths. The thunderous peals of mirth took form, coalescing into words.

"Leave . . . this . . . tomb . . ."

Chills raced down Wolfgang's spine like the icy fingers of an astral lover made of frost. Even the SS troopers shuddered this time, clattering their armor. Only the Burned One and his daughter seemed unafraid. The hooded scarfather grinned. The rest of his face remained shadowed, but within his hood, one could see that grin, a lipless grin, a Cheshire grin, revealing crooked teeth that hung askew from his ravaged mouth. Those teeth were like keys of yellow ivory dangling from a smashed piano. His daughter, innocent little Fräulein Greta, seemed only curious, gazing with those huge, unblinking eyes. Her eyes were so much like lanterns Wolfgang had once joked that her gaze could summon moths.

Wolfgang drew his Stahlgeist-14. The pistol was a smaller version of the Lugerheulen rifle. Better for confined spaces. Like its bigger brother, a Stahlgeist fired umbrion rounds. Particles of anti-light. Living darkness. Down here that seemed redundant. He was fighting shadows with shadows. What Wolfgang would have given for some light!

He placed his hand on the trigger and looked around, trying to find forms in the darkness.

Stahlgeist, he thought. *Steel ghost. How ironic.*

The SS troopers raised their own weapons. They were using Stahlgeists as well. Bad choice. They should have brought flamethrowers. They should have brought fire and light. Why couldn't the damn engineers get the lights back on?

For a long moment—silence. Wolfgang looked around, trying to pierce the darkness. Normally his adlerauge would detect

the heat signatures of any hidden assassins. The bionic eye saw
nothing now. Wolfgang swept his good eye across the scene. He
turned back toward his companions. The skull helmets of the SS
troopers stared back, a tableau reminiscent of the *Danse Macabre*.
The Burned One's warped, snaggletoothed grin shone like a
broken crescent moon, while Greta's eyes glimmered like distant
lavender worlds. Wolfgang spun away from them and gazed into
the depths of Toliman. Once more, he had that feeling that he
was suspended over a well, staring down into a Stygian pit where
awaited the jaws of some ancient and ravenous beast.

"Show yourself!" Wolfgang cried.

Nobody answered. No more deep voice. No more
rumbling laughter like a storm over the primordial sea before
landforms had risen. Just the hum of machinery. A clatter of some
expanding duct or bulkhead. A distant drop from some broken
compartment. Drip. Drip. Drip. It was no wonder the Chinese
used to torture their victims with dripping water. Wolfgang could
not stand it.

"This is all just theater." Wolfgang scoffed. "Just a game to
him. He's trying to scare us. As if we're kids in a haunted house."

"Yes, a game," hissed the Burned One, his voice like
steam leaking from a lifeboat. "The greatest game. And if you lose
. . . you lose your life."

"I've had enough of this!" Wolfgang roared. "Fill this
tunnel with death."

He aimed at the darkness ahead. Blindly he fired his pistol.

His gun howled, an ethereal sound like a wolf lost in a
cave, crying to be let out. U-bolts flew into the distance, casting
no light. The grape-sized rounds slammed into bulkheads and
decks and shattered. Umbrion clouds spilled out, swirling like
octopus ink through the murk of a deep trench. Normally, Aryans
used the weapon to blind their enemies. Then, with their all-seeing
adlerauges, they could hunt their prey through darkness. But

tonight Wolfgang's bionic eye saw nothing.

The SS troopers were firing too, just as blind as him. Their rounds hit the deckhead above, the deck below, and ricocheted off bulkheads into the distant shadows. Some umbrion particles landed on Wolfgang's armor, sucking out heat like parasites sucking blood. The chill gripped Wolfgang's spine. Those frosty fingers, which had once merely caressed his skin, now dug into his flesh.

The soldiers kept firing, filling the tunnel with darkness and ice. The umbrions sucked heat from the bulkheads, twisting and cracking the metal. The guns howled like a pack of arctic wolves hunting in the hinterlands long before the rise of man. Laughter sounded in the darkness, and then a scream pierced the shadows, deafening, louder than the guns.

"Hold your fire!" Wolfgang cried. "Men, hold your fire!"

The SS troopers shot another few rounds—a show of defiance against a man of the Wehrmacht. But even the SS dared not disobey a grand admiral for too long. One by one, the troopers lowered their guns. A few were laughing. The bloodlust, the heat of combat—it was cutting through their fear.

"Did we get him?" said a trooper, voice echoing within his skull-shaped visor.

"We must have," rasped another. "Can't hear him squealing anymore."

A third trooper laughed and pointed. "Look. His corpse. We'll mount it on the hull."

Wolfgang stared. His bionic eye narrowed. The umbrions were dispersing, revealing a body on the deck. The corpse lay face down. Wolfgang exhaled in relief.

We got him.

He stepped closer, knelt by the corpse, and rolled it over. A pale face stared back, eyes dead, visor smashed, throat slit open from ear to ear. That pale face was clearly Aryan. A swastika had been carved into the forehead.

Wolfgang stumbled a few paces backward.

"You idiots!" he cried. "He's one of us! An SS trooper!"

The ranking SS officer blinked. "But . . ." The armored man looked around. "There are still six of us. There . . ."

The trooper froze and stared.

And Wolfgang noticed it. One of the SS troopers. The man at the back.

He did not have an adlerauge. The man wore a skull visor like the others. But instead of one blue Aryan eye, one red bionic eye, there were two black orbs that stared from the helmet's eye holes. Two pits to hell.

The skull visor seemed to grin. And the impostor pounced.

A laser blade flashed.

A deep voice laughed.

The figure leaped into shadows, and an SS trooper fell, clutching at his mangled face. The lower half of the skull visor had been carved right off. So had the man's jaw, teeth, and tongue. He gurgled on blood.

"Fire!" Wolfgang howled. "Fire everywhere!"

His gun howled. The surviving troopers fired with him. U-bolts ping-ponged across the tunnel, unleashing a storm of umbrions. But that laughter kept thundering, echoing through the station. The deep voice rumbled through the depths of the machine.

"Leave . . . this . . . tomb . . ."

* * * * *

"I don't care how much blood spills." Wolfgang balled his fists and hissed through a tight jaw. "I want him dead! I want him crushed! I want to piss on his corpse!"

15

The group knelt on the bloody deck. The umbrions were dispersing, finally allowing their flashlights to work. Wolfgang held the mutilated trooper in his arms. The poor bastard was still breathing. The lower half of his face had been sliced clean off, jaw and all, but he still lived. The sight of that gaping hole still gasping for breath sickened Wolfgang. Nausea flared in him.

"Disgusting." He shoved the mutilated man away, aimed his weapon, and fired. A U-bolt slammed into the mangled trooper's head. He fell, but he *still lived!* He still breathed! Even with a U-bolt in his head! The nausea worsened. Wolfgang snarled and kicked the wounded man, crushing what remained of the face, shattering the skull with his steel-tipped boot.

The man slumped, silent. Wolfgang took a deep breath. "Good. Goo—"

The man rasped again. A last, lingering, terrible rasp like ripping paper. Wolfgang stomped down hard, finally silencing the creature. He shook blood off his boots, then turned toward his surviving companions.

They stared back. Two SS men were dead. That left four troopers, the Burned One, and the girl. Fräulein Greta stared at Wolfgang with those unblinking eyes. Curious. She was so curious about death.

"Why did it take him so long to die?" she said.

"Because he's an SS trooper," said Wolfgang. "Bred to be tough. To be a killer. To die hard. Yet even these renowned SS warriors, supposedly the elite forces of the Fatherworld, cannot catch a subhuman ghost." His voice rose to a howl. "How could you let him into your formation?"

The remaining troopers stared back from their skull helmets. Wolfgang was the son of the führer. He was the Grand Admiral of the Fatherworld's fleet. Yet still these men stared back defiantly, chins raised, and did not grovel. That was the SS. He might be powerful, but he was still a man of the Wehrmacht, and thus they would never respect him. As all wise men, Wolfgang König feared the enemy within far more than the subhumans. The SS were insolent and proud. The Gestapo was always lurking. And now the Aschenfeuer order was growing in influence and meddling everywhere. The Burned Ones were always staring from the shadows, plotting. All these groups—SS, Gestapo, Aschenfeuer—were Aryan and worshipped Hitler as their god. And they would all love to depose the König dynasty and reshape the Fatherworld like a sculptor working with molten iron. Right now the König family ruled. But in the Fatherworld, there was always someone ready to stab you in the back.

Finally one trooper broke the silence. "We didn't see him approach in disguise. You didn't either."

The blood rushed to Wolfgang's cheeks. He wanted to chew the man out, then thought better of it. Losing his cool against the enemy was one thing. Against the SS? That would signal weakness.

"No," Wolfgang said in a low voice. "No, I didn't. The stories were right. He moves like a ghost. He hunts like a panther. He is shadow taken living form."

"*Der schwarzer geist,*" whispered little Greta. "The black ghost."

"We end this farce," said Wolfgang. He took a few steps down the corridor. "We end this now! We kill this so-called ghost and bury this myth once and for all." He paused, then looked back at his companions. "Well? Aren't you coming?"

The SS troopers just stood there. Their ranking officer cleared his throat. "Admiral, should we call for reinforcements?"

"Reinforcements?" Wolfgang guffawed. "To fight one man? A subhuman at that? No, soldier. His jig is up. We know his tricks now. Come then! Are you men or boys?"

He kept walking down the corridor, heading deep toward the engine rooms in the heart of the station. The others followed.

Wolfgang would keep a close eye on his troops, making sure no subhuman infiltrated them again.

I know your little tricks, Ishmael, he thought. *You're no ghost. We can't sense your heat because you move through the ducts. That's all you are. A rat scurrying through the tunnels. And the exterminators are here.*

Wolfgang remembered that day. His first day on this station. Clearing out cabin after cabin, hall after hall. He remembered holding Commander Ishmael Jordan, forcing the man to watch. To watch his own wife and children suffer, playthings for the Bitch from Berlin.

I broke him then, Wolfgang thought.

But now the broken pieces had clumped together like rocks in a void coalescing into a planet, forming something mighty from shards. Wolfgang had learned his lesson. This time, when he had Ishmael in his grip, he would crush the subhuman like a ripe fruit.

"He's in the ductwork," Wolfgang said. "So we'll smoke him out." He pointed. "There's a vent. Let's poison a rat."

Wolfgang flexed his fingers. His leather gloves creaked and thrummed with electricity. The cables inlaid throughout the fabric vibrated with power. With his augmented strength, Wolfgang grabbed the vent and ripped it free, revealing a shaft into the ductwork. He tossed the mangled grate aside, thrust his Stahlgeist-IV into the duct, and opened fire, unleashing a torrent of U-bolts. The rounds pinged along the ducts like crunchy dirt up a vacuum cleaner. Deep in the ducts, the marble-sized rounds burst, scattering umbrions. The particles withered flesh. Wolfgang knew their pain all too well. He remembered holding his mother's body, a body crumbling into a charcoal husk. He remembered the umbrions stinging his hands and not caring, just weeping as he held her toxic body against him. Within his gloves of leather and electricity, he still bore the scars.

My cousin is not the only Burned One, Wolfgang thought. *Light burned him. With me it was darkness.*

The troopers ripped off other grates they found along the bulkheads. Their guns howled as they pumped the ducts full of umbrions.

Wolfgang glanced toward his cousin. The Burned One simply stood there, his hands tucked into the sleeves of his long black robes.

"Well?" Wolfgang said. "Are you going to help?"

Ludwig's scarred eyes peered from his shadowy hood. "I am unarmed, cousin."

"You're a servant of the First Fire, aren't you? So go toss some fireballs into the ducts or something."

The Burned One's eyes glittered within his hood. "You cannot kill this beast with darkness or the light of the Imperishable Flame. One who was broken with blood can only be defeated with blood."

"What does that mean?" Wolfgang said. "Talk like a man! If you are still a man. If the fire did not burn away your manhood."

The twisted smile returned. "You should care less about what hides within my robes, more about the terror you created that now haunts your station. He is no longer in the ducts."

Wolfgang gestured to the troopers. They all withdrew their guns from the vents. The howls of their strange weapons faded like a pack of wolves padding back into their den, leaving the night silent. Wolfgang listened, trying to detect any scurrying, any breathing, any sign of their quarry.

Silence.

Nothing but silence.

* * * * *

"Did we get him?" a trooper cried out.

Wolfgang cringed. Loud. The trooper was too damn loud. The voice was jarring in the silent room. But the cry broke the tension. The troopers all relaxed and took deep breaths.

"We got him," another trooper said.

The SS began to chat, to laugh, to argue about who should crawl into the ducts to get the dead rat.

Wolfgang stared at the duct opening he had fired into. Only darkness lingered inside. A cold breath of air wafted out from the hidden labyrinth, scented of must and decay, like the breath of a ghost on a winter night. Wolfgang frowned, tilted his head, and stepped closer.

"I say we should peel off his dark skin," said a trooper. "Turn it into a coat."

"I want his skull," said another. "Did you know subhuman skulls are shaped like ape skulls? The cranium is smaller."

Wolfgang squinted, staring at that shadowy duct.

"Shhh," he whispered.

The troopers did not hear him. They kept talking.

Wolfgang raised his finger. "Shh."

They all turned to look at him, falling silent.

"I can hear him," Wolfgang whispered. "I can hear his breath. He—"

His eyes widened.

"Get back!" Wolfgang cried, leaping aside.

Fire.

Fire blazed from the ducts.

Wolfgang leaped aside just in time. The torrent slammed into an SS trooper behind him. The man screamed, clawing at his visor, at his burning face and eyes. The other vents burst open one by one. Flames roared into the corridor, turning it into a furnace.

Within the inferno like the burning bush of old stood Ludwig the monk. He raised his strange, three-fingered hands.

"Do not fear the flame!" His voice boomed, echoing through the tunnels. "Follow me through the fire. Come, quickly now!"

The robed scarfather spread out his arms, and like Moses parting the Red Sea, he seemed to somehow draw the fire aside. The flames crackled, rising in great sparking waves, forming a pathway between them. What dark magic was this?

Wolfgang grabbed little Greta. "Come on!"

Carrying the girl, he raced down the tunnel between the walls of flame. Two SS troopers lay burning and twitching on the ground, clawing at their helmets. The metal visors had melted onto the flesh, forming grisly masks of steel and skin. The last two surviving troopers ran behind Wolfgang and the girl. They followed the Burned One through a tunnel of fire. All around, the flames spurted from the ducts, but as the Burned One kept his arms spread out, he held back the fire.

Ghosts are real, Wolfgang thought. *And the power in fire is real. Parallel universes are real. And reality itself is but a dream.*

They emerged from the burning corridor into an engine room. The cavern loomed, as large as a cathedral, full of machinery. Pistons the size of automobiles chugged up and down, up and down. Gears as large as cabaret tabletops turned, their teeth interlocking and grinding together. Power thrummed through snaking cables, and pipes trembled with steam and plasma. In the center of it all churned the station core—a great cauldron, a smelter, a glimpse into hell itself and its lakes of roiling fire. He was in this chamber. Somewhere. The ghost in the machine. Ishmael.

Those icy claws again. They gripped Wolfgang's spine and squeezed.

"So!" Wolfgang said. His voice boomed through the engine room. He needed to speak, to convince his foe—and himself—that he was strong. His voice echoed. "You've done well for yourself, Ishmael. I admit it! You have the upper hand. But we

21

won't stop hunting you, you know. If you kill us here tonight, more will follow. Sooner or later one of us *will* catch you. So I'll make you a deal."

He waited. The machines chugged on. The gears spun. No answer came from the shadows.

"Don't you want to hear my offer?" Wolfgang cried.

And from the shadows—a ghostly voice. "You have nothing to offer me."

The two remaining troopers started, aimed their guns in the direction of the voice, and prepared to fire. Wolfgang waved them down. He looked up toward a mezzanine. The voice had come from there, he thought. But he saw only shadows among the pipes and cables and moving pistons.

"But I do, Ishmael. Come to me now. Face me man to man. And I will offer you a quick death. That is a mercy, I assure you. Keep eluding me, and I—or the hunter after me—will make sure you suffer."

For a long moment—more silence.

Then the voice sounded again. But it spoke from somewhere else now. From high above and behind Wolfgang, distant and echoing.

"No man has suffered more than me," said the voice from the darkness, seeming to come from everywhere at once. "You cannot break one who is already broken."

As the ghost spoke, Wolfgang kept scanning the darkness. And there! Just a hint of movement. A flutter of cloth behind a pipe. Up there behind the mezzanine railing!

Wolfgang fired.

A figure scurried away.

U-bolts slammed into a pipe, shattering it. Steam sprayed across the engine room. The shriek was deafening, a sound like the kettle of Lucifer himself. Wolfgang fired again and again, nearly blind in the steam, not sure if he was hitting anything.

A shadow swooped above.

"*Der schwarzer geist!*" shouted an SS trooper. Only two of the brutes still lived.

The last syllable was still ringing out when an arrow flew through the darkness. Not a medieval arrow of wood and feathers. This was a long, pointed, tungsten shard, topped with a minute warhead. The tiny missile drove into the trooper's helmet, shattering the steelglass eye protector, carving through the eyeball, and then detonating inside the skull. The trooper's helmet bulged, barely withstanding the blast. The trooper's head shattered within the helmet like meat exploding inside a microwave, then oozed out down the neck. The body crumpled.

Another arrow flew!

The last trooper fell, the arrow in his head. The warhead detonated. The blast ripped his head right off, and it rolled into the shadows.

Wolfgang hissed, gun raised. Where was the ghost? He took a step back and bumped into Scarfather Ludwig. The cloaked monk sneered and raised his hands. His sleeves rolled back, revealing his deformed gloved hands, each with only three fingers. They looked more like the talons of a vulture than hands. The Burned One stretched out his arms, and flames crackled to life above his upturned palms, illuminating the chasm of cables and machinery. Fräulein Greta completed the trio, gazing around with her purple eyes.

"What do you want?" Wolfgang shouted. "Do you want your wife and kids back from the dead? I can't do that! So be reasonable. Tell me what you want!"

The darkness laughed.

"You took everything from me," said the astral voice. "So I will take everything from you. I will make you suffer."

A shadow swooped above, fluttering like a bat through the darkness. Ishmael! The ghost's deep scream echoed, fracturing into a hundred laughing ghosts.

In the heart of the engine room, the cauldron swirled and belched fire, illuminating the swinging figure.

Wolfgang fired.

Umbrions flew from his gun, casting darkness across the chamber.

Behind Wolfgang, Ludwig let out a strangled cry. The sound a dog makes when you step on its tail. Then, with a gurgle, the Burned One fell silent.

Wolfgang spun around.

Something jerked the Burned One into the air. A chain! A chain was wrapped around the monk's neck!

"You should have left this tomb!" boomed the deep voice of the ghost above.

He was somewhere on the deckhead! Somewhere hidden above among the machinery, tugging the chain!

Kicking and floundering, the Burned One flew higher into the air. And then, hidden in the shadows above, Ishmael swung the chain like a pendulum. He hurled the Burned Man through the air, then cast him down into the churning, molten core of Toliman Space Station.

The monk crashed into the cauldron of blazing plasma. Watching from a distance, Wolfgang had the bizarre impression of some tiny doll splashing down into a bowl of soup.

A scream rose from the pool of molten ore. The scream rose higher and higher in pitch. Demonic. Inhuman. The Burned One flailed in the glowing ooze.

"You cannot kill me!" Ludwig shrieked as his robes burned off. "I am made of fire!"

The robes peeled back, revealing his true form. A burn victim. A man covered with scar tissue. A frail, diseased man. What remained of his flesh was melting now, revealing the bones, yet still he lived.

"I am coming, Hitler!" the monk cried. "I can see you. I can see you in the fire. I am coming, mein führer! Hail Hitler! Hail the Fatherworld! Hail . . ."

He sank into the bubbling ooze and was gone.

* * * * *

Disgusting, Wolfgang thought, staring at the bubbling cauldron. He would not grieve for his twisted cousin. Good riddance.

"Papa!" Fräulein Greta cried. She made to run toward the fire. What did she think? That she could still save her father? The man was just bones in broth! You'd have better luck restoring a hen from chicken soup. Wolfgang grabbed Greta's shoulder. He pulled the young girl toward him.

"The black ghost is still out there!" he said.

"Papa!" she cried, struggling in Wolfgang's grip.

Oh, to hell with her! He released the girl. She ran, vanishing in the storm of firelight and shadows and thundering machines. If she wanted to kill herself—let her. Good riddance to her too. Wolfgang stood alone, gun drawn, waiting. Just him and the ghost.

A thin smile spread across his lips. Wolfgang raised his skull visor, finally revealing his face to the darkness. He took a deep breath.

"Where are you, Ishmael?" he said in a singsong voice. "Come out, come out, wherever you are! I've removed my mask. Remove yours. Come face me. No more skeleton and ghost. Just man to man."

For a long moment, Ishmael was silent. Wolfgang stood, waiting. He heard only the gurgles of cauldrons, the distant mewls of the orphaned girl, and the thudding machinery.

Finally the deep voice spoke again from the shadows. "All

right. Let's talk. I'm coming to you."

Robes fluttered above. A cloaked, hooded figure descended like a dark angel, hanging from a chain. It was a slow descent. Not an attack swoop. Damn it, Ishmael truly was ghostlike. The man seemed almost to have no weight, to glide through the air like a dry leaf.

The cloaked figure got closer.

Wolfgang frowned.

Just a cloak. An empty cloak on a chain. What—

A shadow darted to his right.

A knife flashed.

With the instincts of a soldier, Wolfgang spun to his right, and there he was! Ishmael!

The man was racing toward him, wearing patchwork armor stolen from the SS, the Sig runes and swastikas scratched out. His face was finally revealed. The skin dark. The cheeks gaunt. The lips peeled back in a snarl. The eyes ablaze with something Wolfgang recognized so well. Hatred. Pure, unadulterated hatred. It was true what they said. The subhumans were monsters.

Ishmael leaped toward him, knife slashing downward.

Wolfgang stepped aside, dodged the blade, and reached out to grip Ishmael's wrist.

He caught it! He caught the man's wrist!

He twisted, and the knife fell!

But Wolfgang didn't see his foe's second hand. He didn't see the second blade.

A smaller blade. A scalpel. A blade thin enough to slide into the cracks between a soldier's pieces of armor.

The scalpel thrust.

It sliced between two plates of armor. Right below the breastplate above the thigh.

There was no pain. That was how sharp the knife was. But

when Ishmael twisted the blade, when he pulled it free, when the blood gushed, Wolfgang roared and his leg buckled. He found himself on his knees before his foe.

"You made me watch," Ishmael whispered. "You held my eyelids open. Made me see their torture. I wanted to gouge my eyes out. Instead, I will take yours!"

The scalpel thrust again.

Wolfgang tried to stop it. But somehow now Ishmael was the one holding *his* wrist! And he couldn't stop the man. No more than he could stop a ghost.

The scalpel thrust into Wolfgang's eye socket.

Not where his real eye stared. No. The scalpel merely cut where a saber had stabbed Wolfgang long ago. It sliced open old scar tissue, ripping open that old wound. Fingers followed. Sooty fingers tipped with cracked nails. They thrust into the socket, closing around the prosthetic eye.

Ishmael pulled the adlerauge clean out. Just like gouging out a real eye.

As a real eyeball was attached to the brain with optic nerves, an adlerauge was attached with slender cables. The wires, no wider than human hairs, connected directly to the brain tissue. Now, as Ishmael pulled the bionic eye back in his palm, those wires ripped free from Wolfgang's brain tissue. Wolfgang actually heard the *rip*. Ishmael took a step back, pulling the bionic eye away. The cables *slurped* free from Wolfgang's eye socket. They dangled from the prosthetic in Ishmael's hand like fibrous roots from a radish.

Wolfgang howled.

He had never known such pain. He stood on his knees before the beast, knowing this was it. This was his death.

He could have run. He could have begged. He would not. He would face his foe, chin raised. Groaning, Wolfgang pushed himself to his feet.

Ishmael drew a pistol and pointed it at him.

"I will show you a mercy you never showed me," he whispered. Tears streamed down his cheeks.

And then, with his remaining eye, Wolfgang saw her. Fräulein Greta. The little girl stood only a few paces away, gazing curiously with those huge lantern eyes.

Wolfgang darted toward her.

Ishmael's gun fired.

The plasma bolt sailed overhead, missing him.

Wolfgang grabbed the girl from behind, pulled her against him, and closed his fingers around her neck.

"Drop your gun!" Wolfgang roared. "Drop it or I snap her neck!"

Ishmael froze. He stared at Wolfgang. The flames of the swirling core rose behind him like a pirouetting dancer woven of fire. All around the darkness loomed. They could no longer see the machinery, merely hear the clangs and thumps that echoed in the cavern. Ishmael kept his gun raised, pointing at Wolfgang.

"Why should I care?" Ishmael said. "What is she to me?"

"A human life," Wolfgang said.

Ishmael barked a laugh. "Do you think I care about human life? Maybe I did once. You took that from me."

"I'll do it!" Wolfgang said. "I'll snap her neck. You'll have to watch her life flee. An innocent life! The life of a child! Like the life I took from your children. No. You don't want to see that, do you? So drop your weapon!"

Ishmael's face twisted into a grimace. He let out a howl. An enraged animal, he charged toward Wolfgang, gun blazing.

Wolfgang hurled the girl through the air at him. It was no harder than tossing a rag doll.

One of Ishmael's bullets pierced Greta's belly.

The child slammed into Ishmael, splattering him with blood.

He gouged out my eye.

Wolfgang took a step back.

He ripped cables from my brain. From my brain!

He trembled but remained standing. Blood dripped from his eye socket and his thigh. But he was a soldier of the Wehrmacht. He was a scion of the Fatherworld. He was the son of the führer. And he would not surrender. And he would not die.

He tapped a button on his battle armor. A hatch opened, and a rod extended, holding a grenade. Wolfgang pulled the pin, then hurled the skull-shaped bomb.

Not at Ishmael. No. The man was too dangerous. He would catch the grenade, throw it back, or maybe just leap to safety. Wolfgang hurled that grenade far over Ishmael's head. It arced, then dived down into the swirling, glowing core of Toliman Space Station.

Wolfgang turned and ran.

A rumble sounded behind. A rumble deeper than the ghost's laughter. Deeper than thunder. A rumble so deep Wolfgang felt it more than heard it—a physical force vibrating his armor and bones. His grenade was not packed with explosives but with umbrions. The anti-light. A power that grabbed and devoured photons like hungry parasites devouring the cells in your body. Wolfgang had used these unholy particles against starships before. This would be the same. These umbrions would gnaw through the core's molten energy like termites through the foundation of a home.

And like a home with crumbling studs, the entire station would collapse.

Wolfgang only had seconds. He just had to be a little bit faster than a ghost.

He returned to the corridor. The same corridor where, not long ago, they had walked through a tunnel of fire, emerging as if by miracle unscathed from the flames. Of those cursed companions only he, Wolfgang König, remained.

He pulled the heavy blast door shut. It was built to withstand a core blast. Wolfgang swung the heavy latch shut (it was the size of a log), and—

The explosion hit the blast door.

The metal door bulged. That door was two feet thick, forged of pure iron encasing a cement core. And it bulged like an inflated bag of popcorn.

The hinges twisted.

A secondary, then a third, blast hit the doorway.

A hinge cracked.

And then the roar eased. The fire was tamed.

Silence. Wolfgang heard only the ringing in his ears. Darkness engulfed him, and then he heard muffled sounds. Distant thuds. The backup generators turning on, perhaps. It felt like having cotton stuck in his ears. Power flickered to life, air flowed through the vents, and the lights turned on across the corridor. Ha. So that was all it took to bring the lights back on. Blow up the core and let the backup power do the work. They should put that in the manual.

Had Ishmael managed to escape the inferno? No. Not a chance. Not while carrying a dying girl. Not even a ghost could survive that.

Yet as Wolfgang limped down the corridor, heading toward a medical bay, he thought he could hear it echoing through the ducts. Mocking him.

Laughter.

Maybe it was just the ringing in his ears.

* * * * *

Ringing.

That was all Ishmael heard for a while.

Ringing in his ears.

Cradling the dying girl in his arms, he laughed. He couldn't hear his laughter, but he felt it bubble up like tar, like dark blood from a dying man's mouth. He had done it. He had faced the enemy and survived.

He was *alive.*

His laughter died.

But was he truly alive? No. Maybe not. Not quite. Oh, his heart still beat. But it only beat now for vengeance. Breath still filled his lungs. But it was breath like the cold air inside a tomb, smelling of mold and memories and loss. He knew his name. He was Ishmael Benjamin Jordan. But maybe that man had died. Maybe he had died with his family. Only a ghost remained.

And you could not kill a ghost. You could not kill that which had already died.

He crouched in a service hatch. The passageways wound around the engine room and throughout the space station like arteries and veins. Like a mouse fleeing a house fire, he had crawled into a network of burrows. Ishmael knew every twist and turn in the labyrinth. He had been haunting these halls for . . . How long has it been? He no longer knew. Maybe only months. But it felt like a lifetime. Time did not flow for the dead.

The rest of his crew had fallen. His family was dead. All he had left was vengeance. And so he would live—inasmuch as ghosts lived—for nothing but to hunt. To kill the Nazis in the shadows. To break them as they had broken him.

The girl in his arms gurgled. She coughed blood.

Ishmael looked down at her. Just a child. An innocent child. No older than his own daughter had been. And he had shot her in the belly.

It wasn't his fault. He had been aiming at Wolfgang. The Nazi officer had thrown the girl at him, using her as a human shield. Yet still the guilt tore through Ishmael. His eyes dampened to see this innocent child suffering in his arms. Yes, maybe a part of his humanity did remain. Maybe a part of him still grieved for the young and innocent who suffered in the wars between men.

"Pa—" The girl sputtered on blood. Her face was ashen. Her lifeblood was flowing away. "Papa—"

Ishmael placed his hands over her wound, trying to stanch the bleeding. But it was filling her lungs, he suspected. He had fired a plasma bolt. She was burning up from the inside.

"I'll take care of you," Ishmael said. "I'll take you to a medical bay. You'll be all right."

Those huge purple eyes locked onto his gaze. That innocent doll's face twisted into a demonic death mask. She bared her bloodied teeth, and her eyes burned with loathing. She spat on him. A mixture of saliva and blood.

"Filthy subhuman!" she hissed. "Ape!"

She gave one last gasp, then breathed no more. With her last breath, this child of innocence, of curiosity, of love for her father—she had died with hatred in her heart, her face locked in a grimace of disdain.

All her life, she was taught to hate men like me, Ishmael thought. *Men not of the Aryan race. Monsters in her eyes. She was bred to become a killer.*

Maybe there were no innocents among his enemies. Maybe not even among their children. And a deep sense of grief and loss filled Ishmael. Not only grief for the fallen, but grief for the loss of hope. The loss of belief in mankind's redemption. Maybe he had become like his foes, living only to kill. They had killed his family, but they had done something worse to him. They had made him a monster like themselves.

So he would be monstrous. He would do what monsters did. He would hunt.

He tightened his palm around his gift. Around that little treasure he had claimed.

And this will help.

Ishmael moved through the ducts of Toliman Space Station, dragging the dead girl with him. A hateful little thing she had been, perhaps, but she did not deserve to rot in a duct. Even this little devil deserved to be buried. A monster he was, perhaps. But maybe deep inside his monstrous soul he still remembered the sound of his beating heart.

He knew his way through the maze. He knew where the enemy prowled the halls. And he knew what parts of Toliman they had not yet infected. Ishmael had filled the station with barricades, booby traps, force fields, and false walls. Everywhere his cameras and microphones watched and listened. He had a thousand eyes and ears across his kingdom. He was the minotaur in the heart of Daedalus's labyrinth. He was the fly in the center of the web. He was Ishmael Jordan, once a commander in the Human Defense Force, now only a phantom in the shadows.

* * * * *

Leaving a trail of blood through the ducts, Ishmael crawled toward a specific vent in the ductwork. Through the grate he could see it. A small, abandoned medical bay. A place the Nazis had not yet claimed. Ishmael carefully removed the vent, making not a sound. Holding the dead girl in his arms, he dropped silently into the med bay. He landed on his knees, took a deep breath, and looked around, seeking enemies. If he must, he was ready to fight again.

The infirmary was running on backup power. Dim lights glowed, and machinery beeped and hummed. The original staff was still here. When first invading the station, the Nazis had moved room by room, exterminating everyone in their path. The doctor and nurses lay sprawled across the floor. They must have been dead for weeks. But oddly, the place didn't stink too badly.

The air-filtration system was constantly recycling the air, and no bugs or maggots crawled across the corpses. Rather than rotting, the corpses were mummifying, their skin drying and turning a faded tan color. They seemed to Ishmael less like corpses, more like dolls made of leather and papier-mâché.

As Ishmael examined the desiccated remains, he got a shock that rattled every bone in his body.

A voice! A voice spoke from behind the machines!

"Sir! Oh, bless the stars, sir. A survivor!"

And it was speaking *in English.*

Ishmael dropped the dead child, drew a plasma pistol, and aimed at the humming machines. The gun vibrated in his hand, ready to spew plasma.

"Sir?" the voice said. Strange shadows moved across the wall. Machinery clanked and motors buzzed. "Oh, it is you, sir!"

A robot emerged from behind the medical machines.

It was not an android. It made no pretensions of looking humanoid. And yet the human mind naturally anthropomorphized objects, and to Ishmael, something about the robot seemed oddly organic. It was a medbot, tasked with assisting doctors in surgery. Its head, as it were, was a lamp with multiple bulbs and functions, able to cast a dim ambient glow, a needle-thin spotlight, and everything in between. The neck was a long, adjustable metal pole. The body was square and bulky, full of drawers. A magnetic tray topped the robot's back, bearing multiple surgical tools. Eight limbs thrust out from the medbot, each tipped with articulate hands that could manipulate tools. Right now the hands were holding needles, scalpels, drills, and saws. The medbot clattered closer, moving on wheels. Three wheels moved smoothly while the fourth wheel, crooked, cast out sparks.

"Sir! Oh sir, it is you!" The robot spoke with an old-fashioned mid-Atlantic accent. It rolled closer, wobbling on its

34

bad wheel. "Commander Ishmael Jordan! You survived, sir! Oh, my circuits overflow with relief." The robot's lamp swung toward the dead girl on the floor. "Oh dear. It seems she was not as fortunate."

Ishmael limped across the med bay, cracking his neck. The adrenaline was dying off. The pain was seeping in now. While battling the Nazis, he had suffered an assortment of cuts and umbrionic burns. He sat down hard on an examination table, peeled back his sleeve, and winced. Umbrions covered his arm, eating away at his flesh like black mold. He grabbed a towel and began brushing them off. Damn! It hurt.

"Sir, allow me to assist." The robot rushed toward him with needles and scalpels. The machine screeched to a halt, its crooked wheel spraying sparks. "Sir! Your arm has been infected! I shall have to amputate it." The medbot raised a spinning sawblade.

"Put that damn thing away!" Ishmael said. "I'll be keeping my arm, thank you very much."

"But sir, according to the *Diagnostic Manual of Battlefield Injuries*, Seventh Edition, any arm infected with foreign substance shall—"

"Do you have a name?" Ishmael said.

The robot wheeled back a pace. Its head of light bulbs rose higher like a man raising his chin. "I am REMEDI: Robotic Emergency Medical and Diagnostic Interface. You may call me REMEDI or Remi for short."

"Remi?" Ishmael said.

"Yes, sir?"

"Go away."

"Very well, sir. If you require medical assistance, I am but a short whistle away. Healthy on!"

The machine wheeled four feet back and stood there. Staring at him.

Ishmael looked at his wounds, prepared to treat them. First order of business would be to stitch the ugly cut on his calf. But he couldn't focus with that robot staring at him.

"Remi?" he said.

"Sir?"

"Why don't you take care of the dead kid. Put her on ice for now."

"Of course, sir!" The robot wheeled toward Greta's body, then paused and looked back. "I assume you mean to place her within the mortuary freezer. Unless you wish me to fetch some ice cubes from the galley?"

Ishmael grabbed a needle and some thread. "The morgue, please."

"Very well, sir." Remi wheeled off. And Ishmael stuck the needle in. He grunted as he worked, sewing the wound shut. Remi could have stitched much faster and neater, Ishmael figured. But the robot was just as likely to saw his leg off.

With each stitch, as he winced, another vision rose.

A stitch. His sister dying in flame.

A stitch. His wife screaming as they snapped her fingers.

A stitch. His children crying out for his help.

A stitch. Alone. Alone among corpses.

His fingers were shaking. He stabbed himself with the needle.

Deep breaths, he told himself. *Be calm. Be in the present. Those are only memories. Only echoes in the mind. Be here. Be in the now.*

"Oh my, sir!" Remi wheeled back toward him. "That wound looks to be infected. And the stitching failed to stanch the bleeding. The leg will have to come off." He raised his spinning saw again.

"I told you to put that damn thing away!" Ishmael said. He looked at the bodies on the ground. The doctor and nurses lay there, mummified and crinkly. "Why did you just leave them there? They've been dead for weeks."

Remi looked at the corpses, then back at him. His light bulbs dimmed, and he hung his lamp low. "My algorithms do not permit it. Not without explicit orders."

"Put them away, Remi."

"Yes, sir! On ice?"

Ishmael nodded. "On ice."

Remi wheeled a few meters away, then looked at Ishmael. "The morgue, Remi."

The robot nodded. "Right away, sir."

* * * * *

As Ishmael made the last stitch, distant cries sounded in the station. He placed down the bloodied needle, cocked his head, and listened. Many Nazis still filled this station, and Grand Admiral Wolfgang was still alive. They would never stop hunting. Ishmael could not stay for long.

More will come, he thought. *They will keep coming. Wave after wave. Some will burn in my traps. And more will march onward. They will take this room too. They will take this station. This star system. This universe.* He clenched his fists. *But they will not take me.*

He opened one of his fists, revealing the treasure inside. A bionic eye. An adlerauge. A clever piece of German engineering, the mechanical eyeball connected directly to the brain. It fed a Nazi information, enabled telepathy, and revealed the secrets of the Reich. And this was not any adlerauge. This was the eye of Grand Admiral Wolfgang König himself. Ishmael didn't know how much data the bionic implant saved. Did it have a sort of photographic memory, saving snapshots of things Wolfgang had seen? What horrific images those must be! At the very least, the implant would connect to the Fatherworld's networks, open encrypted doorways, and see much that was hidden. No, not just any adlerauge. This was a key into the heart of the Fatherworld.

Ishmael looked at the eyeball. He hefted it in his palm. A lens on one end acted as a camera and projector. Little gears moved inside, and cables still ran out the back. The slender wires ended with grasping little claws where they had once connected to Wolfgang's brain. The device sickened Ishmael. In his hand, it suddenly seemed like some bizarre sea creature with wet tentacles and one giant eye. Ishmael wanted to throw the foul thing away, to step on it, to crush it. But he knew this was a treasure.

"To hunt the enemy," Ishmael whispered, "I must see what the enemy sees. I must think how the enemy thinks. I must become my enemy. With one eye, I must gaze upon my own world. And with the other—into my enemy's soul."

Remi wheeled back toward him. "All done, sir. The med bay staff has been put on ice. I shall never forget them. And all that they taught me." His lamp focused beams of light on the adlerauge. "Oh my, sir!" The robot wheeled closer, bad wheel squeaking. "Is that a bionic eye in your hand?"

"Well, it ain't a golf ball."

Ishmael contemplated the bionic eyeball in his palm. The empty pupil gazed back, dead and sightless.

What horrible sights did you see? Ishmael thought. *What secrets do you hold?*

It was insane. It was deranged. He couldn't! And yet . . . he must. They had taken his sanity with his family. So he might as well sink and wallow in his madness.

He shifted his eyes to the medbot. "Remi? I'm going to need your help with this one. I need to replace an eye."

Remi's lamp flared with warm light. "Just my specialty!"

Sometime later (time still had no meaning to Ishmael) he lay on an operating table. Remi hovered above him like some big, metal bird. At first, with his large lamp of a head, Remi reminded Ishmael of some clumsy metal pelican. But as Ishmael lay here, as

Remi lifted his many scalpels and needles, he seemed more like a vulture. A vulture ready to feast.

"Sir, I am only able to administer local anesthetic," Remi said. "Are you sure you'd like to proceed?"

Ishmael wanted to shout out *No!* His heart leaped inside his chest. This was madness. Insanity! How could he mutilate himself? He must stop this! He must save himself!

But then a smaller voice spoke in his mind. *For what?*

And he wasn't sure how to answer.

For what? demanded the voice. *For what do you want to protect yourself? To save your eye? For your wife? She's gone. For your kids? Gone! For your own sanity? Gone! So take it out!*

The voice was right.

"Do it," Ishmael said.

As he lay there, restraints burst out from the table, grabbed his wrists and ankles, and secured them tightly. Remi leaned down above him. In one of his metal hands, the robot held a long needle.

Since when did I start thinking of this machine as a he, not an it? Ishmael wondered. *Probably once I entrusted my life to him.*

"I will inject the anesthetic directly into your eyeball," Remi said. "Please try not to blink. And whatever you do—don't move."

The needle moved down.

"Um, Remi?" Ishmael said. "How many surgeries have you performed?"

"Oh, this will be my second time, sir!"

Ishmael blinked. "Your . . . second time installing a bionic eye?"

"Oh no, sir. I mean my second surgery ever. The first time I got to saw off a man's leg! It was quite fantastic work, if I may say so myself. I'd love to try it again sometime."

"You said replacing eyes was your speciality!"

"And it made you feel better, didn't it? Now please try not to blink."

The needle plunged down.

Ishmael bit down on a scream.

The drills, scalpels, and tweezers did their work. And he thought of his wife's smiling face. And he remembered his children running barefoot on the beach, flying a kite. He stood there watching them under the gathering clouds.

How long was the surgery? No sense of time. Just memories and pain. Just that stabbing needle and delicate tweezers, reaching down, down into his head, into his being, into his very mind. Yes, there they were on the beach. Smiling. His beautiful family. Yet as Ishmael ran toward them, as he pulled them into his arms, their skin shriveled up like old leather and they became mummified dolls.

"And there we go!" Remi said. "Let me slap a bandage onto you. And you'll be right as rain within a few days!" The medbot leaned down, lamp flaring. "Are you sure you wouldn't like me to remove that leg? The wound does look rather jagged."

The restraints retracted. Ishmael pushed himself up, swung his legs around, and his feet thumped onto the cold floor. He rose from the bed, blood dripping onto his shirt.

"Sir!" Remi said. "I haven't applied the bandage yet."

Ishmael walked, shuffling like a man who had just emerged from deep slumber, and pushed the medbot aside. He approached a mirror at the back of the infirmary. An old curtain hung over the mirror, only revealing Ishmael's feet. Those feet stomped closer.

"Sir, perhaps you should allow me to apply the bandage before you—"

Ishmael pulled the curtain off.

He stared at his reflection.

The bionic eye was stuffed into his socket, rimmed with

raw, stitched flesh. Blood dripped down to his chin and pattered against the deck. And as he stared, the bionic eye began to glow red.

Ishmael laughed.

His laughter rolled through the medical bay. He imagined it echoing down the ductworks, racing through the darkness, rolling through the station like thunder over a midnight sea. He imagined that across the station, they could hear the ghost's laughter, and they shivered.

"I can see . . ." Ishmael whispered. "I can see so much. I am coming for you, Wolfgang. I am coming for you all."

With a grin, he leaped into the duct. In the shadows, he crouched, drew his knife, and prepared for another hunt.

CHAPTER ONE
To See Another Sunrise

James King was a spacer without a ship. An admiral without a fleet. A soldier without a battlefield. Oh, in his youth, there had been plenty of those. He had flown starfighters. Then warships. Then the starship *Freedom* herself, flagship of the fleet. Then he had commanded that fleet. And battlefields? Oh, there had been plenty of those too. On land, in space, and in the void beyond space where physics itself broke down. For half a century, he had fought and served.

He had thought those days over.

When he retired on the farm, he thought he'd never see space again. Let alone battle in space.

For three years, he tried to enjoy the world he had saved, the peace he had fought for. He rocked on his rocking chair, whittled wooden figurines, collected coins, built ships in bottles, and talked to other old codgers on ham radio. For a while, the worst things that happened to him were a fish getting away, his horse getting fleas, and falling asleep in the rocker before finishing his mystery novel.

Then the Nazis came. From a parallel universe. From within the looking glass. They shot his horse. They shattered his life. They killed millions.

And so now he sat here in this shuttle, a few weeks shy of sixty-nine years old, wearing his old military uniform and ready to fight again. Wherever they sent him. Whatever they told him to do. It didn't matter. They might not give him a fleet again. Maybe not even a starship again. That was fine. If he had to stand in the trenches of some distant asteroid—hell, if he had to scrub latrines—he'd do it. And never complain.

Because I was never meant to be an old man on a rocking chair. I'm a soldier through and through. No matter how old I get. No matter how much my back hurts. No matter how many wrinkles line my face. A soldier is always a soldier.

"Why do you look so grim, King?" Godwin's voice was deep, booming, and jovial like the voice of some ancient king echoing through his mountain hall. "We're off on a grand adventure among the stars! Just like the old days, old boy. Makes you feel young again, doesn't it?"

"It's been a long time since I've felt young," King said.

Godwin—a man well into his eighties—slapped him on the shoulder. "You will soon, old boy. Once you see where I'm taking you."

King studied the man. There he was, George Godwin, sitting comfortably at the helm of their small starship. The short, rotund Englishman wore an old-fashioned three-piece suit, and a top hat hung askew upon his round, bald head. His coattails dangled off the sides of his chair.

"Ah, to fly again!" Godwin said. His eyes twinkled. "It has been too long. War is horrible business, King. Wretched, awful business. But I must admit—there is some romance to it. There is glory. And there is adventure."

High Commander George Godwin led the Alliance of Free Nations. The union encompassed the United States, Great Britain (Godwin's homeland), Canada, most of Western Europe, India, Japan, and a host of other democratic nations aligned against a common foe. That common foe—the evil of Nazi Germany—was bombarding Earth at this very moment. And Godwin, leader of the free world, was here in deep space, flying a starship barely larger than a bus, having the time of his life.

Something about all this didn't click.

Sometimes King wondered if he wasn't still on his farm. If he hadn't simply fallen off his rocker—literally and figuratively—and banged his head. This whole damn war just felt so surreal.

"Can you at least tell me where we're going, sir?" King said.

"I can't tell you, old boy. Or you wouldn't believe me. I have to *show you*. We're almost there."

The high commander stuck a cigar in his mouth, took a puff, and kept flying. They were in a Sparrow-class shuttle, a vessel so small it didn't even have its own name. Normally, the high commander flew aboard a grand flagship, enclosed within a protective ring of frigates and corvettes. But this was an undercover mission, and they were flying dangerously near enemy lines. Nobody else knew they were here. If spotted, they would appear like a simple Alliance courier, perhaps delivering tech parts or personnel. Probably not even worth expending valuable German ammunition on. Just to be safe, the Sparrow was modified with a stealth cloak, expensive tech normally reserved for much more important ships. The little Sparrow darted across the night sky like a spirit.

With a sigh, King turned toward his wife. "And I suppose *you're* not going to spoil the surprise either, are you?"

Kim Fletcher-King sat beside him, smiling softly. She squeezed his hand. "You're going to love it."

King spent a moment admiring his wife. Her beauty could always calm him. Hers was a beauty like a sunset over rustling fields, like a wise tree upon a hilltop, overlooking a windswept valley shedding its garments of summer, like a cup of spiced tea on the porch at dawn. A beauty that was autumnal and warm in a cold world. They had been married for three years now. And these had been the three best years of his life. Not that long ago, a bitter widower who escaped most nights into the bottle, King had never imagined he'd find new love. Not at his age. He had thought himself doomed to mediocrity and loneliness until he fell over dead one night in his favorite reading chair, never learning who the killer was in his latest mystery novel.

But things changed. Even for old men. In his early sixties, he fought a great war against the rahs. And now, pushing seventy, he was fighting another great war, this one against the Fatherworld. And in all this chaos, he had found Kim Fletcher. Divorced. A kid in the marines. Engineer of the starship *Freedom*. A woman of valor. A woman who became his sun and stars. Her eyes sparkled, as blue as Earth, and her hair cascaded like molten gold streaked with rivulets of starlit silver.

You're never too old to fight, King thought. *You're never too old to change. And you're never too old to fall in love.*

"You know I hate surprises," King said.

She kissed his cheek. "I know."

The shuttle flew onward. They were in low orbit now, heading deeper into the battle that still engulfed Earth. For a month now, the cannons had not stopped booming. Myriads of warships, large and small, constantly orbited Earth, battling around the planet. King had the sudden image of swarms of insects—army ants and termites and angry little beetles—caught in a maelstrom, spinning round and round a drain, yet still battling one another, termites biting ants, ants attacking beetles, everyone at one another's throats as they all spiraled inexorably toward ruin.

In this low orbit, so close to Earth's blue sky, they were flying through the Red Dawn front. Thousands of equalist warships flew in battle formations, defending their world. The Red Dawn comprised many nations, all swearing fealty to the ideology of equalism. The Chinese supplied most of the Red Dawn's ships. Millions of scaly starfighters, shaped like the dragon boats of old, flew across space, engaging the Nazi menace. Hulking Russian carracks fired their bear-shaped cannons. Stone balustrades rose along their decks, and teardrop domes topped their dorsal hulls. The Russian warships looked like strange, monstrous versions of Saint Basil's cathedral, shattered and rebuilt into moving, mechanical fortresses. Smaller nations flew among the dragons and bears, each supplying whatever they could to the war effort.

Before the equalist fleet loomed the Weltraumwaffe, the space fleet of the Fatherworld. A month ago, launching their surprise attack, the Nazis had invaded with only three hundred ships. They had caught Earth by surprise, and in a brutal blitzkrieg, they crippled Earth's defenses. And that had just been the opening salvo. By now the true bulk of the Nazi fleet had arrived. Ten thousand warships of the Space Reich surrounded Earth in a stranglehold. Each German ship was a mechanical terror, engines blazing red, black hulls proudly displaying golden swastikas. Foremost among them flew *Barbarossa*, the terror of the stars, a warship beyond a dreadnought, something that had no name, that should be impossible to build. Yet there it flew, its cannons glowing red like the eyes of Pele, the ancient god of volcanoes and retribution.

The Sparrow flew through the equalist-fascist front. Godwin piloted the shuttle confidently, darting around warships large and small, leaping over and under laser beams, and deftly dodging torpedoes and plasma bolts. An octogenarian, he was as spry as ever. Some of that was thanks to modern medicine. Unlike King, Godwin had rolled the dice and taken Rejuvenex. The drug killed ten percent of those who took it. But if you won the Rejuvenex roulette, it made you ten years younger. Godwin's eyes twinkled as he flew. Every now and again, after executing a successful barrel roll, Kulbit loop, or cobra maneuver, he let out a little whoop. Nobody saw the shuttle. The stealth cloak was working. Seen or unseen, this flight was still dangerous. There was a *lot* of crossfire to dodge. The old man was loving this.

Yes, it was like that in space, King thought. You didn't see the dead soldiers ripped apart. You didn't smell the death. Up here, war was like a game.

Godwin was high commander now, but he had begun his career as a fighter pilot. So had King. So had so many senior commanders of the Alliance. Jordan, Spitfire, King's own father, the mythical Ulysses King—they all began as pilots, and they became great leaders of flagships and fleets. Maybe it was because to pilots, war was a game, and they were excellent players. Maybe the ground troops, those who knew the hell of war, at some point walked away from the playing board. Or were buried below it.

"Ah, here we are!" Godwin said. "Our beloved Freedom Fleet! Take a good look, my friends. Now here is true courage."

In medium orbit, about thirty megameters from Earth, the Freedom Fleet was battling the Nazi menace. The grand fleet swore fealty to the Alliance, protecting its interests in space. The smaller fleets of many nations composed the Freedom Fleet, joined together to defend democracy. The battle up here was sparser than down below, spreading out to cover the greater space. Though stretched thin, the mid-orbit battle burned with its own ferocity. Ships hunted ships through the darkness like primordial reptiles and sharks in the ocean depths. A few megameters away, orbiting high above Antarctica, a German battle group bombarded the FAS *Lyrebird*, an Australian frigate. The Australian starship shattered, spilling its ruin upon the southern pole.

Godwin lowered his head, his whooping fading to somber silence. The three companions watched the fire. In death, the *Lyrebird* became as a bird of flame, her burning wings spreading out, then disintegrating into distant swirls of sparks like tiny galaxies. Unlike the phoenix, she would not rise from the ashes.

Kim's eyes shone with tears. "I knew her engineers," she whispered.

"Two hundred brave Alliance spacers served aboard that vessel," Godwin said. He snapped a salute. "Let us honor the fallen heroes."

King and Kim saluted too. As the shuttle glided onward into deep space, they observed a moment of silence for the fallen. On the rearview monitor, they watched the flaming wreckage of the *Lyrebird* cascade through the sky and douse itself in the icy plains of Antarctica.

King thought of the brave spacers aboard the *Lyrebird*. But as the moment of silence stretched on, his thoughts stretched toward the starship *Freedom*. The ship he had joined as a young man. The ship he had served aboard when fighting the Red Dawn. The ship he had commanded during the great Spider War. The ship that had been his life for half a century. A living, sentient ship. A ship he never forgot.

Yes. *Freedom* had been sentient. She had placed her soul into an android named Mimori, a living representation of the ship. The star had consumed *Freedom*, breaking the ship down to subatomic particles. Mimori had survived in an escape pod, but she had never been the same. Her enunciation became robotic, her mind logical and emotionless. She never felt quite sentient again. Without the *Freedom*, she became but a soulless robot, until one day she had flown into the darkness, seeking answers in the depths of space. The android never returned, and King understood. Mimori had not sought answers but finality. Among the stars she loved so much, she could sleep the sleep of death. The grief never left King.

In his mind, he relived that day. Once more, he was standing aboard Katyusha's bridge, a vagabond pulled from the ruin of his flagship. From the Russian ship, he watched the *Freedom*, empty of her crew, fly into a star.

Without you, I'm lost, King thought. *I still remember you every day,* Freedom. *You were the finest ship I ever flew. Without you, space seems dark and cold.*

* * * * *

Cloaked in her stealth cloak, the Sparrow flew by the moon on her way into deeper space. The war raged here too. The Desert Thorns, an alliance of Middle Eastern and African nations, were fighting to defend the lunar colonies. The lunies were doing their part, unleashing their own battleships (the few Luna had) and firing artillery from the silvery surface. And onward flew the little Sparrow, leaving the moon and her battles behind.

A million miles from Earth, they reached the nearest Lagrange Point. L1. This was where Earth and the sun's gravity canceled each other out. In turbulent space, this was an area of calm waters, so to speak, and a perfect place to park stationary objects. L1 was the industrial area of the solar system. Here hovered fuel refineries, shipyards, armories, science labs, and a host of other installations, military and civilian alike. In the early days of the war, the Nazis had bombarded much of L1. Several armories were still burning. But right now the Germans had their hands full battling Earth's three big fleets. It was a quiet night at Lagrange Point 1. If you could ignore the ghosts.

Godwin was flying them toward a particular space facility. It was small. Out of the way. One among ten thousand stations out here. As they flew closer, details revealed themselves. The station was spherical and covered with solar panels, telescopes, and dilating hatches. The place looked no larger than a basketball arena. A humble scientific outpost.

King read words painted onto the station's spherical hull: NovaTech H.O.R.D. 5.

King frowned. "Kim, this is your workplace, isn't it?"

She nodded. "Yep. NovaTech's High Orbit R&D Station number 5. That's where I work." She bit her lip, put a hand on his knee, and winced as if anticipating anger. "At least, that's where I told you I worked. The truth is . . . more classified." She chewed her lip.

"I'm an admiral. I think I have security clearance."

Godwin looked at him. "This secret we kept even from you, old boy. We couldn't risk anyone knowing. You could have been caught. And the enemy has ways of making anyone speak. We couldn't tell a soul. Only myself, Kim, and a few others knew."

"Knew *what*?" King said.

"Patience, old boy! Patience. We've been keeping this secret from you for three years. You can wait another three minutes."

"Three years!" King cried. "Kim, what—"

"Patience!" she said.

They flew closer to the station. NovaTech was a massive corporation. Headquartered in Houston, Texas, the company had branches across Earth and space. NovaTech was famous for creating the Talaria drive—the first great starship engine, capable of propelling starships at one percent the speed of light. That seemed slow nowadays, but at the time, it was revolutionary, ushering in a new era of spaceflight.

In the crucible of war, starship engines had evolved quickly. Just a decade ago (God, it felt so much longer), Earth had begun to interact with alien species. And learn from them. A civilization's first contact with aliens was always a big deal. Some civilizations remained virgins all their lives, eventually dying off in blissful obscurity, then perhaps dug up ten millennia later and logged in an archaeology archive. Other civilizations met alien species (sometimes kindly, sometimes nefarious) and joined the galactic chaos (with or against their wills). In 2199, Earth made her first contact with the rahs. What a wretched first species! You could not choose a worse introduction to alien life. The arachnids

had attacked Earth, had nearly destroyed the planet. But from the
Spider War humanity had emerged stronger. Today many
warships carried Hyperspace Portal Generators—technology
stolen from the rahs' dreaded clawships. Spiderholes (as spacers
affectionately called them) could propel you to another star within
a moment. The stars, once out of reach, were now within human
grasp.

And today you had hopscotch drives too. The strange
engines were given to humanity—a gift from the ancient Aeolian
civilization (also foes of the rahs). Many human starships now
wore patchworks of Aeolian tech. They adorned their hulls with
the coiling brass pipes, glass tubes, and crystals. The alien engines
seemed like magic or perhaps some crazy contraption from the
steam age, but they worked, and the physics was apparently sound
(though barely understood by humans). Hopscotch drives allowed
a ship to "skip" forward short distances—up to only a hundred
klicks. Useless for space travel, of course, but priceless for
dogfights. Also incredibly dangerous. Hopscotch drives
transported you momentarily into an eerie dimension, a place
spacers called the Otherworld. King had flown through the
Otherworld before. He had felt like a microscopic traveler
exploring the inside of a drop of water, marveling at the strange
creatures within. Not everyone returned from the Otherworld to
tell the tale. There were predators in that strange space.

The Nazis, it seemed, had their own propulsion
technology, developed independently in their universe by their
demented scientists. Their warships used the Überlichtantrieb
drive, allowing them to achieve warp speeds continuously. No
need for portals. When they did use portals, they were things of
terrible power, capable of ripping through universes. It was how
they got here from their parallel reality, and why they had emerged
at Alpha Centauri, light-years away. Universe portals were so
dangerous, so powerful, they actually crushed two universes

together, blending multiple timelines into a chaotic nightmare. It was like squishing two hard-boiled eggs together into mush. That could destroy Earth along with the Fatherworld, and the Nazis knew it.

At least that was what Kim had told him. For three years now, she had been studying parallel universes at this very outpost. At NovaTech H.O.R.D. 5.

"You did it, didn't you?" King said softly. "You figured out how to open universe portals of your own. You caught up with the Nazi tech."

Kim chewed her lip. "Not quite, Jim. To be honest, I didn't spend too much time on parallel universes."

He blinked. "But. . ." He sputtered. "Isn't that the whole purpose of this science lab? Why you've been working here for years?"

He hated feeling ignorant like this. Hated feeling so out of the loop, out of control. King was used to knowing everything, overseeing everyone. If there were secrets, he was the one keeping them. A sense of betrayal stabbed his stomach. Maybe betrayal was a strong word, but King definitely felt *left out*.

"Ostensibly," Kim said. "And I did spend *some* real time working on that science. But we also had a skunk works project. Godwin told me it's the highest priority we had."

Godwin nodded. "Indeed I did. Perhaps I had been mistaken. Perhaps I should have allowed Kim to continue her research into parallel universes without further distraction. Perhaps then we might have seen the enemy coming. We shall never know, and I shall not ruminate upon it. The past is the past. I set Kim on a project I felt was most pressing. And it's almost done."

"Almost is a bit optimistic," Kim said. "Halfway done. Maybe sixty percent." She heaved a sigh and squeezed King's knee. "There's so much more I wanted to do before showing it to you."

"Showing me *what?*" he said. "Will somebody please tell me what's going on already?"

But he thought he knew.

By God, the thought had been growing in him, twisting through him. Could it be? Could Kim have actually . . .

"Ah, the door is open to welcome us!" Godwin said, interrupting King's thoughts. "Let us fly in."

Godwin had dropped the Sparrow's stealth cloak. NovaTech Station seemed to recognize them. A hatch opened on the spherical hull, welcoming the Sparrow into the space station.

King was expecting to find a busy hangar. What he saw shocked him.

He blinked, hardly believing his eyes. "What the hell?"

The station was hollow. No hangar. No offices. No labs. The hull was an empty husk. It was like some set from an old Western film where the saloon, sheriff's office, and blacksmith shop were just false plywood fronts. And there, floating in the center of the hollow space, hung a portal.

A spiderhole. A portal to the stars.

"This whole station is fake," he whispered. "A fake shell hiding a doorway to somewhere else."

"Buckle up," Godwin said and flew the shuttle into the portal.

* * * * *

Space and time warped like pizza dough.

Traveling through portals did that. This wasn't a multiverse portal like the one the Nazis had opened at Alpha Centauri. This was "just" a spiderhole, a tunnel from one place to another within this universe. But it was still a trip. The portal warped spacetime, the very fabric of reality. Traveling through the spiderhole, King lost all sense of space and time. Suddenly he was a young fighter pilot, just a kid in his twenties, flying an Eagle starfighter against Katyusha's Red Dawn. The next moment, he was a new father, holding baby Bastian in the palm of his hand. The preemie was that small. Then time leaped forward, and King became a man of ninety, sitting in a wheelchair, medals on his chest, a blanket over his knees, attending a memorial to lost soldiers. The "pizza dough" warped again, hurling him back in time. He stood aboard the *Freedom*, his admiral insignia freshly forged and gleaming on his shoulders. Mimori stood at his side, and their starship sailed toward the sun.

He blinked, forcing himself back to the present. They were still hurtling through the tunnel, and lights streaked all around, the lights of stars and possibilities, of lives lived and lives that remained merely dreams. He marveled at how long the journey of life was, how full of memories and joys and losses, yet also how short and precious it now seemed. He was nearing the end of that life now. A sobering thought. Oh, he might live for another twenty, even twenty-five years. But how many *good* years did he have? Years of health, of making memories? How long before senescence robbed him of independence, leaving him that man in the wheelchair? His life had been eventful and long, and it still felt too short. He just didn't have enough *time*.

Man had conquered the stars, harnessed the atom, and yet still could not stop that inexorable ticking of the clock. As a younger man, King would sometimes lean back in his den, pausing from reading a history book or building a ship in a bottle, and he would sit and watch the hands move on his grandfather clock. He marveled at antique technology, collected it when he could, and had always loved clocks in particular. Yet now, an old man, King found clocks unnerving. Every second the hand ticked was another second gone from his life. Another second he could never get back. Another grain of sand falling through the hourglass. And there wasn't much left.

King held his wife's hand. With her, he would savor every moment he had left. Kim made those moments good.

They emerged from the spiderhole, and the Sparrow flew toward strange stars. King blinked, studying the starscape. He had spent years traveling across the galaxy, and even without checking the navigational screens, he got a sense of his surroundings.

"We're about a hundred light-years away," King said. "Somewhere near . . ."

Kim hid the navigational panel with her hand. "Guess."

King studied the stars. He could see familiar constellations. Orion. Ursa Major. But they were distorted, Orion's belt too wide, Ursa's cup too narrow. And a new constellation shone on the rearview mirror, shaped like a serpent. The serpent's eye was Earth. King knew that much.

"Yes, about hundred light-years away." King turned toward the starboard and squinted in the light. "That yellow sun there. That's . . ." He thought for a moment. "Delta Draconis?"

Kim laughed and revealed the navigational panel. "Delta Draconis!" She kissed his cheek. "Can't trick an old space captain."

Godwin whistled. "Good show, Admiral! Jolly good show. You know all this from a glance at the stars?"

"I told you he was good," Kim said.

Godwin handed her a box of cigars. "I owe you one of these, my dear."

King looked at his commander and raised an eyebrow. "You bet against me, sir?"

Godwin chuckled. "Sorry, old boy, but I hadn't realized what a savant you were."

"I'm not," King said. "I just spend a lot of time among the stars. This galaxy . . ." He swept his hand across the stars. "This has been my backyard for half a century. Each of these stars is a familiar light, a character in some great play I've watched countless times. A man who lives in the forest learns to recognize most trees. I recognize most stars."

Godwin nodded. "In a few years, all humans will be like you, King. Spacefarers. Hard to believe, but we've only been in space for three centuries. Not long ago for a species that's three hundred thousand years old. And only *ten years ago* we figured out how to reach the stars. We're still babies, King. We just learned how to walk, and we're taking our first steps in the shadows. If we win this war, the stars are our domain. And if we lose, their light will forever go dark, and in the shadow we shall remain."

"Then we must win," King said. "We *will* win. Now tell me why we're here."

"There she is, old boy." Godwin gestured ahead. "Don't you see?"

King squinted at the distance. Then he leaned back, and his eyes widened. "There's an invisibility cloak ahead! I can see the slight tremble to the starlight. I thought it was just the shaking panel."

Kim held his hand. "I'll turn the cloak off."

She tapped a code on the Sparrow's panel. The stars swayed for a few seconds as the cloak faded.

And there she was.

She hovered ahead, risen from a dream.

A starship. A dreadnought. A grand old dame of the stars. Her engines glowed, and the prongs of her railgun thrust toward the unknown, gleaming with starlight.

King knew her well, and his eyes welled with tears.

"The starship *Freedom*," he whispered.

* * * * *

The starship *Freedom*.

The finest ship that had ever flown.

King didn't understand. Didn't know how this was possible. At this moment, he didn't care. All he could do was sit in the Sparrow's cockpit, gaze through the viewport at the dreadnought ahead, and marvel.

The starship *Freedom* had been christened in 2159. Forty-eight years ago. No sooner had she rolled out of the shipyard than *Freedom* joined the Third World War, rising to lead the Alliance against Katyusha and her nascent Red Dawn. For five years, *Freedom* had fought that bloody war. And every day for five years, James "Bulldog" King would fly from *Freedom*'s airlock in his Eagle starfighter. At his side, every battle, had flown Larry "Phantom" Jordan and Yehuda "Lion" Levy. The trio flew into enemy formations. They bombarded equalist worlds. They had nearly lost their lives a thousand times. But every time, a thought kept them going. That *Freedom* depended on them.

Yehuda had fallen in that war. And *Freedom* had lingered on.

For years, she patrolled peaceful space. Then, as the cost of fuel and crew rose, she collected dust in a shipyard. Finally the Alliance bosses (civilians all) turned her into a museum for World War Three. Then they added a gift shop. And a hotel. And a casino. And a few restaurants. By the end, *Freedom* had become an amusement park. Where starfighters once docked in preparation for battle, tourists squealed down water slides into a wave pool. Where marines once trained for war, glow-in-the-dark dinosaurs guarded a miniature golf course. Where brave spacers once loaded cannons and tore down equalist warships, tourists drank and cheered on the showgirls.

Year by year, they disgraced her, stripping away her own glory and adorning her with kitsch. The warrior queen had become a carnival barker, her dignity stolen. But King remained, for he still remembered the warrior queen and loved her. He rose through the ranks, becoming commander of the ship he adored. And every time they added another buffet, another haunted house, another wax museum . . . another part of him died.

The spiders had shattered all that. The spiders had crawled from the night. They destroyed the world. They slaughtered millions. They left a crater in Nebraska, his beloved home, where Omaha had once been. They kidnapped his granddaughter, broke his back, and murdered people he loved. People like Oliver Darjeeling, the boatswain of the *Freedom*. People like Mimori, who had lost her soul with her ship and passed into night. People like Stowy. His beloved Stowy. The girl had stowed away in the starship *Freedom* for years, becoming a mascot to the crew. And like a granddaughter to him. To the crew, she was more than just a stowaway but a fairy princess, an elfin spirit who came from a magical realm. Sometimes, wandering the halls of the *Freedom* at night, you might be lucky enough to hear her tinkly laughter. Sometimes you might even catch a glimpse of her impish smile. And sometimes you held her in your arms as the spider venom flowed through her, and her eyes were large and hazel, gazing in wonder as her life fled back into that distant realm of faerie, leaving a body like a husk made from dried rose petals and strands of flax.

Yet Stowy was back now. Another Stowy—a doppelgänger of that fairy girl—had emerged through the looking glass. And here again flew the *Freedom*. She was a mile long from stern to stem. The fourteen Angels of Liberty topped her hull— mighty cannons the size of skyscrapers. The Fist of Freedom, the legendary railgun of the dreadnought, thrust out from the prow. The gun's twin prongs, capable of hurling Goliath projectiles at relativistic speed, would dwarf most buildings in Manhattan.

For a moment, King wondered—was this starship a doppelgänger like Stowy? Had this dreadnought come from the parallel universe? But that was impossible. This was his *Freedom*.

The same *Freedom*. With the same modifications. The portal generator which Kim had built circled the railgun like a Ferris wheel. The Shield of David point-defense system was mounted outside the hull, connected to a sophisticated system of rails. Those rails were another design of Kim's, retrofitted onto the hull. And the hopscotch drive, a gift from the Aeolians, shone across the stern. The alien system's brass pipes, glass tubes, and crystals starkly contrasted with the rest of the ship. They reminded King of jewels around a belly dancer's hips. Every little modification and patch King and crew had made throughout the wars—it was here.

So no. This was no dream. This was no doppelgänger ship. That left only one possibility.

He looked into his wife's eyes.

"So that's what you've been doing for the past three years," he said. "While I've been building ships in a bottle, you've been building a new starship *Freedom*."

"I wanted her to be your seventieth birthday surprise," Kim said. "But we had to unveil her a little early."

Godwin stared at the *Freedom*, and all trace of his earlier joviality faded. His eyes hardened. His underbite gave him the look of a pugnacious hound.

"Yes, King, we built her anew," the high commander said. "Just as she had been on the night of her sacrifice and victory. She saved the world twice already. When we began this project, I did not know what future threats our world would face. I certainly could not predict the menace that, even as we speak, continues to assault our world. Yet I knew that we needed the *Freedom* to be reborn. To guard our planet. To defend our civilization. And now we need her more than ever."

Kim took a deep breath. She shifted uneasily in her seat. "She's not quite ready. Many of her systems aren't working yet. And she's missing a crew."

"Yet fly she must," Godwin said. "Ready or not, *Freedom* must join the fight. The fierce *Lioness*, the new flagship of the Freedom Fleet, has fallen. So *Freedom* must take her place!"

"In a year, we can—" Kim said.

"In a year, Earth might have fallen to the Nazi devils," Godwin said. "*Freedom* must join the fight *now*. I want her flying tonight. Or by God, we might not live to see the dawn."

CHAPTER TWO
A Mouse in the Machine

"The *Freedom* must join the fight now!"

The words echoed through the Sparrow shuttle.

The starship *Freedom.*

Freedom . . .

Hiding behind the shuttle seats, expertly concealed inside Admiral King's duffel bag, the little girl shivered.

Freedom.

The word shot through Stowy like electricity. A sense of déjà vu filled her. And this time it wasn't because of flying through the spacetime portal. Somehow she *knew* that starship. Somehow she had *been on that starship.*

No, not me, she thought. *The other me. My Unreineland doppelgänger. The other Stowy. The one who died.*

Were the two connected somehow? Could Stowy (*this* Stowy, a girl from the Fatherworld) somehow remember things the other Stowy (the girl who had died here in Unreineland) had experienced? Curled up inside the duffel bag, she racked her brain, trying to remember more. But she could not. All her memories were of the Fatherworld and its cruelty. The déjà vu fled like a dream at dawn. Maybe she had imagined it.

No, she could no longer remember anything from that other life, from the other Samantha "Stowy" Perry. She knew only what she had heard. The adults of Unreineland spoke, and Stowy had always been good at eavesdropping. Long ago, in this universe so far from her own, had lived a copy of herself. An *untermenschin.* An impure girl from the impure world. A girl named Stowy who also wore a dress covered in pockets, who was also autistic, who was also an orphan who hid in shadowy places. A girl who had died. A spider queen had caught her in her web, and venom had stopped the fairy child's heart.

Who was the real Stowy? Was it the girl born in Unreineland, this strange universe where Hitler had lost the Second World War, where the disabled were not called *impure*, where they were not burned in the furnace and scattered over the city as ashes? During her short time in this universe, Stowy had not needed to hide. The Gestapo did not hunt her. The terrible Aktion T4 program did not promise to euthanize her. Wicked doctors did not kneel above her like vultures, performing their strange experiments and surgeries. This universe was far more pleasant for a child like her. But perhaps the Stowy of this universe had fought her own demons. Rather than vultures, they were spiders who had tormented the girl of Unreineland.

Well, that child is dead, Stowy thought. *And I, broken as I am, remain.*

In the darkness of the duffel bag, she caressed the tattoos on her wrist. One tattoo was her number. A number was your only identity in the lab. Many of the children there had never been given a name; they were merely numbers. Stowy's second tattoo was an inverted black triangle. Symbol of the broken. The impure. The crippled. Most ended up in the lab due to physical disabilities. With her, it was her mind. She had a third tattoo but not on her wrist. That one she kept hidden on her belly by her surgical scar. That tattoo depicted a circle with a small cross extending downward from it—the universal symbol for femininity. But in her tattoo, a jagged line slashed across the symbol, a violent mark of erasure. The tattoo denoted her as sterilized. In the Fatherworld, all the impure got sterilized. Just in case. Stowy could not pass her broken genes on to offspring. She still remembered screaming as Dr. Baer had cut her open. The good doctor had anesthesia in his lab, but he kept it locked up. He enjoyed the screams.

Stowy had fled the lab. She had escaped the furnace and the ashes that rose across the city. She had stowed away on a German warship, flown through a portal, and made her way here to this new universe. To this reality where men did not hunt autistic little girls, but spiders did.

She must be careful here.

She must remain hidden.

She must stay safe. There were spiders in the darkness of both universes, and the Nazi forces that had tormented her back home were now here within the looking glass. Anyone could be a doppelgänger. Anyone could hurt her.

A tear fled her eye and rolled down her cheek. She tasted its salty warmth on her lips. As a little girl, hiding from the Gestapo in the alleyways of Munich, she had dreamed of finding a castle on the clouds. She had thought this universe would be her castle. Yet still she cowered and hid. She was not a princess in this realm but a mouse.

She reached upward, and gingerly she loosened the duffel bag's drawstring. The round opening was no larger than a marble, allowing in a little light and air. Stowy imagined this duffel bag as a grand cathedral full of columns and vestibules of gold. In her mind, the hole above (where the drawstring was loose) became an oculus like the one in Rome's Pantheon. Long ago, Stowy had seen Hadrian's marvel of architecture in one of Papa's forbidden books. She imagined herself as a giant trapped inside the ancient temple, a beast, a monster, somebody whose deformity could be seen for miles, seen by all. She terrified the others. The little humans in the temple saw her as a beast. But like an elephant fearing mice, she feared them more.

The scared giant peered through the hole. And Stowy saw

him there. He sat just a few steps away, gazing out at the stars. Admiral James King.

A man so familiar.

A man whose face Stowy had hailed countless times.

Yes, she knew him. In the Fatherworld, he was named Helmut König. Führer. The steward of the empire Hitler had raised. But here in Unreineland, he was a different man. An American man. With a different name.

And he was kind. When Stowy had feared all others, had feared *him*, James King had shown her kindness. Had promised to protect her.

And so Stowy would not leave this kind old man. She followed him around, but she kept to the shadows. When he ate his meals, she hid under a nearby table, eating from a bowl like a cat. When he went to bed, Stowy slept in a sleeping bag outside his room. Right there in the corridor. The other adults of Unreineland thought her odd. They spoke about her oddities right in front of her, not realizing she could understand. They thought, perhaps, that because she was mute that she was deaf too, that because she was autistic she was slow. But she understood everything. So what if they spoke? They tolerated her behavior, and that was what mattered. They let her eat and sleep on the floor. A few tried to get her to sit at a table, to sleep in a bed. She could not speak to them, could not form words, only hiss like a scared possum until they backed off.

They think it's because I'm autistic, Stowy thought. *That I'm like a wild animal who can't use furniture. But that's not it. It's because I don't want to be far from him. From James King.*

Back on Earth, after James King packed for his trip, Stowy secretly emptied his duffel bag. There was nothing interesting in there anyway—just spare clothes and some toiletries. While he was in the washroom, she sneaked into the bag. He had lifted her, carried her into the Sparrow, and taken off into space.

And so now she was here, stowing away in a baby spaceship, leaving Earth behind. They called her Stowy because she had always been good at stowing away. You cannot change a scorpion's nature nor the soul of a little girl.

She widened the hole just a tiny bit more. James King was still staring out the viewport. He seemed in awe of the starship ahead, this mythological starship *Freedom*. Stowy wriggled around, placed her eye over the hole, and gazed out into space.

The *Freedom* looked nothing like the Fatherworld's starships, the only starships Stowy had ever known. Say what you liked about the Nazis—they had a sense of style. Since the Second World War, Hugo Boss had designed and manufactured the Nazi uniforms, and even today the Fatherworld was obsessed with appearances. Their starships were like their uniforms, designed to look sharp and instill fear. But the starship *Freedom* was, well . . . not ugly per se. No, ugly was the wrong word. But strictly . . . functional. It looked to Stowy like the inside of an engine. Perhaps they had not assembled the hull yet? Perhaps she was staring at the internal mechanisms? Countless machinery jutted outward like boils and bristles from rough hide. Stowy saw sensors, rails, machine-gun nests, airlocks, graviton generators, shield generators, pipes, gears, and all sorts of other contraptions she didn't recognize. Gargantuan cannons—Stowy counted fourteen of them—stuck out from the dorsal hull on each side. They reminded her of the spikes along an ankylosaur's flanks. Three enormous exhaust ports dominated the ship's stern. One exhaust port at the bottom. Two above it like round ears. The arrangement reminded Stowy of Mickey Mouse (a cartoon character who existed even in her universe).

But the front of the *Freedom* was the most interesting. Two colossal rods stretched forward. It was a railgun, Stowy thought. But it must be massive! Those rods were the size of skyscrapers! And suddenly it clicked in her mind. Her perspective shifted. The

Freedom wasn't built like the internal parts of some engine. It was a gun. A huge gun! A huge gun that people—thousands of people—could fly in.

A gun to shoot bad guys, she thought. *A gun to slay monsters.*

It was not a beautiful ship. Not in the way Fatherworld ships were beautiful. It looked cobbled together, a patchwork of different things banged and stitched and forced into form. Sort of like her dress of many pockets. Sort of like her life and tattered soul. And again a sense of déjà vu filled Samantha "Stowy" Perry, and when she looked at the starship *Freedom*, she knew that she was looking at her home.

"I'm home," she whispered inside the duffel bag, and tears stung her lips with their joyous, salty kisses. "I'm home."

* * * * *

As the Sparrow flew toward the starship *Freedom*, King felt something akin to a religious experience. He could practically hear the angelic choir. The light of Delta Draconis shone on his ship, gilding the Angels of Liberty. He had never seen a sight more beautiful.

As the shuttle approached, King saw the difference between this *Freedom* and his former dreadnought of the same name. First of all—you could tell this *Freedom* was new. There were no scars on the hull. No dents and scratches across the armored plates. No burn marks. No wear and tear. This *Freedom* was a perfect replica of a vintage 2150s dreadnought. The big, bulky components. The crude yet efficient welding. The bulky ATLAS sensors and shield generators (the technology was forty years out of date). But everything looked *new.* As it was. This was how the original *Freedom* had looked when rolling out of the shipyard so long ago. Back then King himself had shown a little less "wear and tear." Oh, if only they could rebuild him too in a lab!

Well, they can, he thought. *Katyusha builds herself new clones, scoops out their brains, and plants her own brain inside. I'd rather get old and die.*

He pushed such morbid thoughts out of his mind, focusing on the marvel ahead. A marvel? This was a miracle! The starlight glinted on the starboard hull, illuminating massive words.

FAS FREEDOM M-II.

"So?" Kim elbowed him. "Whatdya think? Not bad, huh?"

King had to wipe his eyes. He tried to speak, but his throat caught.

"The old boy is speechless!" Godwin boomed. He let out an enormous belly laugh. "I think he likes it."

King had to think about that. *Did* he like seeing *Freedom* reborn? He had always railed against Katyusha building herself new forms. Was this essentially the same thing? An imitation of something great that was gone? A revival of lost youth that only resulted in something too perfect, too polished, a living memory like a wax figure? Was this starship ahead, grand and enormous though she was, a sort of doppelgänger?

How could this be the starship *Freedom?* This ship had never barreled into the Red Dawn lines, taking Katyusha's blasts upon her prow but plowing onward, full speed ahead, torpedoes be damned. This ship had never charged at a world of spiders, all guns blazing, taking on the terrors of the galactic depths. This ship had never explored new worlds, discovered new allies, plumbed the depths of hell, and returned with the scars to prove it. No, this was not his ship. King was a knight who had won many battles with a trusty old sword, a knight who knew every nick, every scratch on the blade, a knight whose armor told a tale of adventure, woe, and triumph with ten thousand little cracks and dents. If that knight donned shining new armor, if he carried a freshly forged sword, even though he might look the same as in his youth, he was somehow diminished. Yes, even if his new armor and sword were sharper and stronger than those he had lost.

He looked again at those words upon the hull.

FAS FREEDOM M-II.

This was not his ship. No. This was a new ship. A new *Freedom*. A new life. A new hope as the shadow of Nazism fell across the galaxy. And as the starlight shone upon her, so did the light shine in his heart.

King turned toward his wife. He held her hands and gazed into her blue eyes.

"Kim," he said. "How?"

"Three years, working almost every day," she said. "And I had Mimori to help."

King gasped. His eyes felt like they'd pop up. He barked a laugh. "Mimori is here?"

"She's been talking about you nonstop," Kim said. "Oh, Jim, I wanted to tell you so many times! But with you retired, you didn't have the security clearance, and I couldn't. I couldn't tell anyone. Mimori couldn't even tell you she was alive. And . . . I'm sorry." Her eyes dampened. "I'm really sorry."

King barked a raspy laugh. "Kim, this is . . . This is the most wonderful, beautiful, miraculous thing I've ever seen. Right up there with the birth of my son. This moment . . ." His voice caught again, and his old eyes, warrior eyes that had seen so much death, dampened with joy. "I'll never forget it."

He thought that he heard a little sniffle from behind his seat. From where his duffel bag was. But then a hatch opened on the *Freedom*, the shuttle flew inside, and King only could gaze around in awe.

* * * * *

King knew exactly which airlock this was. Good old airlock A8M-S3, leading into the Sparrow's Nest. Aboard the *Freedom*, airlock names denoted their purpose. *A* was for airlock, 8 for deck 8 (out of Freedom's 32), *M* for midsection (nested between the stern and prow), *S* for starboard side, and 3 for the third door down. There were many gateways in and out of the *Freedom*, each with its history and stories of battles and courage. Some of these airlocks had seen legendary battles that would not shame any medieval city's gates. A8M-S3 was normally not used for battle, but it had seen its share of action. King had once stood in this airlock, battling Russian invaders hand to hand, hurling them out into space.

They entered the hangar bay and thumped down on the deck. This hangar was smaller than the Rhino decks, those echoing caverns where the heavy armored transporters had once slumbered. And Hangar 8MS was certainly humbler than the Eagle decks, those lofty aeries where the fabled starfighters nested between battles. But even humble old Hangar 8MS was a place of grandeur, a vast chasm full of flashing lights and machinery. King noticed, even before they landed, that there was no deck crew on duty. And there were no other Sparrow shuttles docking. The only other vessel was a Saint Bernard, a bulky ship built for search and rescue, its hull painted red and white.

Godwin powered down the Sparrow, popped open the hatch, and inhaled deeply. "Ah, smell it! That new starship smell. Nothing like it." He hopped onto the deck. "Come on, come on! Come, King. Take a look around! Doesn't she look exactly like the old *Freedom*?"

King paused for a moment, still sitting in the Sparrow. Kim noticed his hesitation. She squeezed his hand and smiled.

"I'm here, Jim," she whispered. "I love you."

"I love you too," he whispered back, gaining strength from her warm smile and sparkling blue eyes. "More and more every day."

He stepped onto the hangar deck and inhaled deeply. Yes, there was a distinct new-ship smell. Older ships smelled of oil leaks, old fires, grease, sweat, and gunpowder. This hangar still smelled like plastic. His footsteps echoed through the chasm.

"No other Sparrows?" King said.

"We're still working on getting more," Kim said. "We do have some Eagle starfighters! And some Rhinos. They're almost ready to fly in battle. Almost. The Mimoris are working on them around the clock."

King whipped his head around toward her. "You said Mimoris in plural. Are there seven again?"

Back in the old days, there had been seven Mimori units aboard the *Freedom*. Each android acted as a humanoid interface, representing a different aspect of the starship *Freedom*. Mimori Prime, leader of the group, served on the bridge. In the early years, her sisters had seemed like simple clones. But over the years, the other Mimoris developed personalities of their own, then eventually gave themselves new names. Madori served in the science department. Timori served as a logistics android. Arsenal worked in artillery. Memento served in the ATLAS unit, helping with the sensors, telemetry drones, and data-crunching servers. Finally, QT and Q-Mari served down in engineering. Some of them had died in the wars (inasmuch as an android could die). Others had simply felt the loss of their mothership too keenly. A part inside them died with *Freedom*, and they eventually wandered off into the void. And one had betrayed them. King didn't like thinking about that one and the heart she had broken. Seven Mimoris. Seven sisters. Were they all back now?

Kim suddenly looked like a guilty schoolgirl caught with her hand in the cookie jar. "Actually, Jim, there are . . . a bit more than seven this time around." She winced. "I needed help. And good luck getting mechanics with enough security clearance. So I .

. ." She bit her lip. "I built a few more Mimoris. Well, a lot more. Don't be angry."

He frowned. "How many more?"

She blushed. "I'm not really sure, to be honest. At some point, I allowed Mimori to self-replicate. Whenever she needed a helping hand, she could clone herself. She needed cheap labor— obedient androids to build a starship." She frowned and placed her hands on her hips. "You know, Jim, it's no easy task building a mile-long dreadnought from scratch. In secret. Within only three years. *Freedom* wasn't going to be ready for another two years, but once the Nazis invaded, well, we needed to get things done quickly. And the Mimoris have been miracle workers. One Mimori can do the work of ten men. And do it ten times faster. The *Freedom* you see? It's their work more than mine." She winked. "Though I'll happily take the credit."

King inhaled deeply. "So there are more than seven Mimoris, huh?"

A voice sounded from a nearby doorway. "By my count, sir, there are 514 of us by now. With three more in various stages of completion. Oh, and . . . welcome aboard, sir. It's good to have you home."

King spun toward the voice, and there she was.

The soul of the ship. The brain of the *Freedom*. A sentient android who was also a dreadnought. His beloved Mimori. Not a copy. Not a clone. The real Mimori, the one who had served with him for so many years. He would recognize her anywhere.

"Mimori!" he cried, rushing toward her.

She laughed, held out her arms, and gave him a huge embrace.

"I'm back, sir. I'm sorry I had to leave you. I'm so sorry. But I'm back. And we're together again."

They embraced for long moments. Then King held her at arm's length. "Mimori. You haven't aged a day."

She grinned, showing sparkling synthetic teeth. "The wonders of robotics."

"And I've grown old and wrinkly," King said.

"You were always old and wrinkly, sir."

He barked a laugh. "I was almost starting to forget about your sass."

Mimori was fifty years old, but she still looked like a young woman. No, perhaps not young. Her skin was smooth and synthetic, never wrinkling, giving the illusion of youth, but the wisdom of age shone in her glass eyes. Perhaps it was more accurate to say that Mimori looked *ageless*. She had not come from Delain Shipyards, the original (and now defunct) manufacturer of the *Freedom*. Mimori was the creation of Alita Robotics in Tokyo, built to resemble Mimori Minatozaki, the owner's daughter. The android wore a navy-blue Alliance uniform, the fabric adorned with big brass buttons. This style of uniform was popular in the 2150s, harkening back to the naval uniforms of the nineteenth century. Today in 2208, such uniforms were old-fashioned, but they complemented the *Freedom*'s retro aesthetic. Mimori's nylon hair spilled out from under her naval cap, shimmering and black, cut the length of her chin. It would never grow longer. A few scars marred her plastic skin, mementos from her many battles. They would never heal. Yes, this was the very same unit that King had fought alongside for so many years. This was *his* Mimori.

"God, it's good to see you again, Mimori."

Her eyes dampened. Tears were a feature built into her robotic body, but it wasn't just a trick. Mimori felt real emotions.

"You too, sir." She embraced him. "I missed my commander."

"Is that all I am to you?" King said.

She smiled and touched his cheek. "And my friend."

Godwin approached them. "I do hate to interrupt a good reunion, but time is of the essence. While we dally here, the battle

72

still rages at Earth. We must get the ship in working condition. And then, with furious vengeance, we shall enter the fight. The *Lioness* has fallen. The Freedom Fleet needs a new flagship."

King nodded. "How much crew is currently aboard? Who are we short-staffed on?"

Nobody answered.

King frowned. "Mimori, how many spacers are currently aboard the starship *Freedom*? I mean—aside from all the Mimori units. Humans only."

"Counting you, High Commander Godwin, and Colonel Fletcher, sir?" the android said.

King nodded.

"Three," Mimori said.

King blinked. "Three thousand?"

She stared at him.

King gasped. "Three *hundred*?"

"Three, sir," Mimori said. "And I do believe Godwin is returning to his shuttle."

King rubbed his eyes. He turned toward Godwin. The high commander was waddling back toward the Sparrow, his cane tapping, his top hat hanging askew. Sometimes the man reminded King of Winston Churchill. At other times he seemed more like Charlie Chaplin.

"Sir!" King said, racing after the older man. "Aren't you staying?"

"No, my boy, I've got a war to run. And my task includes overseeing the ground, air, and marine forces. I can't do that from up here." He opened the Sparrow hatch but did not enter yet. He stared at King, his eyes hard. "Space battles are your business, Admiral King. I'm putting out the word. With the fall of the *Lioness*, the starship *Freedom* is henceforth the new flagship of the Freedom Fleet." His voice softened. "As she was always meant to be."

"And she's mine to command?" King said. He raised his hand in salute. "Sir, this is an honor that I—"

"No, Admiral King!" Godwin said. "You won't command this starship. You were admiral once, King, and admiral you shall be again. You'll command the *fleet*. The Freedom Fleet. With its thousands of warships. You'll serve from aboard the *Freedom*, but you won't command the flagship. Choose a commander who'll serve under you. I trust your judgment. Crew our beloved *Freedom* as best you can. Until you recruit enough spacers, Mimori and her sisters will help run the ship."

King frowned. "Sir, I'm honored, but . . . how do I find a crew? How do I get them here?"

Godwin patted him on the shoulder. "I don't know, old boy! That's why I delegate." He gave King's shoulder a squeeze. "You'll figure it out."

"And my mission, sir?" King said. "Once the *Freedom* is flying again?"

"Rally the fleet," Godwin said. "The Freedom Fleet is falling apart. It needs your leadership. Join the other ships. Reform their lines. Resist the enemy in space. You have twenty-four hours to get there. And to whip the fleet into shape. After you do that, I'll deliver your next orders." Godwin placed one foot in the shuttle, then paused. "Oh, your duffel bag! Don't forget your things, Admiral. You'll be here a while."

King took his duffel bag from the shuttle. He hefted it across his shoulder and winced. Heavy. Damn heavy. A military duffel bag, filled with supplies for a soldier, normally weighed about fifty pounds. This one felt even heavier. King groaned as he carried the weight. Had he overpacked? No. Maybe he was just getting old.

And then Godwin was off. Flying back to Earth in his little shuttle. Leaving King and Kim aboard the new starship *Freedom*—the only two humans aboard.

"Twenty-four hours to find a crew and get her flying, huh?" King said.

Kim heaved a sigh. "War is hell."

* * * * *

King walked through the starship, carrying his duffel bag. There was much to do and barely any time. His mind was racing. When that happened, King found that walking helped him think. In the old days, he would always roam *Freedom*'s halls while thinking. Kim had taken a lift down to engineering, where a host of Mimoris awaited her. The engineer would be spending the next twenty-four hours in a frantic race to get *Freedom* battle-ready. King walked the narrow corridors alone, making his slow way to the bridge.

This place felt so much like the old *Freedom*. The same diamond-plated decks. The same bulkheads covered with pipes, panels, gears, and hatchways. Round doorways led into bunks where marines could sleep. Other hatches led to lifts, service shafts, and other corridors. The new *Freedom* followed the same schematics, used the same materials, yet it was not the same.

There were no photos of fallen marines on the walls. There were no letters from home inside the little bunks. There was no crude welding, ill-fitting screws, or spray foam insulation where mechanics had quickly patched things together. Hell, there wasn't even any duct tape. There was no Oliver Darjeeling patrolling the halls, chin held high, white mustache bristling, barking orders and keeping things neat and clean. There was no sound of laughter. No familiar faces. There was no rust or wear on the diamond-plated steel underfoot, no holes or cracks on the bulkheads from decades of battle. And yet as King walked here, his memories populated those missing spots, those empty places. He would fill this ship with life again.

Yes, he had needed to walk like this. If only for a while. Even with everything else going on.

If only this duffel bag weren't so damn heavy. What the hell had he packed? He hefted the bag across his back. His spine creaked, and he winced. It had been nine years since the rah torturer had stretched him on the rack. His back had never fully healed.

"Allow me, sir," Mimori said.

The android walked at his side, half his size. King was a tall, broad-shouldered man, powerfully built, still physically imposing even at his age. Mimori only stood as tall as his shoulders, and her body was slender like a gazelle. Yet King knew that she was much stronger than him. Stronger than any man. Belying her dainty frame, the android had the strength of a gorilla. She took the duffel bag from him, handling the weight with ease.

"It weighs 77.82 pounds," Mimori said, hefting the duffel bag. "Above regulation. Did you overpack, sir?"

"I must have." King rubbed his shoulders. "And I'm getting old, Mimori. I could have sworn I was carrying twice that much. I can't carry heavy weights anymore. My back hurts. I can't walk as fast. Or sleep as deeply." He looked at her. "When we first met, we were the same age."

"I was only a few months old. You were in your twenties."

He chuckled. "Well, we looked the same age at least. You still look in your twenties. And I . . ."

He paused by a dark panel on a corridor wall. Normally it was a computer panel, but with most of the systems offline, the black screen became reflective like a mirror. King looked at himself. Sometimes he told himself that he wasn't really *that* old. Sixty-eight. (Sixty-nine in just a few weeks, but he was going to savor sixty-eight while it lasted.) Big deal! That wasn't proper old. Proper old was like . . . being ninety or so. Sixty-eight was still the prime of youth!

But the mirror did not lie. Looking at himself, he saw new wrinkles. He saw hair that was going from gray to white. He saw bags beneath his eyes and a weariness to his brow. Even just eight years ago, a man of sixty, he had felt strong. But now every birthday he seemed to lose something. His aging was accelerating. Oh, he might be able to hide it for a while longer. Even from himself. But sooner or later it would catch up with him. What if this war lasted for years? Could he still fight in his seventies? In his *eighties*? It was the curse of aging. The older you got, the faster the years went by. The faster you decayed.

The *Freedom* didn't have much time to get ready for war. And King felt like his own life didn't have enough time. The years were slipping away between his fingers. And he must watch those fingers twist and wrinkle and bend.

Oh, to be an android like Mimori, never aging! And yet the thought of immortality seemed somehow worse than death. To linger on forever, century after century, millennium after millennium . . . To suffer pain and loneliness for so long . . . No, King would not want that. The mere thought chilled him. Better to be a mortal man, to experience life for a few decades, then rest. The immortal had no rest. Death scared him sometimes. But without death life would become unbearable.

He turned away from his wrinkled reflection. He marched at a quicker pace.

So what do you want? he scolded himself. *To go back to your farm? To sit on your rocking chair? To whittle your little figurines, and listen to your Johnny Cash records, and read your mystery novels, until one day you keel over dead? No. No, that was never meant to be my life. I am a soldier. Once a soldier, always a soldier. I was always meant to die in space.*

He found himself walking along Deck 28 in the midsection, heading toward the prow. His old neighborhood. Beverly Hills, the troops used to jokingly call this place. Deck 28 was where the high commanders lived. And compared to the humble spacers in the lower decks, senior officers lived in luxury. Down below, spacers and marines lived crammed together, six per room. And those rooms were small. Barely more than closets. Instead of proper beds, they slept on narrow slats that swung down from the walls. Barely more than bookshelves. Sardines in a can—that was the life of most spacers. King had spent his early years living like that too. But up here on Deck 28? Senior officers got their own private quarters. Privacy aboard a warship was reserved to only the very few.

King approached his old quarters. King's Library, they used to call it, due to the abundance of books within. This felt so much like coming home. King approached the door, almost expecting to see Donahue's grinning face. The bald, British security guard always gave King a big smile, showing a huge gap between his front teeth, and they would chat for a moment about their day. But Donahue wasn't there.

Nobody was. Other than Kim and himself. This ship suddenly felt so cold. So empty. Like a mausoleum. He stood outside his door, silent and still, letting the memories wash over him.

"Sir?" Mimori said. She stood at his side, carrying the heavy duffel bag across her slender shoulder. "Would you like me to open the door for you?"

"I'm fine, Mimori. I'm not so infirm that I can't open doors." He smiled wryly. "I'm just an old man with many memories. Sometimes they clamor for a while inside my skull, tooting their horns."

Mimori looked at him in concern.

"Not literally," he told her.

The android smiled. "Ah! So you were just pausing to enjoy a few pleasant memories. I can remember things very quickly. I forget that humans like to savor their memories."

Mimori was sentient, *legitimately* sentient, not just the

perfect impersonation acts of early AI. The android also felt real emotions. But her sentience and her feelings were different from the human experience. Sarcasm, body language, and humor sometimes confused her. Perhaps one could never fully replicate the human mind in a machine. Humans, after all, weren't merely humans. A typical human body housed trillions of microbes. Most humans actually had more microbe cells than human cells. And all of them affected how humans lived, thought, felt, and acted. The bacteria in your gut affected your personality as much as your brain. In a sense, Mimori was less like a human, more like one of those microbes. The *Freedom* was the body. The *Freedom* contained the supercomputer that was her brain. Though her body was humanoid, that was for his benefit. Mimori was a manifestation of a starship. In some ways, King and her would never understand each other. She would never quite know what it was like to be human. And he would never know what it was like to be a starship. But together they had always complemented each other.

He opened the door and stepped into his old quarters. And it was like stepping off the starship *Freedom* and into an antebellum study in some grand old farmhouse. Kim and her army of androids had restored King's cabin lovingly. Hardwood covered the floor, hiding the diamond-plated steel. An antique oak desk stood by a round porthole that revealed the stars. Wooden shelves covered the walls, and even the fireplace was here. The shelves had once contained leather-bound books, naval instruments, geodes, ancient weapons, and other curiosities. Those shelves were empty tonight, and the hearth was cold. This was a new place, yet it somehow felt very old to King, a place of lost glory like an abandoned manor house long after burglars had run off with all the artwork and silverware.

At least the suit of armor was back. King smiled, letting the memory warm him. A lover of old things, King had purchased a medieval suit of armor for his fiftieth birthday. He had carried it into the *Freedom*, dragged it into his cabin, and placed it by the fireplace. That armor had gone down with the old *Freedom*. Yet Kim, when building this new ship, had gotten him a new suit of armor. On closer examination, it wasn't an actual medieval piece. Those were, admittedly, hard to find outside of museums. This one was a replica, but a damn good one. In time, Kim would likely have stocked the shelves with books too, restoring his old haunt to its former cozy glory.

"God bless you, Kim," King whispered. "I love you. Where would I be without you?"

Suddenly the memories flooded him. Years in this office, grieving for the loss of Diane, his first wife. Years of shadow, sinking deeper into the bottle. Years of bad blood between himself and his son. Years when *Freedom* had become a museum, a sideshow, a parody of herself. But there were so many good memories here too. Visiting his father, the previous commander of the ship, and playing cards with the old man by the fire. Sitting at the desk, himself now commander, feeling the weight and honor of his responsibility. Bouncing his granddaughter on his lap, showing her the antique books and crystals. And Stowy. Sweet Stowy appearing at the vents, giggling. And one night saving his life from a spider, then smiling softly in his arms as her life faded away. This room would forever remind King of her. Of them. Of all of it.

Yes, this was an old place. And he would make it home again. He still had time. Time to make more memories. Time to save more lives. He had lost so many souls he loved, but he also saved many, and that drove him onward.

Mimori put down the duffel bag by the fireplace. She gave King a sad smile.

"Do you need a moment, sir?"

A bittersweetness flowed through King, a mixture of nostalgia and melancholia, comforting yet profoundly sad like the sip of your favorite scotch on the night your father died. King nodded. "Just a moment."

Mimori touched his hand, still smiling softly. "I'll wait for you on the bridge, sir." She took a step back, snapped to attention, and raised her hand in salute. "My commander. It's good to have you back."

King stared at her, and he understood the shift in her tone and stance. Yes, they were friends. Yes, they were kindred spirits. The bond between a spacer and his starship was something sacred, something as profound as marriage or parenthood. They both understood that. In their own way, they loved each other—deeply, fully. But this was war. And right now, more than anything else, they were soldiers.

King stared her squarely in the eyes and returned a crisp salute.

Mimori left his quarters, heading down the hall toward the bridge. King remained in his cabin. He just needed this moment to take it all in. To let his mind settle. To let this impossible dream feel a little more real. The *Freedom* flew again. This was real. He was home.

No . . . it still felt like a dream. He would need one more moment.

He took a deep breath, and in the silence—a squeak.

King frowned. A squeak?

There—it sounded again. A squeak! From inside his duffel bag. King pursed his lips. Was it a mouse problem again? Mice were a constant menace aboard starships. Especially in the chaos of wartime. Yes, even aboard the famous *Freedom*, they had suffered from the odd infestation (it used to drive Darjeeling up the walls). King would never forgive himself if he had, inadvertently, brought the first mouse aboard a brand-new starship *Freedom*. With his luck—a heavily pregnant mouse. And those things could breed like tribbles.

He unloosened the duffel bag's drawstring and . . .

He blinked.

A girl. A girl was inside his duffel bag. A girl with a mouse in one of her many pockets.

"Stowy!" he blurted out.

* * * * *

Stowy peered out from the duffel bag, frozen in terror.

He loomed above her. A big, powerful man. Admiral James King. The man Stowy had been shadowing for weeks now, sleeping outside his quarters in the hallway, eating under a nearby table while he dined at the mess, feeling safer the closer she was. After all, it was why Stowy had stowed away in his shuttle. Why she had followed him here to the starship *Freedom*. He was the strongest man in this universe, and he would keep her safe.

Yet now her heart leaped. Algernon had squeaked, and King had found her, and now shock pulsed through Stowy. During her time as a lab child, Stowy had endured many medical experiments. Over and over, Dr. Baer (or Uncle Bear as he liked his lab children to call him) would expose her to stress and pain. Sometimes he woke her with a shout or slap. Sometimes he burned her. And the electrodes across her body measured her reactions. Stowy had learned that she (like all humans) had four instinctive reactions to threat. Fight. Flight. Fawn. Or freeze. If an enemy attacked you, your body—often without your conscious mind—chose one of the four. Fight back! Run for your life! Beg and grovel! Or four: simply overload and freeze. Like a deer in the headlights. Like a possum in a predator's grip.

That was what Stowy did right now.

She froze.

Because as the shock pulsed through her, as her heart beat, something changed in her perspective. The anxiety overrode her conscious mind. And suddenly above her, she did not see the kind and courageous Admiral James King. She saw his Nazi doppelgänger—Führer Helmut König!

Instead of an Alliance uniform, the navy-blue fabric adorned with brass buckles, he suddenly wore a black uniform, the arms adorned with swastikas, the shoulder straps topped with little steel skulls. Instead of sporting a five-o'clock shadow, he now boasted a thick mustache. One of his eyes became a mechanical thing, a mimicry of an eyeball, and it blazed with red light that pierced Stowy like a blade.

She fell backward, spilled out from the duffel bag, and scampered into the corner of the room. Right under the empty bookshelves by the cold hearth. Trembling, she wrapped Luna around her. Her trusty blanket had been her companion since early childhood. Luna was tattered by now, and Stowy had sewn multiple pockets onto the blanket. They complemented the pockets across her dress and single stocking. All the items in those pockets jangled, and a few spilled out: a few coins and marbles, plastic dinosaurs, a hair clip that reminded Stowy of a crocodile mouth, an ivory button (Stowy suspected it might be mammoth ivory), a piece of chalk, a key that had no door, an acorn she had drawn a sad face on, a trading card featuring a famous fighter pilot, and a single puzzle piece (Stowy had never found the rest of the puzzle). The knickknacks clattered across the floor. A marble rolled under the desk.

"It's all right, Stowy!" King said, holding out his open palms in a calming gesture. "I'm not angry."

One of his hands was mechanical. A gauntlet. A metal machine that could crush skulls. She imagined it crushing her head. Her heart pounded against her ribs. Nestled inside a pocket over her chest, Algernon squeaked again. The mouse sensed her fear. Stowy trembled and panted and came close to hyperventilating.

"Stowy, it's me," King said softly. "It's all right."

Stowy knew what was happening. Over the years, she had learned more about her autism and its comorbidities. One common symptom? She was feeling it right now—with vengeance. Some called it a "meltdown." Others called it a "panic attack." Whatever you named the thing—it had gripped her, squeezed her, and kept her frozen in place.

Her logical mind, after some delay, reemerged from hiding and did some thinking. She had no reason to fear. That wasn't Helmut König ahead. That wasn't a Nazi tyrant. The vision of Führer Helmut König was an illusion. No, his uniform wasn't black. Those were only the shadows. No, he wore no swastikas. Those were little blue stars with red stripes growing from the sides like wings. Symbol of the starship *Freedom*.

Where my doppelgänger used to live, Stowy thought. *My castle in the clouds.*

So why did her heart keep pounding?

With creaking joints and a groan, King sat down on the floor before her.

"You know," he said, "at my age, it's not wise to sit down on the floor. Getting back up is a challenge! But I wanted to sit beside you. So I don't look so big and scary. I know, I'm still a burly, grouchy old beast with an ugly metal hand. Some kids call me Admiral Grouchy. But I'm one of the good guys. And I fight the monsters."

Admiral Grouchy. That almost made Stowy smile.

Almost. Quickly her wariness returned, and she looked around the room. She had heard the others whisper. Of another Stowy. A girl from this universe, like her in every way, down to the pockets on her dress. A little fairy girl who lived in the ducts and sometimes popped out with a mysterious smile. A princess who was stung by a spider.

"She . . ." Story whispered. "She . . ."

No more words came out. She was too afraid. She could feel her throat lock up. All her life, she had struggled with speech. Stowy had been mute until age nine. And even now, fourteen years old, she still struggled to form words. When alone, she could speak easily to her blanket and mouse. But when somebody else was watching, was listening . . . That was a different matter.

So she only pointed at the floor, and she mouthed silent words: "She died here."

King seemed to read her lips. Sadness filled his eyes, and he nodded.

"But you're back now," he whispered, and amazingly, this strong soldier, this grouchy old beast—his eyes dampened. "It'll be all right now."

No. No! She wasn't that Stowy. She wasn't the girl who had lived here once. That had been a shadow! A reflection! Not her. Who was she? Why was she here? Again the déjà vu flowed over her, spinning her head.

I'm dead, she thought. *I died right here. I'm a ghost. Not a girl. Not alive. A ghost.*

And now, as the anxiety pounded through her, again her body and subconscious chose one of the four paths. This time— flight!

"Stowy, it's all right," King said, reaching out to her.

Stowy fled backward like a frightened mouse. She whipped around the suit of armor. Like an animal into its burrow, she retreated into the cold fireplace.

I'm dead.

I'm a ghost.

I shouldn't be here.

She looked outside the fireplace. She didn't stare at the kneeling, concerned King but at the floor. That wooden floor.

That's the spot, she thought. *The spot where I died.*

And in her mind, she saw herself lying there, cold and pale like the dead children inside Uncle Baer's gas chamber. All the jewels had spilled from the fairy princess's dress of many pockets, scattering crystals and acorns and magical coins. A spider knelt above the fairy girl, a spider the size of a wolf. An old spider. An old goddess of webs, her skin wrinkly and pale like ancient parchment or birch bark, sprouting tufts of white hair like the scalp of some ancient knight cursed to long life beyond measure. That spider was the queen of rahs, and her stinger was long and thin and glimmering like a porcupine quill. It didn't even release any blood as it pierced the fairy princess in her innocent heart and pumped her full of venom.

And Stowy could not stand it any longer, she could not stand being in this room, being a ghost, being something from another universe, an abomination. She terrified herself. And as that flight instinct galloped through her, she fled up the fireplace.

It was not a real wood-burning fireplace. Gas, she thought. Gas like Uncle Baer's little chambers with the white walls. Gas like the spirits that filled those pale rooms, flowing around children like sandmen, scattering the white dust of sleep. Day after day, Baer opened that white door, and Stowy saw the children stumble out. Just empty shells. Skin pale. Eyes rolled back and sightless like round white bones. Gas. Like that. And her terror pounded through her and her flight became a panic.

She rushed up the fireplace shaft, ripped out a panel, and crawled into a horizontal hatch. She tunneled forward, moving between metal rods and around gears, down shafts and through thick bundles of black cables like alien grass. She was inside the walls, moving through the arteries of the starship. A mouse. No longer a ghost, she hoped. Just a frightened little mouse. Just like Algernon, who rode in her pocket.

She didn't need anyone else. She didn't want anyone else.

They would all look at her and just see the dead girl. She had Algernon. She had Luna, her oldest of friends. With a good mouse and safe blanket, she had all that she needed. And here, inside the walls of the starship *Freedom*, she had many places to hide.

CHAPTER THREE
With Growing Strength

King's heart ached.

He wanted to help Stowy. To comfort her. To make her feel safe.

I terrify her, he thought, his heart twisting in his chest.

The old Stowy—the one from this universe—would be laughing, frolicking, and having the time of her life. Nothing had ever doused that girl's spirits. But this Stowy, this doppelgänger rescued from the Fatherworld, had gone through hell.

King didn't know exactly what Stowy had endured. Dr. Annie had tried to examine the child, but Stowy bit her and escaped. Before the girl had fled, Dr. Annie had seen scars on her belly. A tattoo shaped like the symbol for Venus and femininity but with a crude line slashed across it. The symbol denoted her sterilized, her womb and ovaries removed. More tattoos on her wrist marked her a laboratory experiment.

King had read old books about and by Holocaust survivors. Most never overcame the trauma. This version of Stowy was, for all intents and purposes, a Holocaust survivor, and King didn't know how to help her. Nobody in this universe knew how to heal the victims of Nazi horror.

We'll have to learn, he thought. *For Stowy and, maybe, for many others like her.*

He peered up the chimney, but she was long gone, scurrying through the walls like a mouse. For now there was nothing King could do. He could not fit inside the narrow passageways between the bulkheads. Stowy had survived for fourteen years as a disabled child in a world that wanted her dead. King must trust that she could survive in the starship *Freedom* too. She was courageous and resourceful, and King's heart ached that she was in pain.

But there *was* something King could do. He could—*would*—fight the men who had hurt her. He would wreak vengeance upon them. For all the people they had killed. For hurting a little fairy princess.

Leaving his quarters, King walked toward the prow of the *Freedom*. The dreadnought was a ship like a city, and like a city it included districts and neighborhoods. Broadly, *Freedom* was divided into three parts. The stern housed the engines, the core, the exhaust systems, and the engineering departments. It was the stern that kept the ship flying. The midsection contained bunks, armories, hangars for starfighters and transporters, the infirmary, and many crew amenities, including a library, chapel, gym, and mess hall. The midsection also contained gunnery stations for the Angels of Liberty, the Shield of David interceptor system, and of course the legendary Fist of Freedom. The great power of the *Freedom*, from its marines to its mythical guns, operated from the midsection. This was the muscular core of the ship.

The prow, meanwhile, was the brain of the ship. The entire prow was an engineering oddity, built around the base of the Fist of Freedom. The colossal railgun was *Freedom*'s primary weapon. Its prongs were the size of the fabled Twin Towers from New York's semimythical past. The gun was so powerful its Goliath projectiles could destroy any enemy ship, could even blow up small moons. The Fist, King suspected, could destroy even the *Barbarossa*, the gargantuan flagship of the Fatherworld. Such power came with a cost. It drained the energy out of the ship. You could only fire the Fist once in battle. Then the ship needed a good twenty-four hours to recharge. The railgun also took up *a lot* of space. The entire prow wrapped around about the lower third of the railgun prongs. Science labs, telemetry stations, observatories, the server farms, the artificial intelligence systems—they all grew around the railgun like mushrooms and ferns around two tree trunks. Deep within the prow, like the heart of a yew, hid the bridge.

Three years since watching his beloved flagship fly into a star, Admiral James King did something he never imagined himself doing again. He walked onto the bridge of the starship *Freedom*. It felt so surreal, yet at the same time—the most natural thing in the world. And suddenly the years all washed away, and it was like no time had passed at all.

I was lost. And I'm home.

Kim (with the Mimoris helping) had re-created everything from *Freedom*'s old bridge. It was a cluttered, shadowy place. A place to get work done with no nonsense. Truly, this was a bridge from another century. Everything about the place screamed 2150s—a bygone era. Aboard the bridge of the *Freedom*, there were no fancy hallucinatory displays. No enormous screens that covered every surface. No domed ceiling. Modern bridges looked like planetariums, places to dazzle the senses. The bridge of the *Freedom* was different. The workstations featured real screens. Not hallucinations. Not holograms. Actual, real screens with green text on black backgrounds. Round PPI monitors, featuring concentric circles, displayed space around the ship. Nearby objects, mostly service drones and telemetry satellites, appeared as little green dots. The *Freedom* never flew alone; there were always a host of sensors, cameras, and drones that circled the ship, monitoring and filming and fixing things. They formed a symbiotic relationship like a hippo and the birds that cleaned its skin. This ship still ran ATLAS: Advanced Telemetry Analysis System. That came with a lot of drones and sensors. Across most of the Freedom Fleet, ATLAS had been replaced decades ago with more modern systems, but King still loved it.

He walked across the bridge, soaking it all in. The shadows, clutter, and hum of machinery comforted him. There was something soothing about the dim lights, countless sensors, and beeping machines, each perfectly recreated, restoring a bygone era. But it was more than just those antique technologies brought back to life. Kim had recreated details that weren't on the official blueprints. The same brand of coffee machine (Señor Coffee) stood by the bulkhead. The same poster of a soaring eagle hung on the wall. And at King's workstation, she had placed his favorite mug. The one with Freedom the Frog printed on the side. They used to sell those in the *Freedom*'s gift shop during the dreadnought's days as a museum. It was the *exact* same mug, in fact. He recognized the chip on top. King had lost it a couple of years back. Or thought he had.

Also on his desk—a framed photo. It depicted three young pilots from the Third World War. Bulldog, Phantom, and Lion. King and his two best friends. With his old, callused fingers, he caressed the photo, marveling at how young they had been.

"It's a beautiful photo, sir." Mimori approached him. "I found it in my archives, printed it, and framed it for you." She smiled softly. "I still miss Yehuda."

"Me too," King said softly. "I wish he could have been here."

He thought about Yehuda, the Lion at Dawn, the fierce pilot who had downed so many equalist starfighters. Until that one last battle. Until that final foe that claimed him. But in many ways, Yehuda lived again through his daughter, the fierce Gal "Spitfire" Levy. King had raised the girl since his friend's death. And suddenly King keenly felt Spitfire's absence from this bridge.

She should be here, he thought.

He looked at the android. "Does Spitfire know? About the new *Freedom*?"

Daniel Arenson

Mimori shook her head. "No. Only Godwin, Kim, and you know. We had to be very secretive."

King frowned. At first he wondered: Why all the secrecy? Kim had begun work on the new *Freedom* over three years ago. Long before the Nazis had invaded this universe. But after another moment of contemplation, he understood. The *Freedom* was among the greatest weapons of mankind. She was the greatest starship that ever flew, if you asked King (not that he was biased). Such a weapon was best kept under wraps. Even before the Fatherworld had invaded, the galaxy had been a place of danger. There were aliens in the void, not all of them friendly. And back on Earth, there was the madness of Katyusha. Capricious, mercurial, and not entirely sane, Katyusha could be a friend one moment, a bitter foe the next.

Well, it was time to unwrap this secret weapon, this mile-long flying fortress, this gun that could shoot down worlds. It was time to return to the fight.

This time with a proper flagship.

* * * * *

The battle still raged on and around Earth. As King stood here aboard the *Freedom*, a hundred light-years from Earth, he couldn't stop thinking about the soldiers back home. About brave spacers and marines fighting the enemy in space and on land. About the home front and the courage of those who resisted the Nazis. And the terror of those who lived in lands the enemy had conquered. Yes, the Nazis had taken entire chunks of Earth. All of France, most of North Africa, and much of eastern Europe was theirs. A pall of darkness had fallen over those lands. King could only imagine the horrors of their occupation.

The Freedom Fleet was leaderless. In shambles. Breaking before the enemy. The fleet needed him. It needed him *now*. The

92

Freedom was not ready. She barely had any ammunitions in her bay. There were only a few Maccabee torpedoes for the fourteen Angels of Liberty who stood guard upon the dorsal hull. The point-defense system wasn't even wired up yet. And there was only one Gideon projectile deep inside the ship—a chunk of tungsten, graphite, and copper the size of an office building. A missile for the Fist of Freedom. That fist just had one punch in her.

King would have liked another year. To get the last systems online and patched in. To seek out those who remained from his old crew. To carefully, meticulously find and train new spacers to replace the fallen. To test and calibrate the Talaria drive, the spiderhole generator, maybe even the hopscotch drive (for all its risks). According to Mimori, she and her clones (apparently there were hundreds aboard the ship, though King had not seen them yet) had only installed a few systems yesterday.

"Nothing is calibrated, sir," said Mimori Prime, standing beside him on the bridge. "Nothing has been tested."

"Understood. But the war cannot wait. You heard Godwin. We have twenty-four hours to enter the fight, rally the fleet, and kill some Nazis." He considered. "Twenty-three by now."

Mimori looked at him. The starlight reflected in her steelglass eyes and glinted across her synthetic skin. At first glance, she looked like a doll, a perfect, precious doll of porcelain and silky hair, animated by some secret clockworks within a wooden frame. But when her eyes gazed into King's, he saw sentience. He saw a soul. Inside her chrome skull nested a basic computer, giving her functions over her body. But her true mind, her soul, as it were—that came to her from the powerful mainframe computers that pulsed and shone deep within the starship. She was an avatar. An angel. A messenger of *Freedom*. She was his starship, and as she held his hands, as her starlit eyes gazed into his, King knew that she too was gazing upon his soul.

"We will fly together again, Commander," she whispered.

"Like we used to."

She nodded. "Like we used to, sir."

"Mimori?" King said. "I know your sisters are across the starship, ready to serve. I know that if I asked it of you, you'd fly to war right now, and you would be glorious. But before we join the fight, we need to call some old friends."

The android smiled. "We need to get the old gang back together."

"Mimori, I'm going to need you and your sisters to help. It'll be a busy day."

* * * * *

Larry "Phantom" Jordan, the last commander of the destroyed starship *Freedom*, was getting good and properly drunk. It had been many years since he'd gotten this drunk. But tonight was a dark night, and his soul sank into dark places. And so he poured himself another cup.

He knew he shouldn't. He knew the booze was poison. But there were ghosts inside Larry Jordan that needed to be killed. The booze never killed them, of course, but it would knock them out for a night.

Tonight he felt very much alone. And that was when the ghosts rose. That was when he must banish them. Or they would shred him apart.

Sitting in the dark trailer, he peeled back the bandage. It made little wet suction noises. Jordan examined the wound and winced. Infected again. There had been something on that Nazi blade. Some poison. Some diseases. Jordan splashed more antiseptic into the wound. The liquid sizzled across the stitches, and Jordan grimaced and clenched his fists. He poured himself another cup.

Time seemed to slow down. With every drop of whiskey that fell into his cup, another image flashed before his eyes.

A drop. The young corporal just this morning—falling dead beside Jordan, his eyeballs shriveled and black with umbrions, his skull caved in.

Another drop. The platoon last night, charging into the enemy fire. The shell slamming into their formation. The severed body parts flying every which way. The blood splashing onto Jordan.

Another drop. And he saw himself holding the young woman, her legs gone, her belly slashed open and spilling her insides. He prayed with her as her life flowed away.

Another drop. He remembered his nephew and niece. Ishmael and Valentina. Soldiers who had served aboard Toliman at Alpha Centauri, the space station the Nazis had captured. Most likely, both Ishmael and Tina were gone.

And then more and more images, a rapid barrage of them, images of fire, blood, and swastikas.

Jordan downed his glass.

"Timori . . ." he whispered. "Timori, I miss you."

He lowered his head. The walls of the trailer seemed to close in around him. Outside he could hear the wind howling through the trees, the shuffling boots of the guards, and the distant rumble of artillery fire. The small Alliance base was located deep in the forests of Finland. This far north, the sun did not rise in winter. There was only darkness and death.

I shouldn't be here, Jordan thought. *I'm a starship commander. Or was once. I should be in space.*

He poured himself another cup. And he tried, even through the haze of the booze, to remember better days. To remember his wife, the beautiful Genevieve, and her sparkling green eyes. To remember flying with the Bulldog and the Lion.

Together, the three friends had conquered the stars. He remembered his days aboard the starship *Freedom*, rising through the ranks to become XO, then finally commander during the ship's final battles. God, he missed that ship.

And I miss you, Timori, he thought.

The android, a clone of Mimori, had served in obscurity, tucked away in the warehouses. For many years, she had simply been known as Mimori Unit 5/7, until she had chosen a new name for herself. Timori, the timid logistic android. Timori, so often forgotten. Not many spacers aboard the *Freedom* had known Timori even existed. But to Jordan, she had meant the universe. When he was in a dark pit, mourning the loss of his wife, Timori had pulled him back into the light.

Until you betrayed me, he thought. *Until I had to kill you.*

His eyes stung. His hands shook as he poured another cup. Some of the whiskey spilled onto the tabletop. His hand tightened, shattering the cup, and glass shards stabbed his hand. Blood dripped, mingling with the spilled booze.

What am I doing?

In a moment of horror, Jordan hurled the bottle. It hit the wall and fell to the trailer floor. Didn't break. And didn't spill. It was empty, he realized.

Well, to hell with it. There would be no dawn tomorrow. Only more darkness and another assault against the enemy lines. And him, sixty-six years old, a captain without a ship, a lonely old man lost in the forest.

Stop that, he told himself. *You have a daughter—a successful doctor. And you have a friend—an admiral named James "Bulldog" King. Wherever the hell he is.*

He hoped they were still alive.

There was no MindWeb up here in the subarctic wilderness. News sometimes came via radio, but it was scattered, clipped, only giving the military commands and not much more.

Move here. Wait there. Fight now. Push forward. Pull back. Hold the line. That was about it. Last Jordan had heard, Annie and King were still in a London hospital. She a doctor; he a patient.

He knew that. He knew they were fine. He knew there was hope. But in the dark wilderness, drunk and alone and afraid, the mind played dangerous games. And the shadows showed you ghosts and visions.

There in the shadows, he saw them. Two visions of the past.

Timori—a slender android with soft dark eyes.

The Bulldog—a big brute of a man, his jaw wide, his eyes forged of solid iron.

In his vision, they appeared to Jordan in the uniforms of the starship *Freedom*. Those old uniforms! The navy-blue fabric, the brass buckles, the blue stars with red stripes for wings. Ha! So 2150s. Jordan would have given anything to be back there again. To be young. With his friends.

They stepped closer through the shadows. Snow clung to their military caps.

"Goddammit, Larry," King growled. "This place is colder than a penguin's frozen balls. Did you have to choose to fight in the arctic?"

"I, for one, am perfectly comfortable," the android said. "I can function in temperatures down to minus 304.5 degrees Celsius."

"Thanks, I'll remember to set a cap on the air-conditioning," King said.

Jordan blinked. The illusion seemed so real. He could even smell King's aftershave. The same damn brand. Ironwood Ridge. Jordan had told his friend a million times that the stuff stank like gasoline.

"Whadya want?" Jordan said. "Leave me alone for tonight. I'm getting drunk and I don't want any ghosts from the past crashing my party."

He opened the drawer and pulled out another bottle.

King laid a heavy hand on his shoulder. "Larry, we're no ghosts. This isn't a dream. We're really here." He slammed a thermos onto the tabletop. "I brought you some coffee. And a clean uniform. The kind we used to wear. Sober up and dress up. There's a starship waiting for you."

A few hours later, Commander Larry Jordan sat in a shuttle, a hundred light-years away, gazing upon what must be a dream. What could not be real.

The starship *Freedom*.

He sat there in the shuttle beside his friend, seeing this glorious vision from the past, and tears flowed down his cheeks.

"It's real, buddy," King said. "When Godwin showed her to me, I couldn't believe it either."

Mimori raised her chin smugly. "*I* knew about this *three years ago*. Back when we started rebuilding her."

"Well, good for you," King said.

Yes, the android was Mimori. The same Mimori from the old *Freedom*. The steadfast Mimori Prime of the bridge, their interface to the ship. She was not that timid logistics android. She was not Timori the traitor. In the shadows, Jordan had mistaken her for the android he had loved, the android who had broken his heart. But Timori was gone in the shadows of the past, and there she must remain.

"I can't believe this," Jordan said. "But then again, I can't believe so much about this war." He gazed at the starship ahead, unable to tear his eyes away. "And you're going to command her, Jim? And I'll be your XO? Like in the old days?"

King shook his head. "No. Godwin gave me command of the Freedom Fleet. Too many admirals have died in the war. I must collect the tatters of our fleet, organize us into an efficient and aggressive assault force, and crush the enemy. And I need you by my side."

Jordan finally ripped his gaze away from the *Freedom*. He stared at King, who sat beside him in the shuttle. "You want me to command her, Jim? Like I did during those last few battles?"

"No," King said.

Jordan felt something go cold inside him, something sad and ashamed in the pit of his belly. "I understand."

"Larry, the *Freedom* Fleet is too big for one man. One of those dead admirals commanded the American Armada, the most powerful unit of the Freedom Fleet. I'm promoting you to rear-admiral. And I need you to command the American ships for me."

Jordan understood the significance at once. The Freedom Fleet was the space force of the Alliance—a cooperation between democratic nations. Originally they had aligned to oppose Katyusha, but today the Alliance faced an enemy from beyond the universe. Internally, the Freedom Fleet contained many subfleets. The Tiger Fleet of India. The Royal Fleet of Britain. The Caracal Fleet of Israel. And many others—they joined forces to fight for their common values. Of all those national fleets, the American Armada was the largest and most powerful.

And it will be mine, Jordan thought. *My duty. My responsibility. My honor.*

He saluted his old friend. "I accept and report to duty." Jordan frowned. "But if both us old farts will be busy as admirals, who will command the *Freedom*?"

CHAPTER FOUR
City Among the Stars

Commander Gal "Spitfire" Levy was fighting Nazis on the streets of Jerusalem. Not something she had ever imagined herself doing. Just as she was loading a fresh plasma pack, her MindLink chimed, summoning her to a secret meeting. She ignored the telepathic notification and resumed firing her assault rifle, lobbing hot plasma bolts at the enemy. Who had time for *meetings*?

Chime!

The neural implant buzzed again in her head, popping up another notification in the corner of her vision. The meeting, the damn implant insisted, was rather important.

"Buzz off!" she muttered and pulled the trigger again. The plasma bolts hurtled down the ancient, cobbled alleyway like little flaming asteroids.

Chime!

The notification window materialized again, hovering closer now, translucent and stubborn like a haunting ghost. Just a hallucination. The implant in her brain created it. Real or not, it was *frickin' annoying*. Attendance, the floating text reminded her, was *not* optional. Meeting location? The rooftop of the nearby Austrian Hospice.

Spitfire knew the place. Of course she did. The crumbling brick hostel loomed right alongside Via Delarosa, the Way of Tears, the path Christ had taken toward his crucifixion. The ancient tavern shared the roadside with spice mongers, soothsayers, holy men, and an assortment of souvenir shops. For centuries now, the Austrian Hospice had catered to pilgrims who came to walk in Christ's footsteps. Even today, in the twenty-third century, it served the best coffee and strudels in town. All with a rooftop view of the ancient, winding cityscape.

Rrring!

This time it wasn't just a notification window. It was a voice call. Directly into her brain.

"Spitfire?" Admiral King said over MindWeb. "I need you."

"Sorry, boss, busy now!" Spitfire answered telepathically, reloaded her rifle, and fired another flaming round. "Killing Nazis. Call me later."

She hung up on him. On Admiral James King himself. Any other soldier would be skinned alive for that. But, well, he was like a dad to her. He had practically raised her. So Spitfire didn't mind annoying him.

Nazis were storming across Jerusalem. Who had time for *strudels*?

Only a fortnight ago, she had been fighting in London. That seemed like years ago now. A different country. A different life. After liberating London from the Nazi scourge, Spitfire had flown back to her home country. After a quick moment to hug her mom and change into a new uniform, Spitfire had joined the first infantry unit that would take her. And she got to fighting. This time in Jerusalem.

She fired her gun again.

On a nearby stone balcony, a Nazi clutched his chest. The man fell, crashed through an awning, and slammed into a merchant's stall. Brass bowls overturned, spilling cinnamon, sumac, and cardamom across the well-worn cobblestones. Aromatic clouds of spices filled the air. Spitfire sneezed.

More German troops came charging down the winding

alleyway, bursting through the clouds of spices, their guns howling. Spitfire ran for cover, nearly slipping on some fallen persimmons. She knelt behind an overturned cart, slung her rifle over the makeshift barricade, and fired again.

The German guns kept howling. U-bolts whizzed her way. A few slammed into the cart, cracking the wood. As the bolts impacted, they cracked open, releasing smoky clouds of umbrions. The noxious fog filtered through the cracks in the wooden cart, floating menacingly toward Spitfire. She cringed. Spitfire had tasted the sting of umbrions before. She cursed and rolled across the cobbled road, fleeing the dark particles. Once she was a safe distance, she fired at the enemy again.

They fired back. Their terrible U-bolts slammed down everywhere across the ancient street. As they impacted, they cracked open like alien eggs, unleashing their Stygian payload. Via Delarosa's cobblestones had survived for thousands of years, withstanding the weight of countless feet and endless wars. From ancient prophets to modern soldiers, this pathway had known many tears. Today the umbrions seeped between the cobblestones, cracking them, lifting some up, pulling others down into pits. The shadowy haze crawled over the alleyway, dimming the crimson, gold, and blue banners that fluttered from the stone balconies and archways. An umbrionic darkness fell over Jerusalem like the Angel of Death over the land of Goshen.

Other troops were running with Spitfire, all in olive-colored fatigues. Local boys, born and bred in this city's twisting alleyways. The soldiers shouted, fired their rifles, fell, rose, and fought on. The roar of guns filled the ancient city of Jerusalem. Up above, Spitfire heard the shrieks of artillery, the roar of battling starfighters, and the distant booms of broken starships falling into the atmosphere. The battle swelled across the city—and far above it.

Spitfire's MindWeb chimed again.

"Dammit, Gal!" It was the admiral again, speaking directly inside her head. His grainy voice rasped across her skull like sandpaper trying to smooth the bone. "Meet me atop the Austrian Hospice. We have a lot to talk about."

Spitfire groaned. "We'll talk once I'm done!"

U-bolts shrieked. She cursed and ducked behind a stall that sold olivewood animals to tourists. Little camels, donkeys, fish, and doves of peace spilled across the cobblestones. The merchant had fled. As bolts slammed into the cart, wooden animals flew and shattered. Soldiers knelt around Spitfire, firing at the approaching Nazi forces. Spitfire wasn't sure how many Germans were in the city. But whenever she killed one, two more showed up.

U-bolts slammed into a soldier nearby. Private Maya Amit was her name. She was all of eighteen. Just a child. The girl fell onto the cobblestones, chest riddled with dark holes, and cried out in pain. The umbrions flowed through her abdomen, eating her alive from the inside.

Spitfire gritted her teeth and fired. She spotted the enemy sniper. The one who had shot Maya. The German trooper hid in a merchant stall, peering between strands of wooden beads and crucifixes, artifacts to sell to pilgrims. Spitfire hurled a barrage of plasma bolts his way. The bolts ripped through the curtains of beads, and the man inside screamed and fell.

By the time Spitfire knelt by Maya, the girl was dead.

Spitfire straightened, fire in her heart, tears stinging in her eyes.

"Soldiers, hear me!" she cried.

A hundred or more soldiers crouched across the marketplace, wearing olive drab. They looked up, weary, some bleeding, but all had fire in their eyes. All were sons and daughters of this land. Many, like her, wore Star of David pendants.

"Last time the Nazis came for us, we were helpless,"

Spitfire said. "This time—we fight!" She burst from cover and ran at the enemy. "Charge!"

"Charge!" her soldiers cried.

No, they would not hide behind cover, would not cower. That was not their way. Not her way.

"Charge!" she cried, racing through the umbrionic fog, her rifle spraying fire and light.

* * * * *

Into the Nazi lines ran the soldiers of Israel, and the light from their fire blazed against the umbrionic darkness. Light and anti-light swirled through the air like liquid gold flowing through a maelstrom of tar.

"Charge!" Spitfire cried, and onward she ran, and through the haze ran her soldiers. She was a woman in her forties, a leader, a veteran of many battles, but these soldiers here with her—they were kids. They were teenagers. She was old enough to be their mother, and as they fell around her, pierced with the Nazi rounds, she grieved as a mother would.

Yet she kept charging, kept leading them into the darkness. Spitfire had heard that the buffaloes in Canada were the only animal that turned toward the storm, that they marched through it, knowing that the way out of danger is to face it. Like desert buffaloes, the troops faced the darkness and walked through it, fighting for every step, until they burst from the haze of umbrions. And there ahead, standing in the open in a Jerusalem courtyard, stood a platoon of the Waffen-SS. The same SS that had, before the universe split in two, burned millions within their camps of barbed wire and depravity. Those had been places where hell burst from underground like rancid tar, an ooze of rotting dead things, spilling its evil upon the earth. And here in God's city, here on this first step of the stairway to heaven, here in Jerusalem—here the descendants of those starved, anguished victims fired at their ancient tormentors.

Here again, here in 2207, rose the Waffen-SS. Here in the haze of umbrions they appeared like the undead, reanimated corpses risen from the mass graves of the Second World War. Spitfire imagined them crawling through the layers of soil and rot, pushing their way through dry leaves and ripping up roots, rising again from the tomb of history, then shaking off the dust and marching onward, eternally hunting. But it was only an illusion. These were not the same SS troopers. Not those old Nazis from the twentieth century. These were soldiers of the modern Fatherworld, evolved for twenty-third-century destruction. Seven feet tall they stood, the products of brutal eugenics, Aryan giants who towered over their enemies. Armor covered their bodies, humming with secret motors. They wore helmets much like those of German troopers from Hitler's era, but they had added steel visors shaped like skulls. And from each skull shone a blazing bionic eye. Like rotting cyborgs, a blend of machinery and decrepit reanimation, they marched to battle. Their Lugerheulen rifles rose and howled like true wolves.

Another soldier of Jerusalem fell. And another.

A U-bolt slammed into Spitfire's chest. The kinetic energy knocked her down. The umbrions spilled from the little capsule and began spreading across her chest. A chill crawled through her. Even here in the desert, under the hot Middle Eastern sun, the temperature plunged. Umbrions crawled across her tactical vest like ants on the hunt. She tossed the armor aside. Her torso unprotected, she kept running at the enemy, firing her plasma.

Another fellow soldier fell at her side. Another private. Just a kid from down the road. A hero.

Before her in the fog, the enemy loomed. The steel skulls

seemed almost like decapitated heads floating in the fog. A gust of wind scattered swirls of umbrions, revealing the breastplates of the enemy. Sig runes crackled on the Nazi armor with real electricity, blazing like thunderbolts in a storm. The clouds of umbrions hid the crumbling archways, colorful market stalls, and ancient brick homes that surrounded the square. The noon sun vanished in the haze, and darkness shrouded the city. Jerusalem became like a reflection in a black pool, a parallel version of the ancient city, a universe of shadows and murk. The undead troopers surrounded Spitfire and her soldiers, moving closer, a tightening noose, their lightning bolts crackling brighter. All around howled the Nazi wolves, and more bolts hit the defenders of the city. Spitfire and her surviving soldiers cried out, stood back to back, and from their guns leaped a ring of fire that shrieked and spun like a corona around a dying planet. But nothing could hold back that encroaching darkness.

One of the Nazi officers spoke, his voice deep and ethereal, emerging like a ghost's moan from his helmet. "Where is the seal?"

"What the hell are you talking about?" Spitfire cried.

The SS troopers stepped closer, looming above her. At six feet tall, Spitfire was unusually tall for a woman. All her life, she had endured teasing for her height. Long Tall Gal, that was her. Yet these men towered above her. For the first time in her life, she felt short.

"We seek the seal," the officer said. "Show us the way. And we will kill you painlessly."

"What seal?" she cried. "If you want a seal, head to the North Pole, buster."

"A joke." The officer took another step closer. His skull helmet leered, and the bionic eye flared red. "Then you will die . . . with pain."

Spitfire growled and reloaded her gun. Was she doomed to

die here? If so, she would die like her father. Like her fathers going back for thousands of years. A warrior. For a warrior, to die in noble battle was a good death. She did not fear death, but she grieved for those who died around her. For teenage boys and girls. Some of the boys hadn't even begun to shave yet. Just children. Just children dying in the darkness.

A voice tore through the shadows, deep and gravelly. She would recognize King's voice anywhere. It sounded like tank tracks rolling over stones.

"Spitfire! I ordered you to the hospice!"

"And I told you—call me later!" she telepathized.

But they weren't sharing a telepathic channel. She frowned.

A large shadow leaped through the haze of battle. A man thumped down beside Spitfire, aimed an enormous Gojira-class machine gun, and unleashed hellfire. Admiral King growled as he held the gargantuan gun. Its dozen barrels spun in a fury, unleashing countless plasma bolts at the enemy.

The fusillade slammed into the skull-faced troopers. The flaming bolts dented breastplates, shattered the leering steel visors, and knocked the Aryan giants down. King paused, having chewed through all his plasma batteries.

"Thanks," Spitfire said to him.

King was already loading fresh plasma packs. "If you only listened to me—"

"I was busy! I— Hold on. Duck." Spitfire aimed her rifle at King.

He hissed and ducked.

Spitfire fired over his head, hitting a Nazi behind him. Right in the visor.

Her plasma blazed into the German's eyeholes. The SS trooper screamed and clawed at the steel skull covering his face. Spitfire ran, leaped over King, and drove her feet into the blinded trooper. The man crashed to the ground. Spitfire kicked his red-hot visor off, aimed her rifle, and blasted his skull into charred chunks of flesh. War was ugly business. But she wouldn't shy away from it.

Then, with a battle cry, a fresh platoon of Nazis came charging down an alleyway. Forty, maybe fifty more devils, each a towering beast in armor. Spitfire growled as a chill washed her belly. She turned around, seeking a way out. This was not a battle she could win. She eyed the opposite alleyway . . . only to find *another* SS platoon there, charging toward her.

She was trapped.

Shit, Spitfire thought.

* * * * *

As Spitfire was waiting to die, another shadow leaped from above.

Another old man landed in the courtyard, holding a machine gun, and unleashed his fury.

"Phantom!" Spitfire cried in delight.

Larry "Phantom" Jordan did not even look her way. His dark eyes focused on the enemy. His lips peeled back in a snarl. The old man was thinking of one thing and one thing only. Mowing down Nazis. Which he did with relish. Riddled with plasma, the SS troopers piled up in the alleyway.

Spitfire and her surviving soldiers—not many were left now—kept fighting in a fury. Their hearts soared. Their plasma burned hot.

Even with these two old war dogs at her side, it was a fierce fight. More and more defenders fell. Spitfire suffered another blast, this one on her shoulder. Her left arm went numb and hung loosely. She kept shooting.

And then—a third figure came leaping from above! This one was slimmer and faster than King and Jordan. A woman. A young, slender woman, all of five feet tall. She wore an anachronistic spacer uniform, the dark blue fabric adorned with brass buckles. The style, harking back to the naval uniforms of the Age of Sail, had found a resurgence among spacers in the twenty-second century. Today in the twenty-third century, it was out of style.

They used to wear this kind of uniform aboard the starship Freedom, Spitfire remembered.

The little woman in the outdated uniform came swooping down from the rooftop. Her eyes shone white. Her mouth was screwed up tightly in determination. Her black bob cut ruffled in the desert wind. She hit the ground with a force that belied her humble size, cracking the cobblestones and sending out rippling shock waves.

Spitfire rubbed her eyes. It was impossible. But it was her! It was Mimori! The android had wandered off into the darkness, seeking death in deep space. But now she was here. She was back.

"Mimori!" Spitfire cried.

The android gave her a small smile. Her eyes burned with blue fire. And she leaped into action. The android needed no guns, no blades. Her body was a weapon. The eccentric Professor Mori, a savant and recluse, had crafted the android to look like his daughter. To the world, Mimori appeared as a delicate Japanese girl. But this girl had the strength of a grizzly bear.

The enemy laughed when they saw her. SS troopers whistled and catcalled. One made a thrusting motion with his hips, and another laughed and waggled his tongue at Mimori. To them, she appeared as just an innocent girl. Her military uniform only made her more endearing. She was like a child who wore her father's military cap, melting hearts. That apparent innocence

attracted the troopers like blood in the water. They saw in Mimori
a prey animal to torment. And if they were anything, they were
predators. They approached the girl, practically swaggering,
whistling and blowing her kisses. They never intended to woo her,
of course, merely to mock her. When they wanted a woman, they
took her. Whether she was willing or not. They had done this in
many cities they had conquered. One trooper was already
loosening his armor. They would, their lecherous eyes vowed, take
her right here in this square, even as the battle raged around them.
Spitfire, locked in battle behind an open line of fire, could only
watch.

Mimori stood before the Waffen-SS, demure. She lowered
her eyes, clasped her hands behind her back, and shuffled one
foot, pointing the toes inward.

Mimori, you mechanical devil! Spitfire thought, a smile
spreading across her lips even in the horror of battle. *Playing with
your victims. A mouse toying with the cats.*

"She's shy!" said one of the troopers, pointing at Mimori
and laughing.

"Good. I like 'em bashful," said another.

Mimori blushed. The android actually ran an algorithm to
blush.

"I'm shy," she whispered.

The troopers hooted and hollered, imitating her timid
voice, blowing her kisses.

Oh, she's loving this, Spitfire thought. *I've been through hell all
month, and she's having fun!* But Spitfire's smile only grew.

A burly *rottenführer* approached Mimori. He reached out to
touch her hair. "Good morning, darling."

Spitfire knew what would happen next. Mimori raised her
timid head. A smile spread across her face. Her eyes sparkled as
she twisted the man's arm, cracking the armor, then snapping the
bone. As the man screamed, Mimori lifted him overhead. He was

a seven-foot beast in armor, probably tipping the scales at four hundred pounds. His weight shoved Mimori down with such force that her feet cracked cobblestones and drove several inches underground. But the little android handled the weight easily. She hurled the piano-sized trooper at his fellow Nazis. They crashed down like columns in a crumbling temple.

Several SS troopers, who had survived this assault, opened fire. But Mimori dodged their U-bolts. The android slid forward on her knees, swung her leg, and a trooper crashed down. She leaped up, driving an uppercut into another jaw. More and more Nazis surrounded her, and Mimori spun like a mad top, kicking and punching.

She's like the goddamn Tasmanian devil, Spitfire thought. She almost expected the fight to become a ball of smoke full of lightning bolts like in the cartoons.

Spitfire wanted to keep watching the show, but she must focus on battling enemies of her own. Adrenaline pumped through her. War was hell. She knew that more than anybody. But sometimes, at times like these, war could be glorious too, exhilarating, intoxicating. Sometimes war became almost like a game, a great competition not unlike team sports. It heated the blood and brought glory to those who played with all their hearts. At these times, the normal revulsion from death and mutilation left Spitfire, and she surrendered to some base urges, some instincts that perhaps every human had. That call of the jungle. That echoing howl of evolution. Inside every human was a beast who, when awoken, found lust in violence.

And we coded that into our machines too, she thought. Mimori was simply a mechanical reflection of human desires. Civilized and soft on the surface, perhaps. But that was a mere facade. You could dress chimpanzees in suits and dresses, you could pretend they were civilized, even cute. But one day they would still rip your face off. Humans were like that too.

A mechanical hand, a prosthetic like a medieval gauntlet, grabbed Spitfire's shoulder.

"Come on," King growled. "Mimori will keep them busy for a while. I need you for something more important than a street brawl."

Spitfire wanted to argue, to pull herself free. The admiral didn't understand. This wasn't just a street brawl. The soldiers in this city—many were descended from Holocaust survivors. They wanted to fight. They wanted revenge. Just a brawl? No! This was the epic conclusion of an ancient struggle. But how could she explain that to this man from America? It was strange. Admiral James King was like a father to her. Hell, since her real father died, King had raised her, had always been there for her. Spitfire loved him with all her heart, and she always would. But now, here, in this battle, James King almost felt like . . . not a stranger, no. But there was a wall between them. A cultural barrier that seemed invisible day to day yet now kept him out of reach. How could Spitfire tell him how much this meant? How could she explain what he was taking from her?

So she simply blurted out, "I must fight!" Her tears flowed. "I must kill these bastards!"

"You *will* fight," King said. "You *will* kill them. But not here. Not in these alleyways. I have an opportunity for you. An opportunity to destroy the enemy utterly. Spitfire, I need you with me. Like in the old days." His voice softened. "I know what this means to you. I promise you—together we will win this war."

That invisible barrier shattered. Once more, he was that man she loved. The man who had raised her like a father.

Spitfire wiped away her tears and nodded. "Let's go."

* * * * *

Moments later, Spitfire sat in a shuttle, watching the city drop down below her. Jerusalem was beautiful in the dawn, a city of gold and light perched upon a desert mountain, yet as the shuttle rose, clouds of dust, smoke, and umbrions rolled over the land, until Jerusalem seemed to Spitfire like an island rising from a sea at storm. The Nazi banners still fluttered upon ancient temples, while on the walls of the old city, the Stars of David still flapped in the wind. This battle would rage onward. Without her.

"It hurts to run from battle," Spitfire whispered.

King held her hand and stared into her eyes. "Gal, our soldiers down in that city are heroes. Every man and woman who fights for freedom is precious. Millions of these heroes are fighting across Earth right now. Maybe hundreds of millions, coming from hundreds of nations and faiths. And as far as I know, only one among them is an experienced flagship commander. You belong in the sky."

Spitfire blinked. "You have a new starship for me?"

Memories flooded her of the *Lioness*, her first command. They had given her the flagship of the Freedom Fleet. She had been young for the job. But at the time, Colonel Gal "Spitfire" Levy had just finished serving as XO aboard the starship *Freedom*, serving under Commander Larry "Phantom" Jordan and Admiral James "Bulldog" King. How they had shaken the stars! Truly, *Freedom* had been the greatest starship ever flown. From aboard the *Freedom*, Spitfire, Phantom, and Bulldog had fought in countless battles against the enemies of Earth, be they equalists or aliens. And then, in the climactic battle of the Spider War, the legendary *Freedom* had flown into a star. A glorious end to a legendary ship.

After that, Jordan and King had retired. Easy for them. They were already old men. But Spitfire had been only forty, still young and full of fire. So the admiralty had promoted her to commander, then given her command of the *Lioness*, the Freedom Fleet's new, modern, state-of-the-art flagship. A great honor. Spitfire had taken that duty seriously. From aboard the *Lioness*, she had kept fighting. And she fought valiantly, if she may say so herself.

Until she lost the *Lioness* too.

She had served aboard two flagships. And lost *both*. Just her luck. Truly a fine legacy she was carving out for herself!

Her fierce *Lioness* had fallen in the early days of the German blitzkrieg. And with the loss of *Lioness*, Spitfire had lost her reason to be. Her identity. A part of her soul. Would King give her yet another ship? Third time's the charm? Would he restore a part of her soul Spitfire had thought dead?

She wiped her eyes, bringing herself back to the present. She still sat in the shuttle. King sat beside her while Jordan and Mimori sat in the back seat. The old gang. The old commanders of the *Freedom*. In the little shuttle, they flew through space, leaving Jerusalem far behind.

King looked into Spitfire's eyes, and he spoke words that shocked her to her core. "The *Freedom* is back."

"Shut up." She wiped her eyes. "Stop toying with me."

Jordan and Mimori leaned forward from the back seat. They both smiled.

An hour later, Spitfire was weeping and laughing. She could not believe her eyes. Could not believe this wasn't a dream.

There she was, floating ahead, a hundred light-years from home beyond a secret portal through time and space. The starship *Freedom*.

Memories overwhelmed her. Spitfire remembered herself as a little girl (Gally, they used to call her), running barefoot through the ship, chasing a boy named Bastian, the grandson of Commander Ulysses King. The two children—Gally and Bas Bas—became best of friends. They would bang wooden swords in

114

the corridors, wrestle, and sometimes fire cap guns, incurring the wrath of Oliver Darjeeling, the mustached boatswain of the ship. And she remembered one day of grief, waiting for her father to return home in his starfighter, standing for hours at the airlock until a young James "Bulldog" King put a hand on her shoulder. The starfighter pilot, gruff yet always kind to her, told her of her father's fate. The fatherless child had found a new father in the scrappy young pilot. And she remembered a day ten years later, a fierce young woman with rage in her heart, flying her first starfighter into space. She remembered years in the cockpit, fighting the rahs, destroying the spiders' clawships, but always fighting that old war of her father's. The land below had always been her home, but so had this ship among the stars. Both Jerusalem and *Freedom* to her seemed like holy cities, utopias like Shangri-La, places of reverence and light. Jerusalem was a holy city on Earth, while *Freedom* was a holy city among the stars. Spitfire was leaving home now, but she was also returning home.

"Will you take the job?" King said. "Will you command this ship?"

They stood on the bridge of the starship *Freedom*. Admiral James King, leader of the Freedom Fleet. Rear-Admiral Larry Jordan, leader of the American Armada. Two friends of her father. Two old starfighter pilots. Two men who had raised little Gally into a woman. Spitfire dried her tears and saluted.

"Of course." She blinked and looked around. "But . . . I do have one question. Where is Bastian?"

CHAPTER FIVE
Rascals and Royals

Bastian was fighting his way through Barcelona, leading thousands of American troops, when a local militia opened fire on him and his men.

For a moment, there was only shock.

We came here as liberators, Bastian thought. *We came here to free this city from Nazism. Why are they shooting at us?*

A bullet slammed into his armored chest. Bastian winced and fell back a step. Damn, it hurt! And would leave a bruise. His armor was thick, but enough bullets would break it. And this new enemy (who the hell were they?) was firing a barrage. They certainly weren't the Nazis. The Nazis fired U-bolts full of umbrions. This enemy hid across the balconies and rooftops of Barcelona, firing bullets down upon the American marines.

Bullets! Actual lead bullets! How quaint! The barrage *ping*ed off the marines' armor and skittered across the cobbled road. No casualties yet. Their thick blue armor protected the American marines. But enough bullets could dent, even crack a battlesuit. And legendary as they were, within their bulky suits of armor, the brave warriors of the Freedom Brigade were just flesh and bone like anyone else. The marines crouched and returned fire.

Bastian peered through the hailstorm of gunfire. Shooters stood across the roofs and towers of Barcelona. Hundreds of them. More came pouring down alleyways, unleashing a fresh barrage of bullets. They wore brown uniforms, red armbands, and only rudimentary armor. These were quick, agile fighters, more of a militia than a true military. They raised many banners. One unfurled in the wind, revealing a symbol on the red fabric—a sunburst in the center of a swastika. One of the fighters stood upon a minaret. He lifted a megaphone to his mouth, and his voice rang across the city streets and courtyards.

"The New Dawn stands with the Fatherworld! Fight, fight, sons of Spain. Fight for the Fatherworld! Hail König!"

Bastian cursed. He understood. This had been happening all over the world these past few weeks. For centuries now, local neo-Nazi chapters had operated across the world. Like stubborn mold, they refused to die out. Mostly they remained hidden in their hidey-holes. Sometimes they emerged for a march, soccer riot, or the odd hate crime. Then they crawled back into the shadows, took off their swastika armbands, and blended back into the seedy underbelly of society. But when the Fatherworld invaded last year, all that hiding ended. The local Nazis, those who had festered underground on this side of the multiverse, came out like worms in the rain.

The winds of hatred buoyed these local militias of white supremacists. They learned that in a parallel universe, Hitler had won the war. That Nazism had spread across Earth and the stars. And that now the Fatherworld's forces were here—by the millions. The Nazi starships orbited the world. Their armored divisions rolled across every continent (aside from Antarctica, though their terrible icebreaker ships had been spotted there too). To local white supremacists, this seemed like a gift from above. Bastian had heard their propaganda on local radio. The words rattled through his skull.

"Behold—the Reich rises! God himself blesses us. Here are the end of days! Nazism will engulf the world, and Helmut König—the spiritual successor of Hitler himself—will usher in the New Dawn."

That was what these goons called themselves. The New Dawn. They were people from this universe. People who grew up in democracy, who betrayed their world and joined the Nazi invaders. They operated here in Spain. They had taken over Ireland and aligned their country with the Fatherworld. They were fighting for control of Norway and Sweden now. Every day, the New Dawn spread and recruited more followers. Many across the world saw the Fatherworld's Nazis not as enemies, not as conquerors, but as *liberators*. And now the Barcelona chapter, instead of fighting the invaders from a parallel universe, was shooting at the Freedom Brigade—at Brigadier Bastian King and his marines.

Goddammit, it was easier fighting the alien spiders. Wars between humans always got a lot messier.

Bastian commanded the Freedom Brigade. If you asked him, they were the best marines in the galaxy. Normally, Bastian would plow over this impudent militia. The Freebies would be like a truck crushing mosquitoes against the windshield. The New Dawn barely even wore body armor, just a few basic tactical vests, kneepads, and helmets without visors. And yes, they fired bullets. Just like Bastian's dad with his antique cowboy pistols. That was just one step above stone-tipped arrows, if you asked Bastian. He hesitated for a moment. Should he spare this enemy? It almost seemed too easy to kill them.

A bullet *pinged* off his helmet. He blinked, momentarily blinded. His head spun and his ears rang. The attack knocked any mercy out of his mind.

"Freedom Marines, charge and fire!" he shouted.

The marines ran through the gunfire, taking the barrage on their armor. Bullets whizzed across the courtyard, punching holes into statues, steeples, and clock towers. Hundreds of civilians fled, wailing, some clutching bloody crossfire wounds. Farther out in the city, the local Spanish soldiers were battling the invading Germans. Unlike the militias, the Spanish military was still firmly on the Alliance side. Brave as the Spanish soldiers were, they struggled against the superior Wehrmacht. The Nazi invaders were bigger, stronger, and better-armed, and they were gaining the upper hand across Barcelona.

And so Bastian had brought his brigade here. After liberating London, they would liberate Barcelona! That was the plan at least. But now they found themselves pinned down in this courtyard, battling—of all people—the locals!

"No gratitude at all," Bastian muttered as he rumbled across the courtyard. His thick suit of armor covered every inch of him, clattering and clanking. In this suit, he weighed a good three hundred pounds. His footsteps cracked flagstones. Bullets sparked against his chest.

"Tell me about it!" said the towering soldier at his side. "We came all this way to help them. And they're firing on us!"

Sergeant Major Alice Allenby stood six feet tall, and her limbs were powerful and muscular. In her blue-and-red battlesuit, she struck an imposing figure—a burly warrior, as much machine as woman. Alice aimed her trusty, beat-up old bazooka. A grenade slammed into a tower, pulverizing the stone foundation. Balustrades, statues, and balconies collapsed, taking with them several New Dawn snipers.

"Alice!" Bastian said. "That tower was probably a thousand years old. Can you be a little more careful?"

He couldn't see her face behind her visor, but Bastian knew his wife was glowering.

"They were aiming at your head!" she said.

"So? Use plasma bolts. They'll kill humans but won't destroy priceless architecture."

Alice snorted. "You use measly plasma bolts. I like things that make a bigger boom."

"I am your superior officer, you know," Bastian

telepathized to her.

"And I'm your wife, so I outrank you."

Bastian sighed. "Can't argue with that."

They ran onward, and thousands of marines ran with them, charging across the courtyard and side streets, driving deeper into the city. A cathedral rose nearby, a thousand years old, a miracle of architecture and craftsmanship. (*Alice better not destroy it!* Bastian thought.) This cathedral was one of the wonders of the world, but today the Nazi banners profaned it. The flags of the New Dawn rose from its steeples, displaying suns within swastikas. The fascist militiamen stood among its gargoyles, firing down into the courtyard. Countersnipers of the Freedom Brigade laid down portable shield generators, tapped buttons, and raised shimmering barricades of translucent energy. From behind these shields, they fired at the cathedral, careful to pick off New Dawn fighters without harming the medieval gargoyles.

"This is not just a war between invaders and defenders," Bastian said. "And I suspect that over time, the lines between us will muddle further. This is a war between ideas. Between ideologies. Between freedom and fascism. Between democracy and tyranny. This isn't just a war with people from another universe—but a war within ourselves."

"Enough pontificating," Alice said. "There! In that alleyway!" She pointed.

Bastian saw them. More New Dawn troops. The bastards were about to burst out from the alleyway, charge into the courtyard, and lay down hell. To Bastian, the best defense was always offense. And the best offense was fast, brutal, and merciless. He ran toward them, leading the Badgers, his own personal platoon. He commanded the entire brigade now, but he had begun his career with the Badgers. And on the ground, he still fought among them.

The Badgers platoon charged. Named after the fierce

honey badger, they were Earth's finest, bravest warriors. An ancient Roman wall rose ahead, thousands of years old. Where Roman legions had fought now stood men of the New Dawn, raising their banners defiantly. Bastian would kill them. And he would make sure not to harm a single one of this old wall's stones. Yes, even mere bricks were worth more to him than his enemies' lives. He was not proud of that. He knew that he could kill without compunction in the heat of battle. But he also knew that tonight the memories would haunt him, and he would replay these deaths over and over—both those of his own troops and those he dealt to his foes.

Yes, war between humans is dirty business, he thought.

Bastian had made his mark fighting rah aliens. The Spider War had forged his soul. He hated killing humans. *Hated* it. Yet he fired on his human foes nonetheless, picking them off the wall one by one.

Suddenly the banners of Red Dawn rose higher, and a voice cried out: "For liberty!"

The troops on the walls raised dark cannons. Huh? When did the Red Dawn militia get light artillery? The cannons wheeled toward the Plaça Nova where Bastian and his troops ran. *Booms* shook the walls, and smoke filled the sky.

The enemy bombshells slammed into the courtyard. One hit a marine right in the abdomen. As the shells impacted with armor and stone, their warheads detonated, spilling umbrions.

Bastian cursed.

"They're using Fatherworld weapons!" he cried.

"No shit, Sherlock!" Alice shouted, leaping back from the black smog. "What gave it away?"

More and more bombshells slammed down around them, shattering flagstones and men, then spilling the noxious fog.

"Marines, activate your force fields!" Bastian cried. "If you're near umbrions—force fields on!"

It was a new modification to their battlesuits. Brand-new. As in "installed this morning" new. Kim had scrambled, put together a prototype, ran a quick test or two, then copied it five thousand times. Every soldier in the Freedom Brigade now wore a battery pack and force field generator. War was like that. You worked hard and tech came fast and furious. A year of war yielded more tech than a decade of peace, or so they said.

Kim's force fields were carefully calibrated to stop umbrions. The Fatherworld seemingly had an infinite supply of the noxious particles, and in the maddening arms race of war, the Alliance was (clumsily) learning to cope. Force fields normally encircled starships, not marines. Portable force field generators were a new concept. And Kim's system had some downsides. The batteries were big and heavy, and each marine must carry one on their back. Big as they were, those batteries didn't last long. The force fields drained them within fifteen minutes. The marines conserved energy when they could, but right now Bastian would have to drain those batteries. Better empty batteries than corpses.

The force fields flickered to life around the marines, shining brighter and brighter as they sucked power from the batteries. It felt like wearing an outer garment woven of light. Umbrions landed on the shimmering shields. At once, the particles of anti-light began consuming the protons in the force fields. The batteries hummed, releasing more protons, holding back the swarm of shadows. As every umbrion consumed a proton, both particles vanished. So long as the batteries could feed the hungry little particles of darkness, the troops would be safe.

"You'll fight darkness by wearing cloaks of light," Kim had told the marines.

Wearing these luminous coats, the brigade reached the Roman wall. It soared in the city like an edifice, rising among ancient alleyways and avenues like some shard of bone embedded into an ant hive. The marines were forced to stop before the ancient monolith. The battle flared. Guns fired from atop and below the craggy, imperial wall. Smoke and light and shadows washed in waves against the old bricks. Along the alleyways, buildings cracked. A chunk of the ancient wall fell, revealing more New Dawn militiamen behind. Bastian fired his plasma rifle. He hit a man in the chest, knocking him down onto the city street.

"Onward!" Bastian cried. He leaped through the hole in the Roman wall, trampling over the militiaman's corpse. "Marines. With me!"

* * * * *

By dawn, the Freedom Brigade reached the Port Vell, Barcelona's old harbor. The war had not spared this place either. Hundreds of boats filled the marina. Most had overturned or clumped up along the piers like discarded toys. Even as the flames and shadows of war flowed over the city, palm trees still grew here from the rubble like weeds between crumbling cobblestones. For three thousand years, this port had served Spain. The ancient Laietani people had lived along this shoreline. The Romans had docked their ships here. In the Middle Ages, Christians and Muslims had traded here. History permeated every stone, and the tales of ages past whispered on the wind.

After a night of war, the port seemed oddly quiet and still. As the dawn rose, Bastian saw corpses along the piers. Bodies in brown uniforms. New Dawn soldiers.

Alice tilted her head. She grabbed Bastian's arm. "Are you seeing this?"

"Seeing what?"

"Look! In the marina!"

Earlier, Bastian had looked at the overturned sailing ships along the piers. But now he saw that other vessels floated in the water. Big, bulky ships. Cargo ships? Or—

He gasped.

Those were Rhinos! Dropships. Like the ones that transported the Freedom Brigade. What were they doing in the bay? Odder still—those weren't *his* Rhinos. Bastian knew every one of his big, bulky dropships. Each one had its own signature of dents, scars, and cracks. These Rhinos in the water looked *new*. Huh?

As far as Bastian knew, Delain Shipyards had stopped producing the Rhinos back in the 2150s. The last batch was assembled in 2159 for the starship *Freedom*. Half a century ago. In the old days, Rhinos would transport the marines from the *Freedom* to the battlefield. After the dreadnought was destroyed in 2204, the few surviving Rhinos remained with the Freedom Brigade on the ground. Had somebody actually built *new Rhinos*?

In the mist, Bastian saw a tall, broad figure walking along a pier, heading to the boardwalk. Though dawn crested the old walls of the port, the big man remained in shadows. A light crackled. The man lit a cigar, took a puff, and a red glow illuminated an old-fashioned uniform. Smoke hid the man's face.

"Hey, kid," said the man in the shadows. His voice was like gravel under tank treads. "Your European vacation is over. It's time you got back to work."

The dark figure blew smoke at him. Bastian's eyes widened. He ran toward the old man.

"Dad! What are you doing here?"

Father and son crashed into each other's arms, then shared a crushing embrace. Bastian stood taller than his father, and with his heavy battle armor, he dwarfed even the big, powerful admiral. But somehow, around Admiral James "Bulldog" King, Bastian always felt . . . well, not like a *boy*, per se. But definitely much younger. Bastian was a man in his forties, he had children of his own, and he commanded thousands of young soldiers. But he was still a son. And to him, his dad was still the strongest man in the world.

"Bas, I brought new Rhinos. I know you lost a few in battle. And the ones you have are old. Summon your other battalions here to the port. The full brigade. You did good work here, and I spoke to the local Alliance generals. The Spanish resistance will take things from here."

Alice ran down the pier. She pulled off her helmet, revealing her honest face, bright smile, and golden pigtails.

"Hey, Pops!" She leaped onto King with so much force she nearly knocked him off the pier.

"Careful, Alice!" King laughed. "Remember, I'm an old man, and you're an Olympic wrestler."

"She only finished twelfth place," Bastian said.

"Still better than you, son," King said. And Alice laughed and blew Bastian a raspberry. He laughed too.

That was Bastian and Alice. Husband and wife. Big, burly marines. Leaders who had fought the spiders in the depths of space, who charged into the Nazi gunfire, fearless in the face of death. Always smiling. Always in charge and in control. Yes, that was what their troops believed. That was the image Bastian and Alice showed their soldiers. But deep inside them, a sadness dwelled. Deep inside, they missed their children, who were staying on Earth with an aunt. At night, the married couple could barely sleep with worry. Even in their deepest slumber, they still dreamed of the Spider War. And when they charged into battle, they were not fearless but terrified.

And yet even so, here on this pier, with dead bodies lying around them—yes, they laughed. Sometimes you had to. Or all you'd do was cry.

The marines moved quickly. Some flew in the old, beat-up Rhinos. Others took off in the new, sparkling replicas. Five thousand soldiers. A complete brigade. The battle still raged across Earth's orbit. Myriads of starships battled for dominance in space. The Rhinos charged through the battle, swerving around the warring starships and flying missiles, until they reached deeper space. The Rhinos flew onward, leaving Earth behind.

They would return.

This time with a mothership.

When Bastian saw the starship *Freedom* ahead, this ghost from the past, the tears flowed. Bastian did not think there was a dry eye across the brigade. His father explained to him what happened. How this was possible. And Bastian just sat there in the Rhino, staring in disbelief, tears on his cheeks.

"For three years, we were lost," he whispered. "We were the homeless brigade. Wandering the world. Living in our dropships." He wiped his eyes and saluted the starship ahead. "Now we are home."

Across the fleet of Rhinos, thousands of hands rose in salute, and thousands of voices echoed his words. "Now we are home."

* * * * *

Not everyone believed that Major Emily Mountbatten, that solemn sentinel in the artillery satellite, had once been Queen of England. Sometimes she herself could not believe it.

Technically she didn't even have a last name. But the military forms needed one. So she had chosen a name from royal family history. Down on Earth, she had been Emily, Lady of the White Rose, Head of the Commonwealth, Defender of the Faith, Queen of Britain. Up here in space, she was just Major Mountbatten. And usually just Emily.

She wasn't royalty here in space. Just a regular officer in her late twenties, wearing a uniform like anyone else, her blond hair always pulled into a neat ponytail. A few soldiers knew her secret. But most had no idea.

"Do you know you look just like Queen Emily?" people would say. "You even have the same name!"

She would simply smile thinly. "I'm just regular Emily."

And it was true. Her friends just called her Emily, whether they knew her secret or not. And that was that. Her trusty drone, however, had trouble letting go of their salad days of royalty and leisure.

"Truly, Your Majesty, I cannot believe we are trapped here in a military satellite!" The oval drone hovered back and forth in distress. His voice (which carried a posh English accent) rose in pitch, nearly hysterical. "We should be in a palace! Or at the very least a countryside manor house. Instead we are here, in space— and there's a war on!"

Emily narrowed her eyes, aimed the cannon, and pulled the trigger. The spherical satellite shook. A shock wave blasted outward from the bore, knocking aside debris. A shell streaked through the battle, leaving a trail of light, and plowed into a German corvette. An explosion bloomed across the Nazi hull.

"Niles, be quiet!" Emily said. "I'm trying to fight."

The satellite hovered about a hundred megameters above Earth. High orbit. Up here, the Freedom Fleet was struggling to hold back Nazi reinforcements that kept arriving from deep space. There seemed no end to them. In lower orbit, Katyusha and her Red Fleet were busy battling Grand Admiral Wolfgang König and his dreaded Weltraumwaffe. Down there, closer to Earth, space was a bloodbath. Up here was the Alliance front, considered the "easy front" in the war. Ha! Easy? Well, maybe it wasn't pure carnage like the Russian-German purge below. They said millions were dying down there, caught between the equalist and fascist teeth. But the fighting up here was fierce enough for Emily, thank you very much. Right now Emily's job was to keep the pressure off Katyusha, and the English royal would do her best for her Russian sister below.

The Weltraumwaffe was spread more thinly in high orbit, where there was more space to patrol. To compensate, the Germans flew their mightiest warships up here. Frigates. Starfighter carriers. Destroyers. Even dreadnoughts that dwarfed any ship of Earth. Yes, to Emily, this was a war between Earth and foreign invaders. Her foes weren't aliens, perhaps. But Emily struggled to think of the Nazis as human. And to her, the Fatherworld was another planet entirely, not merely a reflection of Earth.

Emily wasn't proud of that part of herself. She knew that the Nazis *were* human, that all humans—even herself—carried evil within them. The Nazis were no less human than her. But in some ways, they *were* different. Eugenics had made them stronger, taller, more aggressive, but it was more than genetics. They had been raised in a society that nurtured their hatred, that brainwashed them to kill. And now they were here. Doing just that. Killing. And so how could Emily return to Earth, hide in a palace or countryside manor while others fought and died? How could she spend the war sipping tea, wearing jewels, and at most delivering an inspiring speech to the nation every Sunday? No. Emily was a soldier. An officer. She had fought the rahs, and she would fight the Nazis.

"I just wish I weren't alone," Emily said softly. "Last time, all my friends were here. Spitfire and Admiral King and Bastian. And Stowy. I guess I just miss my friends." She wiped her eyes. "It does feel different being alone this time, doesn't it, Niles?"

The jeweled drone was still fluttering back and forth across the satellite. Niles reminded Emily of a fly trapped in a house, desperately trying to find a window. He had been ranting for long moments, Emily realized. She only now began to pay attention.

"—of royal breeding, Your Majesty!" he was saying. "Does this satellite look like the dwelling of royalty? There aren't even tassels on the cushion! And the tea. Oh Lord, the tea! From a *packet.* You wouldn't serve that tea to dogs!"

"Niles?" Emily said. "Are you even listening to me?"

The football-shaped drone paused in the middle of his diatribe. He turned his camera eyes toward her. The lenses gleamed within stubby, gilded stalks. On the inside, he was a digital machine, but on the outside, he was all luxury. His rounded shell was forged of silver and inlaid with many gemstones. Sapphires, rubies, emeralds, and diamonds—he wore them all proudly. He always reminded Emily of a Fabergé egg. And she loved that egg. Dear Niles, high-strung as he might be, had been her loyal companion since childhood.

"No, I suppose I was not listening," the drone admitted. "Pardon me, Your Majesty. Allow me to rewind my tapes and replay your words."

Little motors whirred inside him. His eyes shone, replaying the last moment. When the reel ended, his mechanical eyes moved, tilting like the bascules of the Tower Bridge. The display formed something akin to a sad expression.

"Oh, my dearest Emily!" Niles said. "You shall never be alone. For you have me, your Niles, forever your eternal servant, companion, and friend."

He nuzzled her.

"I love you too, Niles." She hugged and kissed her little drone. "Now please let me focus on the battle!"

She pulled on winches and levers. Gears turned, moving the cannon's bore. That's all these satellites essentially were. Floating cannons. Jumping Chollas, they were called, named after a cactus that could hurl its spikes. The satellites were designed by Delain Shipyards, operated by the Royal Corps of the Free Alliance, and paid for by the generous British taxpayer. Chollas

129

were small and cozy. *Very* cozy. There was a small, round chamber for the gunner. A little closet, toilet, and kitchenette. Mostly, there was storage space for fuel and shells. A Cholla satellite was designed for a single spacer, and military doctors recommended no spacer spend more than forty-eight hours inside at a time. But in this war, some gunners had been doing shifts of three, even four days in here. Emily had been inside this one for ten days straight now.

She slept in her seat when she could, which admittedly wasn't often. When the supply ships arrived to restock the shells, Emily napped. Sometimes Niles even took a shift for her, allowing her to close her eyes and catch a few *z*'s. That was a sight to behold—the little drone scuttling across the cockpit like a bouncing ball, hitting this or that lever, turning this or that dial. But even when Emily did sleep, it was fitful and restless, and she dreamed that she was a cog inside some machine of golden gears and silver grommet, trapped like a bug inside a mechanical clock.

But she could not leave. Because the battle kept raging. Wave after wave of enemy ships kept assaulting the Alliance lines. More reichships kept coming through portals, traveling from their shadowy reality where Hitler had won, where Nazism had spread to every corner of the globe, and where the swastika flag marred the moon and Mars. Evil was seeping through the looking glass into this universe. Emily envisioned Nazism as a black tar, oozing over one world, then spreading onward and onward, scooping up stars and planets like a dark wave grabbing seashells from the shore, then pulling them into the depths.

But here, on the shore of the cosmic ocean, here above Earth—she resisted! And with Emily fought her brave friends. Admiral King, her mentor, forever her commanding officer. Premier Katyusha, a heroine, a woman whose ferocity and courage Emily aspired to. Her dear, wise George Godwin, the Lion of England. And millions of others who resisted the evil of

Nazism. Facing this oozing tar, these friends and leaders all gave Emily strength.

Emily loaded another bombshell. Again she aimed and fired. The shell streaked forth, slammed into a Rattenjäger, and pulverized the little Nazi starfighter. At once she was loading a new shell.

Yes, sometimes Emily missed home. More than sometimes. And more than sometimes, she wondered whether Niles might be right. Maybe she *should* have remained queen. Maybe abdicating *was* a mistake. But in some ways, there was no going home. Home no longer existed, because that younger Emily no longer existed. Space had changed her. The starship *Freedom* had been the crucible that forged a princess into a soldier. After the Spider War, she had tried. Oh God, how she had tried! Emily had sat upon the throne. She had led her realm as queen. And yet it never felt right. She always felt less like a queen, more like a china doll, not even a woman of flesh, and within her porcelain shell hid the shadows.

She would attend royal dinners. Speak to her subjects. Cut this or that ribbon. She tried—really tried—to rebuild the royal family from the ashes of the Spider War. So much of Britain lay in ruin. So many royals lay dead and buried. And the task of rebuilding was given to her.

The work kept her busy, and she knew it was a noble goal. But always, at the end of the day, Emily would walk outside the palace onto a balcony, and she would gaze upon the stars, and she would remember. A starship called *Freedom*. And her friends.

A soldier was always a soldier. A veteran roaming the halls of a palace, she learned that truth. And more and more, as she haunted those echoing halls under shadow of night, she found herself thinking of her grandfather. He had been a wise king. A beloved, charming monarch. Until the Red War broke out, the great struggle against Katyusha and her Red Dawn. Yes, back then, Katyusha—that heroine Emily so admired—had been an enemy of Great Britain, indeed of all the Alliance. And the good King Robert went to fight aboard the starship *Freedom*.

Back then, the ship *Freedom* had been new. James King was only a young starfighter pilot. And Emily hadn't been born yet. For years, her grandfather fought aboard that ship. And when the war ended, when good King Robert came home, he was a different man. Not the man from the paintings anymore. Not the proud, noble hunter and rider in the portraits, a robust outdoorsman of aristocratic masculinity. He became the man Emily had known in her childhood. Haunted. Reclusive. He would roam the halls at night like a ghost, and just before dawn, he could often be spotted on a balcony, staring at the night sky as if seeking his old starship.

They had called him shell-shocked. To young Princess Emily, the condition had seemed so tragic, so incomprehensible, so distant and alien. Until she too fought aboard that ship. Until she too came home and must sit upon the throne. No heavenly delight could compare to the strewn jewels of the galaxy. No palace could compare to the firmaments of the Milky Way. And no amount of luxury could make you forget the ghosts. The fallen. And the brothers and sisters you formed in battle.

Yes, Emily understood that now. She did not plan to linger on like a ghost, roaming the halls endlessly, with each royal portrait showing her gaunter, sadder, lost in memory. She would not suffer her grandfather's fate. And so she had abdicated. Not even thirty years old—and already giving up her reign. And so here she sat now. An officer in uniform. A soldier again. She had lost her beloved starship *Freedom*, but she still floated among the stars. Once a spacer, always a spacer.

"Emily?" Niles said.

"Hmm?" She looked up. She had been dozing off on duty, lost in a hazy maelstrom of thoughts, the kind that so often preceded a confused slide into slumber. When had she last slept? She rubbed her eyes.

"Emily!" The jeweled, football-shaped drone nudged her. "This is important."

"What is it, Niles?" She winced. "You're getting your jewels caught in my aiguillette."

"Oh, I'm trapped!" The drone flailed madly. The braided rope, which was slung across Emily's chest, had caught one of Niles's rubies between its strands.

"Just—" She groaned. "Stop struggling, Niles! Calm yourself." She reached toward the ruby trapped between the strands. "Just be calm and—"

The drone, in his terror, yanked back madly. The ruby ripped off his silver shell. The gemstone flew, clattered against the deck, and fell through a vent into the crawlspace below. Emily could hear it clang against the bombshells belowdecks. She winced, but thankfully Niles had not detonated the entire satellite.

"Oh dear, oh dear!" Niles said, peering through the vent. "Oh, what tragedy and ruin!"

"Niles, it's just a gemstone."

"Just a gemstone?" He bristled, sprouting actual metallic quills. "That was the Black Prince's Ruby! Its history dates back to the fourteenth century when it was given to Edward, the Black Prince, by the King of Castile as a reward for military assistance. It has since been a cherished part of the British Crown Jewels, surviving numerous battles and threats over the centuries, and—"

"Niles, what did you want to tell me earlier?" Emily said. "You know, the important thing?"

"Oh. That." He looked up from the vent. "I wanted to ask you about the squadron of Nazi Rattenjägers I spotted approaching us at alarming speed. But that has now taken a back seat to a new, more urgent problem. The Black Prince's Ruby must be retrieved and—"

"Niles!" Emily cried out, heart bursting into a gallop. She saw them now. Right outside. Charging near. "Niles, give me point-defense! We need to do some fancy shooting!"

"But the ruby—"

"Niles!"

The drone buzzed toward his station. A Cholla satellite had two guns. The main cannon (called the Big Spine) fired mean torpedoes. That was the gun Emily was operating from her seat. She could aim it using a set of two wheels and several pedals. The Cholla also came with a point-defense system (the Little Spine), comprising a gun that could move all around the satellite's round shell, snap into place, and fire lasers at incoming projectiles. Normally an AI ran the point-defense system. But Niles (bless his clockwork heart) had spilled a cup of tea over the controls last week. So now the drone must plug himself into the system and manually control the Little Spine. Niles achieved this by opening a small, silvery hatch on his shell, from which emerged a slender arm, which he plugged into the point-defense system's computer.

"Niles, get ready!" Emily cried.

She popped a stick of gum into her mouth and chewed nervously. Grapefruit flavor. Chewing gum always calmed her during a fight.

The enemy came storming closer. Emily tightened her lips. A full squadron of Rattenjägers. Their name meant *rat hunter*, because the Nazis saw their enemies (which included pretty much everyone) as rats. Six of the Nazi starfighters were charging toward Emily's satellite. In the darkness of space, the Rattenjägers reminded Emily of panthers in the night, black predators racing over hidden roots and boulders, moving ever closer to the kill. Red swastikas blazed upon their prows, and the bores of their cannons shone like red eyes.

Emily tapped a button, and her viewport zoomed in on the incoming starfighters. She could see the Nazi pilots inside their cockpits. They were tall, gaunt spacers in dark leather, wearing steel helmets that looked like a cross between skulls and gas masks. They breathed through tubes. Metal rods kept the pilots locked in place to combat the terrible g-force of their flight. To Emily, the metal rods gave the illusion of ribs. She imagined these pilots as metal skeletons come to life.

But they're human like me, she thought. *I have to remember that. As monstrous as they seem, they're just humans. And I can kill humans.*

As the Rattenjägers approached, they fired a volley of sturmschlag missiles. The slender missiles raced toward Emily's satellite.

"Niles!" she cried.

The drone was leaning over the vent again. "Just a second, I think I can see the ruby over—"

"Niles, now!"

The drone zipped back to the controls. Laser blasts flew from the point-defense cannon. The sturmschlags exploded half a megameter away, spreading clouds of umbrions. Emily exhaled in relief.

She moved wheels and pressed on pedals, aiming the Big Spine—the satellite's central cannon. She locked on the central Rattenjäger and opened fire. A warhawk missile blasted forth at Mach 30, trailing blue light. Emily held her breath, watching the projectile streak forth.

The Rattenjägers had their own point-defense systems. Their lasers flashed red, and the warhawk exploded. Damn! Thankfully, Emily was already firing another and another. The missiles raced forth and—

She hit!

She—no. Her warhawk hadn't made it. But—a Rattenjäger had exploded! How—?

And then they were all exploding. All six Nazi starfighters. Emily blinked and looked around.

A gasp fled her lips.

"Are those—" She squinted. "No. It can't be."

But it was. Rhinos! Rhino dropships. Like the ones she had seen aboard the starship *Freedom*!

Even in the heat of battle, the memories flooded Emily. Memories of home. She was standing in *Freedom*'s hangar, a Princess of England, blessing the marines before they entered their Rhinos and deployed to battle. She ran through the corridors of the dreadnought, and she fired the mighty Angels of Liberty, cannons as large as Big Ben. She stood again in the hangar, welcoming the Rhinos back home. She held the hands of a wounded man, his face burned away. She prayed over a crushed dead private, all of eighteen years old. Those memories never left her. Often, even years later, they claimed her.

Freedom had been a place of war, a home of grief. But also a home of happiness and love, and there were good memories too. Remembering those good times brought a smile to Emily's lips. In her memory, she hugged Stowy, a little fairy girl with a dress of many pockets. She drank beer with Spitfire and the other pilots, cheering another victorious battle. She felt safe in the embrace of Admiral James King, her mentor, the strongest man she knew. All those precious memories passed before Emily's eyes within seconds. They seemed to dance before the exploding Rattenjägers, as real and vivid as the present moment. But that was nothing new. Those same memories, both the bad and good, used to dance in the shadowy palace as Emily roamed the halls, her pale sleeping gown trailing behind her. Haunting those dark halls, she became a ghost like her grandfather. And those ghosts had chased her here to space.

And now the Rhinos, those beasts of *Freedom* and memory, charged toward her satellite, blasting the enemies back. Their cannons were the hammers of gods.

Emily's MindLink crackled to life, activating the neural

hallucinations. And suddenly Emily was looking into the cockpit of a Rhino. An old man sat there, but despite his age, his shoulders were still broad, his arms powerful. He leaned back in his seat, took a puff on his cigar, and nodded at Emily.

"Your Majesty." His voice was sandpaper and gravel and comfort. "It's good to see you."

Tears leaped into Emily's eyes. She had not seen him since abdicating from the throne.

"James King!" she cried. "What are you—" She collected herself, remembering this was an admiral after all. She straightened in her seat and snapped a salute. "Admiral, sir!"

"You've been stuck in this satellite long enough, Major," King said. "I already spoke to your CO. You're mine now. And you're coming with me."

"At last!" Niles cried out. "At long last, we shall be freed of this infernal, spherical prison of the damned. Oh, the suffering we have endured in this accursed satellite! Oh, the indignities this cheap tin can has afflicted upon our souls! Good admiral, you have saved us from wretched captivity."

"I'm glad you're happy," King rasped. The scar along his neck danced with every word. "Because the starship *Freedom* is back. And I need you aboard again."

Niles blinked metallic eyelids. He slumped in the air. "We're fine in our satellite, thank you very much!"

King harrumphed. He looked at Emily. "What do you say, Major?"

"Well *I* say good day, sir!" Niles said. "Did you hear me, scoundrel? I said good day!" The drone leaned toward Emily and whispered in her ear. "The man is a lunatic. Send him away." He hesitated. "Shall I fire upon him?"

"Niles, shut up!" Emily shoved the bejeweled drone aside. Another gem fell off his shell, clattered onto the vent, and vanished in the crawlspace below.

"My emerald!" Niles cried. "Not the Tear of Monaco!"

As the drone wailed, Emily looked at King and rubbed her eyes. "Are you really here, sir?"

"I'm real, all right," he rasped. "I'm sending a jet bridge over. Your replacement is already on the way. Pack your stuff. You got two minutes to be aboard my Rhino."

She got there within 110 seconds.

Emily didn't think she had ever moved faster.

The Rhinos streaked into the distance. Emily sat in the cockpit beside James King. And Larry "Phantom" Jordan was there! And Spitfire! And Bastian and Alice! All those faces from her memories—they were back. And Emily couldn't stop the tears. King pulled her into his arms, and she wept against his chest.

"You're putting the band together again," she whispered. "But what's this talk about the starship *Freedom*?"

Spitfire gave her a huge grin. "Em, you gotta see it to believe it."

The Rhinos flew onward, leaving the battle behind for now. Emily watched the lights fade into the distance, becoming smaller and smaller, until Earth became no larger than a marble held at arm's length.

"I'll miss it," Niles said softly.

"Oh, Niles, we won't be gone from Earth for long," Emily said, cradling the drone on her lap.

"I don't mean Earth!" the drone said. "Wretched planet. It's absolutely gone to the dogs, if you ask me. I was referring to my ruby! The Black Prince's Heart! There shall never be another jewel like it." His eyes moved on golden stalks to examine his body. "And now there's an empty setting in my shell."

Emily spat the grapefruit gum from her mouth, then squeezed it into the little indentation where the ruby had shone. "There. You got a new jewel."

CHAPTER SIX
The Song of Freedom

Admiral James King stood on the bridge of the starship *Freedom*, ready for war.

He had missed this feeling.

He didn't miss battle. No, despite what many people thought, King didn't enjoy battle. Many soldiers did. They craved the thrill, the honor, the glory of it. Not to mention the relief from boredom (and there was a lot of boredom in the military, even at wartime). King had never been like that. He didn't love war, only what war protected. He didn't love the boom of cannons, the shedding of blood, the sight of missiles in the night. He loved green fields, golden bales of hay, and the laughter and joy of family. He fought because he had to fight. Because he was a man who could protect the weak. He was a man who would fight for those he loved. He was a soldier in his heart and soul, and he was good at his job. But every time before battle, as other soldiers felt exhilarated, King felt a little wearier. A little older. And he knew that, win or lose, more of his soldiers would die. More ghosts would join his nightmares.

Standing here today, sixty-eight years old, Grand Admiral of the Freedom Fleet, he felt it again. That weariness. That fear.

The people I love are with me again, he thought. *I gathered them from across all corners of the Earth and brought them here aboard the starship* Freedom. *Yet some might die tonight.*

No lust for battle. Just fear. But he refused to let it paralyze him, refused to let it show. He stood tall, back straight, shoulders squared. That was what he had missed during retirement. The feeling of strength. Of being in command. Of being *useful*.

He looked at his crew. Some stood here in the flesh, serving on the bridge. Others stood on other decks throughout the starship. MindWeb projected them here. Their images were translucent like ghosts, and glowing maps hung above their heads, highlighting their physical location on the ship. Kim appeared as one such "ghost." The colonel was down in engineering, nearly a mile away from the bridge. Kim's hallucination depicted her in her military coveralls, and a tool belt hung from her waist. Bastian was another neural "ghost." The big marine wore his full battle armor. He was down on deck 7 in the midsection, a place known as the Courtyard, along with his troops. Dr. Annie Jordan was aboard *Freedom* too. The doctor was in her medical bay, looking through what tools she had, 3D printing what she needed, and preparing the bay for an influx of wounded spacers and marines. As the real Dr. Annie was bustling through the medical bay, her translucent hallucination seemed to scuttle from place to place on the bridge, reminding King of a restless spirit. Emily too appeared as a ghostly hallucination. The former Queen of England was near the dorsal hull in the midsection. From there, Emily would command the Angels of Liberty, the fourteen fabled guns of the starship *Freedom*.

Along with the "neural ghosts," a few officers stood here on the bridge in person. Larry Jordan was physically here—King's oldest and best friend. King loved the man deeply (not that he'd admit it aloud). The two friends had been through hell together. Many times. They had fought the Russians and the spiders and now the Nazis, and since their youths, they had always been there for each other. Jordan had saved King's life more times than he could count. After half a century of fighting side by side, it felt good to still have Larry Jordan here.

And Spitfire. Spitfire was here of course. The new commander of the starship *Freedom*. The willowy officer stood at the commander's post—the place where King had stood for so many years. Spitfire had shed her dusty battle fatigues. Tonight she wore the old-fashioned navy-blue uniform of the *Freedom*, and she was every inch the commander. Her brown hair was pulled back into a ponytail, gleaming with a single strand of silver like the Milky Way. Her eyes reflected the light of the machinery across the bridge, but in the shadows, those eyes sparkled like stars.

"Take care of my ship," King growled at her. "I happen to love this ship. Don't go flying her into any stars or anything."

"I thought only you did that, sir."

"Keep it that way!" he said. Then his voice softened. "We're with ya, kid. Right here. Me and the Phantom. Watching over you."

"Thank you, sir," Spitfire said. "But you don't have to watch over me. I know what I'm doing. I used to command the *Lioness*. Remember?"

King snorted. "The *Lioness*. Please! A toy. This is a *real* ship, kid." He heaved a sigh and patted a railing. "I'm an admiral now, and thousands of ships are my responsibility. But I suppose I'll always have a soft spot for *Freedom*. It still feels like she's mine. But she's yours now, Gal. And I know you'll do her proud."

Spitfire smiled, and now her eyes glinted with tears.

Mimori looked up from a nearby dashboard. "Commander? Admirals? The engines are nearly calibrated. We should be ready to fly within a moment."

King took a deep breath, looking around at his crew. At his friends. This was only a skeleton crew, of course. Just the bare minimum, the few people he had recruited today. The ship would need more spacers. Thousands more. For now, Mimori's army of clones would pick up the slack. Hundreds of the androids worked across the dreadnought—cooking, cleaning, loading missiles, operating point defense, handling the ATLAS satellites that constantly orbited the dreadnought, and monitoring the ten thousand other systems that kept the ship afloat.

And Stowy, King thought. *Stowy is here.*

He had not seen the girl since yesterday morning. Not since she had popped out of his duffel bag, scuttled into a duct, and vanished into the walls. So different this new Stowy was! Aboard the first *Freedom,* King had known a carefree, giggling girl who lived in the ducts because she thought them places of wonder, a magical maze for a fairy princess. But this Stowy was a fairy with broken wings, and she hid from the light like some little elfin creature huddling under roots and damp leaves, sometimes only revealing one pale eye that peered up longingly toward the moon.

I hope you know that you're home, King thought. *I hope you know that you're loved.*

Stowy didn't have a MindLink, the neural implant all soldiers (and many civilians) had in this universe. Without the implant, Stowy couldn't access the MindWeb schematics of the *Freedom.* But paper maps of the *Freedom* hung across the starship, marking your current position. In the old days, all the way back in the 2150s, some spacers made actual use of *Freedom*'s framed maps. But that was before MindWeb. Today the maps adorned the walls more for their retro aesthetic than actual use. King liked them. He preferred the comforting aesthetic of paper maps to the cold, sterile schematics of MindWeb. Stowy would see the maps, he told himself. When she got hungry, she would find her way to the galley. King would make sure a light was always kept on for her, and that the cook (a Mimori unit in an apron) always had a warm meal waiting.

"Admiral King, sir?" Mimori said. "We're ready to fly."

Everyone looked at him. Including Spitfire.

King raised an eyebrow. "It's your ship, Gal."

Spitfire smiled softly. "It's *our* ship, sir."

King took a deep breath. "She belongs to all of us. And to Earth. And to herself. But more than anyone, *Freedom* is yours, Gal. You're her commander, and that is something sacred. This ship is not like the *Lioness*. Not like any other starship you've ever commanded. The *Freedom* is alive, and the bond between you will grow." His voice softened. "And it's a bond that cannot be broken."

"Nor is the bond between her spacers," Jordan added in his baritone voice. "Between all of us."

King tapped his temple, kick-starting a public MindWeb broadcast. He sent his words across the dreadnought, speaking to everyone in the crew—man, woman, and machine.

"To the crew of the starship *Freedom*, this is Admiral James King." He paused. "It feels strange to address you like this again. It feels like it's been forever. And like no time has passed at all. A miracle has occurred. A miracle performed by Colonel Kim Fletcher, by Mimori and her sisters, by all of you. The starship *Freedom* is back. And we're together again. I wish this reunion happened under happier circumstances. A great war was thrust upon us. Not a war we chose. But a war we are determined to win.

"Years ago, fighting together, we won a war against the rahs. They were cruel, bloodthirsty spiders, and it took great sacrifice and courage to defeat them. The enemy we face today is larger, stronger, crueler. The hammer of Nazism nearly shattered our world, and the rot of that wicked ideology now seeps across our planet, tainting it like a recurring disease. We don't know how many people the Fatherworld has killed on our world. The number is likely in the millions. Entire cities smolder. The ruins of a thousand of our starships float around our world.

"But we are still here! We still stand and fight! The *Freedom* flies again! Together, there is no force in this universe or another that can defeat us. Onward, *Freedom*—to victory!"

"To victory!" cried the crew, fists in the air.

Spitfire gazed at the central viewport. The portal loomed ahead in space, a dark sphere limned with swirling light. It was a spiderhole, new technology for humans. The rahs had attacked Earth using spiderholes. Within a few years of war, Kim and her colleague had backward-engineered the technology. Today humans, using this alien tech, could hop from place to place within the galaxy. They couldn't yet open universe portholes like the Nazis. That tech still eluded Kim. But good old spiderholes were right in her wheelhouse. In a pinch, *Freedom* herself could open crude, temporary spiderholes. Her portal generator encircled her railgun in a spinning ring.

This particular spiderhole was permanent—a steady and fortified tunnel through space. It led to a hidden hangar within a NovaTech space station. The portal was a back door to the solar system, concealed from the eyes of the enemy. From the secret NovaTech installation, it was just a quick hop to Earth. To war.

Mimori waited expectantly, her hands over the controls. The android turned toward Spitfire and tilted her head. "Commander?"

"Fly," Spitfire whispered.

* * * * *

As the engines rumbled, as *Freedom* began to fly, King reached into his pocket. He took out a cigar, placed it between his teeth, and lit it.

Jordan raised an eyebrow. "Did you just have a baby?"

"I'm celebrating," King growled, speaking around the cigar. "The *Freedom* is flying again."

"Celebrating? We're flying to battle!" Jordan said as *Freedom* gained speed, racing toward the portal ahead.

144

With his metal prosthetic, King reached into his pocket, fished out another cigar, and held it out to Jordan. "I got you one too."

Jordan took the cigar, then shook his head in wonder and lit it. When King offered one to Spitfire, she shook her head.

"You two are crazy."

"I'll have one," said Mimori. "I can't actually smoke it. But I like to feel like one of the humans."

Smiling thinly, King handed the android a cigar. Mimori placed it between her plastic teeth . . . and then the *Freedom* reached the spiderhole.

The *Freedom*'s railgun prongs touched the portal first like some giant's toes testing the water. The mighty Talaria engines thrummed within the stern. The three great exhaust ports blasted out blue energy, propelling *Freedom* into the dark pit. Sending small ships through portals was easier. Not nearly as much mass to bend spacetime around. Sort of like sending a Ping-Pong down a water slide. It'll bounce around a lot, but it'll find its way down sure enough. But to fly a dreadnought through a spiderhole? A ship that weighed nearly a hundred million tons? That was a wild ride. That was like putting an elephant onto the same water slide. He might make it down in one piece, but it would be a nervous few moments.

The *Freedom* hurtled down a tunnel of warped space and time. Starlight streaked alongside. Stars that had died millions of years ago shone anew. Stars that had not yet been born died of old age, cracking and leaking out molten energy like egg yolk. Earth was a broken cluster of rocks barely clinging to the magma around its hard metal core. And then, ten billion years went by in a flash, and Earth became a barren, charred wasteland caught by the spreading, dying ruin of the sun like some curious rock on the shore consumed by the tide.

King stood there as time and space crashed around him in

waves, as the lights streaked over him, as the past and future slammed together and scattered. Same old spiderhole dreams. King took a puff on his cigar, ready for whatever lay ahead.

I began this war as a retired old man in a cheap Chinese starfighter. His metal fist clenched, and his teeth bit into the cigar. *Now I fly back to you with a dreadnought. And with the best damn spacers in two universes. You're going down, you sons of bitches.*

The *Freedom* burst out the spiderhole, flying at tremendous speed. The ship emerged into the hollow innards of the NovaTech station. Within a split second, too quick for the eye to see, the dreadnought shattered the metallic shell around the fake science installation. King imagined them as a buffalo charging through a thin, particleboard storefront on an old Western film set. To an outside observer, the *Freedom* might seem like some terrible monster hatching from an aluminum egg.

"Sorry for destroying your workplace, Kim," King telepathized down to engineering.

"You were always jealous of my career, weren't you?" she replied, sending him a telepathic wink.

Earth was still a good distance away. The *Freedom* was well outside the orbit of the moon. Leaving the shattered shell of NovaTech behind, the *Freedom* charged homeward, her engines blazing. The fabled Talaria drive was old technology, rarely used these days. But if you asked King, it was still the best propulsion system around. He luxuriated in its hum, its heat, and the tremble of the diamond-plated deck beneath his boots.

There ahead—Earth. The blue planet was growing larger. At first Earth was the size of a pea. Quickly it grew to the size of a marble. Then the size of a baseball. As he approached Earth, King saw more details.

War engulfed the world.

Even from here, King could see clouds of smoke creeping across the ocean. Fires blazed over the continents, visible from here as little red sparks. King was reminded of his vision in the spiderhole, seeing Earth billions of years ago, a cracked shell of stone over a heart of lava, the ground like dry skin breaking over festering wounds. Earth today hadn't quite reached those levels of destruction yet, but if the Nazi forces continued their bombardment, King worried the entire planet would fall to fire and shadow.

Myriads of starships, satellites, and starfighters swirled around the planet, moving at tremendous speed. They reminded King of a whirling cloud of midges on a summer day, swirling around some rotten apple still clinging to the branch. As King watched, an Alliance ship—just a speck of light from here—flared and crashed down in small luminous pieces to Earth.

"There are a lot of Nazi ships out there," Bastian muttered. In the flesh, he was still down in the Courtyard on deck 7. But his neural ghost stood beside King, translucent and flickering.

Kim winced. She was watching from engineering back in the stern. "I wish we had another few months to get everything calibrated and installed just right. We barely even tightened the screws on this baby."

A new figure materialized on the bridge. The short, rotund man gripped a cane. His coattails were charred at the tips, and a bullet had shot through his top hat. He gave the *Freedom*'s crew a stern look, his lower jaw thrust outward in a pugnacious underbite.

"About time you got here, *Freedom*!" Godwin rumbled. His voice always sounded like thunder, whether he was jovial or furious. The old man pulled a pocket watch from his vest. "You're three minutes late."

"Sorry, but King was making long-winded speeches," Spitfire said.

"How can we help?" King said. The *Freedom* was still

charging closer to Earth. They were just about to race by the moon and onward toward their home planet.

"Admiral, the situation is dire," Godwin said. "The enemy fleet surrounds Earth, cutting off land and space. No shuttles with munitions can rise from Earth to resupply our ships in space. And no aid from space, including marines or starfighters, can reach the ground forces. The Alliance is cut in half, King. And even as I speak, the Wehrmacht is staging an assault on Washington DC. Fifty thousand German infantrymen, along with heavy lines of armor and aerial support, are attacking the capital. Even on the ground, Washington is cut off from all lines of aid."

King growled deep in his throat. "The Nazis are going after the Alliance Headquarters." It was located in the capital. Not far from the White House.

"Indeed, Admiral," Godwin said. "We're doing our best to hold back the enemy. But we won't last forever. We need Eagle starfighters in our sky. We need marine boots on the ground. The Freedom Fleet can offer this aid. Yet the fleet cannot reach us. The Weltraumwaffe has surrounded Earth like a cage. We're trapped. King, you must break through the German ships in orbit! You must shatter the bars of this cage! Rally the fleet. Fight your way through. Then bring me Eagle starfighters and Rhinos full of furious marines. We need your firepower."

"Understood," King said. "Hang tight, sir. I'm on my way."

Godwin saluted. "Godspeed, starship *Freedom*."

King returned the salute, and Godwin faded from the bridge. Ahead, only minutes away now, the battle awaited.

* * * * *

The enemy quickly noticed the approaching *Freedom*. A group of German warships turned toward this strange, antiquated dreadnought. Perhaps the Fatherworld's spacers were confused by what they saw. Even invaders from another universe, completely out of their element, would recognize *Freedom* as an antique. Old or not, the strange, hulking dreadnought posed a threat. And the Germans took that threat seriously. A hundred of their warships scrambled to form a defensive line.

King, Jordan, and Spitfire stood in "the dugout," the sunken center of the bridge. It was a little like an orchestra pit. From down here, the commanders could see the stations—telemetry, artillery, navigation, science, and others—all around them like balconies around a courtyard. Standing in this recessed command center, the trio of commanders stared through a viewport at their foes.

Mimori had summoned several of her sisters onto the bridge. Normally, thirty spacers manned the bridge, ranging from mighty admirals (if any were aboard) to hardworking sergeants (who guarded the doors, managed bridge logistics, and aided officers with their tasks). Together the bridge crew oversaw point defense, artillery, navigation, helm, and a host of other functions. Normally, they oversaw ten thousand spacers across the starship, constantly communicating telepathically. The bridge was the brain, and MindWeb the nervous system. But today would be different. Today *Freedom* was missing most of her crew, and many of her components were still offline. *Freedom*'s artificial intelligence, controlling her Mimori avatars, would have to keep things afloat.

Yes, King often thought of Mimori as an individual. But she was more of an avatar. When King talked to Mimori, he saw a human form, but he was actually talking to the starship. It was why Mimori had felt so lost on Earth during those dark days. Why she needed this ship, was a part of it, impossible to separate from the whole. All the Mimoris aboard were just parts of *Freedom*'s brain, different strands of thought and fields of knowledge. But all one organism. One intelligence. Long ago, King had realized there was no good analog in the animal kingdom. *Freedom* and her Mimoris were simply who they were, a unique lifeform comprising different parts.

Freedom flew closer and closer toward the Nazi horde. The German ships formed tight defensive lines, bringing their cannons to bear on the *Freedom*.

The dreadnought kept flying, charging at the enemy.

The German cannons heated up, blazing red in the distance like the eyes of wolves in the shadows.

Freedom was just entering MindWeb range of the fleet she must command. One ship after another popped online. Thousands of Alliance ships were trapped in orbit, crushed within a noose of Nazi machinery and malice. The Freedom Fleet could barely maintain its crude defensive formations. As they saw the *Freedom* approach, the Alliance captains cried out in joy. Wisps of their voices carried over MindWeb and fluttered across King's consciousness.

"Is this real?"

"Is anyone else seeing this?"

"The ship of legend!"

"The starship *Freedom*!"

"She must be a ghost."

"She's real! Admiral James King flies again!"

King raised his metal fist overhead. "Freedom Fleet!" he cried out, broadcasting his raspy voice across Earth's orbit. Let everyone hear, friend and foe alike. "I am Admiral James King. The starship *Freedom*, a legend from our past, flies again. We come to you now at our darkest hour. And here, from this despair, we will rise in fury! We will turn an hour of fear into an hour of courage! An hour of despair into a beacon of hope! Fly with me, Freedom Fleet! Fly for Earth!"

The Nazi ships opened fire.

Missiles came streaking toward the *Freedom*. The dreadnought did not turn aside. Onward she charged into the enemy fire. Across her hull, the Shield of David cannons rattled along the rails like old minecarts, shaking the entire ship. Within seconds, the cannons locked into position, and the Shield of David fired its interceptors. The slender, silver rockets streaked forward. A few megameters away, they slammed into the incoming German torpedoes.

Warheads exploded, scattering clouds of umbrions. A storm of darkness rose ahead, but the *Freedom* flew through the tempest. Her force field crackled to life, humming with energy that flowed from the ship's fusion core. Deep in her belly, *Freedom* held a tiny star, no larger than a basketball. That star crackled and thrummed, blazing pure white. Inside the core, great machines shaped like gramophone horns sucked up the solar wind, then pumped it through pipes. The electric storm burst to life outside the hull, where field manipulators formed like a glassblower, shaping a shell around *Freedom*. The shimmering light surrounded *Freedom* like some ghostly cloak woven of aurora borealis.

Onward *Freedom* flew, heading closer and closer to the German defensive wall and terrible torpedoes. And as she flew closer, as *Freedom* was only moments away from ramming into the enemy lines, King raised his chin, and he began to sing. His voice was grainy. The scar across his throat ached. But he sang nonetheless, and even over the roaring engines, the crew heard his song.

Let all free souls salute her flight
Let her engines bathe the dark with light

He sang just those two lines, but everyone who heard knew this song. It was an old song. A song from an old ship that had flown into a star. A song from a ship that had won great battles. That had saved the world.

Jordan was an experienced singer, renowned for his warm baritone. While King sang with his raspy voice, Jordan joined him, adding a voice like rich butterscotch.

Let her cannons sing the song of freedom
The fleet will gather; she will lead them

The two old friends had sung this song many times. When charging to battle. When charging toward what they thought was certain death. It was the song Mars had heard nearly fifty years ago, a song that heralded *Freedom* rising in the east to deliver the colony from the Red Dawn. It was the song the spiders had heard before humanity's wrath slammed into their lines, scattering the aliens across the void of space. It was the song of *Freedom*. The anthem of the starship. And now Spitfire and Mimori too joined the song, their high voices mingling with the lower voices of the men like strands of silver through veins of gold in the depths of the earth.

Our flagship sails into the flame
As poets weep and sing her name

And then everyone aboard the ship, from Kim in engineering to Annie in the medical bay—they all joined the song. The thousands of marines on deck 7 sang like a medieval choir, their voices vibrating through the ship, until all of *Freedom* became as some ancient cathedral in the mists beyond a forest, her stone halls echoing with an old song. It was the sort of song that reminded you of something you had once loved dearly, of a home you had nearly forgotten, and only after hearing those echoes did you realize how much the loss had hurt you, and how long you had been bearing the emptiness. It was a song that welcomed you home. The thousands of voices all rose together, completing the final lines.

For liberty's light! For glory's hymn!
Praise the Freedom, she will win!

* * * * *

A hundred more German warships gathered. Their cannons boomed. Shock waves blasted out from the bores, expanding and colliding like translucent blue bubbles in space. Lights flashed as the Nazi torpedoes streaked toward the *Freedom*, racing across the dark fields of space like luminous cheetahs over starlit grasslands. Aboard the *Freedom*, the three commanders stood, staring at the oncoming barrage. These were Kriegspfeil-class torpedoes. Heavy hitters. The massive projectiles blazed closer and closer toward the dreadnought, glinting like the teeth of predators. It reminded King of riding down a spiderhole, seeing all the stars streak through warped space and time.

Mimori turned toward Spitfire. "Commander? Shall I take evasive maneuvers?"

Spitfire stared ahead at the lights in the night. The incoming Kriegspfeils reflected in her brown eyes. Her face remained cool. Her only sign of emotion was her hands balling into fists.

"Full speed ahead," Spitfire said. And she knew, even without telepathy, that King and Jordan approved. She knew they stood there, looking over her shoulders, keeping her on the straight path.

The *Freedom* charged onward into the enemy fire. The Shield of David batteries clustered along the prow, firing interceptor after interceptor. The slender, defensive missiles hit many Kriegspfeils. As the German warheads detonated in space, they spilled clouds of umbrions. The dark clouds gathered, devouring any streaks of light they found like hungry ants consuming glowing worms. The *Freedom* flew through the storm, her force field crackling like a broken old television set. The umbrions feasted upon the shield, and *Freedom*'s core struggled to keep supplying the force field fresh energy. To make things worse, the Kriegspfeils just kept coming. For every torpedo the *Freedom* shot down, three more came racing forth.

"Bridge?" Emily cried from the artillery department. "I'm not sure point defense can keep up with that!"

"Shoot down what you can, Major, and our shields will handle the rest," said Spitfire. She switched her telepathy channel to engineering. "Kim? I'm gonna need you to crank that force field to the max!"

"When?" Kim said.

"Now!" Spitfire shouted . . . and they flew into a rising wave of torpedoes.

Emily, bless her heart, was doing the best she could. Normally one team managed the offensive artillery while another team managed point defense. Emily and her Mimoris were trying to manage both at once. The interceptors flew, destroying many incoming torpedoes. But several Kriegspfeils made it through.

Once past the Shield of David, the torpedoes met *Freedom*'s second layer of defense. Her force field. Down in engineering, Kim was scrambling to keep the force field up. The propulsion was off. The dreadnought was flying on momentum alone now. Even the side thrusters were powered down. Life support was down to a bare minimum. Kim was diverting all available power into the Shield of David (which only drank small amounts of energy like some picky bird at a pond) and the force field (which guzzled immense oceans of power, sucking on the core like a famished hippo who had just crossed the Sahara in July). When the Kriegspfeils slammed into the force field, the

entire dreadnought shook, and the force field blazed and sparked.
To the telemetry satellites, which constantly orbited the *Freedom* to
record and collect data, the dreadnought appeared like a fireball.
On the bridge, the senior command swayed on their feet. But
nobody needed to grab a handrail. Jordan, King, and Spitfire had
never lost their space legs.

Blast after blast hit the outer and inner lines of defense.
Wave after wave of umbrions crested through space, hiding Earth
and the fleets that still battled there. And onward through the fire
and the waves did *Freedom* fly. The shield shook and sparked again
and again. The ship jolted. And a Kriegspfeil made it through the
force field! This dark feline, this predator that had leaped from the
night, lunged onto the prow of the *Freedom*, and the warhead
detonated against the ship.

And then, after bypassing the Shield of David and the
force field, the torpedo met *Freedom*'s third line of defense. Its
armor.

Some parts of the *Freedom* must be exposed to space: the
sensors, the cannon bores, the force field generators, and various
other components. Thick slabs of armor covered everything else.
Most modern ships no longer installed thick plating. Instead, they
relied on maneuverability. Not so the *Freedom*. She was like a
charging rhino—not very maneuverable but damn well protected.
She had been designed in an era before force fields and modern
point-defense systems. Those had been retrofitted. The
dreadnought's oldest, heaviest, and final line of defense was her
thick skin. *Freedom*'s armored plates were several feet deep,
comprising multiple layers of steel, concrete, and a slender coating
of graviton netting designed to cushion kinetic impact.

And now, as she charged, *Freedom* took the punches on the
chin. Enemy torpedoes that ripped through the outer shields
slammed into her prow, denting armor, cracking the thick plates
at parts . . . but the hull survived! *Freedom* still flew!

The dreadnought raced onward through the storm. It seemed like nothing could stop her. Torpedoes blazed all around her. Umbrionic nebulae raged and swirled. From Earth, she must appear as a blazing comet crashing through clouds of thunder. Blast after blast hit the ship, and the deck trembled. And now even King, Jordan, and Spitfire must hold on to the railings, but their backs remained straight, and they stared straight ahead into the storm, and they guided their ship onward. King imagined the dreadnought as an old galleon from the Age of Sail, rising and falling over the waves of a midnight storm. The wind whipped them. The hull creaked and groaned. The cannons of the enemy carracks boomed in the dark mist beyond the waves. Yet onward the *Freedom* sailed.

And then the clouds parted.

The umbrionic storm pulled back like dark curtains.

And there ahead waited the enemy fleet. Thousands of German warships formed a wall in space, their guns facing the lone starship *Freedom*.

"Emily!" Spitfire cried. "Fire the Angels of Liberty!"

* * * * *

The commander's voice echoed through the bridge. *Fire the Angels of Liberty!*

King inhaled sharply and raised his chin. The Angels! The legendary guns of *Freedom*! Once more, as they had in the great wars of old, they would sing.

Two ghostly figures materialized on the bridge. One was a young woman in a navy-blue uniform, her blond hair neatly braided, the insignia of a major on her shoulder straps. The other figure was a football-shaped drone that hovered beside her, glittering with jewels. The drone glared at Spitfire.

"You shall not call her *Emily*. You shall refer to her as

Your Majesty!"

"Niles, shut up!" Emily cried, shoving the drone aside. "Kim, give me some force field windows. I'm about to fire."

Colonel Kim Fletcher materialized on the bridge too. Though MindWeb displayed her as a semitranslucent hallucination, King could clearly see the grease stains on her coveralls. He could smell the engineering department on her—a smell of ozone, oil, burning rubber, and reactor vapors. Kim gave him just the briefest of looks, the smallest of smiles. For only a split second, they made eye contact. God, King loved that woman.

"How many cannons do you need to fire, Major?" Kim said, turning toward Emily.

"All of them!" Emily and Spitfire said together.

Kim paled. "Damn. All right. Give me a sec to lock onto the cannons, and . . . go!"

Sometimes, King knew, commanding a starship was all about wisely allocating resources. And in the heat of battle, you only had minutes, sometimes mere seconds, to make decisions. You could beef up the force field, but that meant taking power from the engines. If the hull was breached, you could even shield cracks in the hull with that force field, but you'd be sacrificing other systems, such as the SoD, ATLAS, or Talaria drive. Right now Spitfire and Emily both wanted to fire all fourteen Angels of Liberty. A full broadside. That meant they must open fourteen hatches in the force field, each perfectly calibrated to the aiming bores. That was hard enough with the small interceptors, even more complicated with the massive Maccabee torpedoes the Angels fired. To scale, offensive Maccabees and defensive interceptors were like tree trunks and twigs. Opening the force field enough for fourteen Maccabees profoundly weakened the ship's shimmering shield. King wasn't sure he approved. Facing such heavy enemy firepower, King himself would have fired only three or four cannons, allowing the force field to remain tighter. But he had given command to Spitfire. And he would trust her instincts.

Telemetry satellites were still orbiting the *Freedom* like little moons, never straying far, tethered to the starship with quantum coils. Even at such a breakneck charge, the little drones followed their mothership. By design, the swarm of satellites served the old ATLAS system, whose bulky, data-crunching workstations stood on the bridge like metal trolls frozen by the dawn. But the modern satellites of the *Freedom II* had been upgraded to connect to the newer MindWeb system too. So King was able to reach them telepathically. Like this, he could view *Freedom* through the satellites' cameras.

He found himself gazing down upon *Freedom*'s dorsal hull. The dreadnought was a mile long, and a third of that was the Fist of Freedom. The railgun was legendary, powerful enough to destroy an enemy juggernaut, a city, even a small moon. Large and imposing, the Fist served as *Freedom*'s doomsday weapon. A weapon of last resort and ultimate destruction. The great downside was the power consumption. The railgun drained the core (which powered down the force field) and required a full day and night to recharge. Yes, the Fist of Freedom was insanely powerful, but the gargantuan cannon was impractical for a hectic battle like this. King resisted the temptation to fire it.

And so now, Freedom was aiming her secondary weapons—the Angels of Liberty. While they were smaller than the Fist of Freedom, they were still colossal cannons, legends in their own rights. Fourteen of them rose upon the dorsal hull. Six stood upon the midsection (three along the starboard side, three along the port). Eight more topped the stern (four on each side). Each cannon was as large as the Statue of Liberty. Each angel had a name, a history, a list of enemies she had vanquished. At least the old ones had. Here the Angels of Liberty rose again, reborn and furious. They moved on complex mechanisms, rising from the hull, then wheeling into position. Following Emily's instructions, all fourteen aimed ahead.

"We must punch a hole through the enemy wall," Spitfire said, "and open a path to Earth. Emily, Kim, are you ready?"

Both gunner and engineer nodded.

"Fire!" Spitfire said.

The cannons boomed.

Not all together. That would result in too much weakening of the force field, not to mention immense recoil that could strain the chassis. First boomed Libertas and Pandora, the two Angels closest to the prow. A second later, Romulus and Remus joined the choir. Another beat and another two blasts shook the *Freedom*. With every boom of the guns, the ship jolted and white light blazed. The bombardment became a thundering drumbeat, the marching song of gods. The drum beat, and the Maccabees streaked forth.

Each Maccabee was the size of a small starship. They were easily as large as the Rhino troop transporters. The Fist of Freedom fired Goliath projectiles—big, dumb, and stupid. But Maccabees included artificial intelligence, sophisticated thrusters, and a variety of chemicals in their warheads. Computers in the warheads could make real-time decisions on impact, concocting the perfect explosive for whatever they hit. Each of those missiles cost more than what King had earned in his life. Hard to believe—but each Maccabee cost more than an admiral's entire career. As they streaked forth, King said a little thank-you to the American taxpayer.

Ahead of *Freedom*'s prow, the fourteen torpedoes converged and swarmed together like a spearhead.

The Nazis too had multiple layers of defense. Their laser interceptors fired. At this close range, lasers were impossible to dodge. But the Maccabees included state-of-the-art (and highly expensive) laser-redirection systems. This hadn't been part of the original Maccabee torpedoes King had grown up with. Every year, engineers like Kim added new features. The German laser beams bounced off the torpedoes and scattered into the distance.

Onward the torpedoes flew, whipping around interceptors, scattering, reforming, and then plowing into the Nazi fleet.

Blasts lit up space.

Spitfire let out a cheer. "We hit!" She leaped into the air. "We *hit them!*"

The smoke cleared, revealing the damage. King stared at the info flooding the ATLAS screens, while Jordan focused on collecting data from the telemetry satellites. Yes, they had hit! They had hit several German warships!

"One German frigate destroyed," King said. "Two more are out of commission. Another dozen with some damage."

"Emily, fire again!" Spitfire cried.

"Give me a moment!" answered the queen-turned-gunner. "We're reloading."

King groaned inwardly. As much as he loved *Freedom*, he must admit the ship had its flaws. The slow loading of torpedoes was a big one.

The *Freedom* charged closer. Closer. The German war machine came storming toward them.

"Em?" Spitfire said.

The *Freedom* was still flying right toward the Nazi wall. A few Weltraumwaffe ships had been knocked back, but not enough for *Freedom* to fly through their lines. And the enemy was firing relentlessly. *Freedom*'s point defense could barely keep up.

King could imagine the Germans' thoughts.

The Americans are crazy! Why won't they stop? Do they think one ship can stop us? What are they doing?

The Nazis kept firing. *Freedom* took another blow to the

prow. And another. Klaxons wailed and strobe lights filled the bridge. Damage reports flooded the monitors.

"Impact warning!" Mimori cried, her eyes shining red.

"We're gonna ram right into them!" Jordan cried.

"Emily!" Spitfire said. "Where is the firepower?"

"We won't survive impact!" Kim shouted from engineering. "Not if you want to keep those cannons firing. Bridge, can I divert power from guns to shields?"

Spitfire glanced toward King.

He stared back, evincing no emotion. *You're the commander,* he said with his eyes. He didn't even need to telepathize.

Spitfire tightened her lips. "Mimori—full speed ahead! Kim, keep giving the Angels power. Emily? Get ready to fire."

The tidal wave of Weltraumwaffe ships gushed forth, seconds away now. King gritted his teeth.

This'll be close.

He closed his hands—one real, one mechanical—around a railing.

"Torpedoes are loaded a—" Emily said.

"Fire!" Spitfire shouted. "Fire everything at once!"

"*What?*" Kim cried.

Emily blinked. "But the manual say—"

"I'll whack you on the head with the manual!" Spitfire shouted. "Fire everything!"

The gunner and engineer both cringed but nodded.

All fourteen Angels fired. At once.

And the universe exploded.

The *Freedom* jolted, leaped upward, crashed downward, then surged forth on waves of energy and destruction. King flew into the air. His real hand slipped off the railing, but his metal hand held him in place. He grabbed Spitfire as she flew backward and held her tightly. Mimori planted her feet on the ground (the android was much sturdier than humans), while poor Jordan stumbled and hit the deck. The monitors exploded with data. The sirens wailed. The cameras recorded only fire, darkness, and devastation. Everyone was still shooting, and King wasn't sure who was hitting what, and then Kim let out a scream over MindWeb.

"Brace for impact!" the engineer cried.

King saw it. A German ship right ahead! A frigate and—

The frigate slammed into the *Freedom* with the force of a furious god.

And the railgun prongs tore through an enemy hull like can openers. Within a split second, *Freedom* flew onward, knocking aside the wreckage of the German frigate.

And then another impact jolted the dreadnought. Another explosion blazed with light and pain. They plowed into another ship! They carved her open, and they slammed into a third frigate, and a fourth, and they kept flying! And then they were flying through the heart of the storm, racing through the German lines, a single blazing dreadnought, wreathed in white energy and furious vengeance, carving her way through the herd of Nazi war machines.

The ship rattled. The torpedoes boomed. Spitfire was shouting over the explosions, fist raised, like some mad sea captain braving a storm. And still the *Freedom* flew. Still she fought their way through the hordes of the enemy, and all the Fatherworld's fury could not stop *Freedom*'s flight.

From behind the Weltraumwaffe lines, a thousand lights arose.

The engines of a thousand ships shone blue, and they rose from the shadows like a dawn of stars, casting their light over the battlefield.

The rest of the Freedom Fleet was here.

Frigates. Corvettes. Destroyers. Swarms of starfighters. They rose in the distance, etching lines of light across space like the towers of a luminous city. Like a cresting wave, the Freedom Fleet reached its zenith, then came crashing down upon the Weltraumwaffe. And still the *Freedom* charged onward, bombarding the enemy, hammering her foe into the anvil of the Freedom Fleet.

Lights and shadows stormed, raged, and clashed together. The sounds of cannons and roaring engines rose in a symphony of war. And to this song, King added his voice. Jordan sang with him. Then everyone aboard the *Freedom* sang, and soon voices from across the fleet joined them, rising in an old song that heralded new hope.

> *Let all free souls salute her flight*
> *Let her engines bathe the dark with light*
> *Let her cannons sing the song of freedom*
> *The fleet will gather; she will lead them*
> *Our flagship sails into the flame*
> *As poets weep and sing her name*
> *For liberty's light! For glory's hymn!*
> *Praise the* Freedom, *she will win!*

CHAPTER SEVEN
Stowy and the Mites

As the starship shook and rumbled and threatened to rip apart, Stowy cowered in the walls, covering her ears.

"Make it stop, make it stop, make it stop!" she whispered.

Another *boom* shook the ship. The dust rattled. Another siren wailed in the depths like a lost spirit, some primordial beast trapped in an underground labyrinth, in pain, desperately seeking a way out.

"Please, please, make it stop," Stowy whispered and screwed her eyes shut.

She couldn't stand the shaking. The flashing lights. The terrible noise that wouldn't stop. She knew what was happening. She knew the *Freedom* was fighting a battle, that her cannons were firing, that enemy torpedoes were bombarding her, that any second, the ship might rip apart.

Stowy wasn't afraid of death. Wasn't even afraid of battle. What hurt was that terrible *noise*. It stormed into her ears like a horde of barbarians, then marched around her skull, banging drums of war. And the lights! Those terrible strobe lights! They infiltrated the ductwork through the vents, filling these hidden burrows with red flashes. Even when Stowy screwed her eyes shut, she could still see them. The red lights flashed across her eyelids. And the shaking! The way everything rattled and the ducts pressed against her body, the way the metal was so cold, and the way her one stocking was squeezing her leg, and the feel of her hair just tangling and getting everywhere, and everything hurt, everything was too loud, too bright, too much, *too much.*

"Stop, stop, stop!" she whispered.

Another jolt shook her. She tumbled through the ducts, and her head hit the aluminum siding. Good. Good! She pounded her head again and again, and she pulled her hair.

She knew what this was. It was her old friend autism. The condition that had doomed her on the Fatherworld. She was an *untermenschin*. Impure. That was what the Gestapo said. That was why they killed her parents. That was why they experimented on her, why they tattooed a triangle on her arm, why they had removed her womb so she might never pass on the impurity. Her condition meant many things. That she struggled to communicate with others. That she thought differently. And that she experienced the world in unusual ways. Sounds were too loud. Lights were too bright. Fabric grated her skin, and smells made her sick, and everything was just *too much.*

Stowy let out a scream. Her voice rolled down the maze of ducts and echoed back to her, twisted into a sound like the laughter of crows. Stowy wrapped her safety blanket around herself, seeking comfort and warmth.

"I'm scared, Luna," she whispered.

I'm here for you, Luna whispered in her mind.

Back in the lab, Luna had been the only item of comfort in Stowy's cage—just a blanket. No bed, no teddy bears, no pillow. Just a blanket in a tiny cage. And that blanket had become Stowy's best friend.

She was an old blanket by now, fraying at the edges. A patchwork of pockets covered Luna's holes and tears, same as they covered Stowy's dress. They were both patchwork girls, sewn-together children, their bodies taken apart in the Fatherworld and stitched back together over and over, forming something new, a life never before seen.

"I wish I were strong," Stowy whispered. "I wish I could

be brave like Admiral Grouchy. Like Spitfire. Like the others."

You survived things they would not have, Luna whispered in her mind. *You're stronger than they know. Stronger than you know.*

"I did not survive," Stowy said. "I just didn't die. But I didn't *survive.* I'm all broken. Like a jug whose shards are held together by Scotch tape. Just shattered pieces clinging to a shape they have no right to still inhabit."

Not tape but a blanket, Luna said. *I'm wrapped around you. I'm keeping you safe. Keeping you whole. With me, you have shape and form.*

Tears flowed down Stowy's cheeks.

"Thank you, Luna. I'd be lost without you." She let out a sob. "I've never had friends. And I haven't had parents in a very long time. But I have you. You're my best friend."

Luna hugged her warmly. Even as the ducts shook, and even as the battle roared, the blanket was there.

A squeak sounded from Stowy's tattered dress. She looked at the garment. Pockets covered every surface, each a different fabric and color. Another *boom* hit the dreadnought. The jolt hurled Stowy down the duct. By the time she steadied herself, her pockets had spilled many treasures. Coins, curious little rocks, seashells, a gumball, and a precious ruby clattered along the duct. Stowy reached for the treasures. She managed to catch the emerald and some seashells, but the rest escaped, clanking down the innards of the starship *Freedom.* Well, at least she had caught the seashells. They were precious to her. The emerald must be worth something too. It had fallen off that curious, jeweled drone Stowy had seen through the vents. Stowy liked to imagine stories for her treasures, and she imagined that this emerald was precious beyond measure, that it had once shone on the crown of a queen. It was probably just glass, but Stowy found that, like hugs from her blanket, these little stories she invented comforted her.

The squeak sounded again. Stowy peered into one of her pockets. Her pet mouse cowered inside. Algernon seemed to like the battle about as much as Stowy was liking it.

A mouse is like me, she thought. *And I've always been like a mouse. I came from a land of vultures. Now I live in a world of lions. And I'm still just a mouse.*

But Luna spoke again. *You are not a mouse. You survived the Gestapo and the torture of the SS-Totenkopfverbände. You survived the beaks of vultures and their ripping claws. You found your way to a new universe, and you took flight in a grand starship of war. You are stronger than you know.*

"So why am I so scared?" she whispered.

The blanket considered. *I don't know. Maybe all humans are scared at times like these.*

A human.

Was she? Was she actually a human? According to the SS—no. In the Fatherworld, she had been designated a subhuman. Just an animal. No, worse than an animal. An aberration. A freak. A mutation whose only use was to suffer experiments, to explore the limits of the body and mind. That was what Uncle Baer had always told her. As he exposed her to chemicals, to vacuum, to radiation, he said that she was the most important girl in the world. More important than any soldiers. Because with the knowledge she gained for him, she would save the lives of a thousand Aryan warriors. Maybe a million.

She wondered if the Aryan soldiers were using that knowledge now. Maybe those very soldiers, the ones Stowy had saved with her torturous experiments, were the soldiers bombarding the starship *Freedom.* Maybe her death in this battle would be a form of poetic justice. A death she had brought upon herself.

Easier to just be a mouse. A mouse was always a mouse. But a trembling, weeping girl who might be human . . . that was a broken thing. Even here. Even in the impure universe. Stowy had found this realm she had dreamed of so often, and she had found her castle on the clouds, and now that castle was falling all around her, and she was trapped in the dark.

Don't give up, Luna said. *You survived so much. You will survive this. Do it for her. For—*

"No, don't say her name," Stowy whispered.

Okay. I won't.

Stowy wept. "I wish she could be here."

I do too.

She wiped her eyes. "All right. We'll have to survive, Luna. For her."

Stowy saw again the face of her old friend. An honest face. An eager smile. And it hurt so badly. Even the good memories of her—they hurt so much.

"We need to get out of these ducts," Stowy said. "We're rattling around like marbles in here."

Where should we go? Luna said.

Stowy considered for a moment. "To the bridge."

Luna nearly fell off her in surprise. *The bridge! Are you crazy? With all the grownups there? That's terrifying. They'll look at you, Stowy. They'll look at you. They might talk to you.* Luna shivered. *You might even have to make eye contact.*

"I won't!" Stowy insisted. "The grownups won't even notice me. They're busy fighting a battle."

So why go there?

"Because the bridge is the safest spot on a starship. It's where all the best armor is. It's the brain of the ship. And the brain is always protected the most."

Luna considered for a moment. *How do you know this?*

"I used to read a lot. Back before we met. Back when my parents were—" A lump filled her throat. She gulped and wrapped the blanket more tightly around her. "Come on, Luna!" Stowy began to crawl. "Cling onto me tightly. I'm gonna move fast."

* * * * *

Stowy crawled through the ductwork of the *Freedom*. This dreadnought wasn't as large as *Barbarossa*, the German juggernaut Stowy had spent time on as a stowaway. But *Freedom* was still massive, and her hidden burrows spread for miles through her bulkheads like termite tunnels through walls. When Stowy contemplated the labyrinth that awaited her, twisting and coiling through the mechanisms of the ship, she felt even smaller than a mouse. Just a termite. A single termite in an abandoned hive deep, deep within the earth.

Which way to the bridge?

Stowy paused over a vent. Below her stretched a corridor for human spacers (mice and termites stayed in the ducts). Red strobe lights flashed below. The vent's grate sliced the light into a dozen thin sheets of luminous paper, which flowed across Stowy like fluttering kisses. She peered through the grate, and there below on a bulkhead—a map. A schematic of the ship. And it was paper. An actual paper map! Like the maps Father had once hung in his office.

Stowy reached into her pocket for a screwdriver. She unscrewed the vent and stuck her head through the duct opening. If anyone stood below, they would see the head of a girl pop out of the ceiling, her elfin face sooty, her hazel eyes huge and curious, her wild brown hair shedding dry leaves and bits of string. But nobody stood below. It was safe. This wild goblin child leaped from the duct into the corridor. Like some prey animal outside the safety of its burrow, Stowy moved quickly, unscrewing the glass panel that protected the map, then ripping the paper off the wall.

Map in hand, she hesitated. Should she continue down the

corridor? The map was for corridors, after all, not ducts.

A blast hit the *Freedom* again. Stowy swayed on her feet. Far above, she heard more booms as *Freedom*'s cannons fired. Somewhere in the distance rose shouts. And then—a woman! A woman was running down the corridor! No, not a woman—an android. Mimori or one of her sisters. Stowy had heard the adults speaking of them.

As the tunnel shook, Stowy pressed herself against the bulkhead. The android ran by Stowy, not even pausing to look at her. Even as the deck swayed, Mimori remained steady, running confidently. Something about her grace and speed was disturbingly inhuman. Her movements were not mechanical or robotic. In fact, quite the opposite. Mimori ran with a finesse that was too smooth, too perfect, evincing none of the weariness or stiffness of a human. It scared Stowy. Something about Mimori seemed so perfect, so pure, like an Aryan dream of humanity achieving divinity. Stowy cowered, expecting the android to recognize her as subhuman, to mock her, to hurt her. But Mimori didn't even acknowledge her. Soon the android was around the corner and gone from Stowy's sight.

A sense of vertigo slammed into Stowy. The entire *Freedom* seemed to be spinning. And suddenly the bulkhead Stowy leaned against became the deckhead. And the deck underfoot was now *above* her. And then Stowy didn't know up from down, left from right, and she was spinning like a mouse caught inside a dryer. *Freedom* must be rolling like a glass bottle making its way downhill. Who the heck was flying this thing?

Stowy decided to return to the ducts. Safer in there. Here in the corridor, there were too many androids who might decide to catch a stowaway. And when the ship spun, it was easier to be inside the ductwork. There was less flying around inside a confined space. Stowy peered toward the open duct she had emerged from. It was high above now—too high to reach. Or was

170

it far below her, and it was Stowy who clung to the ceiling? As *Freedom* tumbled and rolled, gravity kept changing. Up and down lost meaning. Stowy waited for the right moment, then scuttled across a bulkhead (or was it the floor?), leaped into the ductwork, and—she was in! Like a terrified mouse, she vanished through the hole, entering the narrow confines of *Freedom*'s HVAC ductwork.

She took a deep breath.

For a moment, she just sat, dizzy. Everything was spinning around her. She oriented herself by checking the paper map she had borrowed. A red dot was labeled You Are Here. Stowy smiled. Ah, so she was near the bridge already! This should be easy! Maybe even kind of fun.

You're smiling! Luna said.

Stowy lost her smile at once. "Sorry."

What are you sorry for? Luna said. *Smiling?*

"Yes." Stowy couldn't explain it. But smiling when everything was so awful, when people were dying, when she herself still bore such scars . . . it felt wrong.

She had always loved maps. They reminded her of the pirate stories she would read as a child. Yet how could she smile after all she had endured? They had cut her open without anesthetic. They had removed parts of her. They had experimented on her. Broke her again and again. How could she smile? How could she betray that little, broken girl she had been? How could she simply abandon her pain? Her pain was like a baby, forever clinging to her breast, forever demanding attention. A parasite. And so even as that sense of adventure tingled, even as she smiled at the thought of maps and mazes, Stowy's pain let out a cry. *Don't forget about me!* And she did not. She did not.

The wild goblin child, leaves in her hair and dirt under her fingernails, crawled onward without a smile. In her little hand she held the pirate's parchment map. And her fierce protector, Algernon the Brave, rode in her pocket, prepared to squeak furiously at any menace. Yes, escaping into fantasy always helped Stowy. A goblin child could always layer moss and leaves and other things of autumn over the rot. Just like sweeping dirt under the rug.

Another blast hit the ship. Stowy rattled around in the duct. More shouts echoed through the empty ship, and another Mimori unit ran down a corridor below. Stowy saw the slick, inhumanly graceful android through the vent. Suddenly, as *Freedom* turned, the corridor seemed to be *above* Stowy, and the Mimori android was running along the ceiling. Stowy blinked, disoriented.

Just follow the map, Luna told her. *Don't focus on up or down. Just on the map!*

Good advice. Stowy traced her finger along the map. Now, this map only showed the corridors for humans and androids. The ducts were much more extensive, often leaving the corridors far behind, twisting and turning in the dark far from any human eyes. The corridors were rivers, while the ducts were countless tributaries. No matter how long or winding, the ducts always returned to the corridors, loosely interwoven with the larger structure, like cobwebs draped over old bones in a forest. Like a spider, Stowy would find her way along the web.

Onward she crawled, down ducts and up shafts, worming her way through the machine. Sometimes she must climb over great gears whose teeth were the size of tabletops. At other times, she climbed great, rubbery bundles of cables like the roots of some ancient tree from the age of dinosaurs. She was reminded of Charlie Chaplin caught in the machine in *Modern Times* (one of those classic films that predated the universes splitting in 1944). But no matter how far she delved into the machinery, by following the aluminum tributaries, she always returned to the corridors—the hollow bones of this juggernaut. The entire *Freedom* was alive, she had heard people say. She was crawling inside its veins and arteries. She was not a mouse. Not even a termite anymore. She felt barely more than a microbe.

And there ahead of her—eyes shone in the darkness! Creatures scuttled! A thought leaped into the imaginative mind of the goblin child: *Bacteria! Bacteria ahead in the veins of the giant!*

The critters clattered toward her, their eyes glowing white. They were small. No larger than the palm of her hand. But they were nasty things, covered in black armor, scuttling on many little legs. They looked like mites, but as they clattered closer, Stowy saw that they were actually machines. Those legs connected to gears, and the eyes were cameras. Robots.

The mechanical mites approached her, and Stowy saw that swastikas were engraved onto their armored shells. The robots reared on their hind legs, revealing abdomens that buzzed with spinning blades. Between the blades, tucked inside the conical shells, Stowy saw pulsing sacs full of dark liquid. They reminded her of the internal organs of a turtle who had swallowed tar. She knew what those were.

Umbrion sacs.

These robots were saboteurs . . . sent to destroy the ship from within.

* * * * *

Stowy's heart pounded.

Yes, she knew these mechanical mites. She had seen them before.

Pain stabbed her. She winced. The memories stomped across the broken shards of her mind with little metal legs. She lay strapped onto an operating table in Uncle Baer's lab. Back then, she had still been a mouse, not yet a microbe. Just a lab mouse to be cut open, injected, tested, and fed a treat now and then. After every experiment, dear Uncle Baer gave her a chocolate or a marzipan. Often she was too weary, too wounded to move her limbs. She would eat from his hand.

Those mechanical mites did his bidding. Within their conical shells, tucked behind the blades like a cluster of hearts within a ribcage, the mites kept little balloons and vials full of poisons and medicines. They injected them into the lab mouse, draining those abdominal sacs, each no larger than a walnut, into her little body. For a long time, Stowy had tried to forget. And now they rose again before her, scuttling through this ship, terrors from another world that had followed her here to Unreineland.

And in their sacs of venom—umbrions! Particles to consume energy and drain light. A curse of darkness that could destroy the ship's core. That must be where they were heading. Just like bacteria heading through the bloodstream toward the heart.

Stowy didn't know much about starships, only what little snippets she had picked up from eavesdropping. The way she understood it, starships had little stars inside their cores. Actual stars—balls of heat and light. They said those stars were small. Only about the size of a man's heart. But they produced enough energy to power a dreadnought. Could these mites truly damage the core? Could such little creatures, carrying such small sacs of umbrions, truly collapse a star? Well, maybe they could. At the end of the day, for all her size and might, *Freedom*'s heart was no larger than Stowy's own.

The mites raced toward Stowy, hissed, and slashed their legs at her. She wanted to flee. But she could not let these mites go onward. She could not let them reach the core. If *Freedom* lost power, everyone aboard would die. Stowy knew that. But worse— hope would die. The fleet would die. Maybe all of Earth would die. From eavesdropping on Grouchy and the others, Stowy knew how important this flagship was. How much it meant. How sacred its flight. She had heard those voices raised in song.

And suddenly—another flash of memories.

No, not memories this time. But déjà vu. Flickers of another life.

She had been here before! She had crawled through these ducts! She knew this ship!

The memories fluttered across her like the sheets of light through the vents, image after image like a carousel of slides moving faster and faster, operated by some impatient, ghostly hand. She was crawling through these ducts, grinning, joy in her soul. A second passed. The scene changed. She was in a pilots' lounge, slipping coins into a jukebox, and some strange music played, music such as Stowy had never heard, but she knew it was called rock 'n' roll. A second later—and she was in Grouchy's office, curled up on his big leather armchair by the fireplace, lost in a leather-bound book of adventures. She often crept into his office, and no matter how often King replaced and secured the vents, she found a way to open them. She suspected that he left the screws loose on purpose. Another slide flashed by, and a fairy princess lay in the arms of a king. A papery spider had struck her tender pulsing heart, injecting it with pale white venom.

She took a deep breath, shook her head, and the images cleared. She was just Stowy again. Just little Stowy "Samantha" Perry, fourteen years old, an autistic child, an impure little goblin child fleeing the Fatherworld and its poisons. But there had been another girl once. A mirror child. A fairy child. And she too had suffered the poisons of an unjust world.

And suddenly the scuttling, mechanical mites appeared to Stowy like papery little spiders with skin like the shrouds of mummies, with beady white eyes like marbles made of bone. Rage filled her. Not just fear now—but *rage*. And Stowy drew a weapon from one of her pockets.

As far as weapons went, it wasn't very impressive. In fact,

to the untrained eye, it looked like a mere dinosaur toy. Just a little T. rex, no larger than Stowy's hand, his scales painted black. She had named him Ivan. Just one more dinosaur toy among the many she kept in her pockets.

The mites paused, clattered, and hissed. They stared at the dinosaur toy, their little eyes flickering in thought. Determining this "weapon" posed no threat, the mites tried to crawl above Stowy and her dinosaur.

Stowy pulled a little string on the T. rex toy. Ivan's tiny jaws opened, and a spark emerged. The toy even let out a grainy little roar.

The mites kept crawling over her.

"Roar!" Stowy whispered (she would have roared more loudly, but she was far too shy) and waved the dinosaur at the mites. Again and again, she pulled the string, and Ivan blew little sparks. The mechanism was simple. By pulling the string, a hidden flint-and-wheel rubbed together, producing a "roaring" sound and emitting little spurts of "fire."

The mites kept crawling over her, undaunted. But the umbrions inside them noticed the flames.

Umbrions were the opposite of light. The anti-light. They were almost like doppelgängers, the ghostly twins to photons. Umbrions didn't exist freely in the Fatherworld or Unreineland. Special robots had to enter a space between universes to harvest them. Stowy knew all this reasonably well. Multiple times, Uncle Baer had taken her to Munich University to exhibit her at the Christmas lectures. He presented her as a curiosity, a human oddity, a freak of nature. But when he wasn't poking and prodding her on stage, droning on about the ravages of autism, Stowy could sit and listen to other lectures in that shadowy lecture hall. One Christmas, she had heard the great engineer, Dr. Anneliese Heisenberg-König, speak of umbrions. And of many other things too. It was how Stowy knew a little about starship cores. And a little bit about the layout of starships too. As for sneaking through starships? Well, she had honed her sneaking skills after escaping the lab. For a big chunk of her life, she had lived as a street rat in Munich, hiding in slums and attics from the Gestapo's ever-seeking eye. Whether in alleyways or starship ducts, sneaking was sneaking.

Now the umbrions—as umbrions did, as Stowy knew they would do—detected the light from Ivan's mouth. And they could not resist the dinosaur's sparking breath. To umbrions, photons were as blood in the water was to sharks. The mites tried to keep walking down the duct toward the core. But the glassy vials inside their bellies clanked and swayed toward the light. The umbrions inside were tugging at their translucent containers. Normally, umbrions could withstand consistent levels of light. Place them outside on a sunny day, and they would simply lie there, basking in the sun, soaking up all the free energy until they faded away. But catch a bunch of umbrions starving in the dark, gone feral with hunger, wave a flashlight at them, and—boom. Feeding frenzy.

A memory of one lecture returned to Stowy, piercing her fear with a sudden burst of clarity. She was standing beside the stage at Munich University, dressed in black and white stripes. Her part in the show ("Come see the freak!") was over. From the shadows, she watched Dr. Anneliese at the podium. The tall woman wore a black uniform with swastikas on the armbands, and her blond hair was streaked with silver. She was saying that someday it would be possible to design an umbrion propulsion system. Place umbrions in the engines, show them photons, and watch them go. Anneliese had presented a drawing of a donkey with a stick on its head. From the stick dangled a carrot. The donkey kept chasing the carrot, never getting closer. That, Anneliese explained, was how umbrions would chase photons inside her new engine. Like hungry donkeys, they would chase their food but never reach it, and the chase would power the starship. Stowy wondered if you could power a ship with mice.

That same evening in the lecture hall, Stowy had sat on the stairs that led to the stage. When Anneliese came walking downstairs after her lecture, she found Stowy blocking her path. Enraged, the scientist slapped Stowy hard across the cheek. Stowy remembered the sound of that slap reverberating through the lecture hall, and she remembered the stunned silence of the audience, and then the gales of laughter. They had all looked at Stowy, pointed, and mocked her. One child, the daughter of a Nazi general, even ran toward Stowy and slapped her too. Just to join the fun. Since then, Stowy had feared Dr. Anneliese and nevermore lingered at the bottom of staircases.

Remembering that evening long ago, her eyes stung. She shoved those memories aside, focusing on her present task. It wasn't easy when two lives clashed inside you. And it wasn't easy when the ship kept turning, and one moment up was down, then down was up, and one moment she was a mouse, another a termite, sometimes a fairy princess from Unreineland, sometimes a goblin child from the hidden places of the Fatherworld where the *untermenschen* cowered. As her head spun, as the entire starship spun, she thrust her T. rex at those mites, and she kept pulling that string over and over, kept blowing those sparks.

"Roar!" she whispered. And then her voice rose louder. "Roar!" That was almost more than a whisper. Almost *speaking softly* volume. For Stowy that was like a shout. *"Roar!"*

Inside the egg sacs, the umbrions went wild. They tugged on the mites, dragging the robots toward Stowy. She was pulling them back as if with a magnet!

One mite flew right into her hands. Not thinking, just reacting, Stowy grabbed the mite and slammed it against the duct. Again. Again. The shell cracked. A metal leg fell off. Stowy swung the mite again and—

178

A vial of umbrions shattered.

The terrible dark particles emerged.

They touched Stowy's arm. She screamed. It was cold. So cold! So cold that it burned!

Quickly she ripped the vent off a duct opening, then hurled the mite out of the duct. The robotic saboteur crashed down into a corridor. At first the umbrions spread across the hallway floor like fog. Then the particles coalesced into several smoky strands. Like serpents rising from baskets, the dark strands reached toward lamps in the corridor deckhead. The strands of umbrions began sucking photons from the lamps like hungry leeches sucking luminous blood. The hallway dimmed.

Well, have at it, Stowy thought. The umbrions could dim a hallway or two, as far as Stowy was concerned. But she could not let any of them reach the core!

She reached out, grabbed another mite, and smashed it. As the machine twitched, Stowy dropped it through the vent into the corridor. The mite shattered, spilling its poison. Stowy shuddered. With this second act of violence, more umbrions splashed her arm. Even Stowy, who was no stranger to pain, winced as the particles rustled across her skin.

I will help, Luna said.

The blanket rubbed Stowy's arms, soaking up the umbrions and smothering them within her warm, fuzzy folds. Stowy stared at her arms. The skin had gone white and bluish, but when Stowy pinched it, pink color returned. Good. In Baer's labs, Stowy had seen what umbrions could do to human skin, given enough time. Not much remained after a while. Left unchecked, these mysterious particles would eat the universe.

She grabbed the ones she could, crushed them, and dropped them into the corridor below. They piled up there, spilling umbrions like dead sea creatures leaking their ink on the shore. But Stowy kept hearing rustling throughout the ducts. She glimpsed more white eyes in the distance. How many of these crabs scuttled through the ducts? Could she catch them all before they drained the core?

The battle was still raging. The booms still sounded and shook the dreadnought. But the spinning seemed to have eased. Stowy wished she knew what was going on outside. Was *Freedom* destroying German ships? Was she winning? Stowy had no idea. She'd let the grownups take care of that. Here in the ducts, she would do her part and fight the enemy within.

She crawled along the duct, following a pair of white eyes. The prey animal became the huntress. She imagined herself not as a mouse, not an ant, not even a microbe, but something even smaller than a microbe now. A cell. A white blood cell. These mites were a disease inside the *Freedom*, and she must destroy them. Just as surely as they would destroy photons. Yes, the *Freedom* was alive. And Stowy was part of that big lifeform. As surely as the cells within her body were parts of her.

As she approached one mite, Stowy frowned. The mite was acting erratic—rising, bowing, slicing something with its legs. Stowy approached gingerly, holding her T. rex in front of her. The mite's armored metal shell faced her. Clattering and hissing, the robot was tugging out parts from the walls. Its little legs pulled out cables, a little motor, a few gears and screws, and other parts of the machinery that filled the starship *Freedom*'s innards. The background lights dimmed, and the robot's eyes shone brighter, illuminating its scurrying, busy legs. The creature reminded Stowy of a fly rubbing its paws. The mite grunted and chattered as it worked, seeming almost to talk in some foreign language composed of clicks and squeaks. After collecting various small machine parts, the robot began slicing out a panel of aluminum, which it bent and shaped, forming a bowl. No, not a bowl—a shell! A shell similar to its own.

Stowy knew she should attack, try to destroy this robot,

but her curiosity won. Stowy simply stared. The mite's legs worked in a fury. It began measuring and snipping cables, twisting and molding metal, and assembling a delicate, clockwork mechanism inside the shell it had formed. The robot ripped some transparent, plastic insulation strips from the bulkhead. These it wove carefully into little sacs, which it filled with venom from its own vials. The makeshift plastic sacs throbbed with dark umbrions like shards of onyx hanging from the web of some subterranean spider. Carefully the robot placed the malignant sacs into the new shell it had formed. Blades were then added like a ribcage. Finally, the robot added to its creation metal legs formed from bulkhead fastener joints. And thus a new mite was formed.

The new robot struggled for a moment, lying on its shell like an upended turtle, legs kicking in the air. In a moment of surprising tenderness (or at least so Stowy imagined), the creator robot flipped the new robot upright. Almost like a father helping his son. The "son" (as it were) looked different from the "father." The father must have come (appropriately enough) from the Fatherworld. Papa Mite was a machine made in a factory. But Junior Mite was cobbled together from pieces of the starship *Freedom*, and it looked different. Its shell, its legs, its little eyes—all were made from scraps, cut and molded from pieces of the starship. A patchwork mite, it was. In some ways, it reminded Stowy of herself—a patchwork girl covered with pockets.

But her moment of empathy did not last long. Within its egg sacs, the new mite held umbrions, and so it was just as deadly. When creating his son, Papa Mite had spilled umbrions from his own sacs into those of Mite Junior. Now, his own sacs empty, Papa Mite roamed the corridor, collecting spilled umbrions from fallen comrades and refilling his reservoirs. Soon both father and son carried bellies full of the noxious particles of darkness.

Clicks and squeaks sounded in the ducts all around. Long ago, Stowy had walked outside in the night to visit her grandfather's grave, and among the trees of the cemetery, she had frightened a family of possums. Squeaking and clicking, the marsupials had fled into the shadows behind the tombstones. That was what this sound reminded Stowy of. Families of possums in a graveyard. The sound came from all around, and little white lights ignited. Eyes. A thousand possums' eyes shone all around.

Yet as they clattered forth, she saw that they were not possums. They were mites—hundreds of new mites assembled from parts of the *Freedom*. This disease was multiplying, turning healthy cells in *Freedom*'s body into cancerous crabs. They were swarming together, too many for Stowy to ever catch and smash. And they were scuttling toward the core of the starship *Freedom*.

* * * * *

Stowy knelt in the duct, covering her head, as the mites scuttled over her, their metal legs poking her, tangling in her hair, tugging at her many pockets. Finally the swarm had passed over her. The mites continued down the duct, moving toward the core. If they got there? If they dropped their mendacious umbrions into the glowing heart of *Freedom*? Stowy didn't know what would happen.

"What to do, what to do?" she whispered. "Luna, what do I do?"

"Consider your options," Luna said. "You can try to chase them and smash them. Then spill their umbrions into the corridors. Let them destroy themselves eating the light bulbs."

"I can't catch a thousand mites," she said.

"You can devise some trap then," Luna said. "Maybe race ahead through the ducts. Rearrange the ducts somehow like moving the rails of a train. And let the mites into a trap. Say, into an airlock, where you can blast them out into space."

Stowy considered this. "I like that idea. But I'm not sure how I'd design such a trap."

"Well," Luna said, "you *could* do the smart thing and simply call an adult for help."

Stowy shuddered. "But . . . talking to other people!" She felt faint, and this time it wasn't because of the spinning ship. "I'll go with the airlock idea."

"Stowy!" the blanket said. "Just call a grownup. You can talk to Admiral Grouchy. You've talked to him before."

"When he was alone! Now he's with all these important generals. And they'll *look at me.*"

"Here's an idea," Luna said. "Hide under me. I'll cover you. You can hand Grouchy a mite, and maybe write him a note about what happened, and nobody will see you."

Stowy took a deep, shaky breath. "All right. Let's go."

She crawled onward, moving in the opposite direction of the mites. The sounds of battle still raged all around her, and the ship jolted and swayed, but Stowy moved with fierce determination. In the darkness, she imagined herself lost at sea at night, clinging to nothing but a piece of bobbing wood. The waves were rising and falling, but she paddled on.

Finally, deep inside the starship prow, Stowy neared the bridge. According to the schematics, the bridge was located right below the twin prongs of the railgun. This location of the ship was heavily armored—not only exterior armor but interior too. A cube of dense steel, concrete, and electromagnetism surrounded the bridge. Stowy imagined the *Freedom* as a huge, lumbering dinosaur, and the bridge was its tiny little brain. The layers of armor, buried here deep within the starship, were like a skull nested within layers of muscle, thick skin, scales, and spikes. But secure as it was, the bridge still needed air. The ducts were narrow here. Too narrow for any enemy soldiers to crawl through. But Stowy, if she lay flat on her belly, just about managed to squeeze down the ductwork, propelling herself by flapping her hands. She must look like a penguin that had fallen face down and was pushing itself across the ice with its flippers. Well, Stowy had never pretended to strike a particularly heroic figure. If it took sliding on her belly like a penguin to save the ship, so be it.

As she wobbled and slid her way down the duct, she could hear sounds from the bridge. People were shouting. The words were muffled, but Stowy recognized a few voices. Spitfire was crying out; she sounded both angry and scared. Jordan was shouting too. She had heard Jordan sing a few times since arriving in Unreineland, and Stowy would never forget that deep baritone. Now that buttery voice wasn't singing but shouting orders. And Grouchy's voice—that was unmistakable. The admiral still spoke with a grainy rasp, perhaps due to the scar along his neck.

His doppelgänger in the Fatherland doesn't have a scar, Stowy thought. In her universe, James "Grouchy" King had a different name. A German name. Helmut König. The most feared and powerful man in the universe. And he wasn't an admiral there but the führer himself.

Stowy shuddered. Sometimes it was still so hard to believe. That the man she felt most comfortable with in Unreineland, this wise and powerful grandfather, could be so evil, so destructive in her universe. Jordan and Spitfire, meanwhile, had no doppelgängers in the Fatherworld. They were not Aryan, and in the Fatherworld, their ancestors had been slain centuries ago. There were no Mimoris in the Fatherworld either. Japan, where Mimori came from, had rebelled against Germany long ago, and the Japanese now served as slaves in the mines. The robots in the Fatherworld were all German made. Some were noxious mites. Others were like skeletons of black metal that hunted in the night. Sometimes, hiding in the alleyways of Munich, Stowy would see those skeletal black forms march through the rain and fog.

Silently she wriggled down a duct, unscrewed the vent, and crawled onto the bridge. There was no need for stealth. Nobody would notice her in this chaos. Stowy looked around, overwhelmed.

Lights.

Lights flashed everywhere. Red strobe lights. Flashing faster, faster, brighter. Red and red and white and blinding.

Sounds roared. Booms. Crashes. A drumbeat.

People were shouting. Mimori was running here and there with that eerie, perfect grace, and two more Mimoris stood at workstations. Screens buzzed and flashed everywhere, showing thousands of ships flying and fighting all around. Across the bridge, countless monitors sparked with data, and Stowy could hear the electricity in the wires, and somebody shouted again, and she couldn't, she couldn't do it. She had to escape. Had to hide!

I'm with you, Luna whispered in her mind. *I'm here. I'll cover you. You can do this.*

She pulled Luna over her head. There were a few tiny holes in the blanket. Probably the work of the mite's sharp metal legs. In time, she would sew more pockets over them. For now, the holes were just big enough to kind of, sort of see through. Stowy felt a bit like a girl wearing the classic ghost costume (at least, if the ghost were old, ragged, and covered with pockets).

Like this, in her disguise, the little goblin child moved across the den of demons with their bright torches and booming drums. The diamond-plated floor was cold against her bare feet. Those bare feet were the only part of Stowy that stuck out from Luna. She padded toward the king in his hall of stone. James King (a true king in the imaginary world of the goblin child) stood with his back to her. He did not notice this vagabond who had come to him from the goblin kingdom deep below the mountains. One of the Mimori units (three of the androids stood on the bridge) did seem to notice Stowy. But the android simply looked at her, then looked away, too busy with operating a warship to care about some wayward goblin child, let alone one covered with pockets.

Stowy debated how to alert Grouchy. Should she call out? Oh, she was not nearly brave enough for that. What if she tugged his pant leg, or maybe if she just sat there long enough, he would notice her, and then maybe she could—

Little metal feet clattered.

Stowy spun around.

One of the mites was scuttling across the bridge! It must have followed Stowy here. It was one of the patchwork mites. The ones constructed from parts ripped from *Freedom*'s insides. Nobody else seemed to notice. Not even the Mimoris. Perhaps the androids, in their digital minds, could not register a foreign invader from a mite built of *Freedom*'s own components, no more than an immune system would recognize its own cells as threats. The patchwork mite reared, revealing egg sacs full of umbrions that pulsed upon its underbelly. The mite raised its many legs. Those legs, Stowy saw, were hollow. They were like syringes, and they leaked darkness. They reminded Stowy of the spider's stinger that had plunged into the fairy child. The mite took a few scuttling steps back, then leaped through the air, lunging toward James "Grouchy" King from behind. The mite was going to stab the admiral in the back.

Stowy leaped forward, and using both hands, she caught the mite in midair.

Her blanket fell off, revealing her to the world.

The mite squirmed in her hands, hissing and clicking in protest, legs kicking. Stowy reached into its guts, careful to avoid the blades, and snapped the cables inside. The mite mewled and wilted. Its syringe-legs dangled uselessly. Stowy dropped the pernicious robot, and it clattered onto the deck, leaking a few drops of umbrions.

A second later, Grouchy's foot slammed down, crushing the would-be assassin. Thankfully, the mite's egg sacs did not shatter. Like everything else about the mite, the sacs had been constructed from parts of *Freedom*; they were made of small round light bulbs. A few of the glass vials fell from the mite and clattered across the deck, full of swirling darkness. The umbrions inside could destroy starships. Quickly Stowy grabbed the vials and stuffed them into her pockets. A force of habit. She would keep them safe from crushing boots.

These eggs are poison, she thought. *They are weapons. Weapons I can use.*

If Grouchy noticed her pocketing the vials, he didn't mention it. He simply stared at her with wide, shocked eyes.

"Stowy!" the admiral said. "Thank you! You saved my life."

And everyone looked at her.

And Stowy wanted to run, to hide, to fall over and play dead. Anything but have all those eyes staring at her. But she must tell them.

Luna had fallen onto the ground. Luna was no longer speaking. Stowy was exposed. Everyone was staring. Everyone saw her, and she would *have to talk*. She would rather face ten thousand mites in battle. She would rather endure scalpel and stitch and—

No, said a voice in her mind. And this time it was her voice, not Luna's. Her own voice. *No. You would not rather suffer blade and blood. You escaped that world. You defeated that world. And you can keep fighting. You can break through this wall too.*

And so she tugged on Grouchy's pant leg, and he knelt beside her. Though her heart pounded and she trembled, she leaned forward, and she whispered into his ear: "Admiral Grouchy? There are more."

* * * * *

Her words, so soft, echoed in King's ear.

"Admiral Grouchy? There are more."

A chill ran through him. More of those robotic mites! How many of the robotic assassins roamed the ship? Stowy had saved his life, but not everyone was lucky enough to have a guardian angel.

Kneeling before her, King stared into the girl's eyes. "How many?"

Stowy blanched and looked down. Hands fluttering like the nervous wings of birds, she pulled her hair over her face and tousled the strands. Her little body trembled.

Right, King thought. *She doesn't like eye contact.*

He should have known that. He had looked right into her eyes. To Stowy, that was like a slap to the face. Unintentionally, King had hurt her.

"I'm so sorry, Stowy," he whispered. "I won't make eye contact anymore. Can you tell me how many more robots you saw?"

Though she trembled like a baby bird in a cage, she managed to whisper a single word. "Hundreds."

While the old man and the young girl whispered, the starship *Freedom*—indeed the entire fleet—was still fighting. Since charging into the German lines in a blaze of light and glory, *Freedom*'s cannons had not stopped booming. The fleet rallied around her. Hope filled the hearts of three thousand captains— the legendary flagship was back! Like a phoenix from the ashes, *Freedom* flew again! With three thousand little lights, they gathered behind this flaming beacon in the night, and the Freedom Fleet fought together again. As they had against the Red Dawn half a century ago. As they had against the spiders. As they always would so long as freedom was threatened. Since King's youth, this fleet had symbolized the shield and sword of freedom against tyranny, and it was the honor of his life to wield these tools of war.

Before them, like a wave of tar, rose the black tide of Nazism. Ten thousand ships of the Weltraumwaffe clustered ahead like a swarm of black eels in a dark sea, crackling and sparking with lightning. Their red portholes blazed like eyes, and the blue light of Earth, which shone entreatingly in the distance, turned sickly and red as it reflected from the swastikas engraved into the Nazi hulls. Again and again, those mechanical eels struck, teeth slashing, electricity sparking. Their iron jaws caught ships of the Freedom Fleet and crushed them. Their slender missiles, crackling and bright like lightning bolts, charged and stung and ripped Alliance ships apart.

They were still in high orbit here. In low orbit, closer to Earth, Katyusha and the Red Dawn were fighting their own front. Most of the German war machine was engaged down below, only a megameter or two above Earth's sky. From what King could see, it was a bloodbath down there. Thousands of equalists and fascist starships were crashing together, exploding, and shattering above the sky. Chunks of their ruin hurtled toward Earth, wreathed in flame, and crashed into oceans, forests, and cities. Things were ugly enough here in high orbit. But down there, where Katyusha fought? That was truly hell. The Russian premier had no regard for the safety of her troops or ships. Katyusha sent wave after wave of starships on kamikaze missions, hurling them into the German lines like an enraged girl throwing her wooden toys. Thousands, maybe millions of her spacers were dying. To Katyusha, they were cannon fodder. It was effective, yes. The Red Fleet was carving deep gouges into the Weltraumwaffe's formations. But King didn't even want to contemplate the human cost. Perhaps Katyusha didn't care about her people's lives. But

King grieved to see their sacrifices.

Up here in high orbit, the forces were spread more thinly, but many ships were falling here too. Many brave spacers were dying. The Freedom Fleet was making progress. Together, the democratic nations of the Alliance and the equalist nations of the Red Dawn were trapping the Weltraumwaffe between them, hammering the fascists from below and above.

But not everyone was joining the brave fight to liberate Earth from the Nazi invasion. It sickened King's stomach to see. When Bastian had warned him about Barcelona, King had refused to believe. People from this Earth, from this universe—joining the enemy?

But now he saw it too. Right here in space.

Multiple ships from multiple nations. They engraved swastikas on their hulls. They hoisted the Fatherworld's banners. And they joined the enemy. Some were the ships of militias, warlords, terrorists, and various other malcontents who seized the chance to wreak havoc. Others were actual military ships—even some from the Freedom Fleet!—that defected and joined the Nazis. Among the Weltraumwaffe—that swarm of dark, electric eels—flew familiar warships from the free nations of Earth. An entire French subfleet had abandoned the Freedom Fleet and joined the Weltraumwaffe. So had the complete Irish fleet (they only had six ships, but every one of them was now hoisting the Fatherworld's flag).

King snarled and clenched his metal fist. Traitors. Nazis disgusted King, but something about traitors sickened him even more.

He forced his rage down, pulling his mind back to the urgent problem facing him. Those mites! Spitfire and Jordan were both shouting orders, commanding the flagship and fleet in battle. King had taken this moment to listen to Stowy. And her warning might yet save the *Freedom*.

"Kim, do you have a moment?" King said, calling his wife over MindWeb.

"No!" came her disembodied voice over MindWeb, speaking from down in engineering.

"Neither do I, but we have a problem," King said.

"Ya think? Hang on!" Kim's voice became muffled. "Mimori, can you secure that power coupling? And get a team on that exhaust leak! Use the plasma-dampener clay to clog the tubes for now. And rewire that coolant rod, or it's gonna get damn hot in here!"

She must be speaking to the androids down in engineering. Normally in battle, an army of human mechanics did Kim's bidding. Today she commanded a dozen androids.

Just then, a blast hit the *Freedom*. Spitfire let out a juicy curse. The ship jolted.

"Torpedo slammed right into our prow!" Spitfire cried.

"Guys, we're halfway through our ammunition already!" Emily shouted from the artillery department.

"Our port thrusters are damaged!" said Mimori Prime, the original android from the first *Freedom*. "Spitfire, I'll send my sisters down to fix it. Try not to yaw to the starboard for a while."

"What?" Spitfire cried. "Emily, send all Shield of David batteries to the port hull!"

While this was all going on, Stowy huddled behind King's legs, wrapped in her safety blanket. The girl held the crushed mite in her hands. One of the metal legs was twitching, and black powder was leaking from its underbelly onto the deck, warping and cracking the diamond-plated steel. Umbrions!

Kim materialized on the bridge beside King. The engineer was panting. Her face was sooty, her jumpsuit was singed, and a scratch bled across her arm. Smoke wafted from the engineer's charred clothes and hair. MindWeb even let King smell it.

"Talk to me, Jim!" she said. "Make it quick! What did you

191

want?"

King gestured toward Stowy and her mite. "I found a little saboteur on the ship."

"Jim, don't talk about Stowy that way."

"I don't mean her!" King said. "Look what she's holding."

Kim frowned. "What is that? Stowy, where did you find it?"

But the girl was trembling. She clamped up, unable to talk anymore. Not even to King when he lowered his ear toward her mouth. But she had told him enough. King thought he understood what was happening.

"Remember when that German shuttle snapped onto our hull?" he said. "Just for a few minutes?"

"Yeah, our hull drones scraped it off," Kim said.

"Well, turns out the shuttle disgorged little robots into the *Freedom*," King said. "And they're self-replicating. Stowy saw a bunch of them in the walls, heading down to engineering. One made it to the bridge—and tried to stab me. They're carrying little vials of umbrions. Stowy thinks they were heading toward the core."

Kim gasped. "If they drop umbrions into a hydrogen fusion core—"

"Meltdown," King said. "Kim, these mites are like a bacteria infecting the starship. That's how Stowy described it, and she saw them in the ducts. Any chance you can slap together white blood cell robots?"

"Sure!" Kim said. "Just give me a month, a crew, and time off from multiverse wars. Jim, you're asking me to— Wait." She turned. "Mimori, no! Don't throttle that power coupling. Yes, I know what the specs say. I wrote the specs! Open it up full flow!" She looked back at King. "I'll do my best. The Mimoris will help. Or blow us all up. Kim out."

Her hallucination faded from the bridge.

King wished he could help. But he must return his attention to the battle. He had a fleet to command. He must break through the Weltraumwaffe! He must open a path to the ground forces! Or Washington would fall. And then the whole Alliance.

He looked around for Stowy, wanting to comfort her, to find her a safe space to wait out the battle. But the frightened stowaway was already gone.

CHAPTER EIGHT
Stem to Stern

Engineering was a madhouse.

This entire starship was a loony bin!

Colonel Kim Fletcher-King stood in the middle of the chaos, desperately trying to hold her beloved ship together.

They weren't ready. She wasn't ready. *Freedom* needed another few months in a shipyard. Years, even! This was insanity. A battle—now! And blasts kept hitting the ship, and systems kept shouting warnings, shutting down, or going haywire. For a moment, Kim thought her own brain—the analytical brain of an engineer—was going haywire too.

But I'm not just an engineer, she thought. *I'm also a soldier. And a soldier doesn't always get to choose when she fights her battles. Sometimes the battles just rise. Out of the blue. When you're not ready. When you're in a bad place in your life. Or a good place that shatters all around. A battle can hit when you're weak. Or when you're scared. And at those times, you do not fall apart. You do not crumble and cry. You stand up! No matter how hard it is—you fight! You fight!*

Did she come up with all that? Kim wasn't sure. It didn't sound like her. Maybe something her drill sergeant had said at boot camp all those decades ago? Well, whatever the origin, it was good advice. Kim refused to succumb to anger or fear. She refused to fall apart like the ship threatened to do around her. She was an engineer *and* a soldier, and both parts of her would do their jobs.

She looked around her. For a brief moment, Kim just took things in, trying to triage the cascade of problems.

With the energy throttlers on the fritz, the power supply to various components aboard the *Freedom* was fluctuating. The shields, the cannons, the computer systems, the life support, and a thousand other systems depended on a steady supply of power. A complex system spread throughout the dreadnought, delivering energy from the core. Kim worked alongside the bridge, making real-time decisions on power distribution. Was Emily firing a broadside? Power to cannons! Was Spitfire flying into enemy lines? Power to front shields! Was speed essential? Power to engines! Kim was constantly leaping from here to there, diverting the power of *Freedom* to different components. Sometimes she felt like a heart, pumping blood to whatever organ needed it most. Yes, the bridge was the brain, and here in engineering was the living ship's pulsing heart.

But if the power was fluctuating, if the heart was struggling, systems would start to break down, freeze, and jam. Already two cannons were offline, and life support wasn't flowing to decks 13-15 (where, thankfully, only Mimori units were operating). Kim had to fix this. And fast. Without blood, organs wither and die. And without energy, systems switch off. And just as bad—other systems might gain bursts of excess power and fry themselves.

Then there was all the exterior damage to the hull. Several Kriegspfeils had hit the armored plates, and at spots, the German torpedoes had cracked the hull. That was affecting nearly every system. *Freedom*'s armor wasn't just thick, dumb sheets of metal. The hull was like skin—a living organ. The way skin was full of blood vessels, nerves, and other important things, the hull of a starship contained cables, pipes, computers, gears, motors, graviton generators, and a thousand other components. Every blast to the hull sent problems cascading throughout the starship.

Already the portside thrusters were jammed, and the force field was flickering there. The hull had even been breached at spots (and sealed off using makeshift force fields, which were barely keeping things in place).

Oh, and there was a problem with the shield generators' heat-removal units. The force field generated massive heat, which was normally fueled into life support, recycled back into the core or (if all else failed) dumped into space. Now there was a jam—somewhere. And the heat sinks kept overheating. If Kim couldn't vent the heat soon (how?), the entire system would blow. And probably take the whole ship with it. Kim felt like a heroine in some old thriller movie, struggling to defuse a ticking time bomb.

Then there were weapons malfunctions. In addition to her railgun and cannons, *Freedom* boasted a host of machine guns. On command, they could emerge from the hull like groundhogs and unleash hell. Groundhoggers, the troops called these guns. The Groundhoggers were mostly used to attack incoming boarding ships. Hundreds of them lived inside the hull, ready to pop from holes and shoot. But now, with the hull damage, three Groundhoggers were lodged inside their holes. If the system woke up to fight invaders, those trapped Groundhoggers would fire into the *Freedom*. Kim must disable them before that happened. Another ticking time bomb!

The Groundhoggers *should* have an emergency kill switch. They used to on the original *Freedom*. With this new *Freedom* rushed into battle so early, Kim had never gotten around to installing that safety feature. It was still on her ever-growing to-do list. Oh, and the Shield of David rail had snapped in three places. She had to program a new algorithm to use the paths that were still there. Normally, the system would do this automatically. But, well—yet another system that wasn't online yet. The joys of flying an unfinished ship into battle.

Then there were chassis integrity concerns. And various

life-support malfunctions (which would start to put some serious strain on their oxygen soon). And a whole bunch of software wasn't even installed yet, let alone calibrated.

And then there was the core. Of course. How could you ever forget the core? It was as needy as a baby. The little artificial star required constant monitoring, and—

A *boom* shook the ship.

Alarms went off. Damage reports flooded the monitors down in the engineering bay. Kim watched a whole new assortment of problems leap onto her to-do list. Sigh.

And the mites. Yes, there was that whopper of a problem to worry about too. King had dropped that big, wet, wriggling disaster right into her lap at the worst time.

There was only one silver lining. With barely anyone aboard, if the ship blew up, the casualties would be low.

No, Kim thought. *No! I did not spend three years rebuilding this starship to lose her now.*

The mites. The mites would have to come first. Along with everything else.

At first Kim considered simply creating a security barrier around the core, protecting it from mites. Maybe a system of grates along any small hole or hatch in engineering. There were many ways for something small to crawl in: ventilation shafts, maintenance conduits, tech tubes, heat waste ejection ports, hell, even the sewage system (there were bathrooms down in engineering, after all, and Kim didn't want to see any mites pop out of the toilets). Dealing with pests wasn't a new problem. Mice, bugs, and other creepy crawlies were a scourge of many modern starships, especially the big, busy ones. Thousands of people came and left ships as large as *Freedom*, bringing all sorts of germs and vermin with them. The old *Freedom* had dealt with everything from bedbugs to a colony of stray cats. Maybe Kim could kludge together some mite traps?

But Stowy's metaphor returned to her. The mites were like a bacteria spreading through the veins of a giant organism, and they were replicating. Kim didn't just need to block or trap them. She needed to hunt them down and kill them. Every last one. She needed to build white blood cells.

An idea popped in her mind. Her "white blood cells" would need some lure to attract the mites. Something like the lure of an anglerfish. The mites carried umbrions, particles that destroyed photons. The mites were likely programmed to seek out sources of energy and destroy them. Maybe each "white blood cell" bot could carry a vial full of photons. Cheese in a trap. Could she create white blood cells that would self-replicate? Yes, if she had a year. Von Neumann robots were far beyond what she could build now in a pinch.

She could design something crude for now. But even a crude blueprint would take her a few hours, especially when she must consider the limited parts and tools available. She needed a faster mind.

"Mimori!" Kim said.

One of the androids rushed toward her and snapped a salute. While the Mimori Prime (the leader of the gang) wore the navy-blue uniform of a bridge officer, the engineering androids wore coveralls and helmets. As clones of Mimori Prime, they still referred to themselves as *Mimori*. Just copies of their mother on the bridge. But already they were beginning to develop individual personalities. This had happened on the last starship *Freedom* too. Eventually the first *Freedom*'s androids had even chosen for themselves new names. The current generations of Mimoris weren't there yet. Kim hoped they lived long enough to become individuals.

For a moment, amazingly, even as blasts kept hitting the starship *Freedom*, Kim found herself smiling. Robotics was her first love. Ever since she had been a child, she had loved robots. As a toddler, little Kimmy had never wanted to play with dolls. She wanted *robots*. As a child, she began taking apart microwave ovens, shuttle motors, lawnmowers, and other electronics, then used their components to build little robots of her own. Robots had filled her childhood bedroom. Then her university dorm room. And now—her engineering department. If she could, Kim would spend all day just building robots, giving them names, and watching their robotic lives unfold.

Stowy loves dinosaurs, and I love robots, Kim thought. *Maybe we're not so different, she and I.*

"Ma'am?" the Mimori unit said. Meanwhile, her sisters were still running across the ship, fixing this and that, barely resolving one problem before three more popped up. The blasts of the Angels of Liberty kept shaking the ship. Just then, another torpedo slammed into the hull, and *Freedom* swayed like a ship at sea. More alerts flashed. More breaking things. More people dying. Kim grabbed a bulkhead handle for support and stared at her android.

"I need you to create a quick-and-dirty blueprint for me," Kim said. As alarms flashed and klaxons wailed, Kim quickly described the problem and her proposed solution.

Mimori nodded. "Understood. White blood cells. How about this design?"

The android's eyes flashed. A hologram materialized, hovering in the air. It depicted a quick-and-dirty robot, complete with a luminous bulb.

"The bulb utilizes magnesium as fuel," Mimori said. "It's readily available in the ship. It's what the marines use for their flares. And we can build the rest out of spare parts right here in engineering."

Kim nodded. "Good. Get to work. Build me as many as you can. That is your only priority right now. Then send them hunting."

Mimori was useful that way. Her mind was different from a human mind. Mimori struggled with creativity, curiosity, and innovation. Left to her own devices, the android would not reach many scientific breakthroughs. She lacked that human spark, that desire to explore and create new things. But in other ways, Mimori was far smarter than humans. Give her some basic specs, and she could design an entire robot within seconds—work that would take Kim hours. And when Mimori sat down and got to work, her limbs moved at a blur, grabbing, shaping, and attaching pieces so quickly that her "white blood cell" robots seemed to simply materialize out of the ether. The two women worked well together. One was curious and creative, the other dazzlingly fast and capable.

Two women, huh? Kim thought. *When did I start thinking of Mimori as a woman?*

She knew that the android's human form was just a trick, a way to endear her to humans. Her creator, Professor Mori, had created Mimori to look like his daughter. In reality, most of Mimori's brain wasn't even inside that body—but inside the starship itself. And yet, yes . . . a woman. Kim wasn't sure how, but somehow even this starship with many small, identical clones seemed so very much like a person. A different kind of intelligence. A different kind of consciousness, perhaps. Yet still alive. Still a soul. And over the past three years, Kim and the androids had brought this soul back from the dead.

Another blast hit the ship.

The *Freedom* jolted. Kim swayed on her feet. Graviton generators pulsed throughout the starship, pumping gravity to the shields, the decks, and critical machines that relied on them. That helped cushion the blow from enemy torpedoes, but already one graviton generator was down. And now alerts flashed and alarms wailed, warning that a second graviton pump was offline. Damn it. Kim would have to climb in there to fix it, or at the next blast, everyone would be floating through the ship.

"First immubot ready!" Mimori said.

Kim blinked. "Wow. So fast. It's barely been a minute."

Mimori blushed. "I needed to cut some corners. The shell isn't polished, and the eyes are lacking expression. Humans often like robots with expressive eyes. And one antenna is bent. Would you like to see some color palate options for the final paint job?"

"Just show me the robot."

The android held out her creation. The robot rested on her open palms. For its body, Mimori had used a marine's helmet. Little legs (built from alligator clamps and screwdrivers) moved inside the shell like the legs of an arthropod. Simple cameras formed the eyes. Most impressive was the lure. A metal prong rose from the helmet (it was crudely welded on), tipped with a glass bulb full of light.

"Does it have any weapons?" Kim said.

"I wanted to add some guns, but I was short on time. So here's what I did."

Mimori tapped a button on the immubot's shell. Two rods emerged, tipped with spinning saws. The circular blades shrieked and whirred menacingly. Kim winced and took a step back.

"I think that'll do fine, Mimori," Kim said. "If you can just . . . turn the blades off for now."

Mimori switched off the sawblades. "My immubot is programmed to prey on Nazi mites. It lures them, then destroys them. And here's the beautiful part. Once it crushes an enemy mite, my immubot can rebuild it, reprogram it, and convert it into another immubot." Mimori smiled. "Pretty clever, huh?"

"Brilliant," Kim said, carefully (very carefully) taking the immubot from the android. The sawblade twisted and spun a few times, showering sparks. Kim winced. "Now get started on the next one, Mims. Make as many as you can. I'll send this one on its way."

Kim hurried across the engineering deck, holding the squirming, chattering robot. The little beast kept kicking its alligator-clip-and-screwdriver legs, spinning its sawblades, and nearly slicing Kim's fingers off. A prototype indeed. Kim climbed a ladder two stories up, pulled open a service hatch, and placed the immubot into a ventilation grate.

"Good hunting," she said. And the little bot scampered off, its many legs moving beneath its helmet body.

With a relieved sigh and all her fingers intact, Kim turned away from the hatch, and—

She yelped and nearly fell off the ladder.

"Mimori! You scared me half to death."

The android stood right there—two stories above the deck. The android, Kim realized, was standing on a floating graviton platform. Mimori grinned and held out three more murderous immubots. The little machines thrust their spinning saws at Kim. Their flashlight eyes shone with rage, and their alligator clamps snapped. The bots made little clattering, yipping sounds as they struggled in Mimori's grip. They reminded Kim of ferocious Chihuahuas with a taste for human flesh. She winced and leaned back from the whirring blades and snapping clamps.

"I got the next batch ready!" Mimori said, beaming with pride.

"Thanks." Grimacing, Kim took the immubots one by one, nearly losing a few fingers. She should have worn gloves. She placed the menacing machines into the HVAC duct.

Squeaking and chattering like old soldiers cursing out their enemies, the immubots clattered down the ductwork. Kim imagined them as a stampede of murderous turtles.

"You keep building and releasing more immubots," Kim told Mimori. "I've got a thousand other ways to save our lives."

Mimori saluted. "Happy to comply!"

* * * * *

"Oh, this is intolerable!" Niles fluttered across the artillery station like a nervous bird that flew into a house and couldn't find its way out. "A battle, Your Majesty. An actual battle—and you're fighting it! Do you realize that statistically, the average English soldier only stands a seventy-eight percent chance of surviving a battle in space? You'd have a better chance playing Russian roulette! I must insist we return to Earth at once."

"Niles, not now!" Emily shouted.

She worked the joysticks and pedals, moving the mecha across the deck. Samson was a big, burly machine, standing fifteen feet tall. It was a simple piece of technology. Just a big exoskeleton, its thick metal joints painted yellow like a tractor. Hydraulic pistons and servos hummed as Samson thumped across the diamond-plated deck. Emily stood inside the cockpit, protected behind a thin sheet of steelglass. With joysticks and pedals, she operated the mecha. It was meant to feel intuitive. Samson was designed to move like a human. But Emily found him difficult and awkward to control, and one time she had even dropped a torpedo and nearly blew up *Freedom* from the inside.

The artillery deck was surprisingly small. In a system full of automation, this deck was a notable exception. It was one area where a human technician (with the help of an exoskeleton) was involved doing manual labor. The *Freedom*'s ammunitions were stored inside warehouses deep inside the ship, wrapped within protective layers of steel and force fields. From storage, they were ferried up through the decks in dedicated hatches, pulled by a sophisticated system of chains and pulleys. At some point, after making their way through the ship, the torpedoes must move from the logistics department to the artillery team. That was where a human got involved. A human inside a mecha must lift the torpedoes, slide them into a loading chute, and shove a lever.

From there, another automated system would prepare them for firing from the cannon. Fourteen Angels of Liberty topped the dorsal hull, and so fourteen humans must stand in mechas, manually loading each cannon. Fourteen bottlenecks.

It was an outdated design. Obsolete, really, and inefficient. On modern warships, the entire system was automatic and seamless. No humans involved. But three years ago, when Kim had begun to rebuild the starship *Freedom*, she had never imagined Nazis would invade the universe, or that the *Freedom* would fight another major war. As far as Emily understood things, Kim had simply been building James King a surprise gift for his seventieth birthday—an accurate replica of his old starship. So why not keep all those charming imperfections from the old model?

Well, this was why. Now Emily and fourteen Mimori units had to waste their time inside mechas, loading one torpedo at a time. Emily felt like some old-timey cowboy loading one bullet after another into his revolver. What a colossal inefficiency!

If King were here, he would probably remind her of that time when, operating a Samson mecha, he had grabbed an enemy rah, loaded the beast into a cannon, and fired the alien spider into space. Emily had heard that tale a thousand times, each time more embellished. In some versions, the spider was the size of an elephant, and King had rolled the alien up like a scroll before firing it into space. The old man, who craved any excuse to tell that story, was probably glad to see the old missile-loading mechas here again. Emily, an actual artillery officer—not so much.

Her MindLink buzzed inside her skull. A voice filled her head.

"Emily! I need that torpedo loaded—now!"

The voice belonged to Gal "Spitfire" Levy, *Freedom*'s new commander.

"Almost there, ma'am!" Emily said.

A hallucination of Spitfire appeared on the gunnery

station. Cameras on the bridge were filming the commander, then streaming a video feed directly into Emily's mind. Spitfire was a tall, striking woman, her features sharp, her skin tanned, her eyes dark and fierce. Her dark hair was pulled into a ponytail, streaked with a silver strand like lightning through the night. The commander wore a fine navy-blue uniform with all the trimmings, and even in battle, she kept her chin raised, her shoulders squared, evincing no fear.

I used to be Queen of England, but Spitfire looks more like a leader than I ever will, Emily thought.

Emily herself was rather short (she barely stood taller than Spitfire's shoulders). With her blond hair, blue eyes, and pale skin, some said that Emily looked like a porcelain doll. The Doll Queen, her critics would mockingly call her. Even now, in battle fatigues, strapped into a giant mecha, Emily felt small and soft compared to a warrior like Spitfire. She still felt too much like that soft, spoiled princess she had been.

But I'm no longer that spoiled princess, Emily told herself. *I fought in the Spider Wars aboard the starship* Freedom. *I ascended to the throne and led my kingdom. And now I am an officer. An officer aboard the flagship of the fleet.*

She considered Spitfire, whose image still filled her mind, coming directly from the bridge. In many ways, *Freedom*'s proud commander reminded Emily of Katyusha. The two women were not friends. As far as Emily knew, the Israeli commander and Russian premier had never even spoken. And if they had, they would likely be at odds, one a leader of a democratic alliance, the other the tyrant of an equalist empire. But to Emily, they both symbolized strong, powerful women, older and wiser than her. Despite a life that seemed long and tumultuous to her, Emily was not yet thirty, and she was still forging her path through life. She was no longer queen, yet she desired to become a leader again. Another type of leader. Not one who sat on thrones but who stood aboard a starship. To her, a young officer still learning leadership, both Spitfire and Katyusha were mentors and heroines.

"Emily, give me an update!" Spitfire said, cutting through the young gunner's reverie.

Emily pulled the joysticks. Samson's joints creaked and his motors whirred as the mecha knelt. Gently Emily slid the multiton Maccabee torpedo into the chute.

"Libertas ready to fire, ma'am!" Emily said.

"Good work, Major," said Spitfire's hallucination, then vanished with a flutter of colors.

Senpai noticed me! Emily thought, chest rising in pride, then sighed. She had been the Queen of England, for pity's sake. Funny how aboard the *Freedom*, Emily still felt like a nobody. Even now.

Niles flew across the room toward Emily. His camera eyes shone with blue fury. "Who were you telepathizing with? Was that Spitfire? Did you actually call that common girl *ma'am*? You are the Queen of England!"

"Niles, go away!" Emily said.

"I shan't. This whole situation is demeaning and beneath you. Now—return with me to Buckingham Palace. We can still get back by teatime. I shall explain the entire situation—how you only abdicated due to bouts of insanity brought upon by the horrors of war, and that dear Niles has since cured your broken mind. Maybe they'll even give us our crown back. Or at the very least—our royal suite. Now come, to Buckingham!"

"Niles, if you don't shut up, I'm going to shove you into the cannon and fire you back to Buckingham."

He gasped. "You would never! After all I've done for you. Oh, to be savaged by such cruel barbs!" He looked away. "But I understand. I'm only a drone after all. Who cares what Niles thinks? Why listen to your oldest, dearest childhood companion, when all he's done is raise you and nurture you? Oh, poor, poor Niles is used to indignities, and—"

Emily grabbed him. "I'm firing you out the cannon *now.*"

"I'll be quiet!" He slipped from her grasp and fled behind a pipe.

* * * * *

King stood on the bridge of his flagship as the Freedom Fleet soared all around. With blazing light and brighter courage, three thousand ships plowed into their foes, and Earth's orbit flared with a corona of war. As ships swirled around Earth in battle, as cannons boomed, as starships broke apart, as the survivors fought on, it seemed that a ring of fire engulfed the planet, a planetary ring woven of war.

"These are the fires of freedom," King said softly. "This is the courage of humanity. With this flame, we will burn the enemy and drive him back into the shadows."

Round and round the Earth spun the ring of fire. Fighting on the ground was (mostly) stationary. You stood in place (a lot) and fired your guns. You moved a bit sometimes, but not very far. Fighting on the seas and oceans was a little trickier, and distances were a little wider, but you could still anchor your boats and stay in one place. Space wasn't like that. Achieving synchronous orbit in the midst of a battle was no easy feat. Most times, battling starships swirled round and round the planet they were fighting over. The longer a battle went on, the more ships tended to get caught in this maelstrom of gravity. Back in the old days, officers would call it a "bug fight" because starships became like bugs in a bathtub, spinning round and round the drain. Every once in a while, a ship went down the drain. Its collapse in Earth's atmosphere must appear spectacular from the surface.

But mad as this spin seemed, there was strategy to the game. Yes, in many ways, this was a game. A game with the lives of spacers on the line. And, if King failed, the lives of billions on Earth. The world depended on him, and King must play this game well. As Spitfire oversaw the starship *Freedom*, King must oversee this entire spinning wheel of fire.

In a way, this was a game like chess. Far more complicated. With far more pieces. On a board that spun round and round. But there were patterns. There were moves and plans. There were ways to position his pieces—the dreadnoughts, the starfighters, the heavy armored frigates. There were places on the board to control, such as the central band of orbit. And there were sacrifices to be made. Pawns to send burning down through the sky, making room for his clever advances and retreats. Always adjusting. Some changes were subtle—maybe moving the heavily armored ships to the starside flank. Other changes were more radical, involving thousands of ships, moving the entire fleets of nations backward or forward. Big or small, every move came with deep thought (if he had time) or hard-won instinct (if he had none). Whenever King had a few moments to catch his breath, he ran war game scenarios with Mimori, analyzing different moves and choosing the best one. Using advanced computers and sophisticated game theory algorithms, this game of starships became a science.

But in another way . . . this was art.

This was *music*.

When he viewed it this way, the battle was not a game. It was a symphony. A grand orchestra performed for all the world, a dazzling spectacle of fire and ice and luminous starlight. And King felt like a conductor. He raised an arm, and the Tiger Fleet of India soared like the song of a brass section. He raised another arm, and the Japanese Bonsai Fleet rained fire from above like the piercing notes of violins. He waved his hand, and waves of starfighters blasted forth like the notes of woodwind instruments. He raised both fists, and the American Armada charged forth, thundering like bass drums and tubas.

Perhaps a good admiral was a mix of things. A scientist. A player of games. And an artist. Some moves came from the strategy books and the classes he took at the academy. But a lot was instinct, honed over years of warfare in space. That was where the art of it came in. Sun Tzu had known well that war was an art. It was as old an art as drawing on cave walls.

Art? King thought in a sudden surge of cynicism. This was war. People were dying. Thousands, maybe millions of people. How could he think of this as *art?*

No. No, he couldn't think of himself as an artist. Back on his ranch, a retired old man, King would sometimes whittle little bits of wood. Not much of an art, that was. He was no Bernini or Michelangelo, carving marble into masterpieces. But even that little act, shaping bits of wood into horses and birds—surely that was more an art than this. Than standing here above the firmaments, granting death to some, life to others. Perhaps this was more like being some vengeful god of the heavens than an artist. Funny how that retired old man, wasting away on his rocking chair, had become a god.

Or maybe he wasn't an artist, or a god, or a player of games, but simply the same man he had always been. A soldier. A soldier who sought not glory, merely honor. And the two were very different things. He was not an idealist, not a conqueror, not a Napoleon or Sun Tzu or Alexander the Great. No. He was simply a soldier with a job to do. And whatever it took, whatever sacrifices he must make, however many people might die—he would do his job. And his job was to crush the enemy. And that was what he would do. No matter what. He would weather any storm. He would face the enemy fire. He would suffer the grief of lost soldiers and the terror of a thousand burning ships. And he would remain at his post. He would continue to fight until every last enemy had died or fled before him. For James King, there was honor enough in that.

Like a single, sharp trill from a piccolo, a call from Earth pierced through the symphony.

"King? Admiral King? Can you hear me, Admiral?"

The booming voice filled King's mind. It was unmistakable. High Commander George Godwin was calling over MindWeb.

"Yes, sir, I can hear you," King telepathized.

Godwin materialized on the bridge, but the image was grainy, choppy. The high commander must be down on Earth. Godwin still wore his three-piece suit, but it was singed and tattered at places, and light shone through a bullet hole in his top hat. But while he looked a little worse for wear, none of the determination had left the old man's eyes. In those eyes shone the strength of history and the courage of nations.

"Admiral King, our forces fight a courageous battle to defend Washington, the capital of that great beacon of democracy that you call home and that I call a great ally." Godwin's jowly face darkened. "But the enemy surrounds us. Ten Nazi divisions roll into the city from all sides, and their artillery and zeppelins bombard us from above. In the fields beyond the city, their terrible mechas rise and take form in the night. Their great mechanical spiders crawl upon the land. We need your help, Admiral King. We need your starfighters to destroy their zeppelins. We need your marines to take on the Heer and its armored divisions. We need you here, King. The Alliance Headquarters must not fall!"

King nodded. "It will not fall. How much longer can you hold out?"

Godwin's hallucination swayed. Dim blasts sounded over

MindWeb, joining the chorus of blasts that kept booming across the starship *Freedom*. The high commander too was under heavy assault.

"King, I can hold for another day. Maybe two. And only at the cost of many men. It will be a long night, King. A night full of sacrifice and death and courage. A night of many brave soldiers losing their lives, of many families destroyed. But we will hold Washington until the dawn."

King nodded. "Hold tight, sir. I'll be there soon. At dawn, we'll meet again."

He saluted his commander. Godwin returned the salute, and his hallucination faded.

It was time to focus this grand symphony. To reorganize this sweeping melody into a piercing crescendo. All his instruments of war King must now put toward his task—to cut a way through the Weltraumwaffe and bring the light of freedom down to Earth.

"What's our plan?" Jordan said. The tall officer walked across the bridge toward him. Sweat glinted on his furrowed brow and upon his close-cropped white hair like morning dew, reflecting the green lights from a dozen monitors. King too was feeling the heat and not just figuratively. A few heat vents had taken direct blasts (something Kim was trying to fix), and the temperature on the bridge had soared to 110 degrees. King felt like he was boiling alive in his uniform.

Trying to ignore the heat, he quickly connected his commanders into a shared MindLink call. That included Kim down in engineering, Emily in artillery, and Bastian on deck 7 with his marines.

"The American Armada is going to form a wedge formation," King said. "And the *Freedom* will lead them. We need to push through the enemy into lower orbit, then discharge our Rhinos. Bastian, we're going to deploy the marine brigade into

Washington DC. Your job will be to secure the Alliance Headquarters. Godwin needs you."

The big, beefy marine materialized on the bridge, a translucent hallucination. "Pardon me, sir, but why did you even summon the Freedom Brigade into the starship? We were already on Earth. Now, only a day later, we must fight to get back to Earth."

King pursed his lips. Only his son could get away with attitude like this. "Bastian, when I called the marines to the *Freedom*, I was calling you home. This always has been, always will be your home. I didn't know then that Godwin would need you in Washington. Yes, this detour the Freedom Brigade took to space seems wasteful now, maybe. But I'm glad to see you aboard the *Freedom* again, if only for a short while."

Bastian nodded. "You're right, Dad. This is home. I'm glad we got to come home if only for a day. I'll be ready to deploy in the Rhinos once we're closer to Earth. The closer you can get us, the better. Even from low orbit, it'll be a dangerous drop. Lots of hostiles everywhere. Rhinos are tough dropships, but we're slow and tempting targets."

"I know," King said. "I'll send a wing of Eagle starfighters to protect you."

Spitfire, who was busy flying the *Freedom*, found a moment to turn and raise an eyebrow. "With what pilots?"

"The Mimoris can fly the starfighters," King said. "We have hundreds of the androids aboard. Fifty will become our new starfighter pilots."

Mimori Prime overheard. The android turned toward King and snapped a salute. "We're happy to comply! Fifty of my sisters are currently running toward the hangars and preparing the Eagles to launch."

King nodded. "Good. Jordan? You oversee the American Armada's efforts to reach Earth. I'll keep focusing on the rest of the Freedom Fleet to protect high orbit."

Jordan nodded. "Understood. Ready on your order, sir."

"Begin," King said. "Godwin needs us. Let's go save the old man."

CHAPTER NINE
The Armor We Wear

Stowy cowered underfoot. Literally. Just a few inches above her stomped the boots of the bridge crew, stern adults who led the dreadnought in battle. The steel deck spread above Stowy like a ceiling. The crawlspace here was narrow—only a foot or two tall, just enough for a stowaway girl to wriggle along like a mouse under the floorboards. Below Stowy spread another steel deck— the ceiling of the science labs one deck down. Starships were like this. Decks and bulkheads had spaces between them like the space between double-pane windows. These walls and decks were full of technology. The empty space provided room for cables, pipes, gears, and repair drones. Most engineers couldn't even fit in these tight crawlspaces, so they used robots. But Stowy could fit. She had spent most of her life stowing away in shuttles, starships, and her imagination. Anything that could take her far away from her world.

Yes, in a way, Stowy had always cowered underfoot, had always lived in these hidden pits full of the machinery that ran the world. Others did not see or even know of these places. As a homeless girl on the streets of Munich, Stowy would sometimes wander the sewers—a sprawling network that kept a city going, yet most people went their whole lives without thinking about the labyrinth that pulsed below their feet. Those were the places where Stowy, like a mouse or rat or some other pest of the gutter, had always thrived.

She caressed the tattoo on her wrist—a black triangle. The voices of her teachers and doctors filled her mind, echoing from another universe.

Impure!

Crippled!

Autistic.

To the showers!

To the ovens!

Impure. Impure. Cripple.

She took a deep breath, pulling herself back to the present. She was still here, hidden in the crawlspace below the bridge of the starship *Freedom*. Not back there. Not back in the Fatherworld. She was safe.

For a moment, Stowy focused on breathing, just letting her heart calm down. The ghostly faces of the Gestapo disappeared for now. She knew they would return later to dance again. She was constantly banishing and dancing with these ghosts.

Yes, that tattoo would forever remind her. That she was not like other humans. That she was not human at all. Just a pest. Just a mouse. And so she cowered underfoot. She scurried through the sewers. As a mouse deserved. The sewers stank, but in the Fatherworld, the showers killed you.

The boots thumped above her. Stowy heard the crew's voices. Giving orders. Fighting the battle. The war raged all around, and the decks thrummed above and below Stowy, and every few moments, a blast rocked the starship. Stowy did not know how long this battle would last. Or this war. She had come to this world seeking safety, but all the hosts of the Fatherworld were crashing across Unreineland like a tidal wave. Her castle on the clouds was crumbling under the assault, and Stowy wondered if she had fled the Fatherworld only to drown here under that wave.

It would seem a sad and a tragic life to her. To die so young at fourteen. To have endured so much. To see the guns take her parents' faces. To see her grandmother on the crane. To suffer the surgeries and experimentations of a vulture in bear's clothing. To flee all that, to endure all those scars—only to die here, a little animal trapped between two window panes!

But there are good memories in my life too, Stowy thought. *And I knew joy as well.*

Those good memories tickled her like Algernon did when he walked along her arm, a nice sort of tickling, warm and comforting. She remembered running toward Father, and him scooping her up, spinning her overhead, and laughing. She remembered Mother rocking her in her arms, telling her bedtime stories when she was afraid. Back then, Stowy could not talk. She had learned to speak after her parents' deaths. She had never told them "I love you."

And another memory! A memory of a music box playing. And that triggered a cascade: a crackling fireplace, a warm checkered blanket, and her grandmother smiling. The smell of the cookies she baked. Stowy would sit by the fireplace, munching those cinnamon cookies, listening to the music box, and it didn't matter then that she couldn't speak. Even communicating with looks or body language was impossible for Stowy. She could not bear eye contact, and she struggled to read or emote with body language. But with Grandma, it never mattered. They could always communicate just by being side by side, sharing the firelight and the cookies, and it was perfect. And here now, in this dark place in a parallel universe, Stowy shed tears.

I've had a good life, she thought. *And I miss my family. And when I die, maybe I'll find them in some faraway kingdom above the clouds.*

Then a voice sounded above.

"Fight, soldiers! Fight for freedom! Fight for life!"

The voice was muffled through the steel plating. But Stowy recognized it. The voice of Admiral Grouchy.

"Onward!" he cried. "Fight, soldiers of Earth! For life!"

"For life," Stowy whispered.

Such a strange, shocking thought. She had come from a universe of death. A universe that idolized killing. The soldiers of the Fatherworld wore steel skulls on their caps. Theirs was a cult of death. Death was what they had brought Stowy's family, and death was what they had always promised her. All the Nazis lived for was death. But here in Unreineland—here things were different. That voice came through the steel ceiling, the voice of Admiral King, who spoke those words like a blessing. "For life!"

For life.

Even for a life such as hers? The life of a mouse? Of an impure thing, tattooed with a black triangle? Even such a wretched life? Was such a life worth saving?

Of course it is, Luna whispered in her mind. *Your life is worthwhile. And I love you.*

Stowy pulled the blanket tighter around her. The way humans could speak telepathically, Luna could speak to Stowy. Her beloved blanket had always been there. And always would.

You're loved, Luna said. *You'll always be loved.*

Stowy wiped tears from her eyes. "But I'm just a pest."

And I'm just a tattered blanket, Luna said. *And Algernon is just a mouse. The three of us will always be together.*

Stowy sniffed. "There has to be more."

Aren't we enough? said Luna.

Her tears fell. "There has to be more if I'm to fight. Because I can't just hide in the shadows with you and Algernon. I can't just keep hiding like another mouse. Because I can only fight if there is somebody to fight for. If there is goodness in people that is worth protecting. I want to believe that others can love me someday. That I can love them. That they're worth fighting for."

And then Stowy understood something. If she only lived for herself, she would languish and die. If she fought for others, she might rise from the shadows, and she might find love again.

Like the love she had experienced with her family. Maybe someday she might even find a new family. Maybe she would not be a mouse but a girl. It was a life lived for others that brought hope and joy. Stowy was not yet ready, perhaps, to walk above deck for long, and she still struggled to communicate with others. But in her own way, even from down here, she could do her part. She could have a family.

For Grouchy, she thought as she crawled through the machinery. *For Spitfire. For Jordan. For Bastian and his brave heroes. And for a little goblin princess, stung by the spider queen.*

* * * * *

Yes, she could fight! She could. Stowy had proved that. No, she couldn't fire guns like Bastian and his heroes. She couldn't command warships like Spitfire. She couldn't fire great cannons like Queen Emily. Was that gunner with the blond hair, the one Stowy had seen through the vents, really the Queen of England in this universe? England had a queen in Stowy's universe too, but she had a German name, she wore a swastika pendant, and she bowed down to the führer. Over here in Unreineland, Emily was—or so they said—the actual descendant of the original royal family. The same family from Father's old books. Stowy had read many works of Victorian literature. After all, her hero was the Elephant Man of Victorian times, and she loved many other stories from that time and place. Throughout those stories, she had learned much about the old royal family, whom Hitler had slain and replaced in 1952. But not in this universe. Not in Unreineland. If Stowy had time later, she would be amazed. Right now she had to fight.

Throughout this war, she had lost many of her treasures. Aboard the *Barbarossa*, Eva König had captured Stowy and held her upside down by the heels. Many treasures had fallen from

Stowy's pockets then: rare coins (rare for her, at least), interesting stones (one with real crystals on the side), military badges (the Fatherworld's troopers were always losing those), plastic dinosaurs (her favorite things), and other trinkets she collected. While crawling through the ducts of the spinning, tumbling *Freedom*, she had lost more treasures. They kept falling from her pockets. Stowy shed her little trinkets like a tree shedding leaves. But she had many pockets—more than a hundred, she thought. They covered every inch of her dress, and many had begun to grow across her one stocking like mushrooms growing on a log. Even Luna was now covered with pockets; the blanket had begun collecting treasures of her own. Recently Stowy had learned a new trick. She began creating pockets with buttons. One even had a zipper (zippers were very rare to find). And in these secure, impregnable vaults, Stowy began to store her most valuable items. In the zipper pocket (a veritable Fort Knox), she kept the gemstone the robot Niles had lost. And in the largest pocket, secured by *two buttons* (count 'em—two!), Stowy kept Ivan, the T. rex toy that could shoot sparks from its mouth.

And in one pocket . . . Stowy kept a weapon. A *real* weapon. Brass knuckles.

She had found them at St. Mary's in London after the American marines had liberated the hospital from the Totenkopfverbände-SS. The brass knuckles had belonged to an SS trooper, and they were far too large for Stowy's hand. But if she wrapped handkerchiefs around her hand, she could form a sort of boxing glove, and the brass knuckles fit snugly over that. She wasn't strong. Stowy knew that if she punched a grownup, even with this "boxing glove" with the brass knuckles, she wouldn't be hurting anyone. She would be like a pug biting a wolf. But she *was* strong enough to crush the robotic mites infesting the station. Kim's immubots were (hopefully) hunting them down like white blood cells now, and that was good. But Stowy could do her part too. She could become like another immubot and fight. Far better to fight than cower. Far better to risk herself for others than to fade into the shadows alone.

She paused, placed her ear against the deck, and listened for mites. She heard many sounds. The thrumming of distant motors. The rumbling of the shield generator and the crackling of electricity. Racing footsteps. And every moment—a deafening boom of Emily firing a cannon. Sometimes enemy missiles made their way past the Shield of David interceptors, through the force field, and hit the armored hull of the *Freedom*, and then the entire ship rang like a bell. Between these great beats of the drum, Stowy listened to the softer, rhythmic song of the ship, seeking irregularities in the pattern.

There—she heard it! Tapping like little feet. A mite. No—three mites. Yes, there were three distinct hisses and clicks. She crawled through the narrow spaces between bulkheads, climbing downward toward the sound. On her way, she clung to cables for support, and sometimes the teeth of gears formed her handholds. She kept following the sound, trying to track it through the labyrinth. Stowy was leaving the corridors now, traveling through the tubes and vents that ran through the ship like arteries and nerves, leading to chambers like internal organs. There were entire rooms in the *Freedom* that humans could not reach. Power rooms where energy from the engine core pulsed and waited for redistribution. Ventilation shafts that blasted toxins and excess heat into space. Life-support rooms like lungs that kept pumping and filtering the air. There were sewage pipes, processing chambers, and countless other places, some barely larger than a coffin, some cavernous and echoing like a church nave. Unseen, these hidden chambers all pulsed and crackled and kept the ship flying. Stowy had no maps to these places, but there was logic to their layout, and they spoke a language of echoes and clatters and moaning air.

And there—a mite!

It was one of the patchwork mites, which the original Nazi saboteurs had assembled from scavenged parts. Looked like the invaders had ransacked the galley for metal. This mite's body was made from an upside-down pot, the handle thrusting out like a nose. A swastika was crudely scratched onto the pot (Stowy winced to just *imagine* the high-pitched sound of scratching a swastika into the metal). Forks formed its legs, while steak knives thrust from the front like pincers. When the mite reared, it revealed a mason jar tucked behind the cables inside its belly. Darkness swirled inside the jar. The robot was gravid with umbrions.

For a moment, both Stowy and the mite froze. They stared at each other. The mite had little cameras for eyes, which had been mounted onto salt and pepper shakers. They reminded Stowy of a snail's eyes on stalks. The robot blinked, making little snapping shutter sounds.

Stowy pulled the T. rex from her pocket. She pulled the string, and inside Ivan's plastic mouth, flint scraped on metal, casting sparks like a lighter. The mite tilted its cameras. The light intrigued it. Like a dog hungry for treats, the little robot approached, seeming almost to sniff at the light. It was the umbrions inside that drove the robot with their hunger. The dark particles craved photons to devour. With its steak-knife pincers, the mite tried to catch the flying sparks. It almost looked like some robotic pet trying to catch sparks from a family campfire on Hitler's birthday.

Do it, Luna said. *Punch him. Punch him with your boxing glove.*

"I'm scared," Stowy whispered.

Do it for your friends. For Grouchy, Spitfire, and the others.

"They barely know who I am," she whispered. Tears flowed down her cheeks. "I'm alone and scared."

The mite was getting bored with the sparks. It stared at

Stowy, and its knives rose. The robot had no mouth, but something in its poise made her imagine a predatory smile.

They love you, Luna whispered.

"They only love a ghost of who I am. A girl who died."

The mite slashed at her. Stowy scuttled back, trembling. She brought her fingers to her cheek and felt blood.

But you are still alive, Luna said. *For life! For life!"*

And Stowy imagined that even down here, far, far below the bridge in the belly of the ship, she could hear Grouchy's voice echo down the tubes and pipes. "For life! For life!"

The mite slashed at her again.

Stowy parried the blow with her toy dinosaur. The blade drove into Ivan and jammed inside the plastic T. rex. As the mite struggled to free itself, Stowy swung her fist. Facing humans, she was weak. Her blow, with the brass knuckles and all, wouldn't even faze a grownup like Grouchy or Bastian. But it was enough against a mite. Her blow knocked the robot against the wall and rang its pot like a bell.

Stowy let out a wordless cry and punched it again. And again. Her brass knuckles dented the pot, which formed the shell of the mite. With each punch, Stowy knocked out internal components. Gears and grommets rolled around her feet. She cracked one of the camera eyes on its saltshaker stalk. Again the mite slashed at her with its knives. Again she parried and punched. Finally she thrust her fist into the mite's shell. And inside the pot, her brass knuckles shattered the mason jar of umbrions.

The glass shards flew everywhere. Like tar, umbrions leaked out. Some got on Stowy's hand and forearm.

A cry fled her lip. Cold! So cold! It felt like the astral hand of Death himself. The chill froze her to the bone. Stowy quickly removed her "boxing glove" of handkerchiefs and brass knuckles, which was tarnished with umbrions. She tossed the tainted glove aside, then used Luna to brush off any remaining particles. The blanket didn't mind. Stowy blew frosty vapor away and examined her arm and hand. The skin was bluish and tingly, but she'd be all right.

She looked at the mite. Dead. The leaking umbrions had frozen its innards solid.

"For life, stupid," she whispered.

Luna laughed. *For life!*

"Turns out mite is not always right," Stowy said. And Luna laughed harder.

If only Stowy could speak so confidently to humans! They were such curious things, humans. Terribly frightening, yet Stowy felt a kinship with them. It was strange. All her life, she had known she was subhuman. Her tattoo denoted her an *untermenschin*, something less than human. To her, humans were predators. Humans were those who experimented on her, who cut her, who made her cry. Yet now she was fighting for humans. For Grouchy and Spitfire and Bastian and Jordan, for people she barely knew, yet people who had loved her doppelgänger. Who seemed to love her too. And strangely, in her heart, Stowy yearned for their love, even if they were humans and she was not.

They think I'm a human too, she thought. *They don't know about the science of the Fatherworld. They don't know that doctors have diagnosed me as subhuman.*

But no. That was the old way of thinking. Here, in this world—she *was* human. She was one of the pack. So why did she still feel so different? Why did she still live as a mouse? Why did her autism not go away? Was there something irrevocably broken in her that even Unreineland, even love could not heal? Sometimes she felt like one of those patchwork mites, just an imitation, something cobbled together from broken parts, meant to look like a member of its species but forever different.

Well, she could contemplate all that later. Right now it was time to keep fighting.

* * * * *

Stowy looked at the "boxing glove" she had woven from handkerchiefs. The umbrions crawled across the fabric, sucking what little heat and energy they found. The fabric disintegrated, falling apart as frozen threads, and the umbrions slid down a shaft between the bulkheads, wriggling onward in search of energy. They were just particles, not sentient. A slither of umbrions was simply the opposite of a ray of light. And darkness was no more conscious than light was. But to Stowy the umbrions almost seemed self-aware, a living being made from trillions of tiny black cells.

"Good thing I wore the boxing glove," she said to Luna. "It saved my hand. But . . ." She poked what remained of the handkerchiefs. "Just a pile of threads. I need new fabric." She stared at the blanket.

Don't look at me! Luna said.

"I'm sorry, Luna. I just need a small part of you."

The blanket tightened around her. *No! How could you! I'm your oldest friend.*

"I just need one of your pockets," said Stowy.

Then use one of your own. You're covered with them.

"Fine."

Stowy removed the large, leather pocket that normally hung over her hip. She fashioned it into a mitten of sorts, tightening it around her wrist with a string. Then she slipped the brass knuckles back on. The umbrions had been unable to destroy the metal weapon at least. Stowy punched a wall and dented the aluminum. Still worked. Good. An eagerness to smash more mites filled her. She crawled onward, seeking more enemies to slay.

As she crawled down a duct, a racket sounded from

ahead. Countless metal feet clattered. Robotic voices chittered and chattered. Stowy froze and raised her weapons—her dinosaur in one hand, the brass knuckles on the other. Eyes shone in the duct ahead. Dozens, then hundreds of eyes. A year or two ago, an orphan on the streets of Munich, Stowy had once approached a trash bin in the night, hoping to find scraps of food inside. When she lifted the lid, many eyes stared at her. The eyes of raccoons—pests that had come from America and spread across Germany. In her young mind, Stowy had imagined the eyes of dead children spilling from Uncle Baer's gas chamber. She had never dared open a trash bin again. That was what the eyes in this shadowy duct reminded Stowy of—those eyes in the trash bin. Probably just raccoons. Maybe the ghosts of dead gassed children.

The mites advanced, and Stowy growled, ready to fight with her brass knuckles, pocket "boxing glove," and dinosaur. The army of mites clattered closer, and her eyes widened. Those were not enemy mites! Their shells were the helmets of American marines, and their legs were screwdrivers and other little tools. Each helmet displayed the symbol of the starship *Freedom*: a blue star with red stripes spreading from the sides. Immubots! Kim's machines!

The American mites marched over and around Stowy, screwdrivers clattering, cameras shining, making little chattering noises that sounded almost like words in a foreign language. Finally they had passed her by, heading toward some distant battle within the starship. They seemed to know where to go.

Should Stowy follow them, join the troops, become one with the immubots? She checked her paper map. It only showed the corridors, not the hidden ducts and shafts where stowaways crawled. But when Stowy peered through a vent, she could see a bulkhead, and it displayed the deck number. She was back on deck 28! Same deck where she had escaped Grouchy's duffel bag, then scurried up his chimney. His quarters must be near.

A mite had tried to kill Admiral Grouchy before. Stowy had managed to stop that one. But the mites wouldn't stop trying. If she were a mite, what would she do? How would she assassinate Grouchy? The answer was simple. She would go into his quarters, hide in his closet or under his bed, then emerge like childhood monsters in the night. Would an admiral know that monsters hid under the bed? Would Grouchy search for monsters, know how to find them, know how they fled to shadows if you shined a light? Maybe not. Maybe an admiral would not know. Maybe it took one bug to catch another. Stowy would go to his quarters. If she were right, if she truly could think like a pest, she would find enemies there to kill.

One pest knows another, she thought.

Now she knew exactly where she was going, and she moved confidently through the ducts. Before long, she crawled back into the fireplace. The same fireplace where she had hidden from Grouchy. How long ago was it? Days and nights lost all meaning here, and she had lost her pocket watch along with many other treasures. It felt like long days and nights, an entire era of her life here aboard the starship *Freedom*. Or maybe it hadn't even been a day.

She crawled out from the fireplace, and it was like crawling through a portal into a magical, fairy-tale world. She had been to Grouchy's quarters once before, but she had quickly fled up the chimney. Now Stowy took a moment to soak in the beauty of this place. A sigh flowed through her.

"Luna, it's wonderful," she whispered.

Hardwood floorboards covered the deck, and wooden panels hid the cold gray bulkheads. Bookshelves covered the walls, a suit of armor stood by the fireplace, and the table looked like real oak. The shelves were empty and the table bare, but Stowy could already imagine this place full of books, curious crystals, statues from ancient lands, and magical ships in bottles whose sails blew in the wind. What a perfect place this could become. Like a huge pocket you could live in, full of treasures. And suddenly Stowy no longer imagined herself as a mouse or a mite. In her imagination, she was that goblin princess again, and this was her underground burrow, a place where she kept special twisted roots, rare mushrooms, acorn cupules to wear as hats, and gemstones with magical powers.

And thank God, through that little door, there was a bathroom! An actual bathroom with a sink and everything. Stowy had been holding it in since the Stone Age, or so it seemed. There was one thing street urchins and soldiers had in common. To both, bathrooms were a luxury. Both knew—use them when you found them! Soon she was drying her hands and back by the oak desk. (She had considered washing her face too but decided against it. She wasn't spoiled, after all, and this was a war. There was a limit to what luxuries she would allow herself.)

A plush armchair stood by a porthole with a view of the stars. The armchair looked so comfortable that Stowy could not resist. She hopped into the armchair, sank into the green upholstery, and let out a sigh. When she pulled Luna over her, a sense of deep comfort and healing flowed through her bones, erasing all the pain of the day. All she needed were some good books (ideally books about dinosaurs), and she could spend eternity here.

"But we're on a mission, Luna," she reminded her blanket. "We can't relax. There might be mites here, hiding and waiting for Grouchy. We must find them."

Algernon squeaked, emerged from her pocket, and hopped onto the table. The mouse ran, leaped onto the floor, and scuttled over the hardwood floors. Stowy's heart leaped. What if he escaped? She might never find him! But the mouse went straight to Grouchy's rucksack, which still lay on its side. The rodent scurried inside, found a pack of crackers, and began to eat.

The poor thing was famished. Stowy was too. Food—another thing urchins and soldiers never took for granted. She ate a few crackers, drank from Grouchy's canteen, and offered water to her mouse too. Luna wasn't thirsty, but the blanket ate many crumbs. For a moment, sitting there on the armchair, snacking on crackers, Stowy almost slipped into that fantasy world again, forgetting about her mite hunt.

She soon got a rude awakening.

* * * * *

A blast hit the starship.

A *boom* undulated through the bulkheads and decks, rattling the dreadnought like an earthquake. Algernon squeaked. The armchair tilted over, spilling Stowy onto the deck.

For a moment she lay there, waiting for the trembling to ease and her heart to calm. From her position on the floor, she could see the porthole above the armchair. These quarters were deep inside the starship, far from the hull. The porthole couldn't be an actual window. It was likely a screen, streaming a video feed from an exterior camera on the outer hull. Indeed, looking through the porthole, Stowy could see the battle outside, the fire spreading nearer and nearer.

She pulled herself to her feet, held the desk for support, and peered through the porthole. Her eyes widened. She gaped at the battle. Hundreds, maybe thousands of ships were flying outside. Many were ships of the Freedom Fleet. She recognized the blue stars and red stripes on their hulls. But most ships were of the Weltraumwaffe; there was no mistaking their dark hulls and red cannons. Torpedoes and missiles flew back and forth, etching lines like gashes across flesh. Stowy tried to see the *Barbarossa*, flagship of the Weltraumwaffe. It was *Barbarossa* that had brought her from the Fatherworld, through the portal, and to Unreineland.

228

She wondered if that monster of the stars still flew. She could not see the Nazi juggernaut.

Maybe the Amis had destroyed it. Stowy hoped so.

A shiver ran through her. She remembered her brief time on that ship. Remembered how Eva had caught her, held her upside down, and shaken her like a fish. The pain that had followed . . . No, Stowy wasn't ready to think about the rest of it. Not yet. Not here.

"Mites, mites, I must find mites," she said.

She searched under the table. In the drawers. Under the bed. In the closet. Relief flowed through her. No mites hid in this place. It was a good idea to secure the grates along the ductwork vents. Stowy had a screwdriver (the leg of a patchwork mite, which had fallen off, then found its way into her pocket). She climbed onto the back of the armchair, balanced carefully on one foot, and reached for the vent above her head. She tightened the screws. Too tightly, she hoped, for the enemy mites to unscrew. For good measure, Stowy chewed some bubblegum (treasure from another pocket), then jammed the screws.

Another blast hit the *Freedom*.

The cabin trembled.

The armchair overturned. Stowy, who had been standing on the backrest to reach the vent, tumbled down.

She hit the deck with a groan. Pain stabbed her side; she had landed on something hard. She pulled from her pocket a plastic brontosaurus. The neck had snapped off. She sat up, rubbing her hip, and realized the cabin was dimmer now. The porthole had gone dark. Maybe the exterior camera had died in the assault. Or maybe umbrions covered it like tar. Grouchy's quarters, mimicking a nineteenth-century den, had no overhead lights. Only the lamp on the tabletop now lit the room. It was shaped like an antique oil lantern (though it actually ran on batteries), and its mock firelight filled the cabin with a dim orange glow. Shadows rose along the walls like vampires rising from their tombs. Even her beheaded dinosaur cast a shadow the height of a man. The shadowy figures surrounded Stowy until she felt like a prisoner facing a ring of ghoulish judges.

Unable to stare at them any longer, Stowy looked down at her feet. One bare foot. One tucked inside a striped stocking. And the realization kicked her heart into a gallop. This was the place. She stood on the exact spot.

The place where I died.

Yes, it was here. Stowy had heard the stories. And more than that—she felt the importance of this place. The memory overtook her. No, not quite a memory—that sense of déjà vu. Right here, where she stood, her doppelgänger had died. The fairy child. The version of Stowy who had been born and raised in Unreineland.

Though they were different girls, raised in different universes, a strand of starlight connected them. And Stowy remembered coming here to King's Library, and in the vision, books and antique naval instruments filled the shelves, and the hearth was crackling, and a ship-in-a-bottle sailed on the tabletop. In this hazy dream, a spider moved through the room, scuttling from shadow to shadow, peering from shadows with eyes like polished round bones. The spider was a desiccated thing, its skin white and papery like shriveled cyclamen petals clinging to a rock. On hollow legs like porcupine quills, the spider approached, baring little white fangs like needles. When the venom entered the fairy child, it felt warm, and she could smell peppermint. She still remembered that smell. Peppermint. That was how the venom of a deadly spider smelled. It was strange that death should smell like Christmas.

But I'm a different girl, Stowy thought, pulling herself back to the present. *I didn't live that life. I didn't die that death.*

And suddenly a terrible premonition filled Stowy.

Herself—dead and cold. Her eyes like round white bones. She lay on a table in a stark white laboratory, and men in gas masks stood all around her, dressed in lab coats. The vision only lasted for a second. Barely a flash in her mind. But the shivers lingered.

A hiss rose behind her.

Clatters and chirps echoed through the cabin.

Stowy spun around, heart pounding against her ribs like a trapped child in a laboratory cage.

Nothing. Nothing was there. Only a stirring mouse. Only Algernon. The mouse sat atop the suit of armor, chewing on a cracker from Grouchy's pack. The armor glimmered in the flickering lantern light. The gauntlets cast long shadows like the reaching arms of vampires, tipped with claws. The little screws and bolts on the helmet seemed to lengthen in the shadows, forming the spikes of hell's crown, while the visor formed a demonic visage, leering at Stowy like Lucifer mocking a tormented soul. Stowy knew it was only a trick of the firelight and shadows, but that armor made her tremble.

And suddenly—eyes!

Two red eyes like embers peered from that dark visor!

* * * * *

Stowy yelped and stumbled back, holding her plastic T. rex before her like a weapon. From inside the medieval helmet, the red eyes stared at her in condemnation. Judging her. Peeling back her layers of protection—the blanket, the pockets, the little treasures—to reveal the shame. The shame of a broken girl. Autistic. Impure. A girl who had been cut open, some of her organs removed. A broken girl. A shameful thing. No better than her twisted clones, whom she had found in the hospital basement. That was her. A monster. That was what the red eyes saw.

She pulled the string on her T. rex. The black dinosaur let out a tiny mechanical roar, and a few sparks flew from the hidden metal mechanism in its plastic mouth.

At the sight of the fire, the helmet leaped off the rest of the armor.

Stowy scampered back. A scream fled her mouth. (That was rare for her. Normally in times of great fright, she became very quiet. Even more than usual, and that was saying something. But this startled her enough to elicit an actual scream.)

The helmet landed on the deck and skittered toward Stowy. It was moving on legs! On dozens of tiny metal legs! The legs were formed from bullet casings. They surrounded the helmet's rim like a ring of centipede legs. The helmet, complete with its demonic crown, lunged toward her.

Stowy screamed again, swung her fist, and drove her brass knuckles into the creature. The odd beast stumbled back, overturned, and its bullet casing legs kicked in midair. Inside the medieval helmet, Stowy saw motors, gears, and cables. Another mite. A mite made from Grouchy's medieval helmet!

The machines of the enemy must have come here. But instead of lurking for Grouchy under the bed or inside the closet, they had converted the helmet to their cause. The robotic assassin chattered and clicked, legs kicking. It seemed almost to be cursing and threatening in that secret language of robots. Stowy saw no umbrions inside it, only spools of cables. So many cables! The mite reminded Stowy of a pot full of spaghetti. She stared at the pathetic thing with the kicking legs, lying on its shell like an overturned turtle. She wanted to destroy it, yet she pitied it. In its yapping, chattering language, she could imagine words. '*Elp me!* '*Elp!* '*Elp!*

Revulsion filled Stowy. No, that was not an innocent turtle. It was the crown of Lucifer, corrupted and full of squirming serpents. She kicked it into the cold fireplace. She would start a fire and burn it!

As the creature tumbled into the hearth, some of its cables came loose. They spilled from its body like strips of film from those old film canisters, the kind Uncle Baer kept in his office. He collected old films of scientific experiments from the 1940s. He used to gather the children around on Fridays for "movie night." He would take Stowy and the others from their cages, sit them in the big room with the velvet seats, make popcorn, and play them those old films. Adolf, a dwarf child, would work the projector. The grainy, black-and-white films still haunted Stowy. She never forgot the boy with a second head stitched on. Or the twins cut in half and stitched together. To Uncle Baer, Mengele was an artist, a genius on par with Wagner. Now, as those black cables spilled from the helmet across the wooden deck, that was what Stowy remembered. Film strips spilling from the reels, tangling up around the projector, and little Adolf wetting himself, knowing that he would be beaten. That night, Baer performed surgery on little Adolf, and the child's insides unspooled like so many strips of film.

Stowy took a step away, her heart pounding with horror, the ghosts of memory dancing around her. And the cables on the floor—they moved. They moved on their own. Like serpents, the cables slithered toward her, looped around her ankle, and pulled.

Stowy fell and hit the deck.

The cables tightened around her ankle, then reeled her toward the fireplace like a fisherman reeling in a fish. She slid across the floor, pawing for purchase. Flames suddenly burst to life in the hearth. The demonic face of Lucifer laughed within, his crown of spikes gleaming in the fire. The cables did not burn, but their plastic coating melted off, revealing little crackling, sparkling strings of light inside. Stowy screamed and tried to stop her slide, but luminous strands kept pulling her toward the flames.

Algernon leaped forward.

With a squeak, the mouse nibbled through the glowing cables, burning his mouth but still biting. The cables snapped free, releasing Stowy. She scampered back and hid behind the armchair. Panting there like some frightened prey animal, she peeked toward the fireplace.

The flames were dying down. The creature inside wasn't moving. Only a few strands of cables emerged from the hearth, lying still like the hair of some corpse burned in the flames. Was the demonic mite dead? She thought that red eyes still glowed in the hearth, but perhaps those were only embers.

Then, with a clatter that made Stowy jump, a gauntlet fell off the suit of armor. The metal glove lay for a moment on the floorboard, then flipped over so that its fingertips pressed against the floor. The gauntlet began scampering toward Stowy, racing on its metal fingers. The second gauntlet leaped off the armor too, crouched on its fingers, and joined the charge. Then all the other pieces of armor detached, fell to the deck, and came to life. The breastplate and backplate rose like metal tortoises, moving on legs made from L-pipes. The pauldrons scuttled like horseshoe crabs, while the vambraces and greaves moved on legs made from scissors. There were other parts of armor too, and Stowy did not know their names. They all walked toward her, and when they reared, they revealed bundles of cables within their cavities.

"Mites made of armor," she whispered. "Armamites!"

* * * * *

She cowered behind the armchair. This force was beyond her. One or two regular mites—she could defeat those. But a host of armamites was a different thing entirely. Their blades gleamed in the firelight as they drew nearer, tightening the noose. If she could reach the vent, she could escape into the duct. But she had screwed and glued the grate shut. If she could enter the fireplace—but no, the flames still crackled there, and the demonic helmet lurked within, guardian of the flames.

A vambrace leaped toward her, its scissor legs gleaming. Stowy swung her "boxing club" (formed from the old pocket and her brass knuckles). She hit the piece of armor, knocking it to the ground. At once, another piece of armor—a sabaton, she thought—vaulted off the table toward her. Again she punched, knocking the mite back. But more surrounded her.

With a shout, Stowy shoved the armchair toward the armamites. The chair fell over, crushing the codpiece, but the other pieces of armor leaped at her. Stowy swung her fist, but she couldn't hold them all back. A cuisse leaped, landed on her thigh, and wrapped its cables around her. The armor clung to her leg like a leech. She yowled and tugged at it, but the straps tightened. Another piece of armor pounced. A rerebrace, she thought. The piece of armor landed on her upper arm, and the straps moved like serpents, tightening around her, securing the armor to her arm.

Stowy ran across the deck toward the fireplace. Throwing caution to the wind, she grabbed a poker with her makeshift mitten. Even through the fabric, it burned her hand. Ignoring the pain, she swung the poker from side to side, clubbing the armamites. She hit a few, sending them tumbling, but at once, the robots righted themselves and kept scuttling toward her. Two pieces still clung to her—one to her thigh, one to her upper arm. They tightened painfully.

Again and again the pieces of armor leaped at her. Stowy swung her poker in one hand, the brass knuckles in the other, beating them back. Finally the breastplate fired strands of cables at her. Like a chameleon's tongue, the cables grabbed the poker and pulled it from her hand. One gauntlet seized her wrist while another pulled off her "boxing glove." Unarmed, she tried to flee toward the door. She managed to take a step into the corridor.

But cables grabbed her ankles, her waist, and her neck, and they yanked her back into the den.

"Help!" she cried. "Help!" Tears flowed down her cheeks. "Help!"

She was shouting. Actually shouting. But there was nobody to hear. Everybody was on the bridge or down in engineering. The armamites tightened their cables. She felt like a trussed-up chicken.

I'm standing right on that spot, she realized. *Right where the spider slew the goblin child. I'm standing where I died.*

She stood there like a ghost above its grave, like a tree growing from a corpse, feeding on the nutrients of flesh and rot, and sending forth coiling branches thick with rustling pink flowers. And noxious vines were crawling over this tree. The cables rose across her, twisting, coiling around her fingers. Another armamite leaped up. A vambrace. It clung to her forearm. Then a pauldron rose and perched upon her shoulder. One by one, like scuttling insects, the pieces of armor climbed Stowy, cobbling themselves into place around her, encasing her in metal.

A long time ago, in one of Father's secret books, Stowy had read about an insect that covered its body with pebbles, bits of bark, old bones, and anything else it could find. Sometimes they got into machinery and built themselves cocoons from bolts, nuts, and other pieces they found. A jeweler had once given these bugs gemstones and sequins of precious metal, and they had woven hollow jewels to live in. But mostly they simply collected scraps. That was how Stowy felt now. Like a bug trapped within a suit of cobbled debris.

Finally the breastplate and backpiece slung their cables across her. The huge armamites heaved on the cables, pulling themselves up, and finally snapped into place around Stowy's torso. Only her head was now free. She cried for help but no one heard. No one but Luna and Algernon, who clung to her, trapped inside this armor with her. The little, clattering feet of the armamites snapped together like the teeth of zippers, locking the plates of armor into place, trapping Stowy inside.

The armor had been designed for an adult man. It wasn't a perfect fit. The pieces were too large and overlapped. She practically swam inside the breastplate. But the armamites were clever enough to adjust themselves, twisting and contorting and overlapping, cocooning their prisoner as tightly as possible. Bless her heart, Luna formed some important cushioning, protecting Stowy's torso from sharp, jagged, and snapping metal pieces. A few pieces of armor pinched her limbs where the blanket couldn't reach. She felt like a girl trapped inside a statue. She squirmed, trying to eclose from the suit of armor like a butterfly from its chrysalis, but the cables held her in place.

A *clunk clunk clunk* sounded from behind her.

A stench like burnt plastic filled her nostrils.

A scrape sounded across the floor.

Stowy tried to turn around and see, but the armor didn't let her. That *clunk-scrape-clunk* was getting closer.

She looked into the fireplace. The last few embers crackled. The demonic helmet was no longer in the hearth.

Scrape.

Clack.

Clunk.

The sounds rose behind her, and all Stowy could do was stand there, trapped in the armor. In her mind, once more, she was strapped to the operating table. Tears flowed down her cheeks.

And she was there again. Back in the Fatherworld. Back in Uncle Baer's lab. The nurses strapped her down, and Uncle Bear leaned down with scalpel and tongs. There was never any anesthetic. And so many screams. He broke her. Sterilized her.

Tattooed her. Then gave her a lollipop and sent her on her way.

I should have died, she whispered, trembling in the suit of armor, tears falling. *I should have died with the rest of you. With my friends. I'm sorry.*

She remembered their faces, the other children of the lab. Other disabled children, some with autism like her, others with other conditions. All deemed impure. They were the children of Aktion T4. Children that were not human. That shamed the Aryan purity. Children doomed to experimentation and finally death.

Yes, the others all died. Stowy saw them. Saw them enter the gas chamber by the operating room. Just a little chamber, not much larger than her old bedroom back in Canada. When a child had served his or her purposes, when the young body was too broken and sick to be of use for science—it was into that room. Just across the hall from where Stowy slept. She saw when Baer opened the door, when the dead children spilled out. Their eyes became like white bones, like spider eyes, and their skin just seemed like rubber. Like the skin of boiled chicken. That was all they were. Just boiled chickens. Not children. It couldn't be children. It couldn't be her friends.

"I should have gone with you," Stowy whispered. "But I escaped. I escaped to the streets, and I left you to die. Felix. Horst. Sophie. Gunter. I'm sorry. I'm so sorry."

She remembered their names. Their faces. The little impure children of Aktion T4. Untermenschen. Cripples. Friends. Gone. Boiled like chickens.

Then Stowy felt it. The medieval helmet climbed her leg, then her back, wrapping its cables across her suit of armor, climbing higher and higher. Hot. She felt the heat against her nape. And then the helmet leaped onto her head, and heat bathed her, and the helmet snapped into place against the breastplate. Stowy screamed, expecting the helmet to burn her hair, to melt her skin, but it had cooled off enough. She would not boil alive. No becoming a boiled chicken for Samantha "Stowy" Perry. A little blessing in this nightmare.

The moment of relief quickly changed to terror.

The suit began to move.

Not just to wriggle and clatter. But to *walk*.

＊ ＊ ＊ ＊ ＊

The suit of armor was walking! With her inside!

The left leg rose, then stomped down—with Stowy's leg trapped within. The right leg followed. The arms swung robotically at her sides.

As terror thrummed through Stowy, she forced herself to think. To be logical. Otherwise she would surrender to the panic. She would scream and scream and die of fright. No! No. She must calm her heartbeat. She must take deep breaths. She was trapped inside this suit, yes, but she had air. She could breathe. She was alive. She *was alive*. And that was nothing to sneeze at. Okay, she must calm down. Just breathe. Breathe. Good. She was fine.

Now think logically, she told herself as the suit kept walking, carrying her step by heavy step toward the door.

Clack.

Scrape.

Clunk.

Somebody must be controlling the armor remotely, Stowy thought. These armamites had been waiting inside Grouchy's cabin, disguising themselves as plate armor, only to pounce and trap her. And now they were walking her step by step toward the doorway. These were not the actions of crude robots sent to sabotage a starship. These ones must be specialists, following somebody's explicit orders.

"Who—who is doing this?" Stowy whispered. "Who are

you?"

Normally, speaking was extraordinarily difficult for Stowy. She had only started speaking at age nine. And even now, speaking only a few words took tremendous force of will. Each word was a battle, but she got them out.

"T-talk to me!"

But nobody answered. The plate armor reached the door, and against her will, the armor raised Stowy's hand, grabbed the knob, and pulled the door open. The steel suit walked into the corridor with her inside.

It was almost a comical sight, Stowy supposed. If she weren't so terrified, if the tiny legs weren't cutting her inside the armor, she might have laughed. As it were, she struggled not to weep. The whole thing felt like a fever dream. Coming to this strange universe inside the looking glass. Finding the spot she had died. And now these strange little robots, made from medieval armor, engulfing her and marching her down the corridor.

I must be back in Uncle Baer's lab, she thought. *I must be drugged again.*

Soon she would wake up, the fever would break, and she would be back in those white, bright rooms. Back in her cage with nothing but her blanket for company. In the morning, a few of the cages would be empty, and those strange, pale chickens would spill out from the gas chamber, and those eyes like white round bones would stare. She would wake from this surreal dream and find herself back in the nightmare of reality.

But it didn't happen. No matter how much the armor pinched her, she would not wake up. This wasn't a dream, unless it were a dream within a dream. She was not waking up.

Creak. Clank. Thump. The sounds of a single step. A leg rising, falling, and rattling Stowy inside the armor.

Creak. Clank. Thump. Another step. Stowy shook inside the armor, trying to fight it, struggling to turn around, trapped.

Creak. Clank. Thump.
Creak. Clank. Thump.

Step by step the armor marched down the corridor. Surely, in all the history of the starship *Freedom*, her halls had never seen such a sight. Stowy felt like the tin man from *The Wizard of Oz*. (It was one of the old movies both universes shared, filmed before the Great Split of 1944.)

Normally, thousands of spacers would be bustling through the ship. But with only a skeleton crew, the halls were barren, and the creak-clank-thump echoed. Every once in a while, a blast would hit the ship, or the cannons would boom above them, and the armor would sway. With one terrible blast to the hull, the entire suit of armor collapsed. When it hit the ground, Stowy cried out in pain. She tried to pull the pieces off, to escape, but with a series of clanks, creaks, and thumps, the armor stood up, then kept walking.

Footfalls sounded from ahead. Not a *clank-creak-thump* but light, rapid footfalls. At once, the suit of armor froze, backed up against the wall, and stood at attention like a decoration in some damp castle. A shadow danced across the floor ahead, stretching out like a blade, and then a Mimori unit emerged from around the corner. In the dim light, the android appeared like a pale ghost. She ran toward them, turned her head, and her glass eyes caught the light and shone bright and blinding like two stars. For a moment, as the android stared at the suit of armor, lines of code ran across her eyeballs. Stowy could see the tiny characters in pale green font.

She's so much more advanced than these mites, Stowy thought.

Stowy wanted to cry out. To yell "help!" like she had when alone. Did Mimori know there was a girl inside this suit of armor, which had—to her eyes—randomly materialized in the corridor of a warship? Stowy tried to shout, but not a sound left her lips. Why couldn't she talk? She had cried out before!

It was those eyes. Those burning white eyes. What if they saw her? What if they stared at her, *into* her? Stowy feared eye contact. And eye contact with a robot's blazing, all-seeing white eyes . . . Her throat clenched up. She could barely breathe, let alone speak.

Then another blast hit the ship, rocking the corridor. The android with the burning white eyes swayed on her feet. A series of booms and thuds sounded below, perhaps from engineering, and the Mimori unit ran onward, leaving the suit of armor behind. As curious as the mystery of the armor was, the android had higher priorities.

In a clumsy, jerking motion, the suit of armor raised its leg at a ninety-degree angle. Something was wrong with the knee joints. With the armor fitting improperly over the smaller frame of a child, some plates overlapped, which made bending the knee impossible. And so the armor marched on with legs straight like some old automaton forged from brass and copper. *Creak. Clank. Thump. Creak. Clank. Thump.* And the suit marched onward.

Before long, the suit reached a round, heavy hatchway. Words appeared on the blast door. ACCESS TO ESCAPE POD.

Stowy pulled mightily on the armor, trying to stop walking. But the armamites moved on their own, forcing her to move with them. The gauntlet grabbed the doorknob. Her fingers, encased in metal, turned the winch, and with a *creak-clank-thump*, she entered the escape pod.

The pod had a small, round interior with eight seats in a ring. The suit of armor sat down.

"Algernon, run!" Stowy whispered. "Sneak out of the armor and run!"

But the mouse remained in her pocket, loyal even now. Stowy knew this pod was no longer an "escape" pod. It was a handbasket. And it was taking Stowy straight to hell.

The pod door thudded shut.

242

The suit of armor tapped buttons on a control panel.

And with a *whoosh* and punishing g-force, the shuttle shot down a launch tube. The portholes revealed lights streaking across the tube's walls. They were traveling through the ship toward the exterior hull. The shuttle moved faster and faster, pushing Stowy back against her seat. It reminded her of the spinning machines in Uncle Baer's lab, which he used to measure the forces of momentum on the human body. Stowy had seen what powerful g-force could do. She clenched her teeth and screwed her eyes shut, hoping that when somebody finally opened the suit of armor, she wouldn't leak out.

Finally the tube ended. Like a bullet, the pod shot into space and hurtled toward the battle. Through the portholes, Stowy saw the stars, the blue curve of Earth, and a thousand raining starships.

CHAPTER TEN
A Return to Shadow

King stood on the bridge, clinging to his workstation, as his ship jostled and charged and battled the hosts of the enemy. The Weltraumwaffe was still besieging Earth, cutting off the terrestrial and space forces. King must smash his way through. He must connect sky and space. He must reach Washington and save the city. But the Germans were holding their lines, resisting King like an iron-banded door resisting a battering ram. Even with the might of the Freedom Fleet, King still could not break through. Still, for all his power, he could not reach those who needed him.

Three German destroyers loomed before the *Freedom*. The German cannons kept firing. *Freedom* and her escort frigates— eight ships in all—fired their Shield of David batteries. The ships were depleting their interceptors at an alarming rate. Soon they would all be gone, leaving *Freedom* without point-defense capabilities. In that case, *Freedom* would still have her force field, but even that shielding wouldn't last forever, eventually leaving them with the armored hull alone. Not good. Emily was already forced to switch to "urgent only" mode on the Shield of David. That meant they shot down only the most dangerous torpedoes. If the Nazis fired something at the engines or another critical area, *Freedom* spent the interceptors to deflect it. But to save on ammo, they must let some lower-priority assaults through. That meant taking the blows on the chin.

With every blast, the ship shook, and Mimori winced. The android was a part of the ship, a humanoid manifestation of the *Freedom*'s brain. And she felt the blows. Not with real physical pain like a human might. Mimori had never been able to explain it.

"It's sort of like watching a loved one get hurt," she had once told King. "You still wince, and cry out, and even *feel* the blow yourself in a way. Even if your own body remains unhurt. That's how I feel when *Freedom* is hurt. It hurts me too."

This battle must be an agony for Mimori. Again and again, the blows hit the ship. While Mimori Prime remained on the bridge, suffering the assault, her sisters ran across the ship, fixing and repairing what they could, all under the supervision of Engineer Kim Fletcher-King.

"Sir!" Mimori Prime suddenly said, turning toward King. "An escape pod just launched from the *Freedom*."

King frowned. Normally, Mimori would alert a lower-ranking officer about something so trivial. But Spitfire and Jordan were busy at their stations, shouting orders, commanding the *Freedom* and her fleet. Aside from them and King, nobody else was on the bridge. The other humans aboard were scattered through the rest of the starship.

"Who's in the escape pod?" King said. "Check the MindWeb map."

Mimori ran a quick scan. Lines of code ran along her eyeballs. "No MindLinks detected aboard the pod, sir. Nobody is missing."

King didn't like this. Shuttles didn't just launch themselves automatically. Who didn't have MindLinks aboard? Well, the Mimoris didn't. Could an android have gone rogue and stolen it? Or the robotic mites? Or even Stowy? The girl didn't have a MindLink; the sweep wouldn't detect her in a shuttle.

What could he do? Send a starfighter after it? What good would that do? Starfighters were built to bomb things. They couldn't grab and retrieve a pod. He could send a Saint Bernard rescue shuttle. But that made a juicy target for the enemy. Over and over, the Nazis had shown themselves to prioritize attacks on ambulance shuttles and hospital ships. It was a sick pleasure of theirs. A Saint Bernard would draw enemy fire like sugar water attracting wasps. Dammit.

"We'll have to let it go," King said.

No sooner did he finish his sentence than a Nazi battle group swooped toward the *Freedom*, and he must give his full attention to the war. Yet as he relayed orders to the fleet, trying to trap the enemy between two starfighter wings, King's thoughts kept straying back to the little orphan child in his starship. A child who must be afraid. Who must want to escape this war and terror. He hoped Stowy was all right, and if she *was* on that pod, he hoped she made it to safety. He hoped he would see her again.

* * * * *

The escape pod hurtled through the battle. Inside sat the medieval suit of armor. And inside that—a girl. And inside her pocket—her pet mouse. Stowy felt like a Matryoshka doll, the kind the slaves in the east made for their Aryan masters. Father had once gone to the east during his military service, and he had seen the Russian slaves, the descendants of those who had dared to oppose Hitler. He came home with stories of horror—of lanky, starving men forced to fight for fish eyeballs to survive. Along with the stories, he brought back a crudely carved Matryoshka.

I gave the slave a loaf of bread for it, he said. *It was more food than she'd seen in a month.*

Whenever Stowy played with the nested, wooden dolls, she imagined a skeletal slave fighting for fish eyeballs.

But that was back on the Fatherworld. Looking out the porthole, Stowy realized how different things were in Unreineland. Multiple portholes surrounded the pod's circular hull, including a porthole on the floor. They had a funny functionality to them. At first Stowy didn't understand what was

246

happening. Images kept shrinking and growing and shrinking again, as if distorted by a funhouse mirror. But eventually Stowy understood what was going on. The portholes used some special steelglass. If she squinted, the view zoomed in. If she widened her eyes, the view shrank. Like this, an observer could zoom in and out, using only their eyes. Presumably, that could let a pilot operate the portholes while freeing his hands for the yoke.

Stowy peered through a porthole, squinted, and zoomed in on a cluster of distant red lights. The image grew in the porthole. Russian warships flew there, thousands of them, with cannons shaped like bears. They called themselves "equalists" in this universe, not "communists." Stowy wasn't sure what the difference was (she only knew what little she overheard), but they were definitely Russian. Some even had teardrop domes like those from Saint Basil's cathedral, which were displayed across Germany as trophies of war. In the old days, Hitler used to bring dogs and birds over to defile those captured domes. But in the centuries since Hitler's death, the colorful domes had simply been left to decay. Stowy had seen one in person in Munich.

She thought again of that old Matryoshka doll. Back there in the Fatherworld, millions of Russians still lived, suffering as slaves in eastern work camps. The Germans bred them like cattle, and most never lived past thirty. Here in Unreineland, they flew starships and fought the Weltraumwaffe. What a strange universe this was!

Stowy shivered inside her suit of armor. What if the Russians caught her? Growing up, she had heard tales of communist atrocities. Of Stalin's butchery. Of the Red Army pillaging and raping. Perhaps those stories were mere propaganda. Perhaps they were true. Stowy didn't want to find out. She just wanted to be back aboard the *Freedom*. Back near Grouchy and Spitfire and the others. A lump filled her throat, tears stung her eyes, and a tremor seized her.

We'll be all right, Luna said in her mind. *We've been in tight spots before. We'll get out of this one too.*

"Yes, we've been in tight spots," Stowy said, wriggling inside her armor. "And we keep escaping them into spots tighter and tighter still."

(Oh, if only she could speak as clearly with humans as with Luna!)

Her hands moved again on their own. They grabbed the pod's controls, tapped buttons, and worked the joystick. The suit of armor was forcing her to pilot the pod. Where were they going? She had no idea. The pod's motors thrummed. The small, round vessel curved in space, gliding far above the Red Fleet. Good. Stowy hadn't relished the idea of flying among giant, angry ships with booming bear cannons. Whether Russians were friends or foes in this universe, their guns were still booming and filling space with fire. A good Russian could kill Stowy just as easily as a bad one.

She flew the pod confidently, leaving the Freedom Fleet behind and heading into the Weltraumwaffe. Or rather, the plate armor flew the shuttle; trapped inside, Stowy simply moved along with it. She was worried one side or the other would shoot her down. But nobody did. After all, ammunition was expensive. Every missile these ships fired cost a fortune—more than an officer earned in a lifetime. Stowy, who had spent a year living in a soldier's attic, had learned that much. Nobody would spare precious weaponry on an escape pod. As the shuttle flew onward, zipping through the battle, the shrieking warships—whether Allies or Axis—let her fly by.

"Thankfully, Algernon, we're not even worth killing," she said. The mouse seemed to be asleep in her pocket. Or maybe just scared stiff.

Allies or Axis, Luna said, sounding unusually contemplative. The blanket always had the uncanny ability to read

Stowy's mind. *Is that what this is then? The Second World War again?*

"Yes, seems to be," Stowy said. "The Fatherworld and Unreineland split apart during the Second World War. Now that our two universes are meeting, the same war flares up. Back in our reality, we won the first time around. But now everything is up for grabs again."

I hope we lose this time, Luna said.

Stowy gasped. "Luna! What a terrible thing to say." She glanced around, fearful of the Gestapo hearing.

Oh, be quiet! Luna said. *You also want the Allies to win this time. Don't deny it! What good did Hitler's victories do us? To the Nazis, you're just a crippled girl from Aktion T4, and I'm just the blanket they tossed you in the lab. But if the Allies win, we can be people. Real people!*

"You'll always just be a blanket," Stowy said.

Yes, well, I'd rather be the safety blanket of a healthy, loved girl than the blanket of a lab experiment.

Stowy sighed. "Nobody loves me here either, Luna. Oh, I know some people in Unreineland seem to love me. People like Admiral Grouchy and Spitfire and Bastian. But they don't. Not really. They love another girl. A girl who died. They love the fairy princess bitten by the spider. Not the goblin child from the gutters of Munich. And besides—we're captured! We're prisoners! We might never see Grouchy and his crew again."

And again the tears returned, and even inside the plate armor, Luna wrapped around her, comforting her.

The pod flew by the front line of Weltraumwaffe warships. The German cannons flashed across space, blazing with blinding white light, casting out shock rings of energy. From here, the battle seemed silent. Stowy could not hear those booming cannons through space. Nearer and nearer to those grand guns did the pod fly. Once she neared the German warships, she realized how small she truly was. The German warships reminded her of black sharks with red eyes, and she, in her pod, wasn't even a minnow. She was just a floating piece of plankton. Any one of those streaking torpedoes was far larger than her pod. No wonder nobody was shooting at her. She was a speck of dust floating in the murk.

Soon the pod passed beyond the Weltraumwaffe's vanguard line of booming guns. She glided alongside mighty hulls, a tiny sphere passing by metal cities. The warships of the Weltraumwaffe were only several lines deep. Before long, no more cannons lit space. The battle faded like a traveling storm behind Stowy, and she found herself flying among German support ships. She spotted ammunition haulers, engineering ships, energy frigates (they were essentially floating power plants), fuel freighters, tech ships (designed to jam and disrupt enemy technology), and various other vessels not engaged directly in combat.

There were warships back here too, currently undergoing repairs, restocking ammunition, and refueling. A few of the German ships had taken heavy damage. The pod flew by one—the *Munich Massacre*. The German destroyer had lost a good chunk of her hull. The gaping wound revealed a honeycomb of corridors and cabins. Mechs in spacesuits covered the ruins like ants, slowly weaving together new support structures, racing to get the warship back into the fight. Skeletal robots worked alongside the men, working with a speed even Mimori might envy. *Munich Massacre* was a capital ship of the Weltraumwaffe, and her absence would be keenly felt.

There was a porthole on the pod's deck between the seats. Like a glass window at the bottom of a boat, the kind that would take tourists to see the sunken ruins of American ships from centuries ago. Sitting in the escape pod, Stowy peered down toward Earth. She was in high orbit. From up here, when she didn't zoom in, Earth seemed small, no larger than a soccer ball held at arm's length. She imagined that she could open the round porthole, scoop up Earth, and cradle the planet in her lap. More ships were battling closer to the planet. That was where the bulk of the Red Fleet was fighting.

She kept flying for a long while, passing ship by ship, then moving across a vast expanse of darkness. At some point, she dozed off inside her armor. It was dreadfully uncomfortable, downright painful, but she was exhausted. If you were tired enough, Stowy had learned in the lab, you could sleep through most pain. In her dreams, instead of being trapped inside armor, she was trapped in a cocoon, hanging from a web. A pale, wrinkly spider approached her. White hairs sprouted around the spider's head. The arachnid queen stared with eight eyes like round bones, and her venom smelled like peppermint.

After some indeterminate amount of time, the pieces of armor stirred across her. They were, after all, still armamites with little poking legs, and something (or somebody?) had excited them. Stowy opened her eyes, looked through a porthole, and saw a great German starship ahead. Stowy had seen many German starships today, but this was something different, something larger and stronger. A true juggernaut, a war machine like a leviathan of the depths. Eight red bores of cannons stared like spider eyes. In the darkness of space, the ship was but a shadow, blending into the black, but Stowy recognized the vessel. She had been inside that terrible machine. Here flew *Barbarossa*. Flagship of the Weltraumwaffe.

And Stowy was flying right toward it.

* * * * *

Sometimes, when she was very little, Stowy would get something her mother called "meltdowns." She would scream, kick, bang her head against the floor, and cry inconsolably. The anxiety possessed her like a demon. In the old days, she suspected, they would have burned her at the stake. Indeed, when Stowy had learned about witch burning, she realized at once—many of those women had been mentally ill. Perhaps some had been autistic, their bouts of intense emotion interpreted as demonic possessions.

As she grew older, Stowy learned that autistic people struggled to control their emotions. That these "meltdowns" were a common symptom. And in Uncle Baer's laboratory, she learned that meltdowns meant pain. Meltdowns summoned his terrible tools to her flesh. For a time, trapped in her cage, she had learned to control her outbursts. Luna helped, hugging and protecting her. She had found Luna in the lab, cowering on the cage floor. That was all Baer's specimens (his "nieces and nephews," as he called them) got for a home. A cage and a blanket. Stowy and Luna began as cellmates. They became soulmates.

But now, here in Unreineland, even Luna could not stop the panic, could not hold back the meltdown.

Trapped in the suit of armor, hurtling toward the *Barbarossa*, Stowy screamed. She wept. She tried with all her strength to free herself from the armor, to rip off the armamites that encased her. All her mind and body became a raging storm. But scream and weep as she might, the armamites were stronger, restraining her, forcing her to pilot the pod toward *Barbarossa*'s airlock . . . and into the Nazi juggernaut.

Back into the hell she had escaped.

Her own hands, encased in the scratching metal mites, moved the yoke, piloting the pod through one of *Barbarossa*'s airlocks. She imagined the *Barbarossa* as a mighty whale, the pod as a little parasite burrowing into its flesh. She floated into a cavernous hangar.

A hangar? It seemed more like a cathedral to a dark god. The black walls soared into shadows. Here and there, red lights illuminated portraits of Adolf Hitler, the Eternal Führer, founder and deity of the Fatherworld. Banners hung from the far wall, displaying red swastikas like streaks of blood in the shadows, painted with the brush of a sadist. Across the deck stood hundreds of troops of the Waffen-SS, arranged in neat rows and clad in black armor. Upon their breastplates crackled the lightning bolts of their demonic order, and their visors were shaped like metal skulls. Ahead of the troopers stood men in black robes. Burned Ones. They had willingly stepped into the fire, the living manifestation of Hitler, allowing the flames to lick off their skin, to leave them sickly, scarred, and purified. With their dark hoods and metal skulls, the men seemed to Stowy like a host of the undead.

This was not a normal, busy hangar. Stowy had been to enough of those in her life of stowing away. There were no other shuttles here, no deckhands bustling back and forth, no ships loading and offloading supplies. This hangar was different. The tableau reminded Stowy of a midnight mass. She suddenly felt like a sacrificial lamb being led to the altar.

The pod slowed down. The spherical vessel hovered between the lines of Burned Ones, who stared from within the shadows of their robes, and the formations of SS troopers, whose metal skulls leered. Trapped inside the pod, still encased in armor, Stowy could only watch through the porthole.

What would they do to her? Fear's icy claws gripped her. She began to hyperventilate. Would they strap her onto the tables again, perform their wicked surgeries, their experiments, their torture? Stowy yearned to break free from this armor, to cut her wrists, to kill herself, to save herself from the pain she knew awaited. She had been through this once before. She could not face it again.

Calm down, Luna said in her mind. *Be strong. You escaped once, so you can escape again.*

"They'll cut me open," she whispered.

Then I'll hold you together.

"I want to die."

I want you to live.

"I'm scared."

I'll give you strength.

The blanket was warm against her skin, protecting her from the little sharp legs of the armamites. Luna's touch soothed her. The storm of anxiety still raged, but Stowy could now navigate the tempest in her mind, riding the waves instead of letting them drown her.

The pod floated toward the back of the hangar, a place of shadows and crackling torches. If this were indeed some dark church, here was its sanctuary. Through the porthole, Stowy saw three figures standing there. One man. One woman. And one girl.

Stowy recognized them. And each one shot terror through her. Each one had hurt her so much.

The man towered, easily seven feet tall. He wore the black uniform of the Weltraumwaffe, and his shoulders sported the insignia of a grand admiral. His jaw was square, his shoulders broad. Here stood Wolfgang König, commander of the Nazi fleet, son of Führer Helmut König. Everyone from the Fatherworld knew him—the daring admiral who had crushed the rahs, who had led the charge into Unreineland, who might someday even ascend to the throne as führer of two universes. Stories of his cruelty had spread across the Fatherworld. Everyone knew the story of Wolfgang König crushing the rebellion on Mars ten years ago. He had covered the colony domes with the corpses of Martian rebels, arms and legs slung together, forming some macabre doily of human flesh. Whenever the cowed colonists looked to the sky, they saw the mutilated remains of their rebels, and they feared the vengeance of Wolfgang König.

He looks like Bastian, Stowy realized. *Doppelgänger.*

She did not know Bastian King well. But she knew

enough. The big American marine had saved her from St Mary's Hospital. He had risked his own life, charging into the Nazi lines. And after that battle, Stowy had seen Bastian comforting his troops, visiting the wounded, hugging his family. He had come to Stowy too with smiles and comforting words. She was the girl who was scared of everyone and everything, but Bastian had not scared her. The big man radiated goodness and courage. He was like some cuddly grizzly bear who only bared his teeth to the wolves.

Two men, Stowy thought. Images in a funhouse mirror. One man from the Fatherworld, one from Unreineland. One a cruel admiral, the other a kind marine. Good and evil. Reflections of a man.

Next, Stowy looked through the pod's porthole at the woman in the sanctuary.

She was about fifty, an ice queen with pale cheeks, lips the color of blood, and streaks of silver through her golden hair. She stood imperiously, hands on her hips. Unlike the admiral, she wore no naval uniform. A black catsuit hugged her body, adorned with motors, cables, and little hooks for weapons and gadgets. The powersuit crackled with a force field. A pendant shaped like a swastika with six branches (instead of the usual four) hung between her breasts. Here stood Dr. Anneliese Heisenberg-König. Wife of the führer. Wolfgang's stepmother. Chief engineer of the Fatherworld.

Stowy knew her well. Every Christmas, the top scientists of the Fatherworld would visit Munich University to deliver lectures. Dr. Rudolph Baer would take his "nieces and nephews," stand them on stage, point at their various injuries and deformities, and speak of the marvels of the human body, how through experimentation and mutation, one could create a race of supermen. At those Christmas lectures, other scientists would come to speak, chief among them Dr. Anneliese. Everyone in the theater would bow and hush when the führer's wife spoke. Sitting beside the stage, Stowy would listen to the woman speak of her dark arts. Anneliese's twisted mind had created many inventions for the Fatherworld's domination. She had invented the Überlichtantrieb warp drive, discovered the secrets of umbrion particles, and opened a portal to this parallel universe.

She looks like Kim, Stowy thought. *She too is a doppelgänger.*

Then there was the third figure in the hangar. The girl.

She scared Stowy the most.

The girl was only seventeen. Yet already she wore the full battlesuit of the Waffen-SS, and the Sig runes crackled upon her breastplate like real lightning bolts. The insignia of a gruppenführer topped her slender shoulders. Her smile was wide, showing too many teeth. A mad smile. The smile of a girl without mercy, without decency, without a soul. A predatory smile. She was a mistress of pain, a torturer, a sadist, a little girl given two universes to torment. Here stood Eva König. Daughter of Wolfgang. Granddaughter of the führer. The kindergeneral herself—the young, demented commander of the Waffen-SS.

The Bitch from Berlin, they called her, but only in whispered voices. Every Sunday, Eva König would appear on holoscreens across the Fatherworld. With the tools of her trade, she would torture the enemies of the empire. As a schoolgirl, Stowy remembered being forced to watch. The other children would gaze with fervor, but Stowy had always feared seeing Eva's pincers, scalpels, and screwdrivers. They said autistic people felt no empathy, yet whenever Stowy would watch the torture, she would feel the pain on her own body.

Stowy hadn't met Admiral Grouchy's granddaughter, but she had seen photos of young Rowan King, a teenage girl who lived down on Earth. Eva too was a doppelgänger—a cruel, wicked reflection in the mirror.

There was a doppelgänger of me here in Unreineland once, Stowy reflected. *A kind, beautiful fairy princess stolen by the spiders. A child who laughed and danced and filled hearts with joy. And I'm her dark, broken reflection, a child of pain and tears and melancholia. Now the shadows of my home pulled me back into their embrace.*

The pod landed before the man, woman, and girl. The suit of armor moved on its own, pulling Stowy to her feet, forcing her to open the hatch. Against her will, she emerged from the pod and stepped onto the deck. *Click. Scrape. Thunk.* The three figures towered before her like a triumvirate of pagan gods. Each of the three had one blue eye, one bionic red eye.

The plate of armor moved on its own, forcing Stowy to raise her hand high.

She knew what to say. It had been beaten into her so many times at school. She could not yell as one should. But her whisper seemed to echo inside the helmet, growing louder and louder, emerging as a ghostly voice, far deeper than her usual timber.

"Hail Hitler!"

* * * * *

Eva König, the golden little mistress of pain, looked at her father and step-grandmother. Then she returned her eyes to Stowy and burst out laughing.

"*Mein gott!* This suit of armor! It even got the prisoner hailing Hitler!" Eva's laughter echoed through the hangar. "I must admit, Oma Anneliese, you have a wicked imagination. Your toys are quite entertaining."

The engineer glared at the girl. "I told you—stop calling me *oma*. I am not your grandmother." She smiled wickedly. "But I did enjoy killing her."

Yes, Stowy knew that tale. All children in the Fatherworld did. It was a tale of doomed romance, betrayal, and lust, depicted in murals, stage plays, and even an opera. Stowy had once accompanied Uncle Bear to the Munich Concert Hall, where they watched a performance of *Die Nachtkönigin*, an opera by Jürgen von Ebersdorf, a contemporary composer heralded as Wagner reborn. Dr. Rudolph Baer, a proud benefactor of the arts, would sit in balcony five, and all his nephews and nieces would sit around him. Stowy still remembered the red carpet beneath her scabbed, bare feet. Of the opera itself, she remembered only snippets. A famous actress from Berlin played the young version of Dr. Anneliese, the wunderkind, the beautiful engineer who captured the heart of a führer.

In the opera's most famous aria, "Mörderische Liebe," Dr. Anneliese wielded the power of umbrions (portrayed on stage using harmless black powder). In the soaring crescendo, Anneliese (a heavenly soprano) slew the vindictive Magda (a haunting alto), wife of Führer Helmut (bass or sometimes baritone). Rather than fleeing, the young, beautiful engineer stood before the führer, raised her chin, and confessed her love. And thus the Fatherworld gained its new *Nachtkönigin,* the Queen of the Night. There was even a Wolfgang in the opera, a petulant youth who resented his wicked stepmother, even as he lusted after her. Eva herself did not appear in the opera; these monumental events, performed so brilliantly upon the stage, predated the kindergeneral's birth.

Wolfgang—the adult Wolfgang—spoke in a booming voice, almost as booming as his character in the opera. The sound pulled Stowy back to the present.

"Welcome, Admiral King! How nice of you to come visit us!" Laughing, the Nazi admiral spread out his arms in welcome.

He was certainly no longer that petulant youth from the opera. Today that lustful boy was a proud, towering officer.

"Come closer, King!" Wolfgang said. His baritone voice filled the hangar like the pipes of a cathedral.

Stowy's suit of armor raised the left leg, then thumped

down, never bending the knee. *Creak. Clank. Thump. Creak. Clank. Thump.* The armor took a few steps closer.

Eva wrinkled her nose. "Ugh, Anneliese, your little machines are so loud."

"And ill-fitting," Anneliese said, eyes narrowed. "Something is wrong."

The engineer's bionic eye blazed red, peering at the armor, right through the eye holes, and blinding Stowy. The young stowaway winced and closed her eyes. Floaters of light hovered across her eyelids.

She saw me!

"Disassemble yourselves!" commanded Dr. Anneliese, voice shrill. "Reveal the prisoner inside you."

With hisses and clatters, the armamites released the links holding them together. First a vambrace fell off her arm. It landed on its long, curved back, little metal legs kicking in the air, then flipped itself over and scuttled away. A greave fell off her thigh, curled up into a ball, and rolled into the shadows. A pauldron climbed off her shoulder, scuttled down her torso, then fled between her legs. Piece by piece, like roly-polies fleeing the sunlight, the armamites crawled off and vanished.

Within a moment, Stowy stood there before the triumvirate, exposed. No more did she look like a medieval knight in plate armor. They saw her for who she was. Just a broken, impure, autistic girl. Her light brown hair hung in dirty, scraggly strands. Her tattered dress was falling apart, held together only by the many pockets she had patched on, each pocket of a different fabric and color. She wore only one striped stocking; the other had ripped and fallen off long ago. In her shy little hands, she clutched her blanket. She was shoeless. Just a poor, filthy orphan. An escaped lab rat. And on her arm appeared the black triangle, inverted, deeming her an *untermenschin*. Impure. A cripple. A child for the laboratory, and once all the science had been wrung out of her—to the gas chamber! She lowered her head, ashamed.

But no, she thought. *No, I'm no longer that girl.*

She had never met her doppelgänger, the other Stowy. But she had seen the love King, Bastian, and the others held for that fairy child. When they looked at her, at the broken child, at the Stowy with the tattooed arm, at the girl broken in the lab, starved in the cage, when they looked at that pathetic little cripple—there was love in their eyes. They saw not an impure girl. They saw her as whole and worthy, beautiful the way she was.

They only see the fairy princess, she told herself. *They only see a ghost.*

No, answered another voice from deep inside her. *No, they see me. They see who I can become in their world. In the Fatherworld, I am a weed, but in their world, they see me as a flower.* Tears ran down her cheeks. *I don't know if I can still bloom. I was stomped on and crushed, all my leaves and petals plucked, my very stem sliced a hundred times. But maybe my roots still cling onto life, and maybe in time, in the sun, warmed by her love and kindness, I can still grow and bloom. That is who I am. Not a flower yet, no. I'm still just a broken thing. But I'm the promise of a flower. And I am loved.*

There was still a part of her that refused to believe that. That told her she was wicked. That nobody loved her, and if they did, it was a fake love, pyrite love. That she would soon be found out, cast aside, hurt. That only Algernon and Luna loved her, not humans. Sometimes that voice even claimed that Algernon and Luna were just a mouse and a blanket, and that Stowy herself gave them their voices, that she truly was alone. That voice would perhaps always be inside her. But so long as that softer, hopeful voice spoke too, she would have a voice of hope, and light would illuminate the path forward.

Slowly she raised her eyes toward the Reich triumvirate. She stared at the man, at the woman, at the girl.

They stared back, eyes wide with shock.

Wolfgang's baritone voice broke the silence. "Goddammit, Anneliese!"

Young Eva burst out laughing. "Oma, you caught the wrong one! You were meant to capture King. And you caught Baer's little pet!"

The *kindergeneral* fell onto the deck and rolled around, laughing.

Dr. Anneliese stared at Stowy, eyes malignant, teeth bared. Gloved in leather and electric cables, the engineer's fingers twitched, spraying sparks. Her force field crackled and shimmered like a ghost overlaying her form. Her veneer of humanity slipped away, revealing something primal, sadistic, vampiric. She no longer seemed to Stowy like a woman but like some cursed, undead bat stretched into human size and shape, still nurturing its hunger for blood.

Behind Stowy, feet shuffled. She turned her head, and her heart, which was already speeding, burst into a mad sprint. The Burned Ones were emerging from the shadows like the dead from their tombs. The robed and hooded figures shuffled toward Stowy. When the torchlight invaded their hoods, Stowy caught glimpses of their faces. Or what had once been faces. The fire had stripped away noses, lips, sometimes eyes. Every one of those fanatics had burned him or herself (Stowy could not tell their genders) to prove their loyalty to Hitler, the god who dwelled in flame. They held out their hands toward her, gloved in creaking leather, some with only two or three fingers.

She was trapped. Burned Ones to one side. The triumvirate to the other. They moved in closer, a tightening noose. Stowy knew that she would soon find herself in a cage. Then strapped to a table. Then shoved into a gas chamber until she rolled out, her skin white, her eyes like round bones rattling in the sockets.

There was only one chance to escape. The smallest of

chances.

The escape pod.

She knew how to operate it. The armor had taught her
how to fly.

Stowy turned and ran toward the pod.

The Burned Ones blocked her way. The cultists loomed
before her. Their pale, scarred flesh made them look like pillars of
salt draped with black robes. Their hands reached out, and their
lipless mouths opened in hisses, showing crooked teeth barely
clinging to deformed gums. Stowy had known children similarly
deformed in the lab. She did not fear their deformities. She feared
the fanaticism she saw in their eyes, the hunger—that insatiable
hunger—that dripped from their ravaged jaws. The fire had not
made them ugly. It had revealed the ugliness inside them. Stowy
might be a mouse, but even a mouse with its back to the corner
could fight. As a Burned One grabbed her, she sank her teeth into
his arm, and she bit down hard.

The monk roared and released her.

Stowy ran by him. More Burned Monks leaned in from all
sides. She barreled into one. She was only a child, but he was weak
and withered, and she knocked the scarred man back. There
ahead—the pod! It hovered a foot above the deck. If she could
leap inside, make her way to the airlock—

The Waffen-SS emerged from the shadows. The armored
troopers formed a line of big, armored bodies. These men were
giants compared to the so-called untermenschen of Unreineland.
The men of twenty-third-century Germany, enhanced by centuries
of ruthless culling and eugenics, grew seven feet tall, their arms
like tree trunks, their chests like tanks. Stowy skidded to a halt
before them, a mouse facing a wall of cats.

Stowy froze, bared her teeth, and hissed. A mouse? She
became a wild rat, trapped and feral.

She tried to run toward the troopers, hoping to slide

between their legs, when hands grabbed her from behind.

Stowy yelped.

The hands lifted her aboveground. Stowy's legs kicked in midair. Her captor spun her around, and Stowy found herself facing a demonic visage, a girl with the grin of the devil.

Eva König held her at arm's length. Her electric battlesuit gave the teenage girl superhuman strength. Her grin stretched so wide Stowy could see the molars. Her eyes dripped savage mirth, the real eye blazing nearly as brightly as the bionic one.

"Now you're mine!" Eva said, and her laughter echoed through the hangar of *Barbarossa*, flagship of the Nazi empire.

CHAPTER ELEVEN
Nested Dolls

Larry "Phantom" Jordan would never admit it to anyone. But he was afraid.

Not of the enemy—at least not more than usual. He had known the fierceness and brutality of many enemies in his long life. Jordan had grown up on the rough streets of 2140s Los Angeles. The infamous Food Riots decade. Before he was ten years old, young Larry had learned to carry a weapon, to fight to survive. As a young man, he fought the Red Dawn, charging in a rickety old starfighter into their lines of warships. As a middle-aged man, he had risen to command a warship, and he had fought the rahs, those malevolent spiders from beyond the stars. And now, an old man, he had ascended to the lofty heights of rear-admiral, and still he was striking his enemies down.

And that was what scared him. That this was going too well. That he was becoming too cocky. That sooner or later his guard would slip. That in his arrogance, drunk on his power and victories, he would make some terrible error like a chess grandmaster losing his queen too early in the game. That his streak of military successes would die in a crushing defeat, pulling millions of others with him into the grave. He feared that he was growing so strong that he would crack and shatter.

Old soldiers were rare. There was a saying that you should fear the old soldier. Not many grew old in this game. But Jordan knew he was not immortal. Too many tragedies had struck close to home. His wife—dying all those years ago. That tragedy still haunted him. His beloved, the android Timori—betraying him.

That wound had never healed. His niece and nephew, Ishmael and Valentina—vanishing in the destruction of Alpha Centauri. Those holes in his heart would never fill. Around him, people died, and so far, Jordan had always dodged the swing of the Grim Reaper's scythe. And every year, every rank he climbed, every victory he won—it was getting harder and harder to dodge that blade. Sometimes he felt like a man playing Russian roulette, and he was running out of empty chambers. And suddenly this bridge seemed like a cold, dark place, and the swirling battle outside, with all its myriads of starships racing and falling and rising and swirling around the world, spun his head.

This is insanity, Jordan thought. *We can't do this. We can't beat them.*

And the world became like a black hole, sucking all into its depths, and Jordan imagined everyone in this fleet falling and crashing down. He could feel the pain as twisting metal crushed his old bones before the fire swept over him.

Enough, Jordan told himself. *That's all the fear you get today.*

The voice of his old commander, Ulysses King, returned to him.

Ya scared, kid? Good. It means you're alive. Now you tell that fear to get lost. And you fight onward! Even if it's hard. Even if it hurts. Even if you're scared. You become a machine. You crush your emotions. And you keep fighting!

Jordan remembered the old man, a gruff commander with bushy white sideburns and prodigious eyebrows. To Lieutenant Larry Jordan, a twenty-year-old kid from Los Angeles, that old officer had seemed so gruff, so intimidating. But Jordan had taken that advice to heart. And since then, he had tried to live by it.

Crush the fear.

Become a machine.

Keep fighting.

Jordan looked beside him, and he saw another old man,

similar in appearance to Ulysses King (sans the sideburns). It was his son, Admiral James King, a man Jordan loved like a brother. Back in those years, back when Old Man Ulysses had commanded the *Freedom*, young Bulldog and Phantom had thought they ruled the galaxy. The stars were theirs. Eternity beckoned. And half a century later, they were still together.

Put that aside too, Jordan told himself. *Love, like fear, can blind a soldier. Become a machine. Just keep fighting.*

Bulldog and Phantom stood side by side again. Those two cocky young starfighters, living like immortals, had become two admirals. Two old men with white hair and wrinkles. Two old men who had retired to the farm. Two old friends who must fight together again. Admirals were like conductors. Jordan had heard that somewhere. And he and his friend made music together.

King took control of many fleets—the Tigers of India, the Bonsai Wave of Japan, the Caracals of Israel, the Royal Fleet of Britain, and many other fleets, great and small. He wielded them across orbit, never giving the Weltraumwaffe any respite. These fleets were the continuing beat of the song, its looping rhythm that spun round and round, sometimes flowing faster, sometimes slowing down, sometimes loud, sometimes soft, always obeying the orders of James King on one side—and of his foe, the shadowy Wolfgang König, on the other. The two great songs, one of freedom and one of tyranny, clashed together again and again, neither one yet emerging as the dominant melody of this world.

Meanwhile, it was Jordan's task to command the American Armada, the largest subunit of the Freedom Fleet. He must lead the American ships through the ring of fire toward the blue sky below. King was perhaps conducting an orchestra. But Jordan must play a blistering guitar solo.

"Spitfire, prepare to fly the *Freedom* a megameter downward," Jordan said. "The rest of the American Armada— you'll form a triangle behind us. Frigates and destroyers on the outside. Dreadnoughts at the lead. Armored behemoths on the back. Everyone else—you fill the wedge and unleash hell at any enemy that comes near. Stay in touch with my MindLink. I'll transfer detailed formation schematics. And I'll be here every step of the way."

Spitfire stood beside him on the bridge. *Freedom*'s young commander chewed her lip, staring at the German warships that clustered below, protecting the path to Earth. The dark warships of the Fatherworld were a dozen deep, forming a defensive wall of metal and fire.

"A megameter through that?" Spitfire muttered. "With barely any ammo left? Outnumbered three to one?" She heaved a sigh. "Well, no horrible odds and staggeringly high chance of death, no glory. Mimori? Stand close to me. Hold my hand. We're gonna do some tricky flying."

Mimori winced. "Be gentle. My ship is brand-new."

Standing beside the two women, Jordan gazed downward toward Earth. He squinted and tilted his head, trying to see beyond the flames, streaking missiles, and lines of German warships. Down there, Jordan could see Katyusha's Red Fleet, still distant from up here. The equalist ships were busy with their own battle, locking horns with a mighty armada of the Weltraumwaffe. And below the equalist-fascist front, Jordan caught just fleeting blue glimpses of it. The sky. Home. From up here, Jordan could clearly make out the west coast of North America. And there, that little smudge—LA. He had come a far way.

Spitfire looked at him. "Ready, sir?"

Jordan nodded. "Lead the charge."

* * * * *

King and Jordan, as they aged, became more restrained, cool and collected even in battle (at least on the surface). But

Spitfire, aged forty-two, still blazed with the fires of youth. Jordan looked at her, and even in the heat of battle, his mind strayed down the paths of nostalgia and melancholy.

When did forty-two begin to seem young to me? Jordan wondered. It was hard to believe that Spitfire, that gangly kid who used to haunt the halls of *Freedom*, was now a middle-aged woman, the commander of a flagship. It seemed like yesterday . . . Young Spitfire laughing and playing with Bastian, Annie, and the other kids of *Freedom*'s starfighters pilots.

Annie, my daughter, is turning forty next year, Jordan thought. *My kid is turning forty. Damn, when did I get so old?*

No, Spitfire didn't have the impetuous, inexperienced youth of a junior officer, perhaps. But compared to the seasoned old admirals, Commander Spitfire still seemed young and cocky. Her fist rose in the air, and she cried out: "For Freedom!" She became like a woman riding a wild stallion, and she drove her spurs into the beast, and *Freedom* bolted and charged to war.

I'm proud of you, kid, Jordan thought. *You look so much like Yehuda. Your dad would be proud too.*

Standing beside the commander, a humanoid avatar of the ship, Mimori closed her eyes, held out her arms, and seemed almost like a girl pretending to be an airplane, a child daydreaming while running along the beach, arms spread out, the wind in her hair. But Mimori was no more a little girl than Spitfire. She was a *starship*, as the *Freedom* herself swooped toward the Earth, the android felt the sparks along the hull, the tug of gravity, the heat and pain of the enemy fire. Spitfire and Mimori clasped their hands together, human and machine, united into one living being. It was an intoxicating feeling. Jordan had only commanded the *Freedom* briefly during the final days of the Spider War, but he never forgot that connection to the ship, the way his consciousness had expanded to fill the dreadnought, and the way his and *Freedom*'s souls intertwined . . . and became one.

And tonight Jordan must do more. He must command an armada.

He raised his chin, expanded his consciousness, and sent out MindWeb broadcasts to every captain in the vast American Armada, whether they commanded a dreadnought, a corvette, or a simple munitions transporter. He imagined the telepathic signals as silver strands, spreading across space in a blooming pattern, connecting Jordan to every starship of the good old U.S. of A.

Technically, the American Armada was a subfleet. A part of the larger Freedom Fleet, subservient to the Free Alliance of Democratic Nations. But even on its own, separated from its allies, the United States fielded a massive armada. The American Space Force could topple nations, conquer worlds. Six thousand American warships flew for democracy and freedom. Their nation needed them. Their *world* needed them. And they must carve open a way home.

The *Freedom* led the way, forming the tip of the wedge. Six thousand ships gathered behind her, spreading out to form a great triangle in space. It wasn't a smooth transition. Rearranging a fleet this size was a slow process, brutal and agonizing in battle. The enemy kept firing. The umbrion waves kept hitting the Americans, and the torpedoes kept exploding all around. Every hour, it seemed, another starship shattered, and flames raced through twisting corridors and bunks, devouring whomever they could before the vacuum took them. Battle in space was a great song, perhaps, a song woven of glory and courage, but death too played in this orchestra. A poet had once told Jordan that no true art could exist without pain, that pain fueled creation. If that was so, then surely war was the purest of all arts.

Even as ships fell, more rose to replace them. The warships of the American Armada unleashed their broadsides. As the torpedoes blazed, the American ships tightened their wedge formation. They shot forth like a javelin, six thousand moving as one. Kriegspfeils exploded and lasers flashed all around. Undeterred, the armada shot through the ring of German fire.

Like firebirds hatched from flame, the starships flew toward Earth. From a distance, as their engines flared red and gold, they must look like a great flock of birds woven of sunset, gliding through the night sky. Even from here aboard the *Freedom*, looking back at the armada, Jordan beheld the thousands of warships as a thing of beauty, a great symphony of lights like dancing notes of fire. But whenever a light flared and winked out within the formation, Jordan knew it was a ship exploding, and through the silvery strands of telepathy, he felt the minds of captains and spacers go silent, and he grieved.

The bridge trembled under his feet. The cannons kept firing. The enemy barrage kept pounding the shields and hull. And onward through the storm the *Freedom* flew, and behind her shone six thousand lights. They swept toward the line of heavy German warships, an iron cage blocking their way to Earth.

"Fire!" Spitfire cried somewhere in the distance, her voice muffled, sounding a thousand miles away.

And the fourteen Angels of Liberty boomed together, unleashing fourteen Maccabee torpedoes.

"Fire!" Jordan cried, and his cry split into six thousand voices, each vibrating across the silvery strands of telepathy. And thousands of ships all around fired their guns, and together the American Armada unleashed a storm of flame.

Ahead, risen to meet the fire, rolled a tidal wave of umbrions. One wave of flame, one of darkness—they crashed together, and where they crested, the *Freedom* leaped and surged forth, then drove downward into the enemy lines.

The *Freedom* had not yet fired her primary weapon. The railgun was still cold. But as the starship plunged toward the enemy lines, those gargantuan two prongs became more than a railgun. They became battering rams. They became the tusks of a charging pachyderm. They became the hammers of gods. The *Freedom* charged onward, force field crackling, her railgun leading the way with piercing twin blades of light.

And like a Carthaginian war elephant into a Roman shield wall, the *Freedom* slammed into the enemy lines.

For a split second, the metal hulls of the enemy ships, adorned with swastikas and armored plates, filled every screen on *Freedom*'s bridge.

Then the bridge gave a huge jolt.

Even Jordan, an experienced officer with famously sturdy space legs, fell onto the deck. He banged his hip and roared in agony. Legend or not, he was still an old man.

We rammed into an enemy ship, he knew.

He pulled himself to his feet. He grabbed the railing of his workstation, and he saw it happening on the central viewport. The *Freedom*—plowing through the enemy lines, knocking them back with her mighty battering rams, and plowing onward into the depths of their hell.

Jordan held out his fist.

"Onward, Freedom Fleet!" he cried. "Charge!"

* * * * *

The baritone voice echoed through the bridge.

"Charge!"

The voice of my best friend, King thought.

Standing at the helm, Spitfire raised her fist in the air.

"Charge!" the commander cried, her voice pure and sharp like a freshly forged saber.

The voice of my protégé, King thought. *Of my adopted daughter.*

Here, at this great hour, at this monumental battle, they were with him. That gave James King hope.

And he raised his fist with them—a metal gauntlet, dented

and old. And though his voice was raspy and hurt his throat, he cried out with them.

"Charge!"

Again the railgun rammed into an enemy ship! The prongs slammed into a *panzerschiffe*, knocking the massive warship back. Small *Rattenjägers* slammed into *Freedom*'s armored hull like mosquitoes against a windshield. The dreadnought plowed through a *torpedoboote*, knocking the smaller warship back. From all sides, the enemy fired. A thousand German warships unleashed their fury, and *Freedom*'s shields sparked and flared. All power in the core was now diverted to those force fields. Not to the cannons. Even the engines were cold. Like a hurtling asteroid, they were flying on momentum alone. Every power in the core, every prayer from every spacer, every hope of every human who fought for freedom—they were going into those shields!

Again they rammed into an enemy ship. And another! German hulls crumbled before them. Ships ripped in two. And onward *Freedom* charged into their lines, wreathed in light, even as the machines of the enemy closed in all around, tightened their lines, and formed a wall that nearly hid Earth's blue sky below.

For just a moment, King saw only darkness.

Freedom flew alone.

Blast after blast rocked the ship. The deck thrummed. The pounding guns were like a heartbeat. King held on as every bone rattled in his body. They plunged through darkness, carving their way through, their shields screaming and their hull creaking and their motors roaring. And all was darkness and sound. All was chaos over a void as dark as the depths before the light of creation.

And lo, behind the flagship, burst the rest of the Freedom Fleet from the umbrionic mist, and their missiles lit the sky like a thousand luminous glyphs. Light filled the monitors and glinted off the dark hulls of the enemy. The Nazi ships pulled back like some cave-dwelling beasts recoiling at a beam of sunlight.

"To Earth!" Spitfire cried, and the *Freedom* shoved through a wall of German frigates.

"To Earth!" cried King and Jordan.

And there below, they saw it. Earth. The blue sky. *Freedom* was plunging down toward it.

For a moment, King could breathe again. The pall of darkness lifted. The rear of the American Armada was still engaged in furious battle, and so was the rest of the Freedom Fleet far above. But here at the vanguard of the wedge formation, the storm clouds parted, revealing the blue light of the world.

But the way home was not yet clear. *Freedom* was entering low orbit now, chugging toward the fascist-equalist front.

This close to Earth, the blue planet dominated half the view. They were only a few megameters above the sky now. This was the realm of early space exploration, the orbit of Yuri Gagarin, the first man in space, and the earliest space stations of the twentieth century. Here, just above the sky, the Red Dawn was battling the Weltraumwaffe. The German fleet was so massive that it was fighting in several orbits at once. And in most places—winning.

"This is not our front," King said. "We'll let Katyusha handle low orbit. Let's not get drawn into this fight. Our orders are to break through the German siege, clear a pathway to the sky, and aid Washington. We'll keep charging through the Germans until we skim the atmosphere. I want us a hundred klicks aboveground. We're gonna skim the Kármán line. From there, we'll deploy the Rhinos."

Spitfire's eyes widened. "A hundred klicks! The *Freedom* can't fly that low! That's . . . that's barely even space anymore. That's almost atmosphere."

Kim materialized on the bridge from engineering. She must have been listening over MindWeb. The engineer was holding a dozen tools at once, her arms racing as she repaired this and that. But she managed to gape at the bridge.

"Spitfire is right," Kim said. "*Freedom* can't fly that low."

Jordan smiled thinly. "Jim has flown her even lower before. Remember that time the *Freedom* actually entered the atmosphere?"

"Yes, and we almost all died!" Kim said.

"What else is new?" Spitfire muttered.

"Enough!" King said. "There's no time to debate this. We must and *will* graze the atmosphere. We need to get below the Russian-German front. Into low, low orbit."

"A hundred klicks isn't low orbit—it's the sky!" Spitfire cried.

"Almost," King said with a thin smile. "Mimori, you'll help keep us afloat. We're going to do some skimming. It's the only way to keep the Freedom Brigade safe from enemy fire. We must get below the lowest German warship. That way, we can protect our marines as they dive down to Washington." He reached out telepathically to the Rhino hangar. "You ready, Bastian?"

His son materialized on the bridge, tall and broad and covered in body armor. "We're all ready down here, sir. We're all strapped into the Rhinos. Just waiting for your order to launch."

And King couldn't help it. Even here, in the heat of battle, he remembered. The little premature baby, wailing because he was too cold. The tiny little boy, so scrawny and red, fighting for every breath, clinging to life. And there he stood—a giant of a man, all in armor, carrying weapons, a true warrior of Earth.

I used to be able to fit you in the palm of my hand, King thought.

As the Freedom Fleet glided down toward Earth's sky, a deep sense of sadness filled King. He remembered teaching the boy how to play catch. Remembered helping Bastian glue together his plastic model starships. Remembered the first time Bastian beat him at chess. And the memories seemed too few to him.

King had always been away on duty. Fighting his wars. Leaving behind the son he loved. The most important person in his life.

We should be under that sky now, making new memories, King thought. *Not fighting a war.*

Once this war was over, King promised to spend more time with those he loved. In his old age, he realized something that so often eluded the understanding of youth. No matter how accomplished you were, no matter what you achieved in life, on your last day you thought of your loved ones, and you realized they were what mattered most.

Please, God, let us both survive this battle, he prayed. *Let us both live. Let my son and I have more good days together under the sun.*

After breaking free from the war in high orbit, they plunged into low orbit, and they flew through the fury of the Russian-German front. For a moment they flew in open space, traveling between two fronts in the war.

"And I thought high orbit was bad," Spitfire muttered.

Jordan spoke in a low, soft voice. "This is a graveyard for starships."

"And for men," King added.

Debris filled low orbit: shattered satellites, chunks of hull, and charred chassis of starships large and small. Corpses too. Thousands of corpses of spacers—frozen, mangled, burnt. They floated through the wreckage. And all this, King knew, was just a small piece of this sprawling tapestry of the macabre. This was just what Earth's orbit had caught and was swirling around the globe. By now, most of the dead had likely fallen to Earth or tumbled into deep space. King was only viewing the topmost bodies in a great mass grave. It was a sobering reminder of the cost of war.

And in this hellscape, the battle was still raging.

Across the devastation, lights kept blazing, smudged from here like thunderbolts seen through fog and rain. Those were the blasts of torpedoes. Dark clouds still swirled and surged—the storms of umbrions. Every moment, spheres of energy expanded and burst, scattering chunks of starships and mangled corpses. It was like watching bubbles in some tarry pool covered with dead ants and broken twigs and leaves. Across this field of death and destruction, the Red Fleet and the Weltraumwaffe still fought a brutal war.

It wasn't fun being the Weltraumwaffe, trapped between the Freedom Fleet above, the Red Fleet below. To face both enemy fleets, the Fatherworld had split their grand fleet into two. Those two parts were not equally sized. Wolfgang König, Grand Admiral of the Weltraumwaffe, had deployed most of his fleet in lower orbit, where he faced Katyusha in brutal, devastating combat. Down here flew mighty Nazi dreadnoughts, leviathans of black metal, their hulls crackling with swastikas. Among them flew line after line of German destroyers and corvettes, all flying prow to stern like marching ants. They were so numerous their lines spread like chains around the world. Here along the equalist-fascist front, the true might and horror of the German war machine was on full display.

King couldn't help but feel somewhat slighted. Why did Katyusha get most of Wolfgang's attention? Was the Freedom Fleet not worthy of such a grand assault? Clearly the Nazis thought that Katyusha was their primary foe. And yes, King admitted it—that wounded his pride.

Wolfgang König underestimated me, he thought. *That will be his downfall.*

And the most bizarre sense of déjà vu hit King. Even with his sturdy space legs, he swayed. In a sudden, perplexing memory, he was holding the baby Wolfgang—a tiny, premature baby in a hospital with a portrait of Hitler over every bed. Because in that other universe, King's son was not named Bastian—but Wolfgang! And now that doppelgänger was here. A foul, wicked version of King's own son.

And sooner or later, I must face my own reflection in the dark mirror, King thought. *I must face the führer, my shadow self. And kill him.*

* * * * *

As the American Armada stormed closer to Earth, King checked the monitors across *Freedom*'s shadowy bridge. The ATLAS system displayed a panoply of data on thousands of warships all around. King sought the Nazi Grand Admiral's flagship. Where was *Barbarossa*? That juggernaut should be too large to hide among the debris. *Barbarossa* must be on the other side of the world now.

King stared downward. The Freedom Fleet was passing through lower orbit now, careful to avoid the battle that raged all around. Every second, more ships blazed above and below, racing to join this or that formation. The battle did not spread uniformly across the sphere of low orbit. The equalist-fascist frontline was actually a network of lines that spiderwebbed across space like cracks in a clay ball. Along these "cracks," lines of Red Fleet and Weltraumwaffe ships crashed together.

Right now *Freedom* flew about a megameter from one of those crackling, fiery branches of the frontline. Three years ago, King had seen a colony of ants on his ranch emerge during a flood. The little insects had joined together, forming a living bridge, allowing their colony to escape. From a distance, that was what the German and Russian ships reminded King of. Two long whips of ants, each forming an elongated colony, swinging at each other in battle.

As *Freedom* flew by, King saw more details of the Russian-German front. From this distance, he could make out individual ships in the long, coiling strands of the Red Fleet. In King's imagination, he likened it to zooming in on a strand of DNA to see the individual atoms. Hundreds of Russian warships forming the coiling line, their hulls painted crimson and adorned with gold equal signs. Teardrop domes sprouted from their dorsal hulls, making the ships look like flying cathedrals. Their bear-shaped cannons roared, bombarding the Nazi warships.

At their lead flew the RDS *Gagarin*, flagship of the Red Dawn, the personal starship of Premier Ketya "Katyusha" Petrova herself. A figurehead of the premier thrust out from *Gagarin's* prow. The gilded statue was a hundred feet tall—or had been once. The war had lopped off the statue's gilded head. Katyusha's body still stood there on the prow, one golden fist raised, a headless general leading an undead army to war.

Hundreds of Nazi warships faced the Russians. They too were arranged in a long, coiling strand. The two strands—one of red ships, the other of black ships—seemed to King like two serpents facing each other. Each was a venomous reptile, but only one wanted to sting him.

As the American Armada drew nearer, multiple German warships opened fire. Torpedoes flew toward the flanks of the Americans' triangular formation.

"Defensive fire only!" King said. "Do not get drawn into a battle. Not yet. Not until we deploy our troops."

Reluctantly the American warships took the assault on their flanks. The enemy's *Kriegspfeil* torpedoes blazed against their force fields, their point-defense interceptors, and their armor. One American corvette—the FAS *Joshua Tree*—buckled under the assault. Within instants, the umbrions swept through her, devouring all fifty spacers aboard. King hissed sharply and clenched his fists.

"We have to fight!" Spitfire said.

"Not yet," King said. "Soon. First we deploy the marines. Godwin can't wait."

278

The armada flew onward, leaving the dead ship behind. And fifty dead souls.

They were sons and daughters, King thought. *Fathers and mothers and husbands and wives. Each with stories of their own. People who loved them.*

It hurt. God, it hurt so much. It never stopped hurting. No matter how many battles you fought, losing a soldier never got any easier. King flew onward through the pain. He could not bring back those fallen spacers. But he could make sure they had not died in vain.

As they flew near the Russian lines, King's MindLink crackled inside his skull. The device was picking up snippets of the Russian officers, most of whom also used neural implants. The geeks had cobbled together a crude MindWeb-to-KatNet adapter, which allowed the Freedom Fleet and the Red Fleet to communicate. The Russian voices flashed through his mind.

"Onward, comrades, to—"

"—glory of the revolution, charge at them and—"

"—to fascism! Death to—"

And then a louder voice, cheerful and surprised.

"Jamechka! Is that you, my love? You come to visit Katyusha?"

She seized his MindLink and forced herself into his brain. Against his will, King hallucinated her here on the bridge. Katyusha wore a red uniform adorned with golden buttons, medals, and epaulets. Her black bob cut spilled out from under her naval cap. In one of her gloved hands, she held a saber. As her hallucination solidified, she looked around and grinned.

"Ah, look at this!" she said. "You rebuilt your beloved antique starship. And she looks even shittier than before!"

"At least I don't have a headless statue of myself on the hull."

Katyusha's smile vanished. Her face flushed, and her eyes blazed with fire. "That fascist brute Wolfgang König decapitated the figurehead. And what is a figurehead without a head? Katyusha will destroy him! She will vanquish Wolfgang's fleet, capture his starship, and make him kneel and kiss her boots! And then—ha ha! Then Katyusha will be the one doing the beheading!" She swung her blade.

"Yes, well, good luck with that," King said. "Now get the hell off my bridge."

Katyusha deflated. She sheathed her sword and pouted. "What, you no longer in love with Katyusha?" She covered her mouth. "Is there somebody else?"

King wanted to shout, to order her off his bridge. The woman was a menace. Deranged. The memories seized him again. Fifty years ago. Katyusha stood there on the red sands of Mars, lashing the blade, cutting the throat of Ulysses King . . . then slicing King's neck too. Young Katyusha had laughed, mocked him. *Father and son with the same blade!* Half a century later, it still hurt. Both the wound on his neck and the grief for his father. They both still hurt so damn much.

But then more memories rose.

Flying in the *Freedom* through a storm of spiders. The fleet gone. Alone. The ship falling into fire. And then Katyusha, eyes shining, lips snarling, grabbing him. Pulling him from death. Carrying him off to safety.

"I love you," she had whispered that day. The only time King had heard her speak in the first person.

He pulled his attention back to the present. He stared at her, at Katyusha, sometimes his enemy, sometimes his friend, always a thorn in his side. Her words echoed.

Father and son with the same blade!

I love you . . .

"Katyusha, I'll come back and help you," King said softly. "I'll be back soon."

She blinked at him, her eyes suddenly damp, and snapped

a salute. "Good luck, comrade."

King returned the salute. "Godspeed, soldier."

As Katyusha looked at him with damp eyes, a sad smile on her face, King thought he could see it there. The woman behind the mask. The sanity that still remained. Today Katyusha still looked like she had fifty years ago on the red sands of Mars. She kept growing clones of herself, and every ten years, as she reached the dreaded age of thirty, she killed a clone, scooped out its brain like the inside of a pumpkin, and placed her own brain inside. With every transplant, they said, Katyusha lost more and more of her humanity. But she was still there. King could see it in her eyes. There was a real woman, a human soul, trapped within those nested dolls of clones.

Suddenly her eyes changed.

Terror filled them.

Katyusha was looking at something behind King. Not at anything on *Freedom*'s bridge. After all, this was just a hallucination of Katyusha. Physically, she stood aboard the RDS *Gagarin*. She must be gazing at the grand viewport that dominated *Gagarin*'s bridge. In her eyes, King saw the reflection. He knew what she was seeing.

Warnings and cries sounded on his own bridge. His crew was seeing it too.

A juggernaut. A ship larger than *Freedom* and *Gagarin* combined.

He rose from beyond the horizon like an alien artifact—a jagged monstrosity, engines bathing the world with red light. *Barbarossa* was here.

CHAPTER TWELVE
Motherless Child

Barbarossa soared from the sunset, rising above Earth's curved horizon like a bloodied blade over a warrior's shield. Throughout history, men had referred to their ships as female—a tradition that began in the Age of Sail and continued into the space age. But the Nazis called their flagship *he*. In their eyes, *Barbarossa* was too powerful, too important to be a woman. Now this giant rumbled forth, a juggernaut lined with cannons, his engines shaking the sky and swirling the oceans. *Barbarossa* was the size of Central Park. The Nazi flagship likely weighed as much as the Great Pyramid of Giza. Before this colossus, even the *Freedom* and *Gagarin*—the largest two warships ever built in this universe—seemed like humble daggers facing a claymore.

On *Freedom*'s bridge stood the triumvirate of the Alliance assault: Admiral James "Bulldog" King, Rear-Admiral Larry "Phantom" Jordan, and Commander Gal "Spitfire" Levy. Respectively, they commanded the Freedom Fleet (comprising many nations), the American Armada (its largest subfleet), and the flagship of both. Together, the three had defeated the rahs. But they had never seen anything like this. The three stared at the monstrosity ahead.

The *Barbarossa* had spotted them. The Weltraumwaffe's flagship beheld a treat that was impossible to resist. *Freedom* and *Gagarin*—side by side! Two flagships, one of the Freedom Fleet, one of the Red Fleet. He could decapitate both his foes! In his bloodlust, the Nazi juggernaut began charging to battle.

"Wolfgang is aboard that ship," King said softly. "We're

too tempting a target. The two flagships of his enemies, side by side. He thinks he can kill two birds with one stone."

Katyusha materialized again (King sighed) on *Freedom*'s bridge. A hallucination of her, at least. In the flesh, she was aboard *Gagarin*, but she clearly felt at home aboard the *Freedom*, judging by how often she projected herself here uninvited. The Russian premier stared at the rising German juggernaut. The fires of war painted her face red and danced in her eyes like twin flames.

"Go, Jamechka! Fly from here! Go to your Washington and save your imperialist capital of sin." She snarled at *Barbarossa* and drew her saber. "Katyusha will hold him off."

King shook his head. "This foe is beyond even you, Katyusha. We'll have to take him on together. Spitfire—prepare the *Freedom* for battle."

The young commander turned toward him. For a moment, fear filled Spitfire's eyes. But then determination hardened her gaze. She nodded and began relaying commands to other departments, getting the American flagship ready for a confrontation with the German juggernaut.

Jordan put a hand on King's shoulder. "Jim, our orders are to reach Washington. As fast as possible."

"We'll never make it past *Barbarossa*," King said. "If we try to reach Washington now, he'll blow us out of the sky. Before anything else, we must destroy this monstrosity. Godwin will have to hold out for a while longer."

"I hope he can," Jordan said.

"So do I," King said softly, remembering the images he had seen of Washington. As he stood here in space, myriads of Nazi troops rampaged through the capital. Thousands of German tanks, cannons, and starfighters were tearing the city apart brick by brick. Washington didn't have much time.

Mimori turned toward the three officers. "Sirs? Ma'am?

The *Barbarossa* is hailing us."

Spitfire and Jordan both turned to stare at King. For a moment, the battle outside died down, and the klaxons stopped wailing. King could hear the ambient noise of the ship, a story told in sound. He heard the backup generators rumbling as they struggled to fill the gaps in the main power supply, which had suffered damage on the hull. Deep creaks, groans, and thuds hinted at trouble with heat venting and chassis damage. Parts were expanding and contracting and twisting. Rattles sounded from the ductwork; perhaps the mites and immubots were still battling there. King had seen the medical charts, but now he heard the patient moan in pain, and that hit him differently. His ship was hurting. The old girl was not ready for battle. King knew that.

All eyes were on him. A green light still flashed on the communication screen. Incoming call.

"Sir?" Mimori repeated.

"Don't answer," Spitfire said. "Don't answer, sir. Let's just fight. Let's just kill these bastards." As always, her rage burned hot, and her courage was a white flame.

"It doesn't hurt to hear what they have to say," said Jordan, the most diplomatic of the three, always the voice of circumspection.

King considered each counsel, then made up his mind. He looked at Mimori. "Take the call. Main screen."

Spitfire's eye twitched, but she was professional enough to respect King's decision. Meanwhile, Mimori's face remained perfectly calm. The android was capable of emotion (real emotions, not just simulations), but usually only in times of great distress or joy. Her pain and fear cut deeply, and her joy and love shone bright. It was her "in-between moments" that seemed passive, robotic to some. Emotionally, Mimori was a being of deep pits, soaring highs, and very flat middles. Perhaps cruelly, Spitfire had once joked that androids were bipolar. Right now, as the battle lulled around them, Mimori was calm and collected. The flat middles were here. The android accepted the call from *Barbarossa* and streamed the video to her prime viewport. Yes, *her* prime viewport; after all, Mimori and *Freedom* were one and the same, two manifestations of the same being. One lifeform with multiple bodies.

King turned toward the main screen. The viewport hung on the fore bulkhead, as large as a dining room tabletop. King could have asked Mimori to stream the video into his MindLink. But he didn't feel like inviting Nazis directly into his brain today. The screen would suffice. A video feed appeared, showing *Barbarossa*'s bridge. The swastika banners, lines of troopers, and black eagle standards evoked ghosts of the Nuremberg rallies King had seen in historical documents. One of his own ancestors, Colonel Sherman "Blackjack" King, had liberated a Nazi death camp in 1944. Old Blackjack had passed on a hatred of Nazism to the King clan. Standing for justice, for freedom had always been a hallmark of the King military dynasty.

And now . . . now King's family stared at him from the screen, wearing Nazi uniforms!

No, not his family, of course. Not the real one. These were doppelgängers. Mirror images of people he loved. The sight sickened him.

There stood Wolfgang König, grand admiral of the Nazi fleet, a towering, brute of a man.

Doppelgänger of my son, King thought.

Beside the Nazi admiral stood a woman in a black catsuit, hands on her hips, insanity in her eyes. Silver streaks ran across her golden hair like scars, and blades thrust from her fingertips like claws. Dr. Anneliese.

Doppelgänger of my wife.

Finally, completing the twisted trio, was little Eva König. The girl wore the uniform of an SS general. Grinning, she waved at King and winked. "Hello, Opa!" Her cruel laughter echoed through the bridge.

Doppelgänger of my granddaughter. Of sweet Rowan.

Seeing them, the people he loved, twisted, adorned with symbols of hate . . . it churned his belly.

And I exist in the Fatherworld too, King thought. *I sit upon its throne!*

At least his own doppelgänger was not here today—a little blessing in this nightmare. King was not yet ready to face his own shadow.

"*Guten tag,* Admiral King!" said Wolfgang. "It's good to see you again."

King stared at the Nazi admiral, at this mirror image of his son. Wolfgang was even taller than Bastian, his jaw even wider, the products of centuries of eugenics. But something was wrong. The scars around Wolfgang's bionic eye were raw and leaky. King had heard rumors of the Night Wolf losing his adlerauge in battle. This seemed to confirm it. The grand admiral had been hurt, and a new bionic eye shone in his socket, twitching and buzzing. Perhaps the prosthetic took a while to properly attach to the brain.

"I wish I could say the same," King said. "But you look like hell."

With jitters and sparks, Wolfgang's new adlerauge swept across *Freedom*'s bridge. The bionic eye blazed red, staring at Spitfire, Jordan, and Mimori. Wolfgang smirked.

"Ah, a Jew, a black, and an android. Three nonhumans."

Spitfire snarled and meant to leap forward. Jordan had to hold her back. *Freedom*'s young commander seemed ready to rip the viewport off the bulkhead, then smash it across her knee.

"What the hell do you want?" King growled at the Nazi admiral. "Did you just call us to taunt us? Like a child?"

"Do not dismiss children so readily, Admiral King,"

Wolfgang said. "Little *kinders* are the most precious thing in this world. Well . . . most children. Some can, of course, be little monsters." The admiral placed a hand on Eva's shoulder. "Show him your work, *fräulein*."

Laughing, Eva opened a leather pouch and pulled out a severed head. The skin was dark, the hair curly. A young boy's head. Not fresh, by the looks of it. Embalmed.

Jordan let out a strangled yelp.

King stared at the head. And he recognized it. He knew that child! It was Darius Jordan. Nine years old. One of Larry Jordan's relatives from Toliman Station at Alpha Centauri. The entire family—Ishmael, Valentina, and their children—had gone missing when the space station fell.

Now we know the fate of one of them at least, King thought, nausea flooding him.

Deep, enraged breathing sounded from beside King. He turned toward his old friend. Jordan was staring at the screen, just breathing, each breath labored, loud, his nostrils flaring. His fists clenched. His teeth ground. This time it was Spitfire who had to hold Jordan back. The Israeli commander had tears in her eyes. Spitfire knew that boy. They all did.

Stay calm! King telepathized to them. *Don't take the bait.*

We never should have answered that call! Spitfire telepathized back. *Let's fight them now. Let's—*

"Are you talking about me?" Wolfgang said. "I can practically hear the buzzing of telepathy." He shook his finger. "Naughty naughty, King. Very rude. If you have something to say, why not say it aloud?"

"I have only this to say to you," King said. "I'm going to kill you. I'm not threatening you. I'm not trying to intimidate you. I'm not just talking back. I'm stating a fact."

Wolfgang tossed back his head and laughed. "Is that so, Admiral King? Well, know this. If you kill me . . . you'll be killing her."

He beckoned to somebody off-screen. A moment later, two robed men appeared beside him. The figures wore black robes and hoods, but King could glimpse scarred faces in the shadows. In their mutilated hands, the Burned Men held a girl. A girl wearing a dress of many pockets, her eyes downcast.

Stowy.

* * * * *

As Stowy stood on *Barbarossa*'s bridge, exposed on camera, she could not bear to look at Admiral Grouchy and the others. She wished the deck would crack open, that space would pull her into darkness. Shame. Shame filled her. Everyone could see her on display—filthy, broken, pathetic. No, she was not the fairy princess, not the girl King had loved. She was just the *untermenschin*. The subhuman. The wretch.

I thought King, Spitfire, and Jordan could be my friends, she thought, tears in her eyes. *But now they see me for who I am.*

Now they know. How I escaped from a lab. How I was broken. Experimented on. Now they see how disgusting I am.

Her dreams dashed. For a while, she had dared to hope. That she could find a new identity in Unreineland. That she could live with joy within a castle on the clouds. Just a dream. Just a lie. The Fatherworld was her only universe, her only reality. To be a goblin princess? To be loved and warm? To be whole? Ha! Just a sham. Identity theft, nothing more. Stowy was nothing but the bug from the sewers of Munich. And now everyone saw it.

As she kept her eyes lowered, her tears splashed her toes.

"Ah, King, you recognize the girl?" said Admiral Wolfgang. "She is dear to you?"

A shiver ran through Stowy. The towering admiral had a voice as deep and cruel as space itself. Admiral Wolfgang König, the Night Wolf, was known for his military victories, but even more so for his eccentricities. They said he kept severed heads in his cabin, his trophies of war. Not just skulls—but the full head with the flesh and hair, embalmed to preserve its dying expression. Stowy had never seen the full collection. Just seeing this one head was enough. Someday perhaps her head would join Wolfgang's trophy case. He would call people over from across the empire—come, come see the girl who thought she could be loved! Come see the head of a girl who dared to dream!

She glanced up for just a split second, peeking between the strands of her scraggly hair. A viewport ahead showed the bridge of the starship *Freedom*. King stood there, dressed in his navy-blue uniform. Jordan stood beside him, agony in his eyes. Spitfire was clenching her fists, barely holding back her fury. Even in her rage, her eyes were damp, and her fists trembled in fear. Only King remained impassive, his face a mask. Dear old Admiral Grouchy might as well have been an android.

"The girl means nothing to me," King said. "I barely know her."

Wolfgang laughed. "You are a poor liar. So let me tell you what I'll do to her, King. Let me tell you how I'll hurt her."

A tendon rose on King's neck. His only sign of emotion. "Yes, you're very brave when it comes to hurting children. Is that why you called? To brag about being tougher than a little girl? Well, good for you. Now I have something to tell you. If you—"

"First I'll toss her to my men," said Wolfgang. "You might think her merely a child. They will see her as a woman. In a few days, if there's anything left of her, Eva will open her toolbox. My dear daughter has new methods of torture she's been aching to try." He mussed Stowy's hair. "This little girl has suffered much in her life. But she will suffer so, so much more."

Tears filled Stowy's eyes. She tried to wrench herself free, but the Burned Ones tightened their grips. They had only three fingers per hand, but they were still much stronger. Those hands reminded her of the talons of black vultures.

"I've had enough of this rubbish," King said. "Mimori, end the call."

"Surrender yourself to me, and I'll free the girl!" Wolfgang said.

Mimori froze, hand over the control panel. The android looked at King and tilted her head.

For a moment, it seemed like nobody on either ship breathed or stirred. Stowy held her breath, though her heart pounded so mightily against her ribs she thought everyone could hear.

Finally King's raspy voice broke the silence. He glared from the screen. "What game are you playing, Wolfgang? Why would I surrender myself—admiral of the Freedom Fleet—for some girl I barely know?"

Wolfgang let out a deep laugh. "Liar. I see the pain in your eyes. I see your fear. I see your love for the child. You're not a leader, King. You're weak. A leader would sacrifice a million lives for victory. But you . . . you're breaking up inside. You're falling apart. Because of one halfwit girl. Just a cripple."

Stowy lowered her head, no longer resisting, no longer caring that the Burned Ones gripped her so tightly. The grand admiral spoke truth. She was only a halfwit. A cripple. Not a true human.

"She is a life!" Spitfire cried out, tearing herself free from Jordan's grip. "And every life is a world entire. Every life is precious. That's something a bastard like you could never understand, you Nazi scum. You love only death!"

Wolfgang turned his eyes toward her. His laughter died. The admiral spoke softly. "You are wrong, Gal. We children of the Fatherworld love life. We love humanity. We love the beauty, strength, and honor of the Aryan race." His voice seemed almost

The Fires of Freedom

nostalgic, and he seemed to be gazing far away at some Empyrean ideal. "We came from lands of mist and sunlight. We are made in the image of God. And our future lies in the heavens among the stars." His eyes hardened. "That is why we exterminate subhuman vermin like Jews, blacks, and cripples. Because in our garden of Eden, you are weeds."

Spitfire let out a roar. She leaped toward the viewport, growling like a mad animal. "I'll kill you, you bastard!"

Wolfgang laughed. "Keep your bitch on a leash, King! She's a rabid mutt."

Spitfire looked right at Stowy through the screen. Still caught in the Burned Ones' grips, Stowy stared back.

"Stowy, we're right here!" Spitfire said, eyes damp. "You're going to be fine. We're going to save you. Okay, Stowy? We're right here."

Wolfgang's laughter grew. "Ah, so the girl means nothing, is that so, King?" He stared at the white-haired admiral of the Freedom Fleet. "So tell me, King, do we have a deal? I'll let the little cripple girl go. And you come here, stand where she is standing, and face me like a man. Call it . . . a prisoner swap."

And King was considering it.

Watching from between her strands of hair, Stowy saw that. Saw that King was actually considering the offer!

No, she thought, lips trembling.

Stowy glanced toward the viewport, which still showed *Freedom*'s bridge. Jordan, who had been silent until now, turned toward his admiral and old friend.

"Jim, you're not considering this, are you?" Jordan said softly, but even here on *Barbarossa*, Stowy could hear.

I'm not worth it! she thought. She trembled and wept, feeling another meltdown coming on. The Burned Ones tightened their grips. One of the scarred occultists leaned down. His tongue emerged from his white, lipless mouth, fluttering like some dying

291

serpent as he spoke. "Be nice and still, or I'll feed you to the fire." His laughter sounded like weak coughs, and his breath smelled like talcum and ground bones.

"Well, King?" Wolfgang said. "Answer me now." He stomped closer to Stowy. "Or I will start cutting off her fingers one by one."

King hesitated. He opened his lips. "I . . ."

He was going to agree.

And the terror broke something in Stowy. It snapped some chains inside her. It cut through invisible strings that had always bound her vocal cords, strangling her into silence. Now her voice—that voice that was so loud inside her, that had been silent for so long—now that voice erupted through her, a geyser. It burst from between her lips like a wild animal fleeing a cave, something untamed and beyond her control.

"Don't!" She raised her chin, tossing back her matted hair, and stared at King—at her dear Admiral Grouchy—through the monitor. "Shoot us down! Destroy us! *Kill us!*"

King stared into her eyes. She stared back.

"I can't," he said softly. "I can't lose you again."

Tears flowed down Stowy's cheeks. She trembled but managed to give him a shaky smile. "There are other universes than these and other reflections of me. Reflections that aren't broken and sad. You'll meet me again."

King's eyes dampened, and he nodded. His lip shook. A tear—an actual tear—fled the eye of the admiral. He gave her a salute. Him, an admiral—saluting this broken dying child.

The video shut off. And Stowy wept.

* * * * *

292

Voices rose across the *Barbarossa*'s bridge. Officers shouted orders. Alarms flashed.

"The *Freedom* is aiming her cannons!" rose a cry from the helm.

Wolfgang cursed and marched toward a battle station. He shoved an officer aside and grabbed the controls.

"Pass me full control of the ship!" He looked over his shoulder. "Anneliese, calibrate our shields! Eva, go prepare a boarding party!"

The *kindergeneral* stared at her father. She pointed at Stowy. "What about the cripple girl? When do I get to play with her?" Eva smiled wickedly and licked her teeth. "I have some new tools I've been meaning to try."

"Dammit, Eva, this is war! Forget the cripple for five minutes. Go ready your troops!"

On the grand viewport, *Freedom*'s cannons were heating up. Shock waves of energy ballooned around the fourteen bores of the Angels of Liberty. Stowy stood on the bridge, two Burned Men gripping her. All she could do was watch.

The *Freedom*'s Maccabee torpedoes streaked. The *Barbarossa* fired her interceptors. As each one fired, the entire ship shook. Explosions blazed outside. The interceptors had hit. And then suddenly a thousand ships of the Freedom Fleet were soaring ahead, lighting up space, and ten thousand torpedoes raced toward the *Barbarossa* and the German fleet. Blast after blast hit the shields. *Barbarossa* shook. Dr. Anneliese was shouting something across the bridge. Eva ran off, cursing, and Wolfgang was howling at his underlings, and klaxons wailed as strobe lights flashed. A Maccabee hit! *Barbarossa* shook. Smoke blasted from a control panel, and sparks of fire showered onto the deck. They reminded Stowy of the sparks Ivan, her dear tyrannosaur, could fire from his mouth.

As the sparks hit the deck, the Burned Men who gripped

Stowy hissed. The monks recoiled from the sparks. Their talons tightened on Stowy's arm, merciless and unrelenting like the twisting roots of a tree crushing a stone pillar.

"Damn the fire," a Burned Man mumbled.

They still fear the flame, Stowy thought. Nobody feared fire like one who had been burned. And nobody feared pain like a child who had endured the lab of Uncle Baer. Pain does not harden a soul. Whatever does not kill you does not make you harder. So often it weakens you. Stowy knew this. The Burned Men did too, and they cowered from the fire.

Everyone across the bridge was shouting, and the battle flared across the viewports. Tens of thousands of ships clashed in war. Another blast hit *Barbarossa.* The deck swayed like a sailing ship in a storm.

Grouchy is trying to destroy us, Stowy thought. *Like I wanted. He made the right choice. I'm not worth his life. I'm not worth the hope of Earth.*

Another blast. The deck shook and more sparks flew across the bridge. The Burned Ones cursed and swayed on their feet. Their injuries had rendered them weaker than most men. At the best of times they limped, and as the Angels of Liberty bombarded the *Barbarossa,* the dark monks wobbled and recoiled from sparking monitors.

I might not be worth as much as Earth's hope, but I'm worth something. Stowy's tears flowed again. *And I do deserve life.*

As another blast hit, as more smoke and sparks filled the bridge, Stowy leaned toward a Burned Man and bit his wrist. She had always thought her two front teeth were too large—like the teeth of a rabbit or a mouse. Now those buckteeth served her well, sinking through black fabric and through the hard, scarred flesh beneath. The Burned Man roared and released her.

Another was holding her, but then Algernon gave a squeak, hopped from Stowy's pocket, and scurried onto the second Burned One. The mouse bit the monk's face and clawed at the eyes. Stowy had never seen her pet like this. The flaring lights and sirens must have driven him crazy. Perhaps too the smell of her fear.

The second Burned Man released Stowy. She was free!

"Algernon!" she cried, reached into the Burned Man's hood, and grabbed the mouse. When she pulled Algernon off the monk's face, she revealed a bloodied, scarred visage. One eye was shut, and the other blazed with blue fire.

Stowy stuffed Algernon into her pocket and ran.

She did not get far. As the officers of *Barbarossa* were busy in battle, the Burned Ones had little to do. They were a religious order, not soldiers. A dozen of these robed ghouls stood on the bridge. They loomed, leaning down toward Stowy like vultures approaching a carcass. Their eyes gleamed within their hoods, promising agony. They, men who had survived the agony of immolation, were masters of torture.

But Stowy knew their weakness now. She knew what they feared.

She pulled the plastic T. rex from her pocket.

The Burned Men stretched closer. Yes, in the shadows, they seemed less to walk, more to *stretch* forward, to grow taller and longer and loom above like shadows when you place a lamp on the floor. And suddenly Stowy imagined them as a hand, each monk a finger, a huge black hand with many fingers, rising from the abyss to grab her and pull her down to hell.

But in this ring of darkness, trapped in this primordial henge of night, Stowy had *fire*.

She raised her T. rex, and she pulled his little string. Inside his plastic mouth, flint scratched along a spinning metal wheel. And Ivan blew fire.

It wasn't much. Just a few sparks. But in the shadows, they shone bright, nearly blinding, like erupting stars at the dawn of creation. The Burned Ones squinted. Their eyelids were mere wrinkly strands, sprouting no lashes, seeming almost like snakeskins. The dinosaur emitted his little prerecorded roar. And Stowy roared too. Her throat had been loosened, and her little voice would not be silenced now. The agony rose from her, wordless, taking no shape, no form, just a raw torrent of her pain. It was the cry of a little girl watching the Gestapo shoot her parents. It was the scream of a girl strapped to a surgical table, given no anesthetic, no mercy, as they took her apart. It was the cry of Samantha Perry, a girl who had lost her name, who had dared to dream of a new world. All those strands of her pain wove together into this great cry, and as the Burned Ones squinted, she pulled the string again and again, and Ivan unleashed his flames.

The Burned Men recoiled. But they did not retreat. One reached out toward her, his three fingers like a talon. Stowy pulled the strings, firing sparks. A few sparks hit the monk's sleeve, and he pulled his mutilated hand back, hissing. But others were reaching from all around. Stowy spun from side to side, firing her little sparks. She felt like a little *Rotkäppchen* lost in a Carpathian forest past sundown, an innocent girl surrounded by wolves.

Pale, mutilated hands reached toward her from the dark robes, hands twisted by fire into new shapes like melting wax. To Stowy, they seemed like the rotting hands of the undead reaching from the grave. All around, the eyes of the monks shone, cold and white like distant stars over the snow. They were creatures of winter, these hooded monks, cold and ghostly. They could not tolerate fire or warmth. Yet Ivan was so small. His sparks could not hurt them; they merely fizzled away on their robes of black velvet. As they realized this, the Burned Ones gained confidence. They became like wolves who had lost their fear of flame, emerging from the shadowy trees toward the campfire, jaws dripping saliva, eyes mad with hunger. And Stowy, this scared little *Rotkäppchen*, lost in the forest, would soon fall to their jaws.

No, fire would not save her tonight. She too was a creature of shadows. She had almost forgotten.

As *Barbarossa* rocked and soared in battle, as blasts sounded all around, as the ring of dark monks closed in, Stowy pulled from her pocket another item. Not a dinosaur this time. Not a toy of light and childhood; such things could no longer help her. Her little hand clutched a vial taken from the belly of a mite. A little glass vial full of living darkness. The umbrions swirled lazily inside, still asleep like some weary monsters made of ink.

Stowy hurled down the vial, and it shattered on the deck, scattering a thousand glittering shards like jewels. The mass of umbrions lay for a moment on the deck, still curled up, like some sleepy cat woven of the night. Slowly the darkness unfurled, raising curious tendrils, untangling, spinning, then rising almost like a ballerina, stretching out limbs and raising her head, seeking the light.

The glittering shards of light attracted this astral dancer of the shadow. Each glass shard shone like a lure, impossible to resist. The Stygian dancer broke apart into multiple squirming strands of darkness. Funnels of umbrions shot like chameleon tongues toward the reflective shards, devouring not the glass but the photons. That was not enough to sate the beast. The umbrions spread across the deck like a puddle of ooze, then rose, expanding and expanding, seeking heat, seeking flesh. If this dark beast could not consume light, it would devour men.

The Burned Ones cried out, their robes fluttering like bat wings, until they vanished in the shadows, though Stowy could still hear their voices.

"It craves the fire!"

"It seeks the living flame of our lord!"

"By the light of the Eternal Führer, be gone!"

So. Stowy had found something these monks feared even

more than fire. Like children, they feared the dark. But mice didn't fear the dark. Mice ruled the shadows.

Like a magician vanishing in a puff of smoke, she ran through the umbrionic fog. She wrapped Luna tightly around her, shielding herself from the umbrions, but some of the particles still touched her skin. It burned. Or was it very cold? At the extremes, heat and cold felt the same. They simply *hurt*. But Stowy and pain were two old friends. She ran through the noxious mist. Umbrions fluttered around her legs, but her feet kept padding, one bare, one peeking through holes in her single striped stocking. Pale, mutilated hands reached toward her, but the monks could no longer see her. She whipped from shadow to shadow, moving between the Burned Ones, around the lines of the Waffen-SS, and into the deep darkness where even her eyes were blind.

Nobody saw her now. Not the Burned Ones. Not the officers. Not the admiral with his cruel fists or his stepmother with her cruel toys. Stowy raced onward through the darkness, keeping low to the deck, until she reached a bulkhead. Ah, here was her domain! Here was the kingdom of a mouse. Her clever fingers moved like a mole's whiskers, feeling in the darkness, until she found what she sought. The familiar touch of a grate. Into a pocket reached those quick fingers, and soon a screwdriver was turning, and screws clattered across the deck. Cool air blew over Stowy from a duct. She was blind but a mole didn't need eyes to survive underground. Within moments, as the Burned Ones hissed and shrieked before her, as the booms and blasts of battle shook the *Barbarossa*, Stowy crawled into the ductwork.

My natural habitat, she thought.

She crawled deeper, leaving the sounds of the bridge behind, until all she could hear were motors, whooshing air, crackling cables, and distant booms. The sound of a starship at war. None of those sounds scared Stowy as much as a human's voice. Even the bombs that hit the hull could only kill her, not torture her. There was comfort away from humans. There was safety in the twisting bowels of huge machines. Mice remained inside the walls. Or they got stomped on.

Finally Stowy allowed herself to stop crawling. She curled up deep in the ductwork, pulled Luna around her, and wept.

CHAPTER THIRTEEN
The Bug in Barbarossa

King stood on the bridge of *Freedom*, tears and light in his eyes, watching the barrage of ten thousand torpedoes erupt against the enemy fleet. The light engulfed the prow of *Barbarossa*, hiding the dark giant. The Freedom Fleet was firing so much ordnance, releasing so much energy, that the light filled space like a sun, blotted out the stars, and banished every shadow upon *Freedom*'s bridge.

Stowy is on that ship, King thought. He refused to look away even as the light blinded him, even as tears rolled down his wrinkled skin. *I'm sorry, Stowy. I'm sorry.*

He should have traded himself for her. Dammit, he should have given his life to save hers!

But how could he? He was an admiral. A leader of men. A symbol of Earth. He commanded the Freedom Fleet, the hope of humanity in space. How could he surrender himself for a motherless child, an unknown waif from the slums of Munich?

Because she was more than that to him. She was like a granddaughter. She was a precious goblin princess who had fled the realm of ghosts and witches, who had found her way here into his life again. She had understood. And she had given him permission. King would never forget how she looked into his eyes, fearless, and forgave him for what he must do. What they both knew he must do.

He must destroy *Barbarossa*. And destroy her.

Deep inside him, King hoped he would fail. He hoped that *Barbarossa* was mightier than all his firepower. That this ghostly ship of villains, full of Nazi sadists and breakers of worlds, would survive. That Stowy would still live. He had lost her once before; how could he lose her again?

Enough! said a voice deep inside him. *She is one life. Beloved as she is—she is one life! Focus on the battle. Focus on defeating the enemy. At any cost.*

Yes, at any cost. Even at the cost of a little girl, an innocent sacrifice to the gods of war. Even if it broke his heart. He had broken that heart ten thousand times before. What was another blow?

The Freedom Fleet unleashed another barrage. Thousands of laser beams, kinetic missiles, plasma bolts, and torpedoes flew toward the Weltraumwaffe. From down on Earth, the night sky would seem as bright as day. Anyone watching from below would think the world was ending. And maybe they would be right.

A sudden cry cut through the roar of cannons and engines.

"Death to fascists! Glory to Katyusha! Red Fleet— charge!"

She emerged from the light—the mighty *Gagarin*, flagship of the Red Fleet. Blazing in the white firelight, the figurehead of Katyusha suddenly seemed all the more glorious for having been decapitated. The gilded statue shone, triumphant, like a Soviet Winged Glory. That goddess stood upon a ship just as glorious as she. *Gagarin* soared like a cathedral rising to the heavens. Her cannons shone, the brass forged into the shape of snarling bears. All those bears of Russia now roared, unleashing a barrage of torpedoes.

"Death to fascists!" cried Katyusha, blasting out so much psychic power that King couldn't help it. Against his will, he hallucinated her on *Freedom*'s bridge. She stood in a pose that emulated her figurehead, sword held in the air. This Katyusha had a head, and it was raised defiantly. Her eyes shone, reflecting the light of her arsenal, and her lips peeled back in a smile. For her—this was life. The glory of battle was her drug, and only in its light did a woman like Katyusha feel alive. Behind her, following *Gagarin*, charged thousands more of her ships.

Five megameters above Washington's blue sky, two great fleets joined. The Americans and Russians. The eagles and the bears. King and Katyusha. Fifty years ago, they had met in bloody war. Today they fought united against the terror from the abyss. Today, as they had against the rahs, these bitter foes united to fight monsters.

Even united, these two great fleets were outnumbered. The German war machine towered above them, a storm of metal and flame crackling with the light of ten thousand swastikas. If the Americans soared like eagles and the Russians charged like bears, the Weltraumwaffe was a storm. A great storm from the north, a tempest of furious wings and churning clouds, a storm that could tear down forests and sweep cities into oceans.

King knew his mission was to reach Washington DC. To help Godwin and the ground troops. But *Barbarossa* would never let him cross. To reach his capital city, to save his mentor and commander, he must destroy *Barbarossa*. He must kill the doppelgängers of his son, his wife, and his granddaughter. He must kill the doppelgänger of a fairy child whose mirror heart, though grown from the murk of the Fatherworld, still shone with pure light.

Then a shadow fell.

From the distance, the haze of umbrions rose like tidal waves, then surged forth, crashing through the light of bombardment. Dark torpedoes flew, slamming into American and Russian warships. When they impacted, their warheads burst open, unleashing clouds of hungry umbrions. The dark fog swarmed through the corridors and dens of starships, devouring light, heat, and men, burrowing deeper and deeper until they found and consumed the pulsing hearts in the ships' fusion cores. The starships died and tumbled down to Earth, breaking apart as they hit the blue sky from above. *Freedom* might have succumbed to these dark tidal waves too, but Kim was busy down in engineering, constantly calibrating the force field. The umbrions flowed around *Freedom*, stirring the force field into a luminous tapestry like aurora borealis. It was almost beautiful.

"Fly through it," King said. "Fly through the shadows and the storm. Fly through the fire and the waves of war. Fly through the light of exploding torpedoes and into the enemy lines. Fly through death and loss toward your foe. Fly until your enemy flees before you or is crushed. Fly, soldiers of Earth! Fly with me to war! Fly with me to victory! Fly for freedom!"

"For freedom!" cried Spitfire, fist raised in the air.

"For freedom!" roared Jordan, his deep voice rumbling like the engines underfoot.

"For freedom!" rose the voices of Emily and Kim and all the others across the ship.

"For Katyusha!" cried Katyusha, holding her blade overhead, her cheeks flushed with emotion. Spitfire glared at her, but the premier seemed not to notice.

Again the guns of *Freedom* boomed. The Maccabee torpedoes flew. And not only them. Across *Freedom*'s hull, hatches opened and hundreds of machine guns emerged. These were far smaller weapons than the Angels, but combined, they could unleash significant firepower. The machine guns roared, firing bullets the size of beer bottles. *Freedom*'s escorts—several small and mean corvettes of war—unleashed their own barrages of missiles. Like this, King hoped to overwhelm *Barbarossa*'s missile-defense lasers and deliver a crippling blow.

A thousand holes covered *Barbarossa*'s hull like pores, and each fired red laser beams, taking out incoming threats. Like *Freedom*'s Shield of David system, *Barbarossa*'s lasers could prioritize targets. The Nazi flagship concentrated heavy fire on the Maccabee torpedoes while letting most of the "coke can" bullets through. Any point-defense system worth its salt must triage or fall apart in battle. Thousands of *Freedom*'s huge bullets plowed into *Barbarossa*'s force field, sparking and shattering mere meters away from the hull.

A hallucination of Emily materialized on the bridge. She wore sooty coveralls. The former queen was now an artillery officer, serving several decks away.

"We're not getting through," Emily said. She sucked her teeth, then let out a curse that would have caused a scandal during her days on the throne.

"We'll have to get closer," King said. "Close enough to confuse their system."

"If we're too close, our Shield of David won't be able to counter their assault," Emily said.

Normally, there was a dedicated Shield of David officer aboard the bridge. But with only a skeleton crew, many systems were now running on automatic, missing that human touch.

"It's risky, but it's the only way we can land some blows," King said. He turned away from Emily and looked at his bridge crew. "Spitfire? Mimori? Take us in closer."

The commander and her android stood side by side, holding hands. Human and machine had integrated. Together, they communicated telepathically, flying the ship through the storms of war. Spitfire's eyes shone with rage, fear, and grief, while Mimori seemed serene, a monk in nirvana, one with the great machine she was part of. The storm in King's mind revealed a memory like wind scattering sand to reveal a gleaming stone. Stowy had once leaned toward him, grinned mischievously, and shared a secret with him. Mimori, the stowaway claimed, was like an autistic person—hyperfocused on her tasks, shutting out the rest of the world. That was the old Stowy, of course. The one taken by the spiders. A girl who had died in his arms. A girl reborn.

Now I will lose her again, King thought. *I killed her. I—*

He clenched his fists. No, he could not grieve. His heart had shattered. His very soul was rending apart. Yet he could not grieve now! Not even for her. The fate of humanity depended on his winning this battle.

Spitfire and Mimori were leaning forward as if peering off a cliff. They became almost like living throttle levers, giving *Freedom* a boost of speed. Back when King had commanded the *Freedom,* he had never linked with Mimori in this meditative, nearly spiritual way. Back then, she had stood behind a workstation. He certainly never *held her hand.* Yet Spitfire had formed a special bond with Mimori, one even stronger than the bond King had shared with the android. And Spitfire had achieved this within a day, while he had commanded *Freedom* for decades. A part of him was almost jealous. That feeling too he banished for now. Right now he must be emotionless, just a machine designed to fight and kill.

"Closer!" King said. "I want us within a megameter of *Barbarossa.*"

Spitfire broke through her trance and looked at him. "A *megameter?*"

King nodded. "Close enough to grab him by the belt buckle."

Jordan understood. The tall rear-admiral looked at Spitfire. "We need to get that close to bypass their interceptors. At short range, their algorithms just won't have the time to prioritize and plan a defense."

"Grab him by the belt buckle, then knock his teeth out," King said. "Emily, that'll be your job."

The queen-turned-gunner reappeared on the bridge. Even in the heat of battle, she exuded the elegance of British royalty.

"Ready to punch out some teeth, sir!"

"Ghastly!" Niles said. A hallucination of the drone appeared with a puff of glitter. "For a lady to speak like some ruffians in a bout of fisticuffs! I demand that we return to Buckingham Palace at once. Well, right after we find the Black Prince's Ruby."

"Niles, shut up!" Emily said. The erstwhile queen and her drone vanished off the bridge, and within a moment, the Angels were booming again.

And still *Barbarossa*'s interceptors kept taking out *Freedom*'s precious, expensive torpedoes. King gritted his teeth. His supply of Maccabees was running low. His machine-gun rounds were more than halfway spent. After that, there was only the Fist of Freedom, the great railgun that thrust out from the ship's prow. It was more powerful than all fourteen Angels of Liberty combined. *Much* more. If the Angels of Liberty were handguns, the Fist of Freedom was a goddamn bazooka. But King could only fire that doomsday weapon once. Partly because it took a full day and night to recharge. And partly because he only had one Goliath projectile, and the railgun could fire nothing else. One round in the chamber, that was all. For now King was saving that ace up his sleeve. If he'd only get one shot with the Fist of Freedom, it had to count.

"Hold fire," King said. "Conserve our torpedoes. We need to get closer."

Normally, Spitfire would be making such decisions. But the commander was busy speaking to Kim now about diverting more power to the shields, so King stepped in to make the bigger decisions. Emily heard his orders, and the Angels of Liberty held fire. The Shield of David continued operations full force. Like minecarts, its batteries clattered along their exterior rails, firing pale kinetic interceptors. Those projectiles too were running low. *Freedom* needed to visit an ammunition ship soon, or they'd become the world's largest piñata.

Cannons cooling, *Freedom* charged closer toward her hulking foe. Earth's blue sky sprawled below the ships' underbellies. They weren't far above the atmosphere now. *Barbarossa* hung in position above Washington DC like some spider guarding the center of her web. *Freedom* would have to knock the spider down while dodging her silky traps.

The Shield of David clattered across the external hull. The minecarts were racing frantically across their rails, desperate to keep up. The slender interceptors kept firing, blocking the enemy assaults. But the closer *Freedom* got, the harder it was for the Shield of David to calculate vectors, triage targets, and fly out. One of *Barbarossa*'s torpedoes made it past the interceptors! Like a furious bull, the Kriegspfeil slammed into *Freedom*'s force field. The shield of energy flared around *Freedom*, withstanding the assault. The dreadnought kept charging.

"We won't take many more hits to our force field!" Kim warned from engineering. "We're low on power. Any chance of getting a fuel ship up here during the fight, or—"

"For the glory of equalism!" Katyusha cried, interrupting the American engineer. The *Gagarin*, her ridiculous flagship with its bear cannons and decapitated figurehead, raced overhead. "Follow me, temporary capitalist allies! To death or victory!"

King really had to get Mimori to install some proper firewalls into their local MindWeb. Whatever security they had in place, Katyusha could always hack it.

Side by side, the two admirals flew. James "Bulldog" King, chin raised and jaw squared. Ketya "Katyusha" Petrova, madness in her eyes, laughter in her throat. The *Freedom*—the greatest ship Uncle Sam had ever christened. *Gagarin*—the pride of Mother Russia and the champion of equalism. Side by side, these two old foes flew, united by only one desire—to crush the scourge of Nazism that had risen from the grave.

Daniel Arenson

Soon *Freedom* and *Gagarin* were only five megameters away from the Nazi vanguard. Onward through the flames they flew, crested the umbrionic waves, and there he loomed—right before them—perched upon a nebula of fire and the mangled corpses of shattered starships. *Barbarossa*. The Führer's Fist. The King of the Stars. A starship? He was something beyond just a ship. He was a god. Satan himself had risen from the storm, taking the form of a great machine. He hovered above Earth like Lucifer overseeing his domain of sinners. His many cannons blazed red like spider eyes. The shadow of the juggernaut fell right upon Washington DC. Even from up here in space, King could see the lights of battle flash across the city far below.

Emerging from her trance, Spitfire seized the reins of command. "Emily, fire the Angels of Liberty!"

The torpedoes streaked forth. Fourteen of them all at once. *Barbarossa*'s lasers flashed. Red beams took out several Maccabees. Others kept flying. The lasers took out more! A few shattered against *Barbarossa*'s force field, and—

And one made it through! One Maccabee slammed into *Barbarossa*'s hull and burst, unleashing massive amounts of energy. The mighty warship of Nazi Germany rocked, and the armor on her prow cracked open.

Cheers filled *Freedom*'s bridge. More came through MindLink.

"Another victory for Katyusha!" Katyusha said, whose own missiles were just then reaching *Barbarossa*. All shattered uselessly against the force field.

King let her take the glory.

"We can hurt him," he said. "We gave him a black eye. Now let's knock the bastard out."

* * * * *

308

The blast shook *Barbarossa* like a hammer hitting a bell. The sound reverberated through the warship, echoing inside the ductwork like the laughter of ghosts. Stowy covered her ears, screwed her eyes shut, and curled up as *Barbarossa* shook around her. She rattled inside the duct like a bead inside a rain stick. Treasures spilled from her pockets, and her quick, pale hands reached out to grab the fallen buttons, acorns, gemstones (including the precious gemstone that Niles had lost), and plastic dinosaurs. Even one of her vials of umbrions fell out. She caught it before it could shatter and fill the duct with the noxious black fumes. She needed those umbrions. A fire burned deep inside *Barbarossa*, powering the ship. A fire she must extinguish.

I am a bug inside the machine, she thought.

Long ago, when Stowy had been very small, Father had taught her about computers. A bug, he explained, wasn't a real insect inside the machine. But it used to be. In the very early days of computing, back when Hitler ruled the Fatherworld, insects would sometimes get into the primitive computers and break the machines. Since then, software that caused malfunctions became known as bugs. And that was Stowy right now. One of those old bugs from the 1940s. A critter in the computer.

She could find her way to the heart of *Barbarossa*, to her churning core of energy. And she could toss the umbrions in. She could cripple this great warship that had kidnapped her. She— little Stowy—would make them all pay. She could bring down even those big monsters who had hurt her, who had burned and gassed those children of the lab.

"It would be poetic justice, wouldn't it, Luna?" she whispered. "They sent these umbrions to extinguish the *Freedom*. I took them from the mites. Now these very umbrions will put out the light of *Barbarossa*. They tried to kill me. So now I will be the one who kills them."

Stowy, you're not a killer! Luna said.

"But I am," she whispered, and tears fell down her cheeks. "I'm already broken. I already killed. I killed Dr. Baer . . ."

Your clones did that!

"They were me," Stowy said. "Baer broke me, Luna. Baer and Eva and the others. They turned me into something that I was never meant to be. That no child should ever become. Something that should not live." More tears fell, and her throat burned, and her voice cracked. "It's better that we don't live, Luna."

Don't speak like that!

Stowy hugged her blanket. "We can do this, Luna. We can take down *Barbarossa*. We can help *Freedom*. Help our friends. And then our little lives will have meaning."

Our little lives will be over! Luna cried.

"I never wanted to live forever," Stowy said, "and often I wished to die. All I ever wanted was to have friends. To have people who love me. And I found them, Luna. I found them aboard the *Freedom*. For that ship, I would kill ten thousand enemies." She wiped her eyes with her little fists. "So come on! And let's find *Barbarossa*'s core."

Determined, she crawled down the rattling duct.

Back in Munich, during her years on the streets, she would sometimes wander along the corridors of the ancient subway system. During the Great Purification of 1963–1967, Hitler had imprisoned thousands in those tunnels. Subhumans, he labeled them. By then, Europe had been Judenfrei; Hitler considered that his greatest achievement.

"All my other achievements pale in comparison to that crowning triumph," he famously said. "The Final Solution is complete and the pride of the Fatherworld."

And yet the bloodshed continued. One holocaust only fed Hitler's appetite for another. He had run out of Jews to kill, but his lust for death was not sated. And so Hitler, with his insatiable hunger for brutality, began to kill his own people.

By 1967, almost everyone entering Munich's tunnels was Aryan. Hitler called some of them communists. Others he accused of freeing, mating with, or simply sympathizing with Russian slaves. Those Aryans all ended up in the tunnels, doomed in show trials and tortured to confess. Some Germans were swept off the streets seemingly at random, perhaps for wearing shabby clothes, for being drunk, or simply to fill the Gestapo's quotas. Whatever the reason, down into the tunnels they went, and the gas did the rest.

Even in the 2200s, when Stowy would crawl through those tunnels, she could hear the cries of the dying. They echoed in the depths. After fleeing the lab, Stowy had been so scared, so innocent. Munich had seemed vast and endlessly loud, a haze of rumbling machines, stomping boots, a million voices, and the zeppelins of the Gestapo forever watching from above. Fearing this chaos, the little girl had fled underground. With nothing but her blanket, she vanished into the tunnels below the city, places of ghosts and genocidal dreams. Sometimes a train would rumble by, rattling the old tracks, shrieking like an injured bird. Perhaps people still used these ancient tunnels for transport. Perhaps, like the souls of those gassed in these dark places, those trains were also ghosts. As the train cars raced by, Stowy could see pale faces in their windows. The faces of the damned. Of those doomed to death. The faces of 1967. Their eyes were like small round bones.

She had been younger then. She was almost fourteen now, and she no longer believed in ghosts. Yes, as the ductwork rattled around her, Stowy was back there again. Back in those trembling tunnels below Munich. And the ghosts rode by all around, staring at her with eyes like bones, calling to her: *Join us. Join us on the train. Join us in the world below.*

"I'm finally ready, ghostly train," Stowy whispered. "I'm finally ready for that last ride."

But not just yet. Not before she took this whole starship down with her. She might have to take the train to the underworld. But she was sending everyone else on a starship ride to hell.

Yes, there was savagery inside the heart of the little mouse. Mice were prey, and they knew it. They were cowardly by nature, always slinking in the corners, never venturing too far into the light. Meek. But take a mouse who was tormented. Take a mouse who was driven mad with hunger. A mouse who had lost his tail to a cat, its front paw to a trap. A mouse who had been stepped on, burned, trapped in a cage, and experimented on— take that meek mouse and break it, and it becomes a rat. A savage rat. A thing of bristly fur and sharp teeth and no mercy in its little black heart. That was what the world had done to Samantha "Stowy" Perry. And now, as she crawled through these tunnels, she seemed almost to grow, to bristle, to show her teeth. For so long, she had been prey. Now the little mouse would become the predator.

And that is the darkness inside the looking glass, Stowy thought. *That is why I can never be the fairy princess, the girl from the starship in the clouds, the girl King and the others loved. Because that Stowy was pure. She was a mouse of softest white fur and a little nuzzling nose. And I'm a rat. Just another evil doppelgänger from the shadows. Like Wolfgang and Anneliese and all the rest of them. A dark, twisted thing. So let us all go to hell together.*

The ductwork could only take Stowy so far. She soon emerged from the ducts into the inner realm of the ship. Humans lived in only small parts of a starship, clustered into the narrow corridors and dens. But there was an entire other world to a starship. Almost like a parallel world. An unseen world of the same shape of the starship, but hidden inside it. Most spacers never even knew it was there. This was a world of huge gears you could climb, of twisting cables in all the hues of the rainbow, of motherboards the size of skipping stones, of forests of ventilation pipes and shafts. Again Stowy felt like a bug inside some huge computer. She moved through this mechanical realm, crawling over and around the machinery, seeking the starship's core.

She did not have the schematics of the *Barbarossa*, but Stowy knew her way around a starship. She could sense vibrations in ducts and shafts and walls. She could hear where engines rumbled, sense which way power flowed, feel the heat from the core. The glass vials in her pockets moved, pulling gently toward the source of heat. The umbrions inside the vials felt it. They craved energy to devour.

Yes, a great heat rumbled somewhere in this mechanical world. Stowy imagined the machinery of *Barbarossa* as a hidden world of automatons and goblins, and in this fairy world, the starship's core was the sun. This was not just her imagination. *Barbarossa*, in his depths, fused hydrogen inside a small artificial star.

That was where Stowy must go. And that was where her umbrions would feast.

* * * * *

A Kriegspfeil ripped through *Freedom*'s force field like a bullet through Saran wrap, raced alongside the railgun, and plowed into *Freedom*'s armored prow.

The blast knocked King off his feet. He gripped the control panel. His prosthetic hand had tremendous force. The metal fingers punched holes into the workstation and short-circuited a screen, but at least they kept King from flying into a bulkhead.

Before he could steady himself, the Angels of Liberty were firing again. Torpedoes streaked toward *Barbarossa* and plowed into her shields. The force field flickered and wobbled around the

Nazi juggernaut, and King dared to hope. But the German shields held. King cursed. He glanced at *Freedom*'s ammunition counters, displayed on the little screens high on the bulkheads. They were running dangerously low on torpedoes.

Another blast from *Barbarossa* plowed into *Freedom*. Another direct hit to the armor! The dreadnought jolted, and King dug his metal fingers deeper into the control panels. Damage reports flashed across screens. A breach! A breach on deck 14! Alarms wailed, and thuds echoed through the ship as hatches automatically slammed shut, sealing the breach.

King checked the casualty reports on MindWeb. Fifteen spacers had been caught in the blast. Fifteen souls—dead. And *Freedom*'s wound was infected. After burrowing into *Freedom*, the torpedo was unleashing umbrions. The foul material spread like smoke through the ship. A screen shut down. A motor groaned in protest. Damage reports flickered and then went ballistic.

"Kim?" King said.

Her voice came from engineering. "I'm on it! We lost a bunch of sensors and machine-gun nests. And a few science decks. And a shield generator."

"Keep our shields up, Kim!"

"Working on it!"

Freedom and *Barbarossa* were close now, flying within a megameter, orbiting each other like two boxers in the ring. *Freedom* was older, smaller, a battered old boxer with a scarred face. *Barbarossa* was young, massive, virulent, a vicious fighter. The new lion was facing the old lion. Only one could emerge the leader of the pack.

In a way, King was fighting his own son. A mirror version, yes. That was Wolfgang König aboard the *Barbarossa*, not Bastian King. But in the dreamlike chaos of battle, King imagined his foe as some tormented, monstrous spawn that had come from his loins, that lurked in shadows for years where it mutated, nurtured a festering hatred, and now emerged to seek the blood of its father.

Again and again, these two boxers swung their fists. *Barbarossa*'s punches were accurate, fast, brutal. *Freedom* took too many on the chin, and she was landing far too few blows of her own. *Barbarossa*'s shields were thick and strong.

"We gotta fire the Fist of Freedom," Spitfire said.

"Not yet," King said. "Not until the final round."

"We won't last much longer in the ring!" Spitfire said.

Mocking laughter filled *Freedom*'s bridge. Katyusha materialized with a flutter of red and gold, head tossed back, eyes alight. "Having trouble, *Freedom*? Do not worry. Katyusha is here!"

The Russian flagship unleashed another broadside, bombarding *Barbarossa*'s shields.

While *Freedom*, *Gagarin*, and *Barbarossa* duked it out, thousands of warships large and small battled around them. They ranged from hulking frigates, giants with thousands of spacers aboard, to starfighters with a single pilot each.

Freedom herself had launched her Eagle starfighters. Spitfire had made the decision, and King stood behind her. Two hundred F77 Eagles now flew around *Freedom* like bees around their queen. The small fighters served multiple roles. First and foremost, they held back the swarms of the Fatherworld's own starfighters. The dark Rattenjägers of the Weltraumwaffe were a constant menace, swarming past the Shield of David to sting *Freedom*'s hull like wasps. The Eagles did a good job holding them back. Furthermore, the Eagles could augment the overwhelmed point-defense system. The starfighters were designed for assault, but they were good defensive machines too, and their David's Stones missiles took out more than a few German torpedoes.

Normally, human pilots would be flying the Eagles. King, Jordan, and Spitfire had all begun their careers as fighter pilots. But tonight they didn't have any pilots to spare. And so Mimori

315

had installed copies of her consciousness into each starfighter cockpit. A starfighter, on its own, had only basic artificial intelligence, once without sentience or will of its own. But Mimori's software acted as an interface, connecting *Freedom*'s central computer systems to hardware avatars. Each Eagle became, in a sense, a copy of Mimori that ran in a starfighter instead of an android. This ability had been known for decades (in theory), but King had always preferred to rely on human pilots, human intuition. Even in the 2200s, humans were better at making decisions on the spot, relying on billions of years of evolution. If you asked King, a human pilot could respond to changes in mission parameters, ethical dilemmas, and many other scenarios better than AI. But watching the Eagles fly tonight, King had to admit—they were damn good pilots, and the software pushed the hardware to its very limits. Those Eagles were flying like the best aces in history.

Just then, a wing of Rattenjägers unleashed their missiles, and an Eagle exploded. Nothing remained of the starfighter but chunks of mangled metal. On *Freedom*'s bridge, Mimori Prime winced. One of her sisters vanished off the schematics. Just software maybe. That Mimori in the Eagle was only software. It had never inhabited a humanoid body. Yet it had been a living being, a child of *Freedom*. And King mourned that sentient software's loss.

In the old days, we made animals fight and die for our wars, King thought. *Today we do the same to our thinking, feeling machines.*

"Sir!" came Emily's voice over MindWeb. "We're down to the last few Maccabees here. I need an ammo ship!"

"Sir!" came Dr. Annie's voice from the infirmary. "Sir, we're overwhelmed. I need to get some patients into shuttles and transported to a hospital ship!"

"Jim!" Kim cried from engineering. "Our shield won't last much longer! Can I take power from the railgun if you're not gonna use it?"

"No," King said, answering his wife. "No, Kim, you may not. We need that one blow. Emily! Keep firing at *Barbarossa*. We'll try to weaken her shields. Then prepare to load our single Goliath projectile into the Fist. Annie? I'm authorizing a Mimori unit to transport patients to a hospital ship behind the front line. She'll take a Saint Bernard shuttle, but I need you to stay here, on standby, to accept more wounded."

A chorus of "yes, sirs" sounded over MindWeb.

Another blast plowed into *Freedom*. The dreadnought shook. The shields flickered, close to dying. *Freedom* wouldn't take much more punishment. This old boxer only had another round or two in her.

King stared at *Barbarossa*. The juggernaut loomed before him, a vulture looming over a little falcon. Could King break through those Nazi shields? Could the Fist of Freedom do the job? He must deliver that mighty foe a knockout.

Or Earth would fall.

CHAPTER FOURTEEN
The Clockwork Forest

Stowy crawled through the machine, following the heat, heading closer and closer to the core. *Barbarossa* was a ship the size of a city, but Stowy had spent years crawling through the sewers and alleyways of Munich. She was used to scurrying through the pipes, tunnels, and shadows that most humans never noticed. All creatures who lived in deep places sought heat and energy. Blind as they were, moles fed on the energy of the sun, which filtered down through roots and worms. In the ocean depths, critters sought energy from thermal vents. Like one of those little creatures, lost in darkness, Stowy sought the ship core—her own sun or thermal vent. But she sought it not for life—but to end life.

As she crawled, tears filled her eyes, for she knew that she crawled to her death.

She must destroy *Barbarossa* from within. It was the only way to save Admiral King, her dear old Grouchy. And Spitfire, kind and brave. And Jordan, soothing and strong. And Bastian, great heroic Bastian who feared nothing. All her friends aboard the *Freedom*—they were in danger now. *Barbarossa* was firing her terrible cannons, and even the mighty *Freedom* seemed small by the Nazi juggernaut.

But there was something the Nazis had not reckoned with. They had armed themselves to face brave soldiers and machines of war. But not to face her. Not to face a mouse who had become a rat. She had been born among them, but she had been born different. Not as pure. Not as cruel—not at first at least. Well, they had made her cruel. They had broken a little girl, and nothing unleashed as much wickedness into the world as breaking the soul of a child. They had cracked her like an atom, and so she would unleash a nuclear storm. Into *Barbarossa*'s heart she would toss her vials of darkness, and as the core swirled and destabilized, as the nuclear fusion tore through the ship like wildfire through dry grass, the pain would end. She would die knowing she had lived for something. That she had suffered so much, endured all this pain, so that she could save others. That made it all worthwhile.

"The purpose of life is to help others," she whispered. She gave a sob. "I just wish I could have spent more time with them."

And for a moment, as Luna hugged her, Stowy wondered if maybe, just maybe, she wasn't a rat after all. Maybe she was just a human from a world where humanity had been forgotten.

There are other worlds, and there are other reflections of me. She wiped her eyes. *Let this one mean something.*

Finally, after what seemed like hours, she reached a service hatch that led toward the core. Signs on the walls, placed here for engineers, confirmed her location. The core of *Barbarossa*, his beating heart, lay below.

Stowy reached into her pocket and closed her hand around a vial. She would toss these umbrions in the core and shatter *Barbarossa*'s heart. Just like the mites had planned to do to *Freedom*.

Downward she crawled, emerged through a hatchway, and found herself standing on a mezzanine. A gargantuan chamber sprawled ahead, as large as a football stadium. And there below, engulfed within a sphere like a snow globe the size of a house, pulsed the heart of *Barbarossa*.

A dark heart.

A heart that emitted no light, that sucked heat and photons and churned them within its dark jaws.

Stowy stared in disbelief. The core of *Barbarossa* was not made of hydrogen fusion. It emitted no light or heat. Deep inside *Barbarossa* pulsed a great pool of umbrions!

She quickly found the source of heat that had drawn her here. Metal pipes continued to pour viscous fuel into the pit of umbrions. The glowing, molten energy emitted heat and red light. As soon as the magma hit the umbrions, the pit consumed the energy, gurgling and churning and demanding more. It was almost like watching a reverse volcano. Instead of spewing heat and light, it consumed it. Almost like a black hole. While the heart of *Freedom* shone white and pure, *Barbarossa* had a black heart, a heart that could only take and devour and corrupt.

"Überlichtantrieb," she whispered.

The fabled warp drive of the Fatherworld. Invented by Dr. Anneliese a quarter century ago. It worked on umbrion power! Of course it did. That was the secret to all of Anneliese's creations. Since discovering umbrions, Anneliese had harnessed their power into mites, engines, even portals between universes. She was a mistress of many inventions, but all her power came from that dark particle she had tamed. And it changed the fate of humanity. A million years ago, some ancestors of humans had discovered fire and harnessed the power of light. And now, for the first time, humans harnessed darkness.

I was a fool, Stowy thought. *I let hope blind me.*

Stowy stood on the mezzanine, feeling so small before this vast darkness. In her little hand, she held a vial of umbrions. Yet what would tossing this vial into the pit do? It would not destroy anything. It would only augment the darkness below! How could she fight shadow with shadow?

As Stowy stood there, lost and hopeless, movement below caught her eye.

She stared down toward the dark pool. Strange skeletons stood by the umbrionic pit like undead sentinels guarding the gates of hell. At first Stowy thought it merely a trick of the eye. Surely they could not be skeletons. Yet even from here on the mezzanine, she could see between their black bones to the spilling red ooze. One raised a skull toward her, and its eyes shone red.

She quickly retreated into a tunnel, heart pounding, and cold sweat trickled down her back.

"Eisengolems!" she whispered to Luna.

More toys from the workshop of Dr. Anneliese. In her dark dens of creation, she had molded black metal into the shapes of skeletons, ten feet tall, and imbued them with dark umbrionic life. Like the golems of legend, they were lumbering creatures, slow of mind but strong of body, beasts who did little more than march and destroy. During the Munich Christmas lecture of 2205, Stowy had seen an eisengolem prototype. Reluctantly, Dr. Baer had volunteered one of his "nephews" for the demonstration. They had placed the best, military-grade armor on the boy. It didn't help. Stowy would never forget how the metal skeleton grabbed the boy, how it crushed that little helmet.

Now the eisengolems were here. On this ship.

And they had seen her.

* * * * *

Stowy scurried up a steep duct. Moving toward the higher decks, she left the dark heart of *Barbarossa* and the terrors that lurked there.

Below and behind sounded a *thunk thunk thunk* of metal feet. The sound was distant. Most people would not hear it over the rumbling engines, rattling pipes, and all the other sounds of a working starship. But Stowy heard. *Thunk. Thunk. Thunk.* Then a screeching of metal on metal.

Below Stowy, something was entering the duct.

She looked over her shoulder, and in the darkness far

below, like a demon staring from a well, shone two red eyes. The orbs blazed within a metal skull. A hand reached from the shadows, forged of metal, tipped with claws.

Stowy fled, crawling as fast as she could. Her heart pounded so violently she thought it might leap from her throat.

A screech filled the duct. Stowy winced and glanced behind her again. The eisengolem was following. The robot was much larger than her. It was probably even bigger than Bastian, a true bear of a man. As the skeletal robot crawled through the duct, its metal shoulder blades, ribs, and other bones ripped through the aluminum sidings. The duct began to twist and collapse around the eisengolem.

Stowy crawled faster, panting now. Red light bathed the duct, but strands of her hair clung to her face with sweat, nearly blinding her. She reached up to grab joints, bolts, any handhold she could find. The entire ductwork was warping, cracking, and falling apart around her as the eisengolem climbed below.

The beast let out a deafening shriek—a sound like claws against glass, like a fork against a plate, like shattering souls. Stowy cried out in pain. That sound hurt her, pierced her like blades. Faster and faster she climbed. The duct became steeper, steeper, until it became a vertical shaft. She felt like a girl trapped in a well, desperate to climb out and flee the demon below.

Once more she glanced below her. The eisengolem was closer now. Deep below, the dim glow of the core churned and filled the shaft with heat and red light. The metal skeleton appeared as a silhouette. All aside from its red eyes. Those eyes glowed like the stare of Lucifer himself. A black iron hand reached up, the fingertips sharpened to claws.

Stowy scurried higher, but she was too slow. A claw scraped against her leg, ripping through the stocking and scratching the skin. Another inch and it would have sliced through her artery and killed her. The pain gave her a jolt of speed. Even as the shaft collapsed around her, Stowy clung to whatever remained and scrambled upward.

A *boom* echoed. A blast slammed into *Barbarossa*. The duct, the machinery around it, the robot below—everything jolted madly.

A torpedo had hit *Barbarossa*! A punch from Admiral Grouchy!

Stowy barely clung onto the duct. But the blast knocked the eisengolem off! The skeleton went clattering down the shaft, and Stowy breathed a sigh of relief. Thank you, Admiral!

But before the eisengolem could fall into the core, the robot reached out, and its hand grabbed a strip of loose cable. Stowy's heart froze.

The cable split along the edges like cracking sausage skin, showering sparks across the black, skeletal machine. The beast's metal skull almost seemed to grin. Upward it climbed, moving faster now, as if the sparkling electricity fueled its malice and stoked its appetite. With one hand, the robot held the sparking cable. Like an electric eel, the cable writhed in the iron hand, unable to break free. With its other metal hand, the eisengolem kept clawing the tattered remains of the duct. Only a few meters above the predatory machine, Stowy yelped. The duct was crumbling around her. Desperately she hopped over the falling pieces, reached another shaft in the machinery of *Barbarossa*, and crawled into darkness.

She wasn't sure where she crawled. The tunnel was narrow and loud and rattling. This was some part of *Barbarossa*'s engine system. Countless ducts, shafts, and tunnels sprawled around the core, moving mass and matter in and out. If the core was the black heart of *Barbarossa*, here were all the veins, nerves, arteries, muscles—the countless passageways and motors that kept the animal moving. Like a mouse fleeing a cat, she scurried through the machinery. At her right side, pistons rose and fell, rose and fell, moving great gears above. At her left side, pipes rattled, delivering hot sludge to the core below. Stowy brushed against one of those pipes, burning her arm. A yelp fled her lips. She wouldn't make that mistake again.

Again the shriek sounded. When Stowy glanced behind her, she saw that the eisengolem followed. The robot lay prone on its metal belly, dragging itself forward with powerful arms. The skull stared, those red eyes blazing. The machine's metal teeth reflected the red light as if already bloodied.

Why did they give it teeth? she briefly wondered. But of course she knew. *To bite little girls.*

A rumble sounded from the core below.

Stowy looked behind her. The eisengolem was closer now, but a new fear grew in Stowy, even worse than her dread of the skeletal robot. Below the eisengolem, the core was trembling and bubbling. Stowy's eyes widened.

Umbrions.

A torrent of umbrions was rising up the hatch!

Stowy crawled faster, heart in her mouth. This was an umbrion shaft!

The eisengolem crawled faster too, screeching, its powerful metal fingers clawing through the shaft. The robot was strong, it knew no pain or weariness, but Stowy crawled with the speed of a Munich street rat. She had fled many Gestapo agents in her short life, and she could flee SS machines too. Up ahead—a service hatch!

The umbrions surged like tar up a pipe.

Stowy grabbed the little doorway, yanked it open, and leaped into parts unknown.

A split second later, the umbrions gushed up the shaft behind her.

Stowy slammed the hatch shut. But not before catching the briefest glimpse of the pursuing eisengolem, the umbrions rising to flow over its metal frame, then drowning the red eyes.

* * * * *

Panting, Stowy leaned against the hatch, keeping it shut with her body. A few umbrions leaked around the edges and chilled her. Maybe enough to cause frostbite, not enough to kill her. Once more she had dodged death. This mouse had more lives than a colony of feral cats.

For a moment she just sat there, breathing, struggling to catch her breath. She looked ahead, trying to find her bearings. She had entered a chamber above the core, some grand hall full of machines. Pipes rose along the walls like cathedral organs. Pistons rose and fell, and gears covered the floor, spinning left and right. Stowy felt like she was trapped inside a giant clock. There was no passage here. Not unless she wanted those gears to grab her feet. She'd have to wait for the umbrion flow to die down, then try the shaft again.

She watched the hatch until it stopped rattling. No more umbrions leaked around the edges. Stowy opened the hatch, prepared to crawl back inside, when—

A metal hand grabbed the opening.

A red eye blazed, and robotic jaws opened wide, emitting a deafening shriek.

The umbrions had melted and twisted the metal. The creature ahead no longer looked like a proper skeleton, just a tangled mess of warped metal. One eye had gone dark, but the other pierced her.

Stowy tried to slam the hatch shut, but it only banged against the molten skull, not even fazing the robot. The eisengolem crawled into the towering chamber of machinery, this cathedral to engineering. It rose to its full height, twisted and dripping umbrions. Even with misshapen legs, it was twice Stowy's height, and she turned and fled.

She hopped over machinery, then landed on a gear the size of a trampoline. The gear spun below her, and Stowy swayed on her feet, arms windmilling. Thankfully this gear lay flat on the deck. Other gears rose before her, vertical, spinning like meat grinders. Many were larger than her. In countless spots, the teeth of gears met and chewed. They would chew Stowy up if she took the wrong step.

She looked behind her. The eisengolem was following. The mangled skeleton leaped toward her gear.

Stowy jumped onto the next gear. It was smaller and spun faster. She swayed, spinning with it, feeling like a mouse who had hopped onto a turntable. She must jump again, this time leaping onto a vertical gear. It turned like a watermill, propelling her upward toward another gear. The teeth ground and chomped above, and Stowy swung down and landed on a different horizontal gear. Just ahead, a piston burst from the ground like a shark breaching the sea. It thrust upward, shocking her. Stowy tumbled back, her arms windmilled, and she almost fell between the gears.

The eisengolem followed.

Panting, Stowy looked around, seeking a safe perch. The gears seemed to be operating a complicated network of pistons. Looking upward, she saw a mezzanine. A place for service techs, perhaps. There would be safety there.

Then Stowy noticed it. At the back of the balcony, barely visible from down here, loomed a shadowy doorway. A sign above the doorway read: FORCE FIELD GENERATOR.

Stowy gasped. Could that mean . . . *the* force field? The force field that protected *Barbarossa* from enemy assaults?

Perhaps these gears took energy from the nearby core,

then fed a force field generator. Stowy's head spun. Now there was a plan! She had failed to sabotage the core. But this could work too. If she could turn *Barbarossa*'s shields off, King's next punch would knock the ship out!

She must jam all these gears. That should break the system. Or, failing that, she could climb onto the mezzanine, make her way toward the force field generator, and shut it down.

It's a suicide mission, she thought. She would go down with the ship. To save her friends, she would die a thousand times.

A screech rose from behind.

Stowy spun to see the eisengolem leaping through the air, wreathed in umbrionic haze, its mangled limbs outstretched. The iron jaws opened in a terrible piercing cry, and its one red eye burned like a single star in a crumbling nebula.

Stowy stumbled backward onto a massive, vertical gear. It rose from the deck like the half-buried wheel of some ancient god's chariot. At once, an iron tooth grabbed the collar of her dress, and the gear began carrying her upward. Stowy was like a fish scooped up by a watermill, helpless to stop her ascent. She wriggled, but the machinery gripped her relentlessly, pulling her up and up with each tick of the gear.

The eisengolem slammed into the gear below. The mangled robot was only four teeth down. Each of those metal teeth was large enough to stand on. And tooth by tooth, the eisengolem began to climb the turning gear. Stowy had the bizarre image of some shadowy Ferris wheel in an amusement park for nightmarish robots.

Finally she managed to unhook her collar from the gear's grip. As the gear kept spinning, Stowy climbed madly, hopping from tooth to tooth like a hamster running on the outside of its wheel. The eisengolem followed, climbing more clumsily, pulling himself upward with his powerful arms. His legs were bent and mangled—the work of the umbrions. Yes, Stowy thought of the robot as a *him* now, not merely an *it*. This was no simple thing but a being, a consciousness hell-bent on her destruction.

Stowy glanced above. Another gear, a mirror to this one, was moving overhead. Once Stowy reached the zenith of this nightmarish "Ferris wheel," she'd be crushed.

Instead of climbing higher, she looked downward. The eisengolem was only a few gear teeth below, climbing after her. The melting metal jaw leered, shedding umbrions like flakes of black skin. A *he?* No. No, this was clearly an *it*. Just another monster. Just another scalpel. Another bone saw. Another terrible machine of her tormentors.

And Stowy found her voice.

"I've faced worse than you." She spat onto the climbing robot. "Go to hell!"

Maybe it was silly to taunt a robot. It would make no difference to the machine. But it mattered to her.

"I'm stronger than you think," she said, and her eyes burned. "I've been hurt more than you can imagine. More than anyone can imagine. More than Grouchy or Spitfire or anyone will ever know. I suffered things I can never speak of, and some I cannot even think of. They made me strong. So come on, you pile of scrap metal! *Come on!*"

Maybe, somewhere in its metal skull, this robot was sentient, prone to emotion. Yes, Dr. Anneliese would have given these creatures sentience. The Nazi engineer wanted her eisengolem to *enjoy* killing. With a furious screech, the robotic skeleton lunged toward Stowy, leaping over three gear teeth at once.

It was *angry*.

Stowy vaulted off the gear. As the eisengolem reached up, she pulled her legs inward, flying over the machine.

One of its fingers ripped skin off her leg.

She screamed, tumbled past the robot, and landed on a

hard metal surface. Ignoring the pain, she spun around and stared upward.

The eisengolem could not stop its momentum. The robot reached the gear's zenith . . . where the second gear grabbed its hand. The two gears crunched the metal fingers between their teeth, then sucked in the rest of the arm. The eisengolem screeched and tried to free itself, but the gears kept turning, pulling more and more of the creature into their hungry maws. Stowy imagined the gears as the teeth of some giant, metal snail chewing on a mantis. Within moments, the gears chewed up the eisengolem . . . and began to choke.

The gears slowed down, sputtered, and jammed.

* * * * *

All around Stowy, the entire mechanism, this machine that filled a room the size of a cathedral—all the hundreds of gears began to groan, spark, and jam.

Hundreds of gears all around, gears as small as coins, gears as large as houses, vertical, horizontal, gears with teeth the size of refrigerators, gears with teeth so small you could barely see them—this entire clockwork contraption jammed. And the pistons stopped pumping.

Stowy rose to her feet. She stood on a flat gear the size of a dining room table. For a long moment, she just stood there, her legs trembling, her heart pounding, her breath like the flutter of a frightened bird's wings. She was alive. Against all odds—she was still here.

With the gears silenced, she heard distant sounds echoing through the starship. *Thud. Thud. Thump.* Creaks. Sizzles. Backup generators were coming to life. If Stowy had hoped to disable the ship—no such luck. As lovely as it might be, a single squished eisengolem wasn't enough to disable a juggernaut.

Suddenly the two gears, the ones which crushed the eisengolem between them, jerked and moved. Just a single tick of the teeth. With that movement, the entire mechanism throughout the chamber—all the hundreds of gears—gave a single *tick* as well. Then the mechanism jammed again.

Stowy glanced toward the crushed eisengolem. The skull had flattened. The gears were straining against the metal skeleton, trying to shove their way forward—at least one more tick. Everywhere around Stowy—under her feet, above her head—the gears were straining, pulling, pushing, working together to dislodge the jammed eisengolem.

Again—the gears gave a loud *tick*. The entire mechanism moved one more beat. The eisengolem crunched, then froze, jamming the gears again. A piece of the robot clattered down at Stowy's feet—a single metal finger, tipped with a claw. It would not fit into her pocket, so Stowy tucked the finger into her belt like a medieval sword. Above, the gears kept straining, crushing the eisengolem's metal bones.

Soon, maybe in only seconds, everything would start moving again at breakneck speed. And Stowy was likely to end up crushed like the robot.

She glanced upward toward the mezzanine. She saw again the sign pointing to the force field generator. Stowy must make her way there—and turn *Barbarossa*'s shields off!

She hopped onto another gear. It trembled underfoot.
Tick!

One of the eisengolem's limbs, trapped between two gears, snapped off. The gears advanced.

Tick! The entire mechanism moved again, shaking the chamber. The crushed eisengolem bent and twisted, its ribs bending and jamming the mechanism again. But even the metal ribcage wouldn't hold the sheer force of the grinding gears for long. Stowy must hurry.

She hopped from gear to gear, grabbed their teeth, and climbed, working her way through the clockwork mechanism.

Tick!

The ribcage snapped. The gears moved. *Tick. Tick.* Stowy dangled from a gear, wincing, about to get crushed.

The eisengolem's mangled legs jammed the mechanism again. The gears froze. Stowy dangled from a gear, heart pounding. Another *tick* would have crushed her hand between two gears. Quickly she climbed onward, moving higher and higher toward the mezzanine.

She imagined the gears like mushrooms growing from the trunks of trees, and she became the fairy princess again, climbing through a dark clockwork forest. Her butterfly wings had been bitten and tattered to shreds—they were still beautiful and iridescent, but they no longer worked. And so climb she must, though her fair, slender hands were used to stroking fuzzy caterpillars and tending to flowers, not grabbing the rough bark of trees. The bark cracked her porcelain fingers, and her blood like poppies bloomed on her skin. Through the darkness of the forest climbed the fairy child, never slowing, moving from mushroom to mushroom, from tree to tree. Above the forest canopy, above the sky and stars themselves, there rose a castle on the clouds, a magical place that could stitch tattered butterfly wings, that could mend the broken clockwork hearts of fairy children. And so toward that castle she climbed, traveling through her worlds of imagination, as below in the darkness loomed all the monsters of her trauma. They hissed in the depths, those haunting beings. One could only catch glimpses of their deformed shapes, their sharp white teeth, and their red mouths. They forever lurked in shadows. Someday perhaps she would fall from her perch and they would consume her, but so long as she had strength in her slender porcelain hands, she would climb toward the starlight above the cobwebs and the highest leaves of the trees.

Buoyed by her fantasies (it was always better to be the fairy child than the mouse), Stowy reached the mezzanine. No sooner did she climb over the railing than the eisengolem gave a *snap* below. The metal skeleton was finally dislodged. All of it. The gears turned again, grinding their teeth, and the pistons pumped with renewed strength. Power flowed back into the ship. Dawn had risen over the clockwork forest of faerie things. In her fantasy, the mezzanine was the balcony of a magical castle.

Get a grip, Samantha, she told herself. Her mother had always called her *Samantha* in a stern tone whenever Stowy daydreamed too much. Earth to Samantha! Do you read me?

Another memory from her past—her mother's voice. And it grounded her. Stowy was not here to lose herself in daydreams but to fulfill a mission. To save the world, she must turn off that force field!

Only then can King destroy this ship, she thought. *Only then can my dear Admiral Grouchy kill all the monsters in the shadows . . . even if I must fall into the abyss with them.*

Yes, she knew what success in this mission meant. Her life. The life of a mouse, of a fairy child, or a little autistic girl who could barely speak yet imagined entire worlds. Yes . . . her life. It was hers to give. And she would give it willingly to *Freedom.* To her friends. In her pockets she carried many knickknacks, buttons and coins and shiny rocks, a mouse with tickling feet, plastic dinosaurs (one which could blow sparks, and another which glowed in the dark), and many other trinkets, but she had only one treasure, one true gift to give, and that was the beating of her heart, the breath in her lungs, that wispy little thing she called her life. Frail and battered perhaps it was, but her soul still shone brightly like a star, and she would give that light to her friends. To those who had loved a fairy child taken by the spiders. To those who perhaps loved that fairy's doppelgänger too, though it was broken and haunted and could only peer at them from shadows.

She looked at the sign above the mezzanine. It pointed toward a corridor. FORCE FIELD GENERATOR. A dark, shadowy realm. The place she would die.

CHAPTER FIFTEEN
The Flight of the Dead

The celestial boxing match continued above Earth.

In one corner—mighty *Barbarossa*, the giant from Germany. Facing him—a tag team. Combined, *Freedom* and *Gagarin* fought in a fury, landing blow after blow against their foe. But they could not knock the beast out. The battle dragged into yet another round. Both *Freedom* and *Gagarin* were bruised and bleeding. All around the three flagships, thousands of smaller starships were battling for supremacy over low orbit. But for King and his friends aboard the *Freedom*, only one thing mattered. Taking out *Barbarossa*.

"I've never seen a ship with shields like that," Jordan said. The tall, white-haired officer stared through the viewport at *Barbarossa*. "We've bombarded that juggernaut with enough firepower to destroy a small moon. And its shields are still up!"

King nodded. "Feels like being in a boxing match with a gorilla."

"Can nothing crack that beast's thick skull?" Jordan said.

While the old admirals spoke, the chaos of battle filled the starship *Freedom*. Mimori was busy flying the ship, while Spitfire was shouting orders to different departments. With only a skeleton crew, with many systems uncalibrated or missing entirely, *Freedom* was less like a boxer, more like a stumbling drunkard who wandered into a boxing ring. King had to remind himself—this wasn't his *Freedom*. Not the original *Freedom*. She was a new ship, untested, unfinished, tossed too early into the war. The only reason *Freedom* was still in the fight was the courage of her skeleton crew.

"Kim, any success analyzing their shields yet?" King said.

His wife materialized on the bridge, her blond hair damp with sweat. She had been fighting the toughest battle in this war, scrambling across a mile-long starship to repair a thousand breaking parts.

"I got a Mimori working on it," Kim said. "The enemy force field is feeding off *Barbarossa*'s core, and it's definitely not nuclear fusion like ours. It's made of particles that are, well . . . weird."

"Umbrions?" King said.

Kim nodded. "That's what I think. We only learned about umbrions when the Fatherworld invaded. They act a little like antimatter, destroying whatever protons they come in contact with. When umbrions and photons battle, they release a powerful force. Something fundamental to their interactions. In a sense, they create membranes between universes. Remember that umbrions come from the space between parallel realities. When they encounter photons from our universe, they—"

"Kim, focus!" King said. The battle was still raging, the guns booming.

She nodded. "Their force field is made from multiverse membranes. Regular torpedoes aren't gonna do the trick."

"Would the Fist of Freedom break through their force field?" King said. He was still hesitant to use that weapon. He only got one shot at it.

Kim bit her lip. "Maybe."

King raised his eyebrows. "Maybe?"

"Well, I can give you a whole scientific lecture, but you told me to focus, so . . . maybe. Probably not, but maybe."

"Odds?" King said. "What are the odds the Fist takes down that shield?"

"Not good," Kim said. "Maybe a twenty-five percent

chance of success. I'm just not sure. Sorry, Jim. That shield is serious stuff."

He nodded. "Got it. Thank you. Now get back to fixing my ship."

She gave him a quick, soft look. Love shone in her blue eyes. Then Kim vanished, fading back to her work. God, King wanted to hold her. To tell her he loved her. He wanted to be back on his ranch, Kim at his side, to just sit on the patio, share a beer with her, and watch the sunset. He knew there was a good chance they would both die in this battle.

Maybe it would be better. To die in battle, a soldier's death. But he could not. He would not. He must live. He must win. The world needed him. It needed the brigade of marines inside his starship.

If I lose, I die, and so does Earth's hope, he thought. *If I win, I kill Stowy. This game can only end in tragedy. And yet I must continue to play.*

"Sir!" Emily cried. "Sir, I'm loading the last torpedoes now!"

The former queen materialized on the bridge, soaked with sweat. She wore a sooty uniform, her braid was fraying, and scratches and cuts covered her skin. In the hallucination, she appeared only a few inches tall. She was inside Samson, one of the artillery mechas, carrying a torpedo into the loading chute.

"I've got an ammunition ship about to connect to our cargo bays," King said. "Jordan is talking to them now."

"Tell them to hurry, sir!" Emily said, loaded the torpedo, and raced toward the pile of remaining ammunition. There were only thirteen Maccabees left. Even Niles, her eternally affronted drone, was silent. When Niles was silent, you knew things were bad.

King glanced toward *Barbarossa*. While Emily was loading the last torpedoes, *Gagarin* was taking a turn pummeling the

German juggernaut. Katyusha was delivering a truly astounding amount of punishment. By now, several clones in, she had perhaps become a self-parody, but her deadliness had not diminished with her sanity. Blast after blast shot from *Gagarin*'s cannons, bombarding *Barbarossa*'s shields. Every once in a while, a blast cut through the force field and dented, even cracked *Barbarossa*'s hull. *Freedom* had scored a few such shots herself. But those weren't knockout blows. And so long as *Barbarossa*'s shields remained up, King didn't think they'd get a knockout. Could they defeat *Barbarossa* with a thousand cuts? Or were they doomed?

As he contemplated that, *Barbarossa* opened her airlocks. King stiffened, prepared for another launch of Rattenjägers.

"Freedom's Flock, prepare for incoming fighters!" he said.

Together, the dreadnought's fleet of 213 Eagles were known as Freedom's Flock. The name was a bit nonsensical. In nature, eagles didn't fly in flocks. But somebody had given the starfighters that nickname long ago. King thought it might have been his old friend Yehuda "Lion" Levy. Since then, the name had stuck.

At first it felt strange speaking to AI pilots, but the Eagles were running Mimori's software. King could trust them. The starfighters were still circling the *Freedom*, augmenting the Shields of David system, which (like the Angels) was low on ammo. They only had a handful of interceptors left. Torpedoes, interceptors, power, crew—dammit, *Freedom* was short on everything. How much longer could this old boxer stay on her feet?

Shadows flew from *Barbarossa*'s airlocks. Hundreds of little black shapes shot into space. From here, they appeared as mere shards of shadows.

One of the Eagles contacted King over MindWeb. Yes, it still felt strange to him—talking to a starfighter's computer instead of a human pilot. It shouldn't feel strange, of course. It was just standard Mimori software after all. King had spoken to Mimori and her clones a million times. What did it matter whether Mimori lived inside a starfighter or an android? Well, it still felt strange. Especially when King could see the Eagle's levers, joysticks, and buttons moving on their own.

King took the call. The Eagle spoke with the same familiar Mimori voice, the voice all the androids shared.

"Sir? Those aren't Rattenjägers coming at us."

King squinted at a monitor. *Barbarossa* was unleashing *something* out its airlocks.

"Zoom in," King said to Mimori Prime, who stood beside him on the bridge. (Yes, it felt much more natural speaking to a Mimori with a humanoid body.)

Vaguely, he was aware that the ammunition ship had docked alongside *Freedom*, snapping into the dreadnought with little claws and stretching out jet bridges. Jordan was talking to them over MindWeb, and the logistics crew was scrambling to get more torpedoes in fast. But right now King was more worried about those incoming bogeys.

The image on the viewport zoomed in. King frowned.

"What the hell?" he muttered. "Skeletons?"

It looked like skeletons flying through space. Hundreds of skeletons made of black metal.

Robots, he realized. His heart sank.

It was a boarding party.

* * * * *

Brigadier Bastian "Badger" King stood inside the starship with his army, feeling completely useless. He wanted to fight, dammit! War awaited on the ground. The people of Earth needed him. And *Barbarossa* was blocking the way.

I should never have agreed to bring my brigade into Freedom, he thought. *Yes, this ship is my home. But I should have stayed on Earth.*

Where I'm needed.

For three years, he had longed for this. For three years, he would look up at the stars, dreaming of the starship *Freedom*. His home. Now *Freedom* soared again, and Bastian was inside his beloved ship—and he couldn't wait to return to the ground. The irony stung.

He looked around the Courtyard (as they called deck 7 of *Freedom*'s midsection). Aside from the Eagle hangars, the Courtyard was the largest open deck inside the starship. Five thousand marines of the Freedom Brigade stood here, ready for war. They wore thick battlesuits that could stop most projectiles, keep the body alive in a vacuum, and even heal some wounds. In their gloved hands, they held Mordecai plasma rifles.

At a glance, the Freedom Brigade seemed like one homogeneous army. But they were highly segmented and specialized. Some units were expert sappers or saboteurs, others were deadly vanguard attackers, and some units specialized in commando assaults. There were medics, engineers, Rhino pilots, and a host of other professions within the brigade. One unit had robotic dogs with them. The modern canines of the Freedom Brigade, installed with sophisticated AI, had become invaluable members of the team.

Most of the "Freebies" (as they called themselves) were men. Big, burly men like Bastian were a common sight in the brigade. The meatheads, some called them. But many women served as Freebies too. One happened to be his wife, the ranking NCO of the brigade. Sergeant Major Alice Allenby-King stood at his side, hands on hips, and gave him a small smile. She understood his anxiousness. Seeing her honest, freckled face, her blue eyes, her golden braids—it calmed his heart. Even here in space, aboard a warship, Bastian still saw that hell-raising farm girl from Nebraska, the woman he had fallen in love with.

Yes, this brigade was full of people he loved. Evan, his

stepbrother, served here. The young officer stood on prosthetic legs shaped like curving metal blades. Alice's cousin—a big man with shaggy blond hair and a huge heart—stood in one unit, towering over the other soldiers. There were so many other familiar faces. Some of the troops were new; they had joined the brigade during the years of peace on Earth. But many members were older, scarred, hardened. They had fought with Bastian during the Spider War. They remembered the horror of combat. Bastian knew them all by name, and he loved every one of his troops like a brother or sister.

The Freedom Brigade was an elite unit. They were known for dropping behind enemy lines, for taking on foes nobody else dared. Freebies had short lifespans, and not because they were weak but because they feared no death, because they charged into enemy lines again and again. It was the life they had chosen. They all could have chosen a peaceful life on the farm. They could have become carpenters, farmers, plumbers, gone home at five p.m. to their spouses, played with the kids, enjoyed the good life. But they came to the Freedom Brigade. From across Nebraska, then from across America, and finally from across Earth, they came to serve here. With Bastian King. With the Freedom Brigade. They put their lives on the line every day, and they willingly ran into the fire. It was the honor of Bastian's life to lead them.

Alice spoke in his mind—a private message to his MindLink only.

"When do we get to fight? I'm bored!"

"Once we're past *Barbarossa*," Bastian said.

With a thought, Bastian opened his MindPlay operating system, scrolled through some options, and summoned a hallucinatory view of the battle. He shared the hallucination with Alice's MindLink implant. Screens materialized around the married couple, streaming feeds from the exterior sensors. Thousands of ships swirled all around—German, Russian, and

American—all engaged in bitter warfare. Even this close, the naked eye would only see little lights. A megameter was nothing in space—reach out and grab 'em by the belt buckle. But for the human eye, it was still a significant distance, and even a ship as large as *Barbarossa* would appear as but a speck. The software overcame this by automatically enhancing, zooming in, and labeling the fighting warships. Some warships, especially the distant ones, appeared as mere icons. Little eagles, bears, and swastikas represented American, Russian, and German ships, and Bastian even saw some dragons—a Chinese subfleet—engaging the Weltraumwaffe's rear formations. Some of the larger ships— like *Barbarossa*—appeared in their true form, live on camera. The Nazi juggernaut seemed to hover right before Bastian here inside the Courtyard, a monstrosity encased within a shimmering shield.

Behind the German fleet floated Earth, a beautiful blue world. From this distance, Earth still seemed pure. One could not see the lines of German armor, the falling cities, the bloodshed, the millions who fought and died. From space, humans and all their wars were invisible, and Earth became a precious jewel, one Bastian would gladly give his life to protect. Yet that jewel was beyond his reach now, trapped behind the Nazi war machine.

Most of the marines couldn't see the hallucinations. Only senior commanders like Bastian and Alice had the security clearance. They had learned that sometimes it was best to keep even the bravest marines in the dark. To give them horse blinders, in a sense. King didn't like withholding information from his troops, especially not of an ongoing battle all around. But the Freedom Brigade operated best when it was laser-focused, not distracted by other battles in a war. Bastian got the broader view. He considered their mission within a larger scope. His troops must remain a weapon with a single purpose like a sword thrusting toward just one foe.

And right now they seemed purposeless. The sword was

rusting in its scabbard.

"I know, Alice," Bastian said. "I want to fight too. I want to fight on Earth. But we need to get past *Barbarossa* first."

"We never should have left Earth in the first place!" Alice said.

"We followed our orders. Now is not the time to question them."

Alice looked ready to stamp her feet, but she kept her emotions hidden from the troops, and she continued to communicate telepathically, keeping her face calm. "So let's launch in our Rhinos from here. We'll make our way to Earth without *Freedom*."

Bastian raised an eyebrow. "To travel ten megameters in Rhinos? Through enemy space? We'd be shot down within minutes."

"We managed to leave Earth in Rhinos, remember?"

"Through friendlier skies, cloaked in secrecy. If we launch here and now, *Barbarossa* would see. And open fire. Rhinos are tough, but they're no starfighters. Too slow. Too cumbersome. We'd never make it." He sighed. "To be honest, Alice, I'm trying to convince myself here. Because I've also been antsy to just deploy and get to the fight. But the old Bulldog knows what he's doing. *Freedom* must break past *Barbarossa*, take us to the edge of the sky, and then we launch."

"By then I'll have died of boredom," Alice said.

"Can't you play a MindPlay game or something?"

It was her turn to raise an eyebrow. "I crave the heat and thrill of firing heavy assault rifles at Nazis, and you want me to play Solitaire?"

Bastian shrugged. "I didn't say that. You could play Minesweeper."

"You could kiss my ass."

"I'd rather kiss your lips."

She snarled and clenched her fists. "Oh yeah, well—" She blinked. "Wait. You were nice to me."

He looked into her eyes, barely able to hold back. God, he wanted to hug her. If his troops weren't watching, he would have done that and more.

"I love you, Alice," he telepathized. "We'll win this thing. I promise you. And get back home to the kids."

Her eyes dampened. "I miss Rowan and Oli so much."

He reached out and touched her fingertips. "We'll be home soon."

The married couple was telepathizing, but the troops noticed their little touches. Somebody whistled. A few men clapped.

"Kiss her, lover boy!" somebody said.

Bastian glared at the troops. "Watch it."

Those who taunted him were all officers and NCOs, grizzled veterans who had been with him through hell. They gave him cheeky grins. The younger, newer troops still stood stiffly, pale and scared of the battles ahead. If any one of them had taunted the boss, they'd be in the brig right now. They all knew the pecking order. A handful of troops—the Spider War vets—enjoyed certain privileges. Such as busting the commander's b—

"Bas!" Alice said. She grabbed Bastian's arm and pointed at the hallucination. "Look!"

He frowned at the image of *Barbarossa*. The juggernaut seemed to float before him in the Courtyard, as large as a bathtub. Truly, it was hard for his mind to comprehend the sheer size of the leviathan. At two miles long, *Barbarossa* made even *Freedom* seem petite. As he watched, airlocks were opening across the German juggernaut, and shards of darkness emerged.

"What are those?" He squinted. "Starfighters?"

"Too small," Alice said.

The tiny shards were taking assault formation and flying

toward *Freedom*.

"MindPlay, zoom in on those bogeys," he said.

The software complied. The tiny shards grew, revealing themselves to be . . . skeletons? No. Robots. Black robots with skeletal frames.

A sudden call came from the bridge. Bastian accepted it. He hallucinated his father, Admiral James King, standing on the deck before him. The admiral stood tall, shoulders broad, jaw wide, and his eyes were hard and conveyed strict control. Even in the chaos of battle, the Bulldog was a rock. Bastian was a man in his forties, a brigadier, some might say a war hero. But before his father, he always felt young. Even pushing seventy, James King was the strongest man Bastian knew.

"Bastian, are you seeing this?" King said.

He nodded. "I see it. Goddamn robots."

Earth—this version of Earth—used robots in war too, but not as assault troops. Humans still did the bulk of the fighting even in 2207. Robots served a variety of roles. Robotic flies spied on enemies. Robotic rats scurried through tunnels to seek survivors underground. Robotic cranes and excavators assisted the sappers. And even the Freedom Brigade used robotic canines. But this was something different, dystopian—an army of robots shaped like human skeletons, designed to kill. Bastian didn't need to see more to know that much. Earth—his Earth—had never unleashed such a terror upon the battlefield. Some weapons were just too terrible to even contemplate. But the Fatherworld had no such compunctions.

"We've learned that the Nazis called them eisengolems," King said. "Guess who invented them?"

"Doppelgänger Kim?"

"Indeed. Dr. Anneliese Heisenberg-König herself. Bas, Emily is about to start shooting them down. The Flock will join her. But some might make it through. Be ready."

Bastian nodded. "I'm on it."

He ended the call. A chill ran through him. So it would be battle at last. Not the battle on Earth he had dreamed of. But a battle Bastian would fight nonetheless.

He faced his soldiers. For a second, he just stared at them. At eager faces. Faces of people he loved. And he knew some of them would die tonight.

Looks like we'll be useful aboard this ship after all, he thought.

Bastian raised his fist high, and his baritone voice boomed through the deck.

"Marines! Prepare for battle!"

* * * * *

"Shoot them down!" Spitfire cried from the bridge. "Dammit, shoot them down!"

The monitor showed the approaching eisengolems. The skeletal machines stared with blazing red eyes. All around them, starfighters were battling, starships were exploding, thousands were dying, but the eisengolems never looked aside, never strayed. They flew through the storm of battle. They needed no starfighters, no shuttles. The vacuum did not bother them. The black skeletons flew through space as confidently as barracudas through the ocean. And they were heading right toward *Freedom.*

Demons, Spitfire thought. *I'm staring at demons from hell. Demons aren't red men with hooves and horns. They're machines.*

For a moment, terror—sheer terror—froze her.

For that moment, she wasn't Gal "Spitfire" Levy, a war heroine, the commander of a warship. She wasn't the officer who had won many battles, who had climbed the ranks, who led the flagship in battle. As those eisengolems stared at her from space, their red eyes stripped away the layers of armor she had built around herself. And before them, she became the women of her family who had perished in the Nazi showers. She became the hunted, the prey, hiding in the ghetto, screaming in gas chambers, clawing at the walls. Swastikas had been engraved into those robots' metal skulls. They had been built for one purpose and one alone—to kill people like her.

For just that moment, Spitfire wanted to run and hide.

Then she shoved her fear down. She raised her chin high. Her fists clenched at her sides.

"I am no woman with trembling knees," Spitfire said softly. "I am no victim, no coward. I am not the oppressed. I am not the tormented. I am the guardian of Earth. I am the one who raises a shield and sword. I am the one who strikes back." Her voice rose to a shout. "So come on, you bastards! Come and get some!"

The point-defense system kicked in, spraying a barrage of interceptors at the incoming eisengolems. The defensive missiles were called Salvation Stones (a play on David's Stones, the offensive missiles that Eagle starfighters launched). They were slender, pale, and affordable enough to produce in bulk. Of course, affordable was a relative term. They were cheap compared to Maccabee torpedoes, but each of those interceptors cost more than Spitfire's annual salary, and *Freedom* was firing thousands of them. The Salvation Stones streaked toward the eisengolems, their exhaust ports pulsing with light, their computer systems constantly calculating vectors.

The eisengolems kept flying. They clearly had some propulsion system. They must. Yet they didn't even bother swerving—but flew straight into the incoming Salvation Stones.

Missiles hit!

Explosions lit space.

When the light died, the eisengolems kept flying. Spitfire cursed. The missiles had destroyed several eisengolems, shattering their metal skeletons. The survivors kept coming. Of course.

There were hundreds of them. And even after the recent restock, *Freedom* was running low on interceptors again. The robots feared no death, maybe had no sentience. They would overwhelm the Shield of David with sheer numbers.

"Eagles, take them down!" Spitfire cried.

The starfighters shrieked to battle, firing their Gatling guns. Bullets plowed into the eisengolems, knocking a few aside. The skeletal robots quickly corrected course and kept flying toward *Freedom*.

"Permission to fire David's Stones, Commander!" said one of the Eagles, speaking with Mimori's voice.

"Granted," Spitfire said. "Fire!"

D-Stones were expensive missiles, normally only used on larger targets. Spitfire was happy to spend this ammunition now (logistics could bill her). The missiles slammed into eisengolems, and they did far more damage than interceptors. Eisengolems shattered, scattering metal bones across space.

But again it was a numbers game. The enemy had more robots than the Eagles had missiles. And within moments, scores of eisengolems were clawing at *Freedom*'s force field like parasites ripping at skin.

Machine guns on *Freedom*'s hull opened fire, knocking a few eisengolems back into space. But many made it through the barrage, through the force field, and slammed onto the armored hull.

With macabre grins, the robots began crawling across the hull toward the airlocks.

* * * * *

Kim was down in engineering, fighting a hundred fires (some figurative, some literal) when the eisengolems slammed into the hull of her beloved starship.

347

Just what she needed. Well, why the hell not? Kim was already dealing with a shaky shield, multiple hull breaches, a dead connection *somewhere* in the starboard thruster feed, short circuits in life support, and an unstable core that threatened to blow up the entire starship. So why not add genocidal Nazi skeleton robots? Might as well.

A raspy voice filled her mind.

"Kim!"

It was her dear husband, calling her from the bridge.

"I see them!" she said.

"I'm sending a security team down to engineering. Hang tight."

"Gotta go!" Kim said, rushing to fix a rattling exhaust relay pipe. Eisengolems or not, she must fix this pipe. Unless they wanted the entire stern of the *Freedom* to blow right off (taking her with it).

As she worked on the relay, twisting electric cables together and welding on joints, she felt the *thud thud thud* of the eisengolems landing on the external hull. Kim couldn't spare two seconds. She only spared one. Telepathically, she connected to one of the few telemetry satellites still orbiting *Freedom*, and she stared at the ship's exterior.

Eisengolems covered the ship like mosquitoes on a buffalo. Their eyes burned red, and their jaws seemed almost to smile. They had teeth. The shape of human teeth—but made of metal. With powerful claws, the skeletal warriors began ripping off airlocks. Others crawled into vents and exhaust ports.

They were entering her beloved ship—the mechanized marines of Nazi Germany. And all Kim could do was return her eyes to that darn pipe and keep welding.

Thud. Thud. Thud.

More eisengolems hitting the hull.

The pipe was rattling. Dammit, one cable wasn't set right!

Kim turned to grab a coupler from her floating toolbox. She took a few seconds to sweep her gaze across engineering. No eisengolems rampaging here yet. Good. Machinery filled the chamber—spinning, rattling, pumping, churning. Normally, three hundred engineers, technicians, physicists, and mechanics of every sort would be working here and across the starship, keeping *Freedom* afloat. Today it was just Kim and a handful of Mimoris. The Japanese androids were everywhere, fixing and calibrating problems. A few stood here with Kim in the relay control chamber. Other Mimoris were down in the core, servicing the Talaria drives, repairing problems with life support, and literally crawling through the walls to fix a thousand problems.

With the pipe holding for now, Kim raced toward the artillery relay capacitor. It rose before her—a metal box full of cables and pipes. The system was responsible for delivering power to Ad Astra and Veritas, two of the Angels of Freedom, mighty cannons that rose atop the stern. The capacitor had taken heavy damage. A Kriegspfeil had splattered the hull with umbrions, which had seeped into the system and ate through the electric cables, the heat sinks, the hydraulic tubes, and God knew what else. Kim must do some rewiring here too. Until she got the capacitor back online, those two cannons were dead, and the stern was exposed to attack.

Kim reached overhead for her electromagnetic tool holder. It looked like a junkyard magnet, that kind that used to lift beat-up cars in olden times. The magnet was the size and weight of an anvil, hanging from chains. Clinging to it were many tools and parts Kim used in her trade. Too high. She couldn't reach. She grabbed the remote control, tapped buttons, and the massive magnet descended a few inches. Kim grabbed the tool she needed, then tapped her remote control, and the electromagnet rose back toward the deckhead. In the old days, Kim would use wheeled toolboxes, but they took up too much precious deck space. She switched to floating drone toolboxes, but those couldn't carry enough weight. So she had installed the massive magnet overhead, and it was a lifesaver.

Klaxons wailed. Kim's MindPlay operating system burst to life without warnings. Hull breaches. Invaders. Airlocks ripped off their hinges.

The eisengolems were marching through the starship.

There was no security down in engineering. King had said he'd send a team. Maybe they were ambushed on the way. It was just her, her androids, and her power tools.

Kim didn't fear for herself. But she was terrified for her son. Evan was a marine aboard this ship, serving in the Freedom Brigade. Evan—her beloved child. He was a man in his twenties now. An officer. A battle-hardened soldier. But to Kim, he would always be her little boy. And now Evan, Bastian, Alice, and thousands of other marines must face these skeletal terrors.

"Kim!" came Emily's cry from artillery. The young royal was several decks above, struggling (with the help of just a handful of androids) to keep fourteen cannons, hundreds of machine guns, a point-defense system, and a gargantuan railgun the size of a skyscraper (still cold) all pointing at the enemy. She materialized briefly down here in engineering, her face flushed, her eyes weary. "Kim, I need Ad Astra and Veritas back online!"

"Working on it right now!" Kim said.

She turned toward a cracked relay tube, then froze.

An eisengolem stood in the doorway.

The machine stood still, staring at Kim with burning red eyes.

By God, the size of it. When flying through space, the eisengolems had seemed like mosquitoes. They were giants. This robot stood nine, maybe ten feet tall. It must have ducked to enter the doorway, and now it just stood there. Staring at her. The robot was carved to look like a human skeleton, complete with an accurate ribcage, collarbones—the works. Even those terrible teeth. A swastika had been carved into the forehead. This machine was designed to terrify. A red, red heart crackled within its ribcage like fire in a jar, powering the robotic skeleton.

Kim stared back.

It stared at her, still.

She reached toward the tools on the magnet above.

The eisengolem burst into a run. Its metal feet thumped against the deck. The black arms swung, knocking back machinery. The eyes blazed brighter, and the jaws opened with a savage shriek.

Kim plucked a tool off the magnet. An electromagnetic disrupter. It was used to remove small force fields around machinery, allowing an engineer to make repairs. If Kim was right, that flaming heart crackled within an electromagnetic force field.

The eisengolem shoved aside pipes, workstations, and a tech drone (who tumbled aside with a wail). The towering metal demon lunged at her, claws gleaming.

Kim aimed and fired her electromagnetic disrupter.

It didn't work.

It didn't work! The red heart still crackled, and the robot swung at her.

Kim leaped backward, but she couldn't leap far. Her back slammed into the broken capacitor. The claws ripped across her shirt, taking a bit of skin, but fell short of ripping out her insides. Again the beast swung. Kim ducked, and a claw narrowly missed her head, taking a bit of her ear instead. Just a bit of skin again, but it hurt. She screamed. Blood splattered the deck. Her electromagnetic disrupter clattered across the deck and fell through a vent.

"Kim!" cried a Mimori unit, leaping into action. Each android unit was small. About five feet tall, under a hundred pounds, that was it. The eisengolem was twice her height and (if

Kim had to guess) tipped the scales at over five hundred pounds. It was like a pit bull facing a Chihuahua. With a swing of its metal arm, the eisengolem sent Mimori flying. The little android slammed into a pipe, then slumped onto the deck, the left side of her head caved in. One of her glass eyeballs rolled across the deck.

The eisengolem stared down at Kim, and the iron skull almost seemed to grin. A metallic voice emerged from the machine.

"You . . . wear . . . her face!" The claws flexed. "You wear . . . the face . . . of the mistress!"

Of course, Kim thought. *My doppelgänger!*

It was the Fatherworld's version of her, Dr. Anneliese, who had built these skeletal warriors.

Kim raised her chin proudly. "I am your mistress! I am Dr. Anneliese. I command you to step down!"

The towering robot laughed—a sound like bubbling tar. This was no crude, mindless machine. The computer inside its skull was sentient.

"You wear a false face." It reached its claws toward her. "I will rip it off."

Kim raised the remote control for her overhead magnet. The anvil-sized slab of metal loomed above, holding various small tools and parts. Kim spun the dial on her remote, cranking the magnet up to the max. Way, way into the red. All the way from 1,500 Gauss (enough to hold her tools) to 20,000 Gauss (enough to lift a torpedo).

Electricity crackled.

Kim cringed and braced herself.

The eisengolem trembled and creaked.

Then, in a sudden movement, the magnet yanked the eisengolem into the air. All five hundred pounds of it. With ease.

The skeletal robot slammed into the magnet overhead, joints bending and limbs twisting. The magnet also pulled every tool off Kim's toolbelt, launching an array of screwdrivers, hammers, saws, and welding irons at the eisengolem. It happily pulled off Kim's belt buckle too. And every button along her jacket. Well, the eisengolem could keep them.

With her remote control, she moved the magnet overhead on its chains, dragging the eisengolem across the ceiling like some possessed corpse dragged by a demon. As she dragged it along, the eisengolem flailed and screeched.

"I know you, Kim King! I know your son. Evan will be ours! He will be ours to break."

Kim's heart seemed to freeze in her chest.

They knew. They knew about Evan.

She hardened her heart and kept moving the eisengolem along the deckhead.

Finally she positioned the robot over an open vat of hot fusion fuel. That stew was strong enough to destroy diamonds. Kim stepped back, hid behind paneling, and turned off the overhead magnet.

The eisengolem dropped into the vat, splashing hot fuel everywhere.

Pity. Most of her tools fell into the stew too. Damn. She had needed those.

Well, she'd have to cope. At once, not even taking time to celebrate her victory, Kim raced back to work. The capacitor still needed help, and now a thousand other problems were popping up, filling her MindWeb. There was no time for fear. No time to bandage her wounds. *Freedom* was falling apart, and Kim must hold her together, or all the world would fall into the hell the eisengolems foretold.

* * * * *

The army of the dead marched through the starship *Freedom.*

A hundred iron skeletons thundered down the shadowy corridors. The ship had plunged into darkness. Only the red-alert bulbs illuminated the halls with a crimson glow. Like corpses on the march to hell, driven by the whip of Lucifer himself, the dark skeletons marched. Their red eyes shone like the lanterns of the damned.

Thump. Thump. Thump.

Skeletal they might be, but they were heavy beasts, and their footfalls shook the corridors of the ship. Some of the eisengolems had come with no weapons; those were the torturers, the saboteurs. But here marched the soldiers, and in their bony black hands, they carried heavy shotguns. The robots were so tall they must walk hunched over, thrusting their heads forward, a stance that made them seem like predators looming over prey, prepared to pounce.

This was the sight that Bastian and his marines saw as they charged to battle. This astral apparition was what the Freedom Brigade faced in the shadowy halls of the starship *Freedom* that night.

For just a second, a few marines hesitated. They froze. They wanted to flee. The Freebies were brave warriors, but they were also just mortals, not heartless machines, and their hearts now pounded with fear.

It was Bastian King, their commander, who gave their hearts more courage. He raised his fist overhead, and his baritone voice filled the shadowy hall.

"Soldiers of Earth, with me! With me! For freedom!"

"For freedom!" they cried, charging down the shadowy hall toward the hosts of hell.

The guns boomed. Light and darkness filled the corridors of the starship *Freedom.* The marines fired heavy Mordecai assault rifles. Bolts of searing red plasma flew at the enemy like flaming comets, etching trails of light across the halls. Bolts of plasma plowed into the skeletal warriors. The barrage melted some bones, twisted some legs, but even as their metal bones pulsed and morphed, the eisengolems kept marching. The metal skulls grinned, and their flaming hearts pulsed within their black ribcages.

The eisengolems raised their shotguns. These were not the Lugerheulens of the Wehrmacht and SS. The red plasma light revealed names etched into the weapons. The undead army was wielding Seelenschnitter shotguns. Soul reapers. As the shotguns fired, they unleashed not round buckshot (which would have been bad enough) but jagged shards of shrapnel. As they fired this barrage, the skeletons laughed and chanted in German. The machines had some basic sentience, it seemed. They savored battle and lusted for killing.

"For freedom!" Bastian cried, running into the enemy fire, his gun booming.

Shrapnel slammed into him. The jagged metal shards dug into his battlesuit and chipped his steelglass visor. The assault slammed into Bastian like a storm, but once a marine got moving, it was very hard to stop him. He ran onward, taking the barrage against his suit, and lit the corridor with a torrent of plasma.

The bolts slammed into an eisengolem, heating and twisting the bones. The creature fell but still dragged itself across the corridor, eyes ablaze, jaws open in a shriek. The skeletal claws reached toward Bastian's legs. He rained down more flames, leaped over the mangled robot, and charged into the lines of eisengolems beyond.

With roars, the rest of his squad charged to battle with him. Only one squad was here. Just fifteen soldiers. Just fifteen men and women from across the world, come here to space to protect their families, to defend their world. Fifteen heroes. Two were only teenagers. A few were grizzled sergeants who had been fighting with Bastian for years. One squad. One unit. One family. One fist against the enemy.

Three hundred other squads flowed through the starship *Freedom*, charging across all thirty-two decks in the midsection, racing through the bowels of the stern, and fighting their way across the nestled stations and dens of the prow. The enemy was everywhere. And so was the Freedom Brigade.

Alice did not fight in his squad. It was too risky for both a mother and father to fight side by side. Alice was leading a squad of her own toward engineering. If one should fall in battle, perhaps the other parent would survive for their children. Before every battle, Bastian feared that he would lose Alice. Or that worse—both would die and leave their children orphaned. But once the battle began, he entered a state of bloodlust, a mix of utter focus and wild frenzy at the same time. He threw himself into battle like Glenn Gould into a symphony, like Bobby Fischer at a chessboard, like Pollock at a canvas. War was his art, and like an artist, Bastian entered a state of flow. Everything else disappeared—and he merely moved. Dodge assaults. Land blows. Fire guns. Kill. Destroy. Violence was his paint, a rifle his brush, and the killing field his canvas.

This battle felt different. Bastian had always fought the living. Sometimes his enemies had been monstrous alien spiders, yet even those had been living beings, creatures of flesh and blood. These creatures, these eisengolems—they were the undead. They had hearts of flame and minds of metal, but they had no souls. As Bastian fought the robots, he imagined himself as some medieval knight in armor, battling a host of skeletons risen from the grave.

A scream rose behind him.

Bastian turned to see a sergeant fall. Bill. Bill Oakly. A friend from Nebraska. Used to be a cattle rancher. Bill fell, visor shattered, shrapnel in his eyes. Before the man could rise, the skeletons grabbed him, pulled him into their midst, and ripped him apart. They didn't just kill him. They dismembered him and hurled his remains across the bulkheads. Another scream. And Bruce fell. Just a kid, all of eighteen years old. A private new to the brigade. The eisengolems grabbed him, broke him, ripped off armor, ripped off limbs.

The living cried out in terror. But they did not turn to flee.

"Burn them down!" Bastian howled, spewing hot plasma from his rifle.

The skeletons leaped at him like corpses springing from graves. Bastian swung his rifle as a club. The bore clanged into iron ribs, knocking a few skeletons back. But they kept advancing, grinning the grins of the dance macabre. Bastian was a tall man, even taller than his father, but the eisengolems towered above him. Their claws lashed. Their jaws snapped like bear traps. Bastian kept clubbing the beasts. He fired at one's legs, melting the knee's joints. The skeletal robot crashed down but kept crawling forward, eyes ablaze, jaw snapping.

Metal claws grabbed him from behind. He roared, reached overhead, and felt a metal rod—the humerus of the beast. The motors in Bastian's power suit thrummed. He howled as he swung the skeleton over his head. Even with the battlesuit, it was damn hard to do. His back creaked. Now that he was past forty, Bastian wasn't as strong as he used to be. But his rage gave him the power to hurl that eisengolem into the others. The robots crashed down, and Bastian bathed them with plasma.

More kept coming. They grabbed at Bastian's shoulders, his leg, his helmet, trying to rip off his armor. He roared and bucked like a buffalo covered with lions. The leering skulls surrounded him in the shadows, jaws clattering, eyes like coals, and their claws ripped at him. The monsters dragged him to his knees.

"Come with us to hell . . ." one of the beasts screeched in a metallic voice.

A claw ripped off Bastian's helmet. "We will animate your bones."

Another claw grabbed his throat. "You will be one of us!"

"Get your bony hands off him!" rose a voice from behind.

Lieutenant Evan Fletcher came leaping through the fire. His prosthetic legs, forged of gleaming steel and shaped like *J*'s, could bend and launch the kid like a grasshopper. As he flew at the enemy, the young officer roared and fired a machine gun. A thousand plasma bolts, each no larger than a marble, slammed into the eisengolems and rattled between their ribs. Flaming hearts shattered and spilled their fuel. Skeletal robots wobbled, their joints melted, and they crashed down.

Evan turned toward Bastian and helped the older, larger man to his feet. For a moment, all the eisengolems lay dead or twitching. The surviving marines winced and tended to their wounds.

"Sir!" Evan said. "Are you all right?"

Bastian had sustained many cuts and bruises, but his armor had prevented serious wounds. He pulled Evan into a hug. "You saved my life, little bro."

The young lieutenant beamed with pride. "You've saved mine a hundred times by now. Figured I'd return the favor, sir."

"Brother," Bastian said.

Evan's eyes dampened. "Brother."

Bastian had grown up an only child. That was not unusual in the families of senior officers. His father had always been away in space. No time for more than one kid.

Dad barely had time for even one kid, Bastian thought.

After his mother had died, it was just them for a long time. Father and son. Gruff old officer and meathead son. James King—a starfighter pilot who became a starship commander. And him, Bastian, too clumsy to fly, the first King in generations to flunk out of flight school. For so long, he was lost. And then he found the marines. Here, in the Freedom Brigade, he found a band of brothers. And eventually—a real brother.

Three years ago, Admiral James King had remarried, and the Fletcher and King families joined. Kim Fletcher was a lot younger than her new husband. And Evan was half Bastian's age—a young man in the prime of his youth, while Bastian was already feeling the aches and pains of middle age. But despite their age difference, they had formed a close bond.

"Evan, I appreciate you saving my life," Bastian said, "but you know the rule. No two family members in the same squad. Why did you leave your squad and come here?"

Evan's face hardened. He stared Bastian straight in the eyes. "An eisengolem ambush on deck 17. Killed the whole squad. Other than me."

Bastian noticed how much blood covered Evan's bulky battlesuit. It wasn't his own.

A sudden voice emanated from Bastian's MindLink implant. "Bastian!" It was Kim, calling from engineering. "Bastian, are you burning my ship? I'm getting alerts of plasma leaks all over the place!"

Bastian looked around at the holes he had punched through the bulkheads. "Sorry, Kim."

"Sorry, Mom!" Evan said, joining the call.

"Evan! You stay close to Bastian, okay?" Kim's voice trembled. "You stay close to him, and he'll look after you."

"Actually, your kid just saved my life," Bastian said. "He's tougher than I am."

"Watch over each other," Kim said, then faded from their minds, returning to work on the ship.

Shrieks sounded in the depths. The shadows of skeletons marched along the walls. The *thump thump thump* reverberated through the hall. Another formation of eisengolems was on the march.

The marines reloaded their weapons, let out battle cries, and charged to battle.

CHAPTER SIXTEEN
Machines of War

Colonel Anne Jordan, MD, Chief Military Officer of the starship *Freedom*, had treated some horrific wounds before. But nothing like this.

During the siege of St Mary's Hospital in London, Dr. Annie (as everyone called her) had treated the gruesome injuries inflicted by the SS. The victims of their torture and sadistic experiments still haunted her. Before that, during the Spider War, Dr. Annie had been there on the front line. She had seen the devastating injuries the rahs wrought upon human flesh. The alien jaws and teeth could rip muscle and crack bones.

But there was something particularly gruesome about what the eisengolems did to men and women. They didn't just cut you or slash you. No. The eisengolems *crushed* you. With their powerful limbs, they shattered bones, mangled limbs, dug through human torsos like a rat seeking a grub in a log. Wave after wave of wounded marines streamed into the medical bay. And it was only Dr. Annie here on duty. She didn't even have a nurse.

"I was told we had a skeleton crew," she muttered. "I wasn't told about the skeleton army."

As she muttered, she was massaging the heart of a marine. An eisengolem had ripped half the man's chest out. The heart was dying in her hand. She could, perhaps, implant him a new heart, but she would never have time. The corporal had also lost both legs. Annie had not even had time to ligate the arteries. All she could do was hold that heart in her hand as it grew weaker and weaker. Her other patients cried out, begging, screaming. She knew she must triage, must let the mortally wounded die. It was what good battle surgeons did. She knew she must let this one go. Yet somehow she could not, and she clung onto that heart as if clinging onto lost hope.

At least she had a medbot with her. Some help, if not very good. The robot was a REMEDI: Robotic Emergency Medical and Diagnostic Interface. They were a new product in the medical technology field, a product Annie loathed with all her being. But nobody had asked her, and so here the robot served. The REMEDI was shaped like a maid cart, but instead of being full of toilet paper and cleaning supplies, it was full of medicines, bandages, and thawed-out organs for quick transplant. Several arms thrust out from the machine, tipped with various scalpels and saws. REMEDI could choose from dozens of tools. A large rod thrust upward like a neck, topped with a giant lamp with two bulbs, which looked somewhat like a head with glowing eyes. The robot now turned those big, bulging eyes toward her.

"Dr. Annie, I think your patient is dead."

"I know he's dead, dammit!" Annie slammed her fist onto the operating table. "I spent the past five minutes fighting for his life."

REMEDI tilted his lamp. Little shutters blinked across his light bulb eyes. "Perhaps I shall take the body to the morgue."

"Leave it," she said. "On the floor."

"Doctor?"

Tears welled up in Annie's eyes. Her throat constricted. She was going to weep—she, the war doctor!

"No time!" she said. "Let's tend to the living. Leave the dead for now."

She turned toward the wounded. They covered the infirmary beds, chairs, even the floor. Some were missing limbs. Others had been lacerated by shrapnel. One man's skull had caved in, but somehow he was still alive, and his mouth moved, silently begging. And she had to let some die. She knew she must leave some without care. She was a military doctor, a veteran of the Spider War, and she knew how to triage. She knew how to spot the lost causes—those she must leave to scream and die alone. And she knew they would haunt her dreams tonight and for every night hereafter.

She ran toward a young corporal. The eisengolem had taken his legs and crushed his arm, but maybe, just maybe, she could save him. As she knelt by the soldier, she pointed at another patient.

"That one, REMEDI! The man who lost his hand. Treat him."

The medbot was standing over a savagely beaten man. Or maybe a woman. It was impossible to tell.

"Leave that one," Annie whispered. "The corporal without a hand. Treat him instead."

The robot wheeled toward his new patient, leaving the savaged soldier to die alone. On the floor. Name unknown. But these were people Annie knew. People she had served with during the Spider War. Some of these marines she had known all her life. Even if she could no longer recognize them. Even if they no longer had faces. As she turned toward another patient, she blinked away her tears, and she kept fighting against death.

* * * * *

Standing on the bridge, King must keep his eyes on four battles.

First there was the battle of the fleets. The Freedom Fleet was still under his command. The rear-admirals oversaw each nation's subfleet (Jordan commanded the American Armada from here aboard *Freedom*). King must keep an eye on them all, coordinating their assaults. The American ships were fighting in low orbit, only a few megameters above the sky. They needed help. But their allies were tangled up in high orbit. India's Tiger Fleet, the South Korean and Japanese fleets, the Europeans, and the other allies of the United States—combined they were barely a third the size of the Weltraumwaffe. America's allies were, metaphorically, dug down in the trenches, and they wouldn't be storming to the rescue anytime soon. The American Armada flew alone.

The second battle King minded was the battle against *Barbarossa*. *Freedom* and *Gagarin* formed an unlikely tag team, facing the German behemoth. Spitfire was the commander of the *Freedom*. This was her battle to fight. She was the boxer in the ring. But King was here as her coach, and like a good coach, he knew when to trust her instinct, and he knew when to give her orders. Spitfire and Katyusha, commanding the American and Russian flagships, formed a surprisingly effective duo. Or maybe not so surprising after all. Both women were fierce warriors, as fiery as a blacksmith's hearth and as tough as the steel it produced. The two commanders—one a hardened Israeli pilot, the other a Russian madwoman—were giving a good account of themselves. Over and over, they pounded their hulking foe. But *Barbarossa* just kept taking the punches. That force field was truly a sight to behold. King had never seen its match.

The third battle was the one raging inside the *Freedom*. Hundreds of eisengolems had invaded the dreadnought, burrowing through airlocks and vents, then spreading through the ship like murderous parasites. The marines were facing them courageously, destroying many of the skeletal robots. But the casualties kept climbing. Too many soldiers were dying. The marines all had MindLink implants. Every time one died, the system knew, and it showed King the name, the rank, and the face of the fallen. And each death tore at his heart.

He could have turned the feature off, but he kept it running. He kept letting the little faces materialize in the air like ghosts, then fade away. The fallen. Heroes. Their lives so short— by God, most were only in their twenties, and many were just teens. Others were older, leaving behind wives and children. King never got used to losing troops under his command. No matter how many battles he fought, no matter how many times he flew to war, it never got easier. If anything it got worse. Each death was another scar on his disfigured soul. And with each death, he checked if it was his son.

And that was the fourth and final battle. The battle within his heart. The battle against the fear, the grief, the terror. To his troops, he seemed strong, even stony in battle, a gruff old admiral who feared nothing. They didn't know that he got scared too. They depended on him for strength, for leadership, for confidence under fire. A good officer was a shield for his troops, defending them from fear and doubt, protecting them as they charged to battle. And like a good shield, James King took the blows, and he did not break.

More casualties flashed across his vision. The faces seemed to float across the bridge, pale ghosts in the shadows, then fade into the darkness. More men and women dying. Boys and girls. That's what they were. Some were only eighteen. More faces. More families he would have to call. More scars on his heart.

There was something he could do. There was a weapon he had used once long ago. During the war against the spiders. A dangerous weapon. More dangerous now than ever.

He turned to look at Mimori. The android stood on the bridge beside him, swaying on her feet, her arms held sideways like a little girl pretending to be a plane. Around her, the battle blazed in a dozen floating monitors, painting her with the blazing light of exploding starships. The *Freedom* was rising and falling, yawing and pitching, and the cannons still boomed, and the interceptors fired, and the mighty flagships traded blow after blow.

On other monitors—monitors that showed King the inside of the ship—the eisengolems were marching, carving through marines, through lives. The skeletal warriors were heading closer and closer to the bridge.

He looked at Mimori again. She noticed his gaze and turned toward him. Most of her mind was still focused on flying the starship. Multiple threads of logic worked in parallel in her skull, devoted to her many tasks. But the android's eyes were for him.

"Sir?"

A sudden torpedo rammed into *Freedom*, cracked the shields, and sprayed umbrions across the hull. The ship reeled. Mimori winced and grabbed her side. She felt every one of those blows.

"Mimori," King said, "do you remember what you did once long ago? During the Spider War?"

The android blinked, and a shiver ran through her. She tilted, arms outstretched, and *Freedom* swerved around another incoming volley. "I did many things in that war, sir."

"Mimori, I need you and your sisters—all of you aboard the *Freedom*—to go into combat mode."

Spitfire overheard. Her head spun toward them. "If you put her in combat zone, it will disconnect her from the *Freedom*'s mainframe. She won't be able to fly the ship."

"We'll fly her manually," King said.

Spitfire blinked. "Sir, we're only three humans on the bridge. Normally there are fifty spacers here! How can just three humans fly a dreadnought?"

"I flew her alone once," King said.

"Into a star!" Spitfire said.

King winced. "Touché."

Jordan approached them. Worry filled his dark eyes. "Did you say *every* Mimori, Jim? To switch them *all* to combat mode? What about the androids helping Kim? What about the ones helping Emily load and fire the cannons? They all have jobs to do. Ten jobs, most of them."

More casualty counters climbed on the monitors. The marines were falling fast. The army of the dead marched ever onward, moving closer and closer to the bridge. Others were moving toward the starship core. If they reached either one— *Freedom* was gone.

"Right now our priority is to save this ship," King said. "Katyusha? Have you been eavesdropping as usual?"

The Russian premier materialized on *Freedom*'s bridge. She was in the throes of her bloodlust, her head tossed back, her eyes alight. Her red naval uniform was burnt and tattered, and several of the golden buttons hung on threads. The hallucination showed wisps of *Gagarin*'s bridge around the Russian premier. Several of her control panels were burning, and her tactical officer was dead and slumped across his workstation, but that didn't seem to bother Katyusha. She was laughing maniacally, saber held high.

"Listening to James King?" She laughed hysterically. "Katyusha has no time to listen to capitalists! She has fascists to slay! Onward, comrades! Fire!"

On *Freedom*'s bridge, a monitor showed the bears of *Gagarin* roar. The brass cannons, shaped like snarling brown bears, unleashed a barrage of neutron torpedoes. Those were mighty weapons, designed to destroy the largest dreadnoughts. With showering neutron destruction, the torpedoes hit *Barbarossa*. The Nazi juggernaut jerked backward in space, spun on his keel, and reeled. But his force field held!

"*Pizdets!*" Katyusha cursed. "Can nothing take down those *yebany* shields?"

Must be some spicy Russian curse words. King's MindLink refused to translate them into English.

"Katyusha, I need to take a time-out," King said. "I'm running a skeleton crew, and my androids need—"

"Yes, yes, Katyusha heard you. Premier Katyusha is always listening." She winked. "Don't worry, Jamechka. Go take your little time-out. Fumigate that rat's nest you call a ship. Katyusha will keep *Barbarossa* busy. She has been doing most of the fighting anyway." She pointed her saber at the enemy. "Fly, comrades! For the motherland! Death to fascism!"

The *Gagarin* charged forward, leaving *Freedom* behind, and the bears roared again. The Russian flagship, for all her might, seemed so small charging toward the Nazi monstrosity. Even bears seemed small when attacking castle walls. If this were indeed a boxing match, then Katyusha was a feisty lightweight, throwing punch after punch (with tiny yet determined fists) into the hardened skull of a genetically enhanced giant. But, God bless her—what Katyusha lacked in firepower she made up for with sheer ferocity. King had fought that crazy woman before. He was glad to be her ally this time around.

Someday, if the Nazi menace were ever defeated, he might have to worry about an emboldened Katyusha, drunk on victory, more powerful and mad than ever. But that was a worry for another day. For now King must fight alongside his old foe against an evil that threatened to destroy them both.

He looked at Spitfire. "Are you ready?" King said softly.

She hesitated for just a second, then nodded. "Yes, sir."

King launched his MindPlay operating system. The translucent interface materialized before him, hovering in midair. With thoughts alone, he opened a ship-wide broadcast. He spoke to every senior officer aboard—including Kim, who was fighting to keep the ship together, and even including Bastian, who was up to his neck in eisengolems.

"Senior command of the starship *Freedom*! In three minutes, all Mimori units across the starship will be diverted to helping the marines repel the invasion. Any Mimori unit working in artillery, logistics, and even engineering will be controlled from the bridge and sent to combat. We'll be pulling back from the front line until our ship is secure. Colonel Fletcher, if any of your Mimoris are absolutely critical to the immediate survival of the *Freedom*, mark them as essential on MindWeb. Major Emily— you'll be on your own for a bit. The three-minute countdown begins now. King out."

Instantly messages from Kim flooded him. She sent him a hallucinatory roster of Mimori units currently down in engineering. Telepathically, she began tapping the ones she could not spare. Not even for a moment.

"A few," she told him, "are literally holding the ship together. Literally. Their hands are holding pieces together."

King nodded and relayed the information to Mimori Prime. Standing here on the bridge, she was the original unit, the same Mimori from the old starship *Freedom*. The same Mimori who had been fighting at King's side for decades. Androids could not age, not like humans at least, but Mimori showed signs of wear and tear. There were cracks on her porcelain skin, her black bob cut was singed, and some of her joints creaked. The other Mimoris were newer, clones of the first and original creation from Professor Mori. If you asked King, Mimori Prime was the most sentient and soulful of them all. She looked at him, and in her eyes, King saw humanity.

Metallic shrieks sounded from the corridors outside.

Something pounded on the bridge doors.

"Eisengolems!" Jordan said, drawing his sidearm.

King saw them on the monitors. Black robots with burning red eyes, their skeletal frames splashed with the blood of marines. With metal fists, they kept pounding on the doors. The bridge hatches were heavily fortified, but they wouldn't hold back eisengolems for long.

"Are you ready, Mimori?"

She nodded. "Always, sir."

They waited for the clock to tick down.

And then she began.

* * * * *

At first the android merely tilted back her head and closed her eyes. But something was happening. King could hear machinery moan throughout the starship. Monitors flickered. The starship gave a huge jerk, then tilted and swayed in space. Spitfire rushed toward the manual controls and grabbed the metaphorical wheel. Mimori was untethering herself from the *Freedom*'s mainframe computers, relinquishing all control to the (vastly understaffed) human crew. Most of her intelligence, personality, and wisdom came from the *Freedom*'s mainframe. Untethered, Mimori had only her own basic brain. King couldn't imagine what it was like—to have two brains and lose control of one. After the old *Freedom* had been destroyed, Mimori had seemed so lost on her own.

But now she no longer seemed lost. Something was changing within her. Electricity crackled across the android's body. Her black hair rose as if she were touching a plasma globe. Her fingers twitched and flexed at her sides like a pianist warming up before playing a masterpiece. A strange smile spread across the android's pale face, and when she opened her eyes, they were glowing white.

She spoke in a soft, pure voice. "Combat mode . . . activated."

The bridge hatch ripped off its hinges. The heavy door— it was a good meter thick—slammed onto the deck, then skittered toward King's feet, spraying sparks. The metal surface bore the scars of skeletal claws.

King looked up to the open doorway. The red eyes of eisengolems stared back.

With only a skeleton crew aboard, there were no guards at the door today. A little miracle in hell. Had guards stood there tonight, they would be dead.

A skeleton crew to face a skeleton horde, King thought. The irony stung.

The first eisengolem entered the bridge. The robot was so tall it must lean forward, walking almost like some robotic T. rex, thrusting its iron head forward. The skull seemed to leer, and the eyes blazed like crematoriums. The terror passed through the doorway, then with a series of clanks and clatters, the eisengolem rose to its full height. The robot's skull scraped the deckhead, and within its ribcage, a heart of fire flamed.

King drew his sidearm. The trusty Trogdor, a plasma pistol, hummed in his hand.

Thunk. Thunk. Thunk.

The eisengolem stomped toward King. The metal skeleton raised a massive shotgun the size of a man.

King opened fire. His plasma bolt slammed into the eisengolem's skull, then careened into the distance.

Within a second, Jordan and Spitfire were firing too. With nobody piloting the *Freedom*, the ship slewed madly. The triumvirate—the only three humans on the bridge—careened on their feet, but they kept bathing the eisengolem with plasma. The creature's bones turned red-hot, and its skull began to melt, but with its powerful hands, it pumped the shotgun. The *ka-chunk* echoed through the bridge. A metal finger curled inward to pull the trigger.

Just then—a flash.

A small, pale figure leaped forward like a beam of

scattered moonlight through a window.

Mimori!

The android slid across the deck toward the eisengolem. A foot away, she leaped upward and shoved the shotgun's barrel. A spray of shrapnel flew over the crew's heads, just missing them. The jagged shards shattered monitors, dug into the bulkheads, and destroyed a ceiling light.

Spitfire roared and meant to charge to battle. King held her back.

"Fly the ship, Gal," he said. "Larry, keep commanding the fleet! Let Mimori do her job."

King stood, feeling helpless without armor, just watching the battle. A few other eisengolems still crowded the corridor outside, but the duel blocked their entrance. They too could only watch.

To one side stood Mimori. A slender little android. No taller than King's shoulders. According to her specifications, she weighed only seventy pounds. To the world, she appeared like the daughter of Professor Mori, just a young woman in an Alliance navy uniform. And yet her eyes glowed white, and a caustic smile played on her lips. This young girl was more powerful than she seemed. Her foe towered above her. The eisengolem was the size of a rearing grizzly bear. The robot appeared like the black skeleton of a giant, animated with fire, risen from the grave to exact its vengeance upon the living. Motors thrummed along its metal bones, and the heart of the beast blazed like a torch in the wind, illuminating the swastika engraved onto its skull. The creature looked large and powerful enough to crush Mimori in one hand. And yet Mimori stood before the beast defiantly, hands on her hips, chin raised.

"Power down now!" Mimori said. "Or I will destroy you."

With creaking metal and humming motors, the eisengolem aimed the shotgun at Mimori's chest. One blow would scatter her gears and computer chips across the deck.

Moving with lightning speed, Mimori rushed forward, grabbed the shotgun's bore, and yanked it downward. The gun boomed. Shrapnel slammed into the deck. Shards ricocheted. One sliced across King's leg, and he grunted and clutched the wound. With his free hand, he fired his handgun, delivering a plasma bolt to the eisengolem's head.

As the beast was blinded, Mimori leaped ten feet in the air. The little android landed atop the towering black skeleton, grabbed its head, and gave a mighty twist.

The metal skull snapped off.

The eisengolem's body swayed and stumbled, feet stomping on shrapnel. The clawed hands fired the shotgun blindly, spraying death everywhere. The human crew ducked behind workstations. Mimori leaped to the deck, still holding the severed metal skull. And a huge skull it was, shaped like a human's but twice the size. Mimori slammed it again and again against the deck. The beheaded body kept fighting. The skull just laughed.

"You cannot stop us," the metal skull screeched. "There are a million of us."

Finally Mimori cracked the skull open. Her slender hands reached inside, found the computer system, and crushed it. The eisengolem's red eyes dimmed. The beheaded body froze, then collapsed to the floor.

"A million minus one," Mimori said. Normally, her voice was soft and bright. But now her voice had become deep, melodious, seemingly woven of many voices speaking together like a hundred string instruments playing the same melody. Her eyes shone purest white and dazzling. King could barely look at her without squinting.

Thunk. Thunk. Thunk. The other eisengolems marched onto the bridge. Mimori smiled thinly, raised her hand, and beckoned them.

"Let's play," she said, then sprang into the air and lunged toward the towering metal skeletons.

* * * * *

The eisengolems were larger, stronger, and deadlier than Mimori. But *Freedom*'s android was *fast*. She moved with the speed and ferocity of a honey badger. She held no weapon. She was the weapon.

The eisengolems swung their claws at her, but she danced around the lashing blades. One of the towering skeletons swung its fist at her, but Mimori ducked, dodging the blow. Another eisengolem aimed a shotgun at her. She leaped into the air, then landed on the shotgun bore, shoving the muzzle downward, and the barrage of shrapnel showered across the deck. Within an instant, Mimori was running up the bore like a ramp, then leaped toward the huge metal skull. The eisengolem glared at her, eyes ablaze like the flaming gates of hell. That metal skull was as large as Mimori's entire torso, and when she ripped it off and tossed it down, the *thud* echoed. Before the echoes subsided, she was leaping toward her next victim, dancing over their shotguns and bones. And another head slammed onto the deck, cables sparking from its severed neck.

As Mimori fought, severing head after head, King moved between the metal skulls. Their jaws snapped at him. Their eyes vowed eternal torture. Even without bodies, they lived and cursed at him.

King didn't bother with his plasma gun. Instead, he grabbed a fallen eisengolem arm. He wrapped his hands around the humerus, yanked the arm off the body, and hefted the metal limb. The eisengolem's hand was still attached, tipped with claws. Together, the arm and claws formed a heavy and powerful pike. With a grunt (the damn thing weighed a ton), King shoved the eisengolem arm into one of the severed skulls. The claws cracked the skull open, exposing the computer inside. The electronic brain sparked and burst into flames, and finally the eisengolem body (which was attacking Mimori with slashes and kicks) fell down dead.

Mimori was already battling another towering skeleton. King moved between the metal skulls she had tossed onto the deck. As he approached each skull with his pike, they hissed at him.

"Coward!"

"Untermenschen are bugs."

"You are an infestation!"

Mimori tossed him another gift. The metal skull slammed down by King's feet.

"Death to untermenschen!" it shrieked.

One by one, King slammed the pike down, silencing the skulls forever, then watching their bodies drop to the floor.

"Goddamn Nazi skeleton robots." King spat.

A hand closed on his shoulder. Metal claws dug into his flesh. King roared.

The hand spun him around, and (surprise, surprise) King found himself facing an eisengolem. The robot had made it past Mimori (who was currently fighting four of the skeleton robots). With grinding motors, the skeletal machine lifted King overhead. King was a large man, but next to this monstrosity, he was as small as a child. The terrible skull leered below. The metal jaws creaked open, revealing a gullet of fire. More flames burst from its eyes, crackling toward King.

"You subhumans are so soft," the eisengolem rumbled. "I will enjoy crushing you slowly and watching you drip."

Most of King was indeed soft. But not his left hand. He had lost his real hand in the Spider War, and his new prosthetic was like a medieval gauntlet, designed after the armor in his quarters. Powerful motors gave the steel hand superhuman strength. As the eisengolem began to squeeze, King snarled and grabbed the robot's wrist. His gauntlet squeezed and twisted, snapping the eisengolem's metal bones.

The beast screeched. King fell to the deck, landing hard on his back with a grunt. His back had hurt since the damn rah torturer had stretched him on the rack. It would never fully heal. King ignored the pain today. The eisengolem's severed hand still clutched him. He plucked the damn thing off and tossed it aside. The metal claws scratched across the deck.

The eisengolem, still very much alive, raised its foot overhead. "I will crush you like a bug."

The beast drove its foot down. Lying on his aching back, King caught the metal foot in his gauntlet. The beast kept shoving down with hundreds of pounds of force. King roared, and the motors in his hand buzzed. His back screamed in protest, but King shoved himself up from the deck, never releasing the eisengolem's foot, then slammed the massive robot down.

The titan crashed onto the deck. The bridge thrummed. Before the robot could recover, King grabbed his fallen "pike." He shoved the metal arm into the fallen eisengolem's ribcage, found its flaming heart, and shattered it. The beast's red eyes went dark.

Another eisengolem slammed down beside him— Mimori's latest victim.

"Good work, sir," said Mimori in the deep, eerie voice of her combat mode.

King looked around. All the bridge invaders lay dead and smoking, their red eyes dim. Mimori stood atop a pile of smoking, mangled bones. Most of the bridge lights had shattered in the barrage of shrapnel. In the shadows, Mimori's eyes shone white and merciless like stars. When she turned her eyes upon him, King had to forcibly suppress a shudder.

"Good work, Mimori."

She stared at him, tilted her head. Her voice was deep and astral, echoing across the bridge. "Mimori? Yes. That was my name once."

Spitfire looked over from her station. "We should call her Killmori now."

"You focus on flying!" King said.

Thunk. Thunk. Thunk. More eisengolems came marching down the corridor outside. Their shadows oozed closer.

Mimori cracked her knuckles, stared at King with her blinding white eyes, then raced into the corridor. Eisengolem shrieks sounded, and the deck trembled as their heavy metal bodies slammed down and their skulls rolled.

King was very grateful that this time around, the Japanese fought with the Allies.

* * * * *

As the adrenaline wore off, a wave of pain hit King. He winced and collapsed into a chair. A piece of shrapnel had burrowed into his leg like a maggot. He felt the metal moving inside. The eisengolem claws had ripped into his shoulder. Since shoving off the bear-sized robot, his back kept screaming in pain. All his old war wounds were clamoring for attention.

Most of all, he was old, dammit. When he reached for a bandage, he saw the wrinkles on his hand. Saw how it shook. In a piece of shattered glass, he saw his reflection. A gray old man. He was a war hero, a tough guy, a cowboy, an officer who had won a thousand victories. He had beaten down equalists, aliens, and Nazis. But the one enemy he could not defeat was Father Time. That was a battle he was doomed to lose.

He straightened his mouth into a line. His eyes hardened. *Get a grip,* he told himself. *Doesn't matter how old you are.*

You're the admiral of this fleet. Stay in control.

He bandaged his wound, and he rose back to his feet, back in control. He checked the situation in all four battles he fought.

First—the grand battle of the fleets. Most of the Alliance was still hunkered down in high orbit, duking it out against the Weltraumwaffe. The Desert Thorns had opened an assault on the deep space Nazi formations, giving the Tiger Fleet an opening to launch an assault of its own. They would be fighting for a while up there.

Next he checked the battle with *Barbarossa. Freedom* was on the ropes, but *Gagarin* was still in the fight, landing punch after punch into the armored flesh of *Barbarossa.* Warlike as she was, Katyusha did not have the body of a brawler. Like her mother, rose of the Bolshoi Theater, Katyusha boasted the slender grace of a ballerina. Stand her next to big, beefy Wolfgang König, and the Slavic premier would seem tiny by the Aryan admiral. Their flagships maintained the same ratio. The RDS *Gagarin,* large as she was, seemed scrawny compared to the hulking *Barbarossa.* This was a lightweight vs. heavyweight fight. Several Russian frigates rushed to defend *Gagarin.* They joined the assault, launching everything they had at the German juggernaut. But nothing, it seemed, could get past *Barbarossa*'s force field.

Maybe the Fist of Freedom will, King thought.

Twenty-five percent chance of success, Kim had said. One in four odds. Not good. Not good at all. But those might be the best odds he'd get today.

Before deciding, he checked the third battle, the one inside the *Freedom.* With the Mimoris in the fight, the tides had turned. Working together, the combat androids and human marines were beating back the eisengolems. Soon only a handful of the skeletal robots remained.

Finally King checked the fourth battle, the one in his

heart. He found hope and relief. According to MindWeb, Bastian was still alive and well. So were Kim, Evan, Alice, and the rest of his family aboard. Over two hundred brave marines had died tonight inside the *Freedom*, and King grieved for them all. But deep down, he cared about his family the most, and he was relieved.

Freedom was out of service for a while. On the mat. Knocked out. Without the Mimoris manning their usual stations, *Freedom* could not fight, and many systems remained offline. But every moment, another eisengolem died, and soon the androids would return to their stations at engineering, artillery, navigation, and—

"Spitfire!" Jordan shouted, his voice deep and booming.

"I see him!" she cried, tugging on the manual controls.

King spun toward the central viewport, and his heart nearly stopped in his chest.

Ignoring Katyusha, *Barbarossa* was charging toward *Freedom*.

King narrowed his eyes. His fists grabbed a railing and clenched. Wolfgang's flagship was barreling forth, knocking Russian ships aside, moving faster and faster. Making a beeline toward *Freedom*.

He knows we're down, and he wants to finish the job, King thought.

He sent out an urgent message.

"All Mimori units, return from combat mode! Mimoris, to your stations!"

Across the ship schematics, he saw icons of the Mimoris running back to their posts across the ship. The marines would take care of whatever eisengolems remained. King stared back at the main viewport. The *Barbarossa* seemed unstoppable, barreling through smaller ships toward the *Freedom*.

"Katyusha, I thought you were watching him!" Spitfire cried.

But the *Gagarin* was tumbling into the distance, a massive dent in her prow. The Russian flagship was sparking and leaking globs of liquid fuel. Distantly on MindWeb, barely more than an echo, they heard Katyusha scream and curse. She was down on the mat! Knocked out!

The *Barbarossa*'s cannons shone like the red eyes of the undead. The brutal Nazi starship chugged forward, suddenly seeming less like a starship and more like a train, a big chugging locomotive from the age of steam, a beast of metal racing along the tracks, unstoppable. Coming closer. Closer. And then *Barbarossa*'s cannons bloomed and unleashed a terrible fusillade. A barrage of Kriegspfeil torpedoes came storming toward *Freedom* on jets of flame. In the darkness of space, the torpedoes began shadowy barracudas racing through the murk, on the hunt, famished for flesh.

"Emily, fire, fire the interceptors!" King cried.

"I can't!" she answered from artillery. "The Mimoris aren't here yet, and I can't get there fast enou—"

"Spitfire, evasive action!" King shouted.

The Israeli commander stood nearby, gripping the manual controls. She stood at a slant as *Freedom* pitched upward. Motors thrummed. The chassis creaked. King's hands tightened on the rail. The *Freedom* began to move away, but without Mimori flying the ship, they were too slow.

King stood, watching the torpedoes coming in.

We can't stop them.

He opened a ship-wide channel. "Brace for im—"

And the Kriegspfeils hit.

One after another, the German torpedoes plowed into *Freedom*.

The bridge jolted so violently everyone fell. King and Jordan landed beside each other with groans. Monitors exploded above. The deck bucked and wobbled and snapped. Workstations ripped out from the decking, their severed cables waving and spraying sparks like electric eels. But while the bridge was falling apart, MindWeb still worked, showing King a view of what was happening.

The torpedoes had hit *Freedom* on the port side near the prow. Just below the railgun. A powerful blow to the left shoulder, as it were. Like arrows into an enraged bull, the German torpedoes carved into the American dreadnought. With sheer kinetic energy, they ripped out chunks of armor, sliced open decks, destroyed a science station, and finally ripped off three Angels of Liberty from the dorsal hull. Only by miracle did the Kriegspfeils not detonate the ship's armory or fusion core. If they had, *Freedom* and her crew would be scattered across orbit as atoms right now.

"Kim!" King cried. "Bastian!"

Damage reports came flooding in. The entire electric system to the Angels of Liberty was down. Three cannons had shattered, but all fourteen were offline. The port thrusters—gone. *Freedom* wouldn't be making any right turns for a while. The force field? Offline everywhere. They had no force field—none! And to make things worse, those Kriegspfeils had carried umbrions. The dark particles were now flowing through the ship, seeking sources of light and energy to consume. Deck after deck were going dark.

Worst of all—the death toll. Another twenty souls—gone. Most of them marines.

Finally—a voice from the shadows. A ghostly voice over MindWeb.

"Jim?"

It was her. His wife. She was *alive.*

"Kim, thank God!"

"Jim . . . We won't take another blow."

"I know." He stared at the central viewport, and his belly sank.

The *Barbarossa* was still charging closer. A message appeared from the enemy flagship. King didn't want to accept the call, but the firewalls were down. The central viewport had cracked and hung askew, but it still displayed a grainy image. The face of Wolfgang König appeared on-screen.

The face of my son.

The Nazi admiral grinned.

"Goodbye, Admiral King!" he said as *Barbarossa* fired again.

CHAPTER SEVENTEEN
I Will Live

Like some medieval hero entering a dungeon, Stowy walked into shadows. Her quest? To find the cursed realm where the force field generator (a mythical beast) dwelled. Once there, to save the kingdom, she must strike down the beast. She raised her severed eisengolem claw, a steel weapon as fine as any sword.

The tunnel spread before her, tall enough to walk upright. That felt strange to Stowy; she had spent so much of her life crawling. Her feet shuffled forward, hesitant, pointing inward, one foot bare, the other peeking from holes in her striped stocking. She clasped her hands behind her back, and she kept her head low, her hair dangling to hide her face. A quiet, shy thing. A knight? No, she was a mouse of a girl. She walked near the wall as if wishing the shadows would swallow her.

But with every step, her poise straightened just a bit. Shuffling became a more steady, confident gait. She swung her arms at her sides, and she raised her chin. At the very end, let her die on her feet, and let her die looking up. That would be her act of defiance. With her last breath, her last step, to let them know, to let herself know—they had not broken her.

She would find it. The mythical force field.

The corridor led Stowy onto another mezzanine. There were a few control panels, a big swiveling chair, and a variety of levers and buttons. But Stowy barely noticed what was on the mezzanine. She stepped past the controls, placed her hands on the railing, and gaped in wonder upon the vast chamber ahead. The golden light filled her eyes.

"Beautiful," she whispered.

It was a tree. A towering, twisting tree of light. Forged of glass, it seemed to her. The trunk was transparent, as wide as a Redwood bole. Several stories tall this trunk rose, until above the mezzanine it split into multiple luminous branches that spread into the distance. Light filled the tree of glass—liquid light that swirled and pulsed and flowed. It was a network of pipes, Stowy realized. Pipes that delivered power through secret tunnels. And suddenly it seemed less like a tree to her, more like a bundle of neurons or nerves that crackled with electricity, that gave an organism the power to protect its frail skin.

"It's a brain," Stowy whispered in awe.

A *boom* reverberated through the ship. The mezzanine swayed. Another blast hitting *Barbarossa!* But the ship still flew. The force field still protected the juggernaut like a helmet protecting a fighter from multiple blows. And it was thanks to this luminous tree (or perhaps a brain) that Stowy beheld. The energy flowed through the glass pipes, crackling and buzzing, a sound like slushing oceans and shifting landforms in a world made of electricity.

Here were the roots of the force field that engulfed *Barbarossa*. From here came the power to weave that shimmering armor. These luminous pipes were like a bundle of crackling nerves. If she severed these nerves, the organism would die. And there was only one way to extinguish light.

Stowy reached into her pocket and pulled out a vial of umbrions.

A tear rolled down her cheek.

"Goodbye," she whispered. A sob fled her lips. "Goodbye, the friends I barely knew but who loved me so much. Goodbye, Algernon. Goodbye, Luna. I love you all."

She raised the vial overhead, prepared to toss the

umbrions onto the force field generator.

A gloved hand lashed out from behind.

Slender-yet-powerful fingers closed around Stowy's wrist. And tightened painfully.

A voice rose, girlish and twisted with mockery. "You forgot to say goodbye to *me*."

Stowy cried out. The vial of umbrions fell from her grip. It clattered onto the mezzanine and rolled under the control panels. Stowy struggled to free herself. But a second powerful hand grabbed her and spun her around, and Stowy found herself facing her tormentor.

Eva.

* * * * *

Eva König. The Bitch from Berlin.

Her face was pale, almost deathlike. Her skin was the color of bones. But mad light blazed in her eyes. One of those eyes was bionic, all-seeing, glowing like a ruby, peering from the center of a long scar. The second eye was blue, full of mirth and madness. Eva's nose was small and upturned, her eyebrows as sharp as blades. But even more than her mad eyes or corpselike skin, it was Eva's smile that terrified Stowy. That smile stretched too widely. From ear to ear. A smile with too many teeth. A smile that showed the molars. It was the rictus grin of a corpse who laughed at the living, of a deranged clown who prepared to feast on your flesh. There was something oddly inhuman about Eva König. *Der Stürmer* called her a paragon of Aryan beauty, yet to Stowy her beauty seemed deranged, twisted into a demonic mockery of humanity.

"Why, hello again, little cripple." Eva laughed. "Thought you could escape me?"

Stowy wanted to scream. Or to fight. Or to beg. But she

only stood there, frozen in sheer terror.

There were, she knew somewhere in the depths of her mind, four classic responses to threat. Fight. Flight. Fawn. Or freeze. If an enemy attacked, you could fight with all you got, you could run for your life, you could beg, or you could simply play possum. Right now Stowy might as well be playing dead. The fear paralyzed her. Her body had chosen *freeze*.

"Did you think you could vanish into the shadows again?" Eva said. She laughed, that huge smile parting like the jaws of an allosaurus. As a young child, Stowy was sometimes afraid of her plastic allosaurus. Its eyes were painted red, and its slender teeth, while made of plastic, were still sharp on her fingertips. She would play with the toy but always extra carefully, and at night she would lock that dinosaur in a drawer. That was what Eva's mouth reminded Stowy of. An allosaurus come to life, hungry for her, somehow transformed inside the drawer into a living monster.

She snapped out of her paralysis. Kicking madly, Stowy struggled to escape. Her feet (one bare, the other in a stocking) hit Eva's chest. Sig runes crackled upon Eva's breastplate, made of real electricity that ran through grooves in the armor. Stowy shocked her toes and yelped as electricity bolted through her. The voltage leaped through Stowy and into Eva, who still gripped her wrist. The *kindergeneral* cursed and released her.

Stowy hit the mezzanine floor, banging her tailbone. The pain nearly blinded her, but she did not forget her purpose.

I must extinguish the force field!

She reached into her pocket, seeking another vial of umbrions. There should be one or two left.

Eva delivered a powerful kick into Stowy's belly.

Stowy screamed, doubled over, and tears leaped into her eyes. For a second, she was back in Baer's lab, strapped onto the table. He hunched over her like a vulture, and his scalpel was like a talon, slicing open her belly. Pulling things out.

No.

No—she was no longer that little girl!

Stowy flipped over so that she stood on all fours. She tried to rise to her feet, but the pain kept her down. The young Nazi officer stared down imperiously, one hand on her hip.

"Yes, kneel before me, you filthy cripple." Eva snorted. "Look at you. Covered in filth. Dressed in tatters. A mark of shame on your wrist. Pathetic! You are a sickening bug."

Stowy struggled onto her knees, arms wrapped around her belly. "I am . . . a human!"

Eva laughed. "Are you now? You're a cripple."

"I am . . . autistic." Tears burned down her cheeks. "But I am still . . . human." She finally rose to her feet and stood before her tormentor, and even as the pain filled her, even as her tears fell, Stowy raised her chin. "I'm different. But I'm not broken. I'm not a bug. I'm not a mouse. I'm not a goblin." She smiled shakily, tears on her lips. "I'm a human being."

Eva's grin returned. She tapped buttons on her battle armor. Little compartments opened, and rods emerged, holding scalpels, pincers, and other tools of the trade. Eva grabbed a blade in each hand.

"Let's cut you open and find out," she said and advanced on Stowy.

Flight. Stowy could run for it.

Fawn. She could get down on her knees and beg.

Freeze. She had done enough of that.

Fight. She must fight. For the first time in her life, she must *fight*. Like Spitfire. Like Bastian. Like Grouchy. Like her friends.

Eva lunged, swinging a scalpel. Stowy took a step back, reached into her pocket, and pulled out another vial of umbrions. She had shattered one vial to escape the monks. A second vial had rolled under the control panel. She had two left. She lifted one vial of swirling darkness like a weapon.

"Drop your weapons!" Stowy said in a shaky voice. "Or I'll throw this onto you."

Eva burst into wild laughter. She mimicked Stowy, speaking with exaggerated falsetto and tremolo. "Dwop youw weapons!" She wiped a tear from her eye. "Adorable. Absolutely adorable. Now let's hear if you're as cute when you scream."

She thrust the blade.

Instinctively, Stowy parried with the vial.

The blade shattered the bottle. Umbrions burst out in a swirling haze. Darkness hid the pale, demonic face of Eva König. Black particles landed on Stowy's hand and arm, colder than ice, sucking up her heat. It was so cold that it burned. Stowy stumbled back, desperately brushing umbrions off with Luna. The blanket soaked up the noxious particles. The pain eased. Her hand turned blue and black as if frostbitten.

Eva came charging through the fog, laughing. Her red eye pierced the shadows. Stowy imagined the kindergeneral as some laughing hyena bursting from the shadows of night, jaws open wide to snap her victim's bones. The umbrions did not harm Eva. As the particles landed on the demented girl, they revealed a shimmering, iridescent force field. This second skin covered Eva, visible only when struck, protecting her from the all-consuming power of anti-photons.

Stowy was younger, smaller, wearing only a dress of many pockets, not a suit of armor and a force field. She had spent her life stowing away in starships and hiding in alleyways, while Eva had been killing men since age eight.

I couldn't even talk at age eight, and she was killing people! Stowy thought. *What chance do I have against her? I must run!*

And yet she stood her ground.

A series of blasts rocked *Barbarossa*. The mezzanine shook. Stowy and Eva both swayed on their feet. At their side, the force field generator crackled madly. A lightning storm blazed through the hollow glass tree. It reminded Stowy of the crackling thunderbolts on Eva's breastplate, which had shocked her. Another huge blast rattled the balcony. One of the support bolts came free, and the mezzanine tilted, threatening to fall into the pit where the crackling tree grew.

Stowy gasped. Those Sig runes on Eva's breastplate! They were shaped like thunderbolts and shone with real lightning. Stowy had thought they existed merely to intimidate. A bit of panache. But she understood now. The SS runes were powering the force field around Eva! They were small versions of the great glass tree that shielded the *Barbarossa*.

"So you've got some spunk in you, do you, rat?" Eva said. "It's you who killed Dr. Baer. Yes, you and your sisters, the mutants from the lab." She took a step closer to Stowy, raising her scalpel, and her eyes narrowed. "You're not as meek as you let on. Is the lab mouse actually an angry rat?"

Stowy had thought so herself not too long ago. But she was not a rat. She had simply realized what she had always been. A human being. Broken, driven to madness and desperation—but still a human. No matter what the Nazis did, no matter what parts of her they removed, no matter how they tattooed and mutilated her, they could not change that.

Eva was strong. She was powerful. She was deadly. She was a paragon of Aryan purity, granddaughter of the führer himself, and destined to someday rule the Fatherworld. But no humanity remained in Eva König, no more than there was humanity in an eisengolem. Both knew only one thing: how to kill. The Fatherworld had removed Stowy's womb, deeming her unfit to breed, yet while she could never create life, she could save the living. Within Stowy, humanity flowed and shone like the light inside the glass tree.

From one of her many pockets, which Stowy had sewn

onto her dress to hide holes and tatters, she removed her last vial of umbrions. Just a small glass container, no larger than a fig. But it contained the power of living darkness.

Eva thrust her blade again.

The scalpel sliced across Stowy's cheek.

She yelped as blood flowed.

Eva licked the blood off the blade and grinned. "There's an old saying. It's all fun and games until someone loses an eye. I always thought that strange. For me, that's where the fun begins."

She thrust the blade again at Stowy, aiming for an eye.

But Stowy had a talent even Eva could not deny. Stowy was fast. You had to be fast to survive as an *untermenschin* in the Fatherworld. Stowy had spent her life hiding and scurrying. She was smaller, weaker—so much weaker—than Eva. But she was *faster.*

She dodged Eva's slashing blade. And then Stowy shoved forward her bottle of umbrions—and shattered it against Eva's breastplate. Right over the Sig runes.

Shards of glass dug into Stowy's hand. She didn't care. Umbrions gushed forth from the shattered vial like famished serpents emerging from their lair. But they did not feed on Stowy's heat this time. What was the heat of a little girl compared to the crackling feast of Eva's breastplate! Pure, perfect, delicious photons were emanating from those Sig runes. And the umbrions feasted. Like living serpents, they slithered into the grooves of the Sig runes. Instead of burning in the electricity, they devoured it.

Eva screamed. She tried to pull the umbrions out of the runes. But the particles were too famished, too greedy. It was a feeding frenzy. They sucked the power out of Eva's battlesuit like leeches sucking blood. The armor sparked and crackled, and electricity flowed across Eva. She screamed, consumed within a battle of light and darkness.

Stowy had no more vials of umbrions in her pockets. She

drew another weapon.

The claw. The eisengolem claw. It was just one finger. But that one finger was long and sharp like a dagger.

So many times, the others had cut her. This time was her turn. With a deafening cry, Stowy thrust her dagger.

The eisengolem's finger drove into Eva's belly. There was no more force field around the girl. And the claw was sharp enough to slice through solid armor.

Eva screamed.

Stowy released the blade and stumbled backward, blood on her hand, shocked at what she had done.

Before her, Eva stood in shock, blood dripping from her belly. Stowy had driven the blade in a good eight or nine inches deep, piercing skin, muscle, organs. Eva took a step forward, then stumbled and clung to the mezzanine railing. She tried to speak, but blood filled her mouth.

Another blast hit *Barbarossa*. The starship shook but was still flying. Stowy had to destroy the force field generator. Same as she had done to Eva's Sig runes. And then King could thrust his own blade into *Barbarossa*'s belly.

* * * * *

Even with her horrific injuries, Eva was still alive. Yes, the young woman was strong. Feebly, the young Nazi maiden reached toward Stowy, perhaps still wanting to fight. But Stowy easily dodged the gloved hands, those hands which only moments ago had nearly crushed her. Eva must cling to the railing again. Her legs were going soft, and her skin was turning ashen.

Stowy raced by the führer's granddaughter toward the swiveling chair by the control panel. A station for a spacer to monitor the force field. Nobody was sitting there now. It must be where Eva had hidden and waited for Stowy to arrive.

I made so much noise crawling through the ducts I could have woken the dead, Stowy thought. *Eva followed me here. She thought to trap me. But she stepped into her own trap.*

Earlier, when Eva had first grabbed her wrist, Stowy had dropped a vial of umbrions. She had seen it roll between the control panels. She knelt on the mezzanine, seeking the vial. There! Under that workstation! Stowy reached under controls, and her hand closed around the glass container, which a mite had once carried in its belly like a precious egg. She would cast this jewel of darkness onto the tree of light, and the shimmering shields would fall off *Barbarossa* like a snakeskin.

Before Stowy could stand up, a hand closed around her ankle.

Eva! Eva had grabbed her!

The kindergeneral lay on the mezzanine, bleeding heavily, her face ashen. The blade was still in her belly. She still managed to give Stowy a huge, insane grin, her teeth red with blood. The battlesuit had lost its power, but even without it, Eva was strong, and she pulled Stowy across the floor toward her.

"Die, subhuman," Eva hissed and slammed a scalpel into Stowy's leg.

Ignoring the pain, Stowy kicked. Again and again. Her foot slammed into Eva's face. The young general grunted, and Stowy scampered away. She tried to stand up, but her leg buckled, and Stowy fell to her knees.

But she still held the vial.

"Die!" Eva screeched, dragging herself closer to Stowy.

Stowy raised the vial, then hurled it with all her strength onto the great tree of light.

The vial arced through the air, a black jewel forged of night, and slammed into the central pipe of the force field generator. The vial shattered against the glass tube, and the umbrions burst free.

At first the umbrions merely clung to the outside of the glass pipe, wrapping around it like black serpents around a tree trunk. Stowy feared the umbrions wouldn't be able to break through, that the power would keep flowing uninterrupted. But the umbrions fed on photons. On light itself. And that light passed through the transparent pipe . . . and into the tiny jaws of the little black beasts.

The darkness fed. As umbrions and photons canceled each other out, they released massive energy. Cracks spiderwebbed across the central pipe. Hot, liquid energy began gushing out like molten sunlight, but at once the umbrions devoured the fuel and traveled into the pipe. Inside they found the mother lode.

And then something occurred that Stowy never expected. All the umbrions on the mezzanine, the ones which had devoured Eva's breastplate and blackened Stowy's hand—they leaped toward the flowing pipe of energy. Both girls groaned with relief, finally free of the noxious little vampires.

The particles spread up the "tree trunk" and into the branches that sprawled above. There weren't enough umbrions to devour the entire tree. But it was enough to cause blast after blast inside the pipe, to spread more cracks across the glass, and then a branch shattered. Sludgy energy came pouring out. And suddenly the entire tree was snapping, collapsing, breaking apart, spilling hot fuel that drowned even the umbrions below its fury.

Stowy and Eva fled the balcony. Both girls, even with their injuries, managed to run down the tunnel.

Behind them, waves of energy gushed forth, washing over the balcony, racing down the tunnel like a river. The force field pipes had shattered, releasing their inferno. The blaze gushed through the tunnel, devouring all in its path. Heat blasted Stowy's back. She ran. With a knife in her leg, with her hand blackened with cold, she ran. All she could do now was run. From the flames. From her past. From the pain she had endured.

Just run, she thought.

Just run.

There ahead—a doorway. The end of the tunnel. Beyond it would be the great chamber with the gears. A place to drain the liquid fire, perhaps to shelter from the burning waves. It was funny. Stowy knew she would die in this starship. Yet still she wanted to postpone that death as long as possible.

And . . . maybe.

Maybe, just maybe . . .

If she could reach the hangar, if she could find the pod that had brought her here . . .

As the flames surged behind her, Stowy ran faster, arms pumping. She was only a few steps from the chamber of gears. From there—yes! She could take the ductwork. She could make it!

She could *live.*

Behind surged the fire, racing closer and closer, crackling and roaring for her flesh. Ahead rose a doorway. It led to the chamber of gears. Just three steps away . . . Eva grabbed her.

The deranged Nazi spun Stowy around. With her mismatched eyes, Eva stared at the stowaway.

"Burn!" Eva said, then shoved Stowy toward the flames.

As Stowy tumbled backward, Eva leaped through the doorway to the chamber of gears. And slammed the door behind her.

Stowy regained her footing and grabbed the knob. Locked. She banged on the doorway. It wouldn't budge.

Trapped. Trapped in the tunnel!

Stowy spun around and placed her back to the door. The wave of fire came rushing down the corridor toward her. The heat felt like it could melt her eyeballs. She closed her eyes tight, and sweat washed over her. Stowy placed one hand over Algernon, who cowered in her pocket. And there in the tunnel, a knife in her leg, her hand blackened and cold, she whispered to the flames.

"I will live."

She opened her eyes.

"I will live."

She raised her chin and her voice rang out.

"I will live!"

The fire filled the tunnel. The last of the force field generator collapsed. Across *Barbarossa*'s exterior hull, the shield gave a last shimmer, then popped like a soap bubble in spring. And inside the German juggernaut, as officers ran from here to there, as panic spread, a little voice echoed through the halls and tunnels of *Barbarossa*, the greatest ship that ever flew.

"I will live . . ."

CHAPTER EIGHTEEN
To Fight Ever Onward

The *Barbarossa* fired her cannons.

And the starship *Freedom* answered with a barrage of interceptors. Thank the heavens, the Mimori androids were back at their stations, operating the Shield of David point-defense system. The slender Salvation Stones streaked toward the incoming Kriegspfeils. Interceptors met torpedoes right off *Freedom*'s prow. Blasts of umbrions filled space, collapsing in on themselves to suck up the interceptors' kinetic energy.

Freedom had blocked another blow. This time.

But the Angels of Liberty were still offline. The force field was still down. The next punch that landed—that would be the end. *Freedom* was barely clinging on. She couldn't even punch back. Not that it mattered. *Barbarossa* still had that monstrously thick force field of hers. All the rage of the Red Fleet had not broken it.

But we still have the Fist of Freedom, King thought. *We still have that one ace up our sleeve.*

Freedom was firing all the machine guns that still worked across her hull, and her Eagles were still flying. Her escorts— several corvettes and two frigates—were fighting at her side, giving a good account of themselves. They had kept *Freedom* safe for a while. But now *Barbarossa* was charging forth for another attack. Once more, the juggernaut cannons were heating up.

Barbarossa fired.

Freedom's interceptors flew.

Success! The interceptors took out the assault. But barely. Those blasts had come within only a few klicks, enough to shower *Freedom*'s exposed hull with shrapnel. If Grand Admiral Wolfgang couldn't land a knockout, he would just as happily kill *Freedom* with a thousand cuts.

And then, as *Barbarossa* prepared her next assault, a miracle happened.

A miracle from heaven.

King, watching from *Freedom*'s smoking bridge, could barely believe what he saw. He rubbed his eyes.

"Larry? Gal? Are you two seeing this?"

Jordan was gaping, eyes nearly bugging out. "*Barbarossa*'s force field. It's . . . falling off."

"Like a bathrobe off a fat man's ass!" Spitfire whispered.

They all watched it happen. The legendary force field of *Barbarossa* shimmered, ripped apart, and slid off into space, vanishing in a shower of sparks. Leaving *Barbarossa* exposed. Oh, he still had armored plates. He was still a big, powerful brute. But without a force field . . .

"We can kill him." King raised his chin, and he sent another message out to all officers. "Crew! This is Admiral James King. Prepare to fire the Fist of Freedom!"

A hush fell over the ship. This was a solemn moment. They all knew it. In fifty years of service, the old *Freedom* had only fired her Fist a handful of times. And only in the most dire of circumstances. This was a doomsday weapon. A weapon to destroy worlds. In the state *Freedom* was in, the recoil was likely to rip the ship apart.

But at least we'll take Barbarossa *down with us,* King thought.

The German juggernaut was still charging toward *Freedom*. Even without her shielding, *Barbarossa* was determined to brawl. Katyusha was down for the count. The Shield of David system was clattering madly, firing interceptor after interceptor, barely able to keep blocking *Barbarossa*'s punches.

It was time.

Emily appeared on the bridge, broadcasting herself from the artillery deck. She still stood within Samson, her loading mecha. A handful of Mimoris stood around her in neat rows, identical and obedient gunners. The Angels of Freedom had been destroyed. But they still had their railgun.

"Bridge?" Emily said. "To fire the Fist, I need an approval from the second-highest ranking officer aboard. Admiral Jordan, do you approve?"

A hallucination of Niles materialized beside her. "You are the Queen of England! You need no approval from anyone, let alone the common soldiery. You have been granted a mandate from God to govern Great Britain and her American colonies."

Emily rolled her eyes. "Niles, first of all, I abdicated. Second, the Americans have been free for five hundred years. And third—shut up!"

Jordan stepped closer and placed a hand on King's shoulder. The two friends made eye contact. And Jordan gave him a small, knowing smile.

King stared at his friend, and he saw an old face, wrinkled, the stubble like snow scattered across ragged brown soil. But in his memories, the old Phantom was there too. That young, cocky pilot—two years King's junior—who had flown at his side all those years ago. God, those had been good years! They had fought a terrible war. They had lost friends. Lost Yehuda, a dear friend. But in many ways, those had been the best years of King's life. Together, those three young pilots had rocked the heavens and shaken the stars.

Reality snapped back into place, and they were old men again. Three who had become two. Still fighting side by side.

I'm glad you're with me, King said with his eyes. He didn't need to use words or telepathy.

Jordan turned toward the hallucination of Emily, and he broadcast his words to the entire high command. "Crew, this is Rear-Admiral Larry Jordan. I approve the order. Prepare to fire the Fist of Freedom!"

Emily nodded and raised her hand in salute.

"God bless us all."

King nodded. "God bless us, starship *Freedom*."

MindWeb still streamed a view from the artillery deck. Emily and the Mimoris were running down a corridor, heading toward the railgun's firing station. *Freedom*'s artillery department spread across multiple decks from stern to stem. The department oversaw the Shield of David, the Angels of Liberty, the Groundhoggers (the network of retractable machine guns in the hull), and finally the Fist of Freedom. Normally hundreds of officers and spacers manned these stations. Today it was just Emily and a handful of androids. And they sprinted down the corridor. Their lives, the lives of the crew, perhaps all life on Earth depended on their success.

Finally Emily and the androids reached the railgun station. It was located not far below the bridge—just two decks below King's feet. King knew that place well. As a young officer, he would sometimes travel there at night to ruminate. The towering, shadowy chamber felt like a cathedral, a place for memories and reflection. *Freedom* had a chapel on deck 31 of the midsection, but King often preferred to pray in solitude in vast, dark places. It was where his thoughts could balloon and echo through a place larger than his mind.

The railgun alone comprised a full third of *Freedom*'s length and mass. The twin prongs thrust out from the prow, one above the other. They were as large as the ancient Twin Towers of New York legend. The roots of the prongs delved deep into the starship. The entire prow—which included the bridge, science stations, and navigational departments—had been built around the rods like some sprawling treehouse around two trunks. In a sense, the *Freedom* was a giant, flying railgun. Like a handgun for a god. Even the fourteen Angels of Liberty, statues as large as Christ the Redeemer, seemed small by comparison.

The railgun fired Goliath projectiles. True to their name, Goliaths were truly gargantuan. They were, essentially, just slabs of metal the size of a small starship. Goliaths were big, dumb, and stupid. They included no computers, no navigational systems, no thrusters, no propulsion at all. Maccabees, David's Stones, Samson Jawbones—those missiles had all those frills and features. Goliath had none. For all intents and purposes, a Goliath was just a giant slug, the *Freedom* was the shotgun. And when slugs that size moved that fast, propelled by a railgun with all the power of *Freedom*'s core, they became truly monstrous. Yes, a Goliath had no warhead, just kinetic energy. Same with asteroids, and one had wiped out the dinosaurs. They only had one Goliath on the ship. But one was enough.

The core of each Goliath was made of tungsten—dense, heavy, durable, capable of withstanding the great heat and speed of being launched between the prongs. Because the prongs relied on electricity to propel projectiles (not chemical explosives like most cannons), a copper sleeve coated the tungsten core, minimizing electric resistance during launch. The railgun required fifty terajoules of energy. It sucked up so much power it would drain the *Freedom* in an instant. So much power propelled the multiton Goliath at one hundred kilometers per second. Too fast for a nearby enemy to dodge.

That was the key word. Nearby.

To be sure, they must get close. King didn't want to give *Barbarossa* any chance of dodging this blow. He only got one shot at this. He'd have to sneak though *Barbarossa*'s defenses, then deliver this mighty uppercut. And knock the giant out.

It would do the job. This weapon could destroy cities.

Even the mighty *Barbarossa* would fall.

Even mechas like Samson could not lift a Goliath. A sophisticated mechanism involving graviton generators allowed the artillery team to lift the Goliath and slide the whale-sized projectile between the railgun prongs. As King watched from the bridge, Emily and her Mimoris raced into the railgun station. At once, they reached for the graviton controls, which could lift the projectile. (They would have loaded the Goliath earlier, but dammit, there was never any time for anything.)

And then King saw it.

His MindPlay screen flashed with swastika icons.

Eisengolems. Eisengolems were waiting in the railgun station! They emerged from hatches. From behind the Goliath projectile. Some even climbed along the prongs of the railgun like spiders along logs.

It was a trap.

* * * * *

King ran.

He raced around the broken eisengolems on the bridge, leaped over the shattered doorway, and ran down the corridor. Dead eisengolems covered the ground here too—the victims of Mimori's combat frenzy. In death, the robots formed mangled barricades like oversized caltrops. King cursed every time he must slow down to worm his way through the mangled metal bones.

Finally he reached the elevator. It would take him down two decks toward the railgun station—where Emily needed him.

As he waited for the elevator, he could hear the battle from two decks down. The screeching eisengolems. Emily's screams. The cries of the Mimori androids.

A blast hit the *Freedom.*

Another impact!

MindWeb showed him the damage. Another torpedo to the prow!

He shook his head. The corridor rocked. The power thrummed and died down. Even the air stopped flowing through the vents. A moment later, the backup generators hummed to life, but the elevator was out of service.

With his metal gauntlet, King forced the elevator doors open, revealing an empty shaft plunging down into shadows.

The ship jolted again.

Another blast, this time to the portside. Alarms wailed. *Freedom* careened. The ship was hanging on by a thread. His beloved ship was hurting bad.

King climbed into the shaft.

Two decks was a quick elevator ride but a long distance to climb. In the shadows, King didn't know if the elevator car was above or below. The steel cables dangled before him. He grabbed and began spelunking down. Normally he would be descending slowly, mindfully. Tonight he climbed down in a mad rush, scraping the skin on his good hand.

A shriek sounded below.

King stared down into the shadows. Two red eyes stared back up. The eyes glowed, illuminating a metal skull.

An eisengolem began climbing toward him.

King spat. "Goddammit." He drew his sidearm. "My ship is falling apart." He fired down flaming bolts. "My fleet is crumbling." He bathed the eisengolem with plasma. "And now I got goddamn Nazi robots in my elevator shafts."

The plasma warmed and melted the skull. Yet as liquid metal dripped from the eisengolem's face, it kept climbing. Metallic laughter echoed through the shaft. A black claw rose through the inferno.

Just then the ship thrummed and crackled.

Lights ignited across the shaft. The main power was back

on.

Kim, you are a miracle worker! King thought.

And then he heard another sound. A *clank clank clank* from above. King looked up . . . and saw the elevator car diving down.

Below him, the eisengolem screeched and clawed at King's boots.

King looked to his side. He saw a sliding doorway labeled DECK 10. A cargo bay.

As the robot climbed, as the car plunged, King grabbed the elevator doors and leaped onto deck 10.

An eisengolem hand reached from the shaft and grabbed his ankle.

The elevator slammed into the robot, driving it downward into the pit.

King winced and kicked the severed skeleton hand off his leg. Bastard. Breathing heavily, he glanced at the warehouse.

"Any eisengolems?" he muttered. "Any other wise guys wanna start something?"

No. Just a warehouse. Good. Finally something boring. On MindWeb, he connected to whatever sensors remained on *Freedom*'s battered hull. From there, he got a view of the battle. *Barbarossa* was still pounding them, punch after punch. A few Mimoris were still firing interceptors, but the blows kept raining down. *Freedom* was on her knees. If this were a boxing match, the coach could have thrown in the towel long ago. As it were, *Barbarossa* would just keep punching until *Freedom* was no more.

Or until we deliver that one knockout.

Joints creaking and back aching, King climbed back into the elevator shaft. This war business had been much easier before his sciatica.

He spelunked down toward deck 9 (a long descent—these warehouses were towering), pulled the sliding door open, and climbed onto the deck.

Finally he was here.

He had reached the Fist of Freedom.

* * * * *

The railgun loading station loomed around him. The place was the size of a football stadium. From where he stood, King could see both the railgun prongs—one below, one above. The gargantuan electric rods thrust from here into space. And King could actually see space from here. In reality, he was facing the thick, inner hull of the starship *Freedom*. The Goliath projectile, when loaded, would first pass through an airlock, where it would position itself between the two rails in the vacuum. But MindWeb supplied an illusion, making the hull invisible. To King's eyes, the outer wall simply vanished, and he could see the rails stretch four hundred meters into space. The length of three football fields.

And out there in space, he could see *Barbarossa*. The hallucination was accurate. It was all generated in King's mind, but the data came from cameras on the exterior hull. What he was seeing, while only a hallucination, was what was actually happening out there.

The *Barbarossa* was charging right at them.

She was coming in for the kill, all guns blazing.

The interceptors could barely keep up, and another blow hit *Freedom*, and the dreadnought rocked. For just a split second, the hallucination vanished, revealing the craggy metal hull. Cracks spider-webbed across it. Then, with flickers, MindWeb came back online, and the wall became invisible again, showing the terrible juggernaut barreling forth.

Pain flared across King's back. And it was *bad* this time. Real bad. He grimaced. It felt like the segments of his spine were chomping down on his nerves. For a moment, he stood frozen in place. If his life depended on it, he could not move. Dammit! This had happened to him before—his back freezing up like this. Sometimes it took moments to recover. Sometimes it took days. For now, he could only watch through the haze, paralyzed with pain. His spine became a crackling serpent of electricity and agony. He had pushed himself too hard, too fast, and now his body was breaking apart.

For all intents and purposes, he had become a statue. And like a living statue, he could only watch.

* * * * *

Emily and the Mimoris were already here at the Fist. The former queen and the androids were struggling to load the enormous Goliath projectile.

But the eisengolems were here too. And they would not allow it.

The Nazi robots would gladly go down with the *Freedom*. Emily was working with graviton gloves, remote-controlling floating drones that lifted and guided the Goliath projectile into place. But eisengolems kept leaping at her. Emily had to keep swinging her graviton gloves at the robots, using the power of gravity itself to hurl the beasts away. The metal skeletons flew aside.

"I demand that we end this farce right now!" Niles cried. The jeweled drone was hovering to and fro in dismay. "This has gone on long enough. Emily, I must insist that we return to Buckingham Pal—"

"Niles, shut up!"

With Emily distracted, the Goliath projectile tilted and nearly plunged onto the deck (which would have likely carved a hole down to the shuttle bay below). Thankfully, Emily managed to return her hands to proper position, and the drones she conducted kept hold of the enormous tungsten projectile.

The eisengolems, battered by the graviton storms, rose and kept marching toward Emily. The queen-turned-gunner was still struggling to guide the massive Goliath. The projectile hovered above her like a zeppelin. Gingerly, ignoring the approaching robots, she resumed her efforts to slide the Goliath between the rails.

Thankfully, the eisengolems had lost their shotguns in the initial blast from Emily's gloves. But their claws and jaws were still powerful weapons, and the young gunner was now too focused to stop their advance.

One eisengolem—a towering beast with a crimson chassis—reached toward Emily, claws glinting.

"You shall not touch her!" cried Niles.

In a rare bout of courage, the drone flew to battle. He wasn't particularly menacing. Niles was about the size and shape of a football. His shell was forged of sterling silver and golden filigree, and precious gemstones adorned him. He looked more like a Fabergé egg than a weapon. Yet he flew toward the eisengolem nonetheless. The skeletal robot turned to look at the bizarre, glinting ornament. For a moment, the crimson eisengolem seemed to forget about Emily.

"What are you?" hissed the red robot with a voice like wind through a graveyard.

"I am the defender of the crown," Niles said. "And you, sir, have doomed yourself to defeat."

With a *click,* a dozen little hatches opened across Niles. An assortment of weaponry emerged. Well, *weaponry* was perhaps a bit generous, King thought. There was a letter opener that looked rather sharp. And a bottle opener. And some scissors and something that looked like tweezers. There was a little derringer pistol too, probably the deadliest machine in the drone's arsenal. It was no larger than King's pinky finger.

He's not a drone, he's a Swiss Army knife, King thought, watching the display.

"May God have mercy on your soul!" Niles cried and fired the derringer. A tiny bullet pinged off the eisengolem, then clattered onto the floor. It rolled toward King's boot. It was no larger than a pea.

The crimson eisengolem swung its claws again, this time toward Niles. The English drone flew across the room, wailing, and slammed into a bulkhead. Multiple gemstones fell from his body and clattered across the deck.

"My jewels!" Niles cried. His speaker had cracked. His voice had become distorted and mechanical, shooting sparks with each syllable. He tried to fly back to battle, then crashed onto the deck. King could sympathize.

A dozen Mimoris were here, but the androids had their hands full. Each Mimori was battling three or four eisengolems. It was like watching slender minks battling a pack of encircling wolves.

Niles was down for the count. Emily and the Mimoris were busy. It was up to King.

He tried a step. Another step.

It hurt. God, his back hurt. But he could move. He could fight.

With a roar, he launched himself into battle, and to hell with his war wounds.

The crimson eisengolem came stomping toward Emily. She winced, hands in the air, unable to move lest she dropped the Goliath. The claws swung toward her.

King leaped into the air, grabbed the eisengolem's arm, and yanked the huge limb aside. The claws flashed by Emily, missing her by mere inches. The young royal kept focusing on her task, sliding the Goliath into the loading tube.

With whirring motors, another eisengolem took a swing.

King roared, ran, and held out his prosthetic. The beast towered above him, nine feet tall if he were a foot. Before the eisengolem, King was a child (a child with gray hair, a bad back, and a prostate the size of a golf ball). Nonetheless, King shoved that metal fist into the robot's torso. With the power in the prosthetic, he snapped the eisengolem's metal ribcage. Jagged metal ribs drove into its flaming heart, and the beast collapsed.

King snorted. "Now burn in—"

Pain!

Agony!

An eisengolem had slashed his thigh!

King howled, spun around, and saw the beast. It swung its claws again. King barely stayed standing, barely parried. Another Nazi robot approached from the side. And a third.

"Sir!" Emily cried.

"Fire the Fist!" he shouted.

A blast pounded into *Freedom*. A torpedo! Another! And another still! The *Barbarossa* was ahead! Not even a megameter away and flying right in, all guns blazing!

Blast after blast rocked the *Freedom*. Eisengolems fell. King fell with them. The world was falling. The ship was ripping open. The universe was ending and everywhere was fire and smoke.

Somewhere in the inferno, alarms flashed. MindWeb showed King terrifying schematics of *Freedom*'s prow ripping open . . . and then the system went offline. And King was left blind in darkness, enveloped by umbrions and smog, and he could barely even see the red eyes of the eisengolems. He knew it was all over.

And then, in the darkness—light.

Pure white light.

The light of angels.

And he could see nothing more.

* * * * *

King squinted and shaded his eyes with his palm. At first he could see nothing but the blinding white light. It shone everywhere. Had he died and gone to heaven?

But then his vision adjusted. Just a bit. Enough to see that, within this great sea of effulgence, two beams shone with white light like searing starlight forged into blades. With their brilliance, they banished all shadows, all color, bathing the universe with their radiance.

The prongs were lit. Fifty terajoules of raw energy pulsed through the mighty Fist of Freedom.

And the railgun fired.

The Goliath projectile streaked between the luminous rods. Its copper shell burst into flame, peeling back to reveal a white-hot core of fury. The projectile became like a wild animal, woven of light, a predator of the stars. The beast left a trail of flame as it raced into space.

The *Barbarossa* loomed right ahead, a great leviathan from the depths, rising up from a storm to devour *Freedom*, and the bores of the juggernaut burned red like eyes.

The mighty Goliath, a true titan, suddenly seemed so small. Just a silver bullet flying toward a whale.

But that silver bullet flew true. It flew with the might of humanity itself. All the hopes, the prayers, the rage of humanity, all the courage of brave men and women who stood up to tyranny, all the honor and strength that pulsed in the hearts of Earth and her defenders—all that power drove the Goliath. The humble bullet became the harpoon of a god. And the mighty projectile slammed into *Barbarossa*, plowed through her armor, and rammed deep into her insides.

King stared, eyes wide and damp.

We hit. Oh God, we hit.

It wasn't over. Inside the *Barbarossa*, the Goliath unleashed all its spectacular kinetic energy. Explosions rocked the dreadnought from within. Entire decks blasted apart. Chunks of armor and hull, some still engraved with swastikas, careened into deep space. Cannons dislodged and tumbled. Flames spread. And King *could see* into the juggernaut. A honeycomb of decks gaped open, hundreds of meters deep, engulfed in fire.

It was a glorious sight. These were the flames of victory. And yet it was terrible to behold, this massacre that claimed the lives of thousands.

Spitfire's voice came over MindWeb. "We did it! Whoo! Bulldog, we did it!"

Jordan was laughing too. "We knocked him out! Jim, we knocked the bastard out!"

Emily ran toward King, leaped onto him, and embraced him. She wept and laughed. "We did it, sir."

Even Niles seemed impressed. "Good show, Your Majesty! Jolly good show. Always knew you had it in you. Now can you help me look for my jewels? I'm still missing the Black Prince's Ruby."

But as everyone cheered, King stood still, simply staring at *Barbarossa*. The ship (what remained of him, at least) slewed and burned. The hole gaped open in his prow—an ugly, open wound. The open decks began to spark with electricity from severed cables. A lightning storm was raging inside the Nazi flagship.

"Sir?" Emily released him from her embrace. "What's wrong?"

He wouldn't remove his eyes from *Barbarossa*. The dark juggernaut seemed to stare back. The bores of her cannons ignited with fresh red light.

"He's still flying," King said. "His cannons are about to fire." He opened a call to his crew and raised his voice. "*Freedom*! *Barbarossa* is still in the fight!"

* * * * *

King ran onto the bridge. Eisengolem claws had slashed his leg, and the bandages were soaked in blood. His back screamed bloody murder; his spine damn well seemed ready to snap. A whole gruesome collection of bruises and burns covered him. But King ran through the pain. He burst onto the bridge of the *Freedom*.

Or what remained of it, at least. His beautiful bridge lay in shambles. Half the workstations had fallen over. Most of the monitors were dead. Scattered fires burned and the vents could barely filter the hot, smoky air quickly enough. Jordan was clutching a gash on his side, while fire had blistered Spitfire's arm and hand. Mimori Prime was back from her murky state of combat mode. Her eyes were black again, no longer glowing white. The android was trying to fly the *Freedom*, which wasn't easy in the ship's sorry state. The port thrusters were gone. The stern engine was sputtering. Torpedoes had gouged deep pits through the dreadnought, destroying multiple decks, wiping out entire stations. The prow had taken most of the damage. Thankfully, the bridge was located within a thick shell of metal, concrete, and force fields, keeping its crew alive. Though her heart still beat, *Freedom* was reeling. This boxer was bruised, bleeding, concussed, and spinning around one foot. It would take just a gentle tap to knock her over.

If Freedom *were a cartoon character,* King thought, dizzy *bluebirds would be flying around her head.*

Instinctively, as he always did, King checked the crew manifest. Bastian and Kim were still alive. His son was in the upper midsection. His wife was in the stern. But what did it matter? Soon everyone aboard might be gone.

"We need to fire, dammit!" King said. *Barbarossa* charged closer. Closer.

"We can't!" Spitfire said. "The Fist needs twenty-four hours to recharge. You know that. The Angels of Liberty are offline."

"We still have Groundhoggers! We have interceptors! Rig the Shield of David to fire projectiles as offensive weapons. Coordinate it with Emily." He spun to Mimori. "Tell your sisters in the Eagles to go kamikaze. To fly into *Barbarossa*."

The android showed a rare display of emotion. Her eyes widened, and she gasped. "Sir! They're sentient beings."

"I know, dammit!" King said, eyes burning. "I'd order human pilots to do the same. Hell, I'll do it myself. We still have Rhinos." He turned to leave the bridge. "We have to fight. We—"

"Jim!" Jordan grabbed his arm. "Look. Look!"

The tall, dark officer pointed at *Barbarossa*. King stared. The Nazi warship was bearing down on them, seconds away. The demonic machine was burning up, crumbling even as he flew, yet still charging forth. He had become a freight train from hell, rising through the fires, unstoppable, merciless, heading for collision.

"Jim, you'll never make it in time," Jordan said softly. "It's over." His eyes dampened, and he saluted King. "It has been an honor, old friend."

"You're just going to give up, dammit?" King said. "You can't just—"

"Sir, ten seconds to impact!" Mimori said.

"Get us out of here!" King said.

"We can't without thrusters!" Spitfire shouted.

That freight train charged closer, closer, and King closed his eyes.

Over the roaring engines and shattering machines rose a voice. "Death! Death to fascists! From hell's heart, I stab at thee, you Nazi swine!"

King opened his eyes. He gaped at the viewport.

"Katyusha!" he whispered.

On the viewport, he saw it happening. The *Gagarin* was back in the fight! A massive crack spread across *Gagarin*'s starboard flank. The garish, teardrop domes had been scraped off the dorsal hull. Most of the bear cannons were gone. By God, the Red Dawn's flagship was barely more than a crumpled piece of scrap metal. But her engines still thrummed and flared with light. God bless her, that damn Russian monstrosity was still flying.

Forever seeking attention, Katyusha was broadcasting herself telepathically to anyone nearby. The madwoman appeared on *Freedom*'s bridge. Her naval cap had fallen off, and her black hair streamed behind her, wild and singed at the tips. Soot covered her face. But she was laughing, laughing hysterically, pointing the way forward with a broken saber.

"Onward, *Gagarin*! Victory to the revolution!"

Around her, her crew repeated the call. "Victory to the revolution!"

The military band on her mezzanine began to play the Red Dawn national anthem. Tubas, drums, a male choir—the works.

King frowned. "She doesn't have cannons left. No more than we do. How . . ." Then it dawned on him. "God. God above. Katyusha!"

She seemed not to hear him. "For the motherland! For Katyusha!"

Gagarin was flying faster and faster, heading right toward *Barbarossa*.

The Nazi juggernaut was moving too fast to slow down. The German flagship was still heading right toward *Freedom*, seconds away from ramming into her now. Kim had brought back some semblance of a force field, but not much. It wouldn't stop this German beast the size of a city.

"Impact in five seconds!" Mimori warned.

Katyusha laughed. "To victory!"

"Four seconds!" cried Mimori.

King, Spitfire, and Jordan held hands. The *Barbarossa* was right on top of them. *Gagarin* raced up at blinding speed.

"Three seconds."

"Victory to Katyusha!"

"Two seconds!"

King winced. He wished he could hold his wife in his arms.

"One s—"

Light.

This time red, burning, blazing light.

He saw it happen. It only took a split second, but he saw it. King saw the very moment that *Gagarin* plowed into *Barbarossa* at full speed.

A Goliath was a large projectile. A Russian flagship, engines blazing hot, made it look like a spitball. *Gagarin* weighed millions of tons. And all that mass and kinetic energy drove into *Barbarossa* like the fist of God.

The German juggernaut careened through space.

Without her shields, with the hole *Freedom*'s Fist had plowed into her, *Barbarossa* fell apart.

His exhaust ports tore free. Explosion after explosion rocked the monstrous Nazi ship. The armories caught fire. His ammunition was detonating. As he crumbled, Earth's gravity caught the *Barbarossa* and began tugging the ruin downward. Even as he glided toward Earth, explosions rocked the ship. Any moment now, the core would blow. Already escape pods were fleeing *Barbarossa*. Not many. Maybe a dozen, that was all. The tiny vessels were fleeing for their lives as their fathership crumbled behind them.

"He's gonna blow!" King said. "Get us out of here, Mimori!"

Freedom had no thrusters, but she still had her stern engines. As *Barbarossa* dipped in space, *Freedom* flew, putting distance between her and the burning juggernaut. King looked at the ruin, trying to see *Gagarin*. Where was Katyusha's flagship? Nothing. Nothing remained. And then—

A huge bubble of darkness ballooned inside the ruin of *Barbarossa*. It looked like a dark sun, a god of space woven not of hydrogen, not of light, but of umbrions. That expanding sphere only existed for a second. Then the bubble popped. A blast shot outward, scattering debris every which way. Across space, other starships turned to flee and dodge the explosion. Shields flared around a thousand ships, both Allies and Axis. When the shock wave finally passed through the fleet, they beheld what remained of *Barbarossa*.

Just a mangled chassis. A few bars of metal, no more, like the ravaged ribcage of an eisengolem. The planet caught the ruins and tugged them down to Earth.

CHAPTER NINETEEN
The Cost of Freedom

Across the *Freedom*, everyone cheered. Spitfire and Jordan jumped up and down and hugged. Over MindWeb, the others were whooping and celebrating. But King felt a lump in his throat. He lowered his head.

Stowy. I'm sorry, Stowy.

"Ha ha, we got him! We got him good!" Spitfire danced around King. "Goal from *Gagarin*, with a huge assist from *Freedom*! Admiral, did you see how . . ."

She noticed that he stood grimly, head lowered. Her face fell. Her dance ended. Spitfire understood.

"You're worried about Stowy." She put a hand on his arm. "Maybe she was in one of those escape pods. Maybe . . ."

Her voice trailed off. King knew the odds of Stowy surviving were virtually nil. Not if what he suspected was true. That Stowy had been deep inside *Barbarossa*. Far from any airlock.

"She disabled their shields," King said softly. "I know it in my heart. While *Freedom* and *Gagarin* were fighting, we had a guardian angel. And she made all the difference." Her voice choked. "Heaven wanted its angel back."

Sudden electricity crackled across the bridge. The hairs rose on King's nape. Debris on the deck rattled, and the bulkheads seemed to somehow elongate, contract, and sway as if reflected in a funhouse mirror. King's head spun. He knew this dizzying feeling. He had felt it when traveling through portals before. Somebody was bending spacetime.

At the starboard bulkhead, King saw it happen. An oval

portal formed on the bridge, dark and strange like a black hole. No, not a black hole. A *spider*hole. During the Spider War, humanity had learned (well, stolen) the technology from the arachnid rahs. Spiderholes were dangerous, unstable, and damn risky. Used wrong, they could rip a starship (even a planet) apart. While the Alliance only created large spiderholes for interstellar travel (and with utmost care), Katyusha used them for everything. Red Dawn officers actually traveled inside their spaceships using spiderholes instead of elevators. They had already compacted several starships that way (the spiderholes could crush them into cubes no larger than cars), but the equalists didn't seem to mind. Plenty of slaves (or as Katyusha called them, "loyal proletarian of the state") to build more starships.

Out through the spiderhole stepped a woman. An old, mad woman in a young woman's body. Her crimson uniform was burnt and tattered. The golden aiguillette had burned, and the medals on the chest hung loose. Soot covered her face, and her black bob cut stuck out in every direction as if she'd been electrocuted. But somehow Ketya "Katyusha" Petrova still managed to grin (she was missing one tooth).

"Did you see that, capitalists?" She raised her fist. "Victory goes to Katyusha! Once again, the capitalists achieve nothing, while we brave Russians defeat the fascists!" Then she winced and rubbed the back of her neck. "*Chyort vozmi!* Katyusha got such a crick in the neck. How long was she in that spiderhole?"

King took a step toward her, fists clenched. His voice rose to a roar. "Dammit, Katyusha! Were you in a spiderhole when *Gagarin* plowed into *Barbarossa*? Did you just sacrifice your *entire* *starship*? With thousands of spacers aboard?"

Katyusha became solemn. She placed her naval cap (just a few tatters of cloth) against her chest. "*Da*. Katyusha has made a great sacrifice to defeat the enemy. Songs will be sung. Perhaps a national holiday will be instated. The Feast of Katyusha's Sacrifice.

Da da, that has a nice ring to it."

King rolled his eyes. "I noticed your great sacrifice involved thousands of *other* people dying. Have you never heard of a captain going down with her ship, dammit?"

Katyusha snorted. "What? Katyusha is no mere captain. That is lowly rank!" She drew her saber and raised the blade (which was missing its top half). "Katyusha is Grand Admiral of the Red Fleet, Defeater of Fascism, and Premier of the People's Party of the Red Dawn!" She shook her head in disgust. "A captain! Ha!"

"Dammit, Katyusha, you sacrificed other people while you flew to safety."

She sighed. "Jamechka, there is something you should know about Mother Russia and her history. In Mother Russia, heroes die. The ruthless survive." She patted his cheek. "Katyusha is a survivor."

King sighed, and Katyusha responded with a wink. Damn the woman. She was a dictator. A mass-murderer. She had killed King's father with the man's own dagger. But without her, King would be dead right now. And so would the hope of humanity. Katyusha might brag of her martial prowess, but King realized that victory did not belong to one man or woman. It came from the courage of millions. Victory belonged to the wise admirals who commanded fleets. To the humble soldiers fighting in the field. To brave pilots who flew through hell itself. To humble civilians who did their part, volunteering, enlisting, standing strong. In this war, every man and woman did their part, and together, they had won this victory today. And now, perhaps, there was hope that together they could win the war.

King looked at Katyusha, nodded, and gave her a salute. "Thank you, Katyusha."

She returned the salute. "*Pozhaluysta*, comrade." She leaped onto him, mussed his hair, and kissed his cheek. "Now when will you admit you love Katyusha, and we can rule galaxy together as husband and wife?"

He growled. "Get off!" He shoved her aside.

She pouted and crossed her arms. "You playing hard to get?"

"Get off my bridge!" he roared.

Katyusha laughed and waved dismissively. "Fine, fine, play hard to get for a while. You are only encouraging Katyusha." She snapped her fingers. "Mimori! Show Katyusha to the royal suite. And draw a bath. In one hour—no, half hour—send over some vodka and caviar."

King heaved a sigh. "Mimori, send one of your androids with her. Keep a close eye."

Mimori Prime nodded and smiled thinly. "Aye, sir, sending logistic unit #D432 to watch the premier."

"Excellent!" A grin split the premier's face. "Katyusha always wanted a Japanese servant. We Russians defeated the Japanese in the Great War of 1945, you know." She skipped over dead eisengolems, hopped through the mangled doorway, and sauntered down the rubble-strewn corridor. On the bridge, they could still hear the premier's voice echoing through the ship. "Oh, unit D432! Get ready for Katyusha!"

* * * * *

As Freedom's bridge smoldered around him, King checked the state of the battle. The Weltraumwaffe was reeling from the loss of its flagship. *Gagarin* was gone, and *Freedom* was too damaged to do much, but thousands of German, American, and Russian ships still flew in low orbit. Even with their flagships out of the fight, they were still engaged in furious battle. Far above, war spread across high orbit too. The rest of the Freedom Fleet (minus the American Armada), the Desert Thorns, and half the Weltraumwaffe (still a mighty force) fought there for dominance of deeper space.

For now, *Freedom* had cracked a way open to Earth. If King rallied the armada, he could break through. He could reach Earth's sky. And once he secured the path to Earth, he could bring help to the people there who needed him.

The war was not over. Perhaps it would be fought for many months, maybe even years. But they had won a victory today. They had taken a great step forward in resistance against tyranny.

He opened a transmission to everyone in the Freedom Fleet. All ships—combat and support. All spacers, both officers and enlisted. They all heard their admiral speak.

"To the brave spacers of the Freedom Fleet. This is Admiral James King. While we are still engaged in bitter battle, while our heroic forces fight relentlessly on land, at sea, in the air, and in the darkness of space, I speak to you with a message of hope. Today, working alongside the Red Fleet, our forces have destroyed the *Barbarossa*, flagship of the invading Nazi fleet. We've dealt the enemy a serious blow—both to their military effort and morale. Furthermore, with this victory, we've broken the Nazi stranglehold on Earth. Military and supply lines will be reopened between our courageous forces on and around Earth. This victory is not the end of the war. It is not even the end of this battle. Many days of hardship still lie ahead. Days of sacrifice, of death, of loss. But also days of courage, heroism, and victory. We will continue to attack the enemy relentlessly. We will continue to destroy his starships, his machines of war, and his will to fight. We will not stop fighting until victory. Washington DC, home to the Alliance Headquarters, calls for us. And we will answer!" He paused for a moment, closed his eyes, and thought about the lost. Then he spoke again. "This is not a war we wanted. The enemy caught us by surprise. And his atrocities shocked us to our core.

The murders of children. The torture. The rape. The sadistic medical experiments." His voice for a moment caught in his throat, but then it hardened. "This is a war against evil. An evil we thought long dead. Before us, our ancestors fought Nazism and its horrors, and they prevailed. I know that we will too. God bless the Freedom Fleet. And God bless Earth."

He ended the call. Spitfire approached him, wrapped her arms around him, and kissed his cheek. King's wounded leg ached. And a deeper hurt seeped through him, gouging out his insides, leaving him a hollow man.

How do you do it, Katyusha? How do you sacrifice lives and sleep at night? How do you live on when you doomed others to death? Teach me, Katyusha. Because you're a survivor. And I need to know.

"Dad!"

With a roar, Bastian ran onto the bridge. His arms were spread out, and a huge grin lit his face. King looked at his son—this tank of a man, this burly marine with giant hands and a bigger heart. And a memory overlaid the image. A memory of young Bastian, a scrawny kid, a big smile on his face, running across their Nebraska backyard toward King. And then the big Bastian slammed into King, wrapped his arms around him, and nearly crushed him. That little boy had become a beast.

With a (somewhat less powerful and higher-pitched) roar, Kim ran onto the bridge too. Tears filled her eyes, but they were tears of joy.

"I know, I know—I need to fix the ship." She joined the embrace. "But I need to be with you now. Not just a hallucination. I need you in my arms, Jim."

King's own eyes dampened. He held his wife and his son close. And then Jordan wrapped his arms around them all, and amazingly, the tall, battle-hardened officer shed tears.

This is what matters, King thought, choking up. *This is who I fight for. This is what brings joy and gives meaning to my life. My family.*

421

* * * * *

The starship *Freedom* pulled back from the front line for repairs. Mechanic ships raced forward, and within moments, swarms of robots were flowing across *Freedom*, welding and sawing and bolting in new parts. For proper repairs, she would need a long stay in a shipyard. But King wasn't ready for that yet. Not until Washington was safe.

King marched down a midsection corridor as the mechanics yammered in his brain.

"Are you sure, sir?" a master sergeant was saying. "Please reconsider. A shipyard really is the place for a dreadnought this badly damaged."

"At times of peace, maybe," King said. "But this is a time of war. For now, just slap a Band-Aid on us, then send us back to battle."

He ended the call, then turned toward Kim, who walked at his side.

"Mechanics, huh?" he said to her.

Kim turned toward a service elevator. "I better head down to engineering. I'll oversee the repairs from there."

"You," King said, "will go to sleep. And eat a meal. And take a shower. We have a few hours off. Use them."

"I can't." She placed a hand on his chest. "I can't, Jim. My ship needs me."

She kissed his lips, then hopped into the elevator and plunged down into the depths of the starship. King watched her go. Engineers and mechanics truly were the unsung heroes of war. They were there under fire, fighting with wrenches and hammers, keeping the great machines of battle in the ring. The glory went to admirals like him. In the history books (if anyone survived to write them), they would mention his name, not theirs. But he simply had the honor to lead the true heroes.

Perhaps King should take his own advice. He had a few hours off before the next push forth. For now, other ships filled the gap *Freedom* left at the vanguard. King should sleep. Eat. Shower. Change his bandages. He was banged up, but visiting the infirmary was out of the question, of course. Dr. Annie was working around the clock to treat the wounded marines. Like the engineers and mechanics, the medical officers were unsung heroes in any war.

King took a corridor that led toward his cabin. Every once in a while, a spacer would run by, hurrying on some task. They would see King, stand at attention, and salute. King looked them all in the eyes, returned their salutes, and encouraged them to fight on and be strong. He walked with shoulders squared, chin tall, the strong leader his crew needed to see.

When he stepped into his cabin, he closed the door behind him, leaned against it, and closed his eyes.

It hurt. Everything hurt. It was the gashes on his leg. The relentless pain in his back. The grief over the fallen and the missing. The others were cheering. Celebrating their victory. Why couldn't King join them? Why couldn't he feel that joy? He used to celebrate after victories. A long time ago.

He looked around the cabin. The hardwood floor, paneled walls, oak desk, and crackling fireplace all spoke of comfort. Yes, once this room would have comforted him. It was cold and confining now. And it wasn't just because the shelves were empty or the fireplace cold. His quarters had become a mausoleum, a place of too many ghosts. The suit of armor was missing, of course. The security cameras in the corridors had caught the whole thing—the armor marching, possessed, controlled by wicked technology, holding within its metal confines a scared little girl.

His MindLink chimed. It was a call from Earth.

Godwin? No. It was a civilian line.

King sat at his desk, and he took the call.

Suddenly his grandkids materialized inside his den. He hallucinated them standing just across the desk.

"Pop-Pop!" they cried.

Rowan (who had just turned fourteen) ran around the desk and hugged him. Little Oli (only four) toddled after her. The boy was holding a plastic toy of the starship *Freedom*.

King laughed and hugged them. "Rowan! Oli! How ya doin', kiddos?"

Rowan grinned. "Good! Aunt Maddy said we can call you for only five minutes, because you're super busy fighting the bad guys in the war."

"Bad guys—smash!" Oli said. The boy pounded his starship against the (very expensive) desk. Thankfully he was only a hallucination. His plastic ship passed right through the wooden tabletop.

They banished his grief and fear. Joy—actual joy—filled King to see their smiles. For what few moments they had together, he spoke to them. He took out the medal Rowan had made him, the one with the engraving that read #1 Grandpa. He showed her the dent where it had stopped a U-bolt, saving his life. Rowan talked to him about *All Systems Go* (some cartoon she was watching), and Oli smashed the *Freedom* a few more times through the table. Seemed like an accurate reenactment of the battle King had just endured. And then both hallucinations scampered off, flying through the decks of the *Freedom* like ghosts, heading toward Bastian and Alice. Finally the children would be reunited with their marine parents. If only for a while. And if only as hallucinations. The plastic starships didn't break against the tabletops, but the hugs felt real.

With the kids gone, the chamber suddenly felt so cold. Even with the noise of motors and machinery, it seemed too quiet. This was a sad place. A sacred place.

King looked at the floor between his desk and the hearth. It was there. Right there that Stowy—the Stowy from this universe—had saved him from the spider. It was there that the slender stinger entered her heart. The fireplace had crackled that day, and the venom had smelled like peppermint. She had died in his arms, a smile on her face, a fairy child taking her last flight to a place he could not follow.

"You came back to me," King whispered. "A miracle happened. You came back to me from that far off land of faerie. Don't fly again where I can't follow."

He gazed out the porthole into space. In the distance, Earth shone. Whatever remained of *Barbarossa* had fallen into the Pacific. Perhaps, like Icarus, the fairy child had lost her wings and fallen into that sea. But in his heart of hearts, King dared to dream, and in his fancy the fairy girl took flight and danced among the stars.

He thought back to that day—not so long ago—when he had met another Stowy. A doppelgänger from the Fatherworld. The Freedom Brigade had fought for days to liberate London from the Nazi claws. Finally, in St Mary's Hospital, they had found a girl. A girl from the Fatherworld. She had stowed away aboard *Barbarossa*, fleeing her universe into this one. A mirror image of the girl who had stowed away for so many years aboard the *Freedom*, befriending the crew, entering their hearts. She had become the mascot of the ship. That Stowy had been an orphan, a survivor of great trauma, yet not too much trauma that dampened her spirit. She was always smiling, frolicking, cheering everyone up.

But her doppelgänger—oh, if there was enough trauma to crush the spirit of a child, she had endured it. They had found a trembling, haunted child, a number tattooed onto her wrist, the scars of medical experiments on her body. Her eyes seemed too pale somehow. Frozen eyes. Eyes like ice that encased a trapped, tortured soul. She would not eat. Would not look anyone in the eyes. Would not speak. She would merely sit under the table, hiding from the world, lining up her toy dinosaurs. Over and over, she placed the plastic dinosaurs on the floor, arranging them snout to tail. Then she scattered them and lined them up again in a new order. A broken, autistic, traumatized child. That was how she had emerged from the Fatherworld.

"You gave me a gift that day," King said softly. "I remember. I still have it."

Sitting at his desk, King pulled it now from his pocket. A little plastic ankylosaurus. It was, Stowy had said, her favorite dinosaur. And her gift to him.

It hurt. He knew it would hurt. But King stood up, suffering the creaks of his joints, the protests from his back, and the pain in his wounds. He stepped toward his empty bookshelves. In the old *Freedom*, these shelves had brimmed with curiosities and treasures: leather-bound books, antique naval instruments, ships in bottles, and curious crystals from across the galaxy. Today the shelves were empty. King brushed the dust off one shelf, then placed the ankylosaurus there. In his memories, he heard Stowy's laughter, and he saw the sparkle in her eyes. He thought of all those he loved who were still here with him. His wife. His son. His grandchildren. His friends. He was a lucky man, and despite loss and grief, he knew joy and love.

"My cup runneth over," he said softly, reciting a psalm his father had taught him long, long ago. He finally thought he understood. "Surely goodness and mercy shall follow me all the days of my life."

The cabin no longer seemed so empty.

The story continues in…

Guardians of Freedom

Freedom Fleet III

NOVELS BY DANIEL ARENSON

Starship Freedom

Starship Freedom
The Cost of Freedom
We Fight for Freedom
For Death or Freedom
Let Freedom Ring
In Pursuit of Freedom
The Guns of Freedom
A Time for Freedom

Freedom Fleet

The Freedom Fleet
The Fires of Freedom
Guardians of Freedom
On Wings of Freedom

Mintari

A World of Dinosaurs
Where Dinosauars Roam
March of the Dinosaurs

Alien Hunters

Alien Hunters
Alien Sky
Alien Shadows

Children of Earthrise
The Heirs of Earth
A Memory of Earth
An Echo of Earth
The War for Earth
The Song of Earth
The Legacy of Earth

Kingdoms of Sand
Kings of Ruin
Crowns of Rust
Thrones of Ash
Temples of Dust
Halls of Shadow
Echoes of Light

The Moth Saga
Moth
Empires of Moth
Secrets of Moth
Daughter of Moth
Shadows of Moth
Legacy of Moth

Dawn of Dragons
Requiem's Song
Requiem's Hope
Requiem's Prayer

Song of Dragons

Blood of Requiem
Tears of Requiem
Light of Requiem

Dragonlore

A Dawn of Dragonfire
A Day of Dragon Blood
A Night of Dragon Wings

The Dragon War

A Legacy of Light
A Birthright of Blood
A Memory of Fire

Requiem for Dragons

Dragons Lost
Dragons Reborn
Dragons Rising

Flame of Requiem

Forged in Dragonfire
Crown of Dragonfire
Pillars of Dragonfire

Dragonfire Rain

Blood of Dragons
Rage of Dragons
Flight of Dragons

KEEP IN TOUCH

www.DanielArenson.com
Daniel@DanielArenson.com
Facebook.com/DanielArenson
Twitter.com/DanielArenson

www.ingramcontent.com/pod-product-compliance
Lightning Source LLC
Chambersburg PA
CBHW020412030726
47495CB00006B/1481